Acclaim for
REALMS OF LIGHT

"In *Realms of Light,* Sandra Fernandez Rhoads uses the best of fantasy fiction to cleverly blend in *Paradise Lost* as a backstory. The result is a fast-paced story driven by intimate portrayals of characters who display a realistic range of human strengths and faults, rich settings that draw in readers, and a vibrant plot that leads to a conclusion that surprises yet satisfyingly ties together narrative threads from the first volume of this duology, *Mortal Sight.*"

— ANGELICA DURAN, President of the Milton Society
of America (2020–2021) and Professor of English, Comparative
Literature, and Religious Studies at Purdue University

"An epic conclusion to The Colliding Line, *Realms of Light* is a beautiful, clever ending to this duology. New friends, new enemies, and new mysteries await in this bewitching tale!"

— GABRIELLA GRAVES, Disney Channel actor

"The dark, fantastic adventure that began in *Mortal Sight* yields new and surprising revelations in this thrilling sequel. Allusions to classic art, Milton's poetry, and Machiavellian philosophy give the book's lore a fresh and fascinating twist as *Realms of Light* twists toward an apocalyptic, pulse-racing climax. Sandra Fernandez Rhoads is a YA fantasy author to watch!"

— RJ ANDERSON, award-winning author of *Knife,*
Ultraviolet and The Flight and Flame Trilogy

"Realms of Light propels The Colliding Line duology to a breathless, dazzling conclusion. What Sandra Fernandez Rhoads began in *Mortal Sight* is expanded, enriched, and deepened in *Realms*. I loved it."

— LINDSAY A. FRANKLIN, award-winning author of *The Story Peddler*

"With nonstop intrigue, new characters who stole my heart, and, of course, the poetic quality of Rhoads' storytelling, I completely devoured this book and all of its mysteries! It is truly a thoughtful and heart-pounding conclusion to Cera's journey in finding a place in the world and ultimately learning acceptance of herself."

— KRISSI DALLAS, author of the Phantom Island series

REALMS OF LIGHT

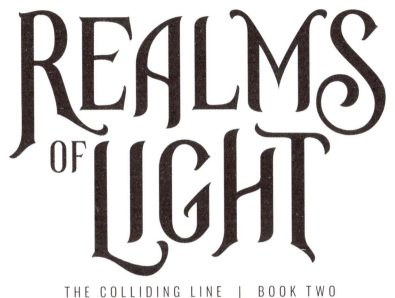

REALMS OF LIGHT

THE COLLIDING LINE | BOOK TWO

SANDRA FERNANDEZ RHOADS

For my mother & my late father
Who taught me to persevere

&

For Donna
Who guided me through the storms

1

URIEL'S SUNBEAM

I bounce my foot as Devon drives us deeper into the forest at a crawling pace. Maddox sits beside me, tapping a restless beat on his knee as the rumbling engine fills the growing silence. Autumn leaves blanket our path, and the bleak horizon blocks out the rising sun, but I know it's there, hiding behind the clouds, waiting to break through.

"Is the wound bothering you?" Harper flattens the edge of the bandage wrapped around my burnt calf. "The serum will probably wear off soon."

"It's fine, really." I'm far from fine. But it's not the wound that troubles me. With every passing minute, I get closer to the Alliance Council Estate—the one place Mom has spent the last ten years keeping me safe from. And I'm terrified.

"Keep watch for any creatures. We're not in the clear yet." Devon's weary eyes meet mine in the rearview mirror.

I've been watching and listening for hours, sandwiched in the back, caught next to Harper, who keeps shooting Maddox a side-eyed stare, making him shift uncomfortably. Every now and then he glances at me, tightening his lips, holding back words his eyes are fighting to say. But words can't erase the awkwardness between us.

I look out the window. No violent wind signals beastly Cormorants overhead, and no misted Legions creep along the prickly underbrush, tracking our path. "We've set good distance. Nothing's in sight."

Pop, who's been quietly resting in the front seat, grunts and adjusts his sunglasses. "Don't use your eyes."

Use my senses, I know. But smells collide in this stuffy car, making it hard to detect any ash or sulfur in the air, so I close my eyes to listen and feel for anything out of the ordinary. But as far as I can tell, "Everything's clear."

Maddox tips his head against the glass to look at the treetops. "Yeah, but somewhere out there, Sage is commanding those things to kill innocent people."

Harper clutches the duffle bag in her lap. "Like he did with me."

I check the sky again. "He can be stopped." At least I hope. If not, then there's no telling how many others will die.

"Our trip to Council isn't about stopping Sage." Devon makes a hard turn, sending me into Maddox's shoulder.

A swarming flutter takes flight inside my stomach as his bold scent of rain envelops me. I snuff out the feeling and hold on to Pop's headrest, clawing into the aged-velour cushion to stay upright. "It's about keeping a half-breed like me out of Sage's hands, I know."

I've decided to offer up whatever I can to help Council's cause and prove I'm on their side. And hopefully in return I'll get training. Maybe even fight in the war.

That is, of course, if they don't kill me at first sight.

Devon suddenly stops the car out in the middle of nowhere. The only thing visible deep inside the woods is a twenty-foot gate overgrown with thorny vines, once built, then forgotten. No fence sprawls out from either side of the aged pillars. No road marks a path. It's simply an obsolete structure abandoned in the middle of the autumn forest.

"Something wrong?" I ask.

Pop grips his cane and sits up. "We're at the gate, Honey."

Verses from *Paradise Lost* race through my mind at that same moment:

> *Three folds were brass,*
> *Three iron, three of adamantine rock*
> *Impenetrable, impaled with circling fire*
> *Yet unconsumed.*

Those lines describe the gates that keep the archfiend bound in hell—not a comforting thought when I'm about to meet the Alliance Council, Milton. But at second glance, his description is spot on. The gate isn't one solid color or material but a twisted mesh of metal and rock, or hundreds of swords tangled together. All that's missing is the fire along the perimeter.

Harper smacks her lips after applying pink lip gloss. "I only see an ivy pillar."

Maddox sinks in the seat. "Those are statues."

I lean forward for a better look out the front windshield. When I do, the flower hairpin Gladys gave me, the one I lost and Maddox found, pokes at me from inside my pocket. I adjust the pin through the fabric and take a second look.

Maddox is right. Two giant statues covered in climbing ivy flank the gate. The one on the right stands on a light ray carved in white marble. Milton nudges me with the verse, *"Gliding through the ev'n / On a sunbeam, swift as a shooting star."* That's how you described the angel of the sun, Uriel. But Uriel guarded earth, not hell.

"Who's waitin' for us?" Pop asks Devon.

"Can't tell." Devon parks the car. "Let me go check."

When Devon gets out of the car, so does Maddox. Harper soon follows, and I can't help but do the same. Maybe taking a better look at the statues will bridge the connection that, without a copy of Milton's poem, feels just out of reach. Not only that, a quick breath of fresh air might settle my nerves. I scoot across the fabric seat, careful not to aggravate my wound.

"Everyone get back in the car," Devon says, before my feet have touched the ground.

"We've been cramped up for hours." Harper stretches her arms over her head with a yawn. "Give us a minute."

"Make it quick." Devon checks the sky and walks toward the gate.

I know the longer I stay outside, the easier it is for the creatures to find me, but the crisp air gives me a freeing burst of energy. And with a clear view of both pillars, I might pick up a clue on what to expect from Alliance Council.

The statues are majestic. Uriel is beautifully carved with sharp eyes and thick ivory locks swept back by the wind. The second pillar is sculpted in charcoal-gray marble. Tangled ivy climbs over his opulent armor and cradles his handsome face as he stares into the distance with a warlike glare.

"*Chief of the angelic guards, awaiting night,*" Milton whispers in my head.

Gabriel? But he guarded Eden, and this place is far from a lush garden. Everything around me, including the woods on the other side of the gate, decays and smells of fall.

Just then, the hazy sun streaks though the treetops and lands on a blanket of leaves strewn on the dusty ground. Tingles ripple over my skin as the ground shimmers, and I'm drawn to the flittering light. It's as if each leaf is dipped in wet gold. What is this place?

Before Devon can scold me back in the car, an older woman with sun-weathered skin and a smooth black bun steps out from behind Uriel's sunbeam. She stays behind the gate, holding a lantern even though it's the middle of the day. Eager flames wrestle inside the glass as she waves the light up and down, then left and right behind the statue. As soon as she completes the last motion, a rumbling tremor pulses through the ground like the earth itself is opening to swallow me whole.

I jump back.

"What is that?" Harper speaks my thoughts, looking about as skittish as I feel.

Maddox, however, is completely unfazed. "It's the gate."

Sure enough, the rusted metal twists apart, opening about a car width. Crazy.

Devon embraces the tiny woman with a hug, lifting her off the ground the way he might have done with his own mother, if she were still alive. He sets her down with a grin as she brushes out her tribal skirt and blousy, mustard-colored shirt.

The woman pats Maddox on the cheek. His smile is warm. "Hi, Lina. It's been a while, I know."

Then she sees me. When she eyes my wounded leg, I squirm. She's bound to know I'm a Blight—an Alliance enemy. I give her a tiny wave and try to smile, regardless.

Devon nods at the woman. "Lina will heal your burn when we get up to the Estate. But for now, get back in the car." He scours the sky and surrounding forest. "You're not safe until we get behind the Circuit Wall."

I look at the gate again. There isn't a wall, only a flimsy wire near the pillars, doing a terrible job at holding back the woods.

"Cera, come look at this." Harper calls me over to the gate. "Have you ever seen a vine like this before?"

Forget the vines, I'm fascinated by the wire border, at how the warping air dances all the way into the treetops, blending with the overcast sky.

"*Impenetrable, impaled with circling fire / Yet unconsumed,*" Milton says in my head, repeating the line about the gate. Sure enough, the air warps above the marking line like heat from a fire. But there aren't any visible flames from what I can tell, and the only pungent smell comes from the car exhaust, not smoke.

"Is the Wall invisible?" I extend my hand toward the distorted air. Heat warms my fingertips. Tingling excitement rushes over me, catching me by surprise.

"Stop!" Devon commands as Maddox lunges toward me, pulling me away, shouting, "Don't touch it!"

"That wire is the outline of the Circuit Wall," Devon says. "But it's more of a guideline than anything else. Don't touch the Wall *or* the gate. Any contact by Awakened, Dissenter, beast or"—he looks at me—"anyone who can see the second realm will explode on contact. The only way in or out of the Estate is through the open gate. It's the only safe way." He is suddenly distracted by Lina.

Her head is tilted to the sky, listening into the distant wind.

That's when I hear it. Over the idling engine and rustling leaves, somewhere deep in the forest comes a faint but unmistakable shriek.

"A Cormorant." I search the woods for the swift crow beast.

Lina shoos us into the car. *"Rápido."*

"Go first." I hang back to let Maddox climb in, but he hesitates. It's only when I say, "Let me have the window to keep watch," that he relents.

As soon as we're all in and Devon jumps in the front seat, Pop makes a grunting sound. "Forget to tell Honey about the Wall, did we?"

"Yeah, a little bit." Devon throws the car in drive.

A stealthy shadow, no bigger than a mountain lion, glides through the autumn forest, tracking our path. As soon as we pass through the open gate, Lina holds the lantern near Gabriel and waves the light in reverse order. The vines shift back into place. But the beast is gaining on us, and Lina is out there, exposed.

"Devon, stop the car." My breath fogs the window as I fumble for the door handle. I can command the Cormorant to fly away and leave Lina alone if I'm close enough. "There's a—"

The black creature frantically beats its wings, keeping its six razor-sharp talons extended. It's working hard to change direction as the vines lock back into place, but instead it tumbles, slamming its lion head and those dripping fangs into the thorny gate. A blast of light, brighter than a welder's arc, sparks against the vines. Burning ashes rain down, extinguishing before they've hit the floor. And just like that, the beast is gone.

"Cormorant?" Devon's confident eyes find mine in the rearview mirror. "Like I said. Nothing gets through the Circuit Wall. When that gate is closed, we're protected."

Maddox slouches with a troubled expression. "If you're talking about Legions and Cormorants, then sure."

Despite Devon's assurance, I turn and keep an eye on the woods anyway. I do a double take. Everything on this side of the gate is . . . vibrant, budding green? How is that possible? There isn't a single trace of a decaying fall. Even the afternoon sun, breaking through the lush treetops, glows brighter.

"When as sacred light began to dawn / In Eden on the humid flowers." Yes, Milton, it's very much a world in the throes of spring. My pulse is electric.

I'm not alone in my wonder. Harper is slack-jawed with her face against the window, staring up at the trees.

Someone in a groundskeeping cart zooms by in the opposite direction, heading toward the gate and Lina, as we slowly drive up the hill. Every rotation of the tires brings me closer to Council. Closer to death. Or closer to defeating Sage.

"Don't worry, Pop and I will smooth things over with Lieutenant Foster. He's in command until the admiral returns," Devon says, his eyes meeting mine again.

I try to smile. I'm not worried. I'm scared to death. But judging by the look on Maddox's face, I'm not so sure Devon is only talking to me.

After several winding curves, Devon turns onto a graveled

path tunneled by trees raining white blossoms. Rocks crumble and pop as we inch up the drive. Maddox's knee bounces. My foot does too.

Maybe the Alliance will kill me at first sight. Maybe Pop can convince them otherwise. But one thing is certain.

My fate waits at the top of that hill.

2
THE ARBOR

The "Estate" is nothing but a summer getaway home plopped in the middle of a botanical garden—a squat, one-story, Spanish-style fortress with a terra-cotta roof and sunbaked stucco walls. The only thing grand about the building is how it sprawls the entire length of the circular driveway. I sit back but don't let my guard down. I'm in enemy territory, and I can't forget it.

Cooperate. Stay alive. Train. Fight in the war.

I recite these words over and over as way to calm down and keep focused as Devon pulls the car around a three-tiered water fountain.

He cuts the engine. "Nothing's changed."

"Hmph." Pop's fingers search the side panel for the handle. "We'll find out soon enough."

When Pop opens the door, an eager breeze whips through the car, cooling the stuffy air. Before I can get out, Devon turns around. "Stay put while we go in and work things out," he says to me. "When you do come in, be quiet. Lay low. Speak when spoken to."

"It's best if she's not left alone," Pop says to no one in particular.

"I'll stay," Maddox volunteers a little too quickly.

"So will I." Harper shoots him another sideways glance.

Devon looks at the three of us crammed in the back seat.

His Caretaker's built-in truth-meter is raging strong. After a scrutinizing silence he says, "If I'm not out in ten, then come in."

"Devon, wait." I lean forward before he gets out of the car. Gladys's hairpin pokes me again. I wiggle it to the side. "Can I use your phone to call my mom?"

"Battery's dead. But last I heard she was transported to Hesperian. We'll talk to Foster, then call Gladys for an update on her recovery."

He shuts the door and then walks off to help Pop navigate the three steps up to the front door. While Harper rummages through the duffle bag, I search for a way to roll down the window. I pull the handle near my knee but nothing happens. I'm about to open the door instead when Maddox reaches over and cranks the handle in a circle. "Roll it down like this."

"Thanks. I can get it from here." I take over, lowering the wonky window on my own, but it gets stuck about halfway. Or maybe that's as far as it goes. Regardless, it's enough to let in the cool breeze that tastes like nectar.

"Go change somewhere." Harper hands me Devon's vintage green T-shirt she pulled from the bag. "I need to talk to Maddox for a minute."

My shirt. I'd forgotten the front was slashed open by the generator coils. I take a quick inventory of the grounds. Besides the forest, my best option is an enclosed pergola about thirty feet away. It's nestled by the side of the house and covered in thick ivy, making it private enough. "Be right back."

Harper eyes the cuts on Maddox's arm and rips open a gauze packet, dousing it with stringent antiseptic. "And be careful with your wound," she adds. "You didn't have enough serum to block the pain much longer."

I stretch and inspect the burnt edge of my jeans. "It feels tight but doesn't hurt." Too much.

A gentle breeze rustles the surrounding treetops, lighting

the greenery with beckoning shimmers like the sprinkled dust of fallen stars. Or maybe it's the morning dew.

"Stay close. Make it quick." Maddox is in full Guardian mode. His serious tone underscores my reality but, for some reason, clashes with the soulful music from a distant cello.

No one patrols the grounds. We're alone as far as I can tell, and I don't see any cameras, but I trust him. Even with the awkwardness lingering between us. "I won't be long."

I hobble to the arbor. Sugary nectar douses the air and lands on my tongue. Out here, my senses sharpen. I feel more alert, alive, aware of every breath. A tiny pulse—no, it's more of a hum, or maybe a heartbeat—thrums through the Garden. Whether it's nerves, something in the air, or there really is an electric pulse riding my skin, I don't know.

When I reach the arbor, that familiar, paranoid feeling of being watched creeps over me. Devon said creatures couldn't get into the Garden when the gate was shut, but I'm on the alert anyhow.

The empty nook is about twenty stones deep and four wide, nothing but a corridor leading to a narrow opening on the far right. Tangled vines net the ceiling. The space looks void of strange shadows or black mist, so I carefully navigate down the steps.

Cold radiates from the stones. The sugary nectar tastes stronger in the damp air. The floral scent is familiar, but I can't place it. Gardenia, maybe? When a slight breeze brushes across the vines, small honey-colored flowers glow between waxy leaves. That's definitely *not* gardenia.

I run my fingertip over a velvet petal. A gentle hum purrs against my skin, and the flower brightens at my touch. I jerk my hand away. The light quickly fades, and the flower shrivels, turning dirty brown. Dead.

"Cera?" Maddox's footsteps skid across the gravel, sounding in my direction.

"Give her a second." Harper's voice carries from the drive.

I peer through the vines. I'm not sure how much they can see, but it can't be much because I only get pockets of Maddox's white T-shirt near the water fountain and Harper's blonde hair as she chases after him.

"Cera can't be left alone," Maddox says, sounding frustrated.

"She's fine." Harper's flats scuffle on the pebbles. "Besides, we have a conversation to finish. We barely got a chance to talk back at the apartment."

"Later. Cera can't be in there."

Why not? The gleaming sun beckons from the narrow opening at the far end of the alcove, lapping the stones and flittering back and forth the way water wrestles a lake's edge. But there's nothing threatening in this cozy space.

"Maddox, please don't walk away." Harper is practically begging. "I just want to know what's going on."

All footsteps stop. "That corridor leads to the Empyrean Well. If a Blade finds her in there, they'll think she was trying to find the source of our Bents. They'll think she's—it's just not safe for her. That's all."

Wait. The source of the Current is around that corner? I inch closer to the arched walkway and poke my head around the entry. Six-foot shrubs line a crushed-granite path into a maze garden, but where did the reflective water come from? An urge to explore tugs strong.

Then something rustles deep inside the thick maze walls. I quickly step back.

Change. Do it fast.

"That's not what I'm talking about." Harper's voice rises. "You said you kissed her because you thought you all were going to die, but there's more to it, isn't there?"

"Can we talk later?" Maddox tries to whisper.

"No, Maddox, we can't. I get that you and I, we're not a

thing. You made that clear, but I just want you to tell me what's really going on—"

"I'm her interceptor. I'm supposed to stay near and guard her."

"Why won't you be honest with me?"

I work the buttons on the flannel shirt and glance through the vines, catching a glimpse of Maddox as he rubs his hands over his face. "I promise we'll talk. Just not out here. Cera needs— Harper? Harper, wait." Hard footsteps grind over the gravel drive. "Harper!" The front door slams.

I change as fast as I can.

He only kissed me because he thought we were about to die? Unbelievable. I was simply one last kiss before death. I really don't need this distraction right now.

In one fluid motion, I slide my arms out of the collared shirt and put on Devon's T-shirt. I shrug the flannel back on for added warmth, leaving it unbuttoned. As I bend down to roll up the torn fabric of my burnt jeans, a warning flare rips through me. I push the feeling aside and adjust my ponytail.

"What are you doing in here?" a deep voice asks from behind.

I spin around, wiping a wayward strand of hair from my face. "I'm—I—"

Why can't I find the words? Maybe it's because the guy is about as cut as the statue of Gabriel come to life and his warrior-like presence suffocates any trace of air. His ice-blue eyes scan me with the intensity of a trained hunter. He's a Blade—and a strong one. I look down at the ground and count the distance between us.

One. Two. Five mossy stones.

"You one of us?" I'm not sure if he means a Blade or Awakened. But in both cases, the answer is no. I consider lying, but that's proven to cause more problems. I clearly can't outrun him. Not with my busted leg. His hand rests close to his hip, weaponless. But he's bound to have something tucked in the lining of his clothes the way all Blades do.

He steps closer. Two stones away. Now one.

"Look at me," he commands.

I lift my eyes, slowly. His sharp jaw is pinpricked with stubble. He's about Devon's age, maybe slightly older. Smells of metal shavings—either that, or it's blood. I work hard to avoid direct contact with his eyes that scorch with a stare so intense, warmth radiates from my face. He'll read my Current and know what I am.

"Cera, you ready?" Maddox appears around the corner. He stops. "Gray." His confident voice wavers. "She's been cleared."

"Not by me." The guy, Gray, lifts my jaw with strong fingers. My face turns hotter than the summer sun.

Then his name slaps inside my head. *Gray.*

Maddox's brother.

The Elite Blade and god-to-all-things-Alliance holds my chin firmly in his hands.

When our eyes meet, the buzzing Current cuts through me with a painful shock. Paralyzing. Stronger than any other. He's assessing. Judging. Deciding.

Maddox is a blur rushing to my side. "She's here to see Foster. Not you." He takes my hand and jerks me away, breaking the intense hold of Gray's Current that's left me shaky. "C'mon, Cera."

"Wait." I wiggle my hand free.

Broken sunlight peers through the netted ceiling, highlighting Gray's spiky hair and striking cheekbones. He doesn't look anything like Maddox. The only similarity lies in the smooth lips and the sharp nose, although compared to Gray's, Maddox's nose might have been broken. I will my heart to slow down. "I was told I should train with you. Kellan said that you're the best Blade there is."

"You brought home a Blight?" Gray completely ignores me. His eyes harden at Maddox. "The gate should have sensed her as a threat. How did she get through?"

"Because she's not a threat," Maddox says abruptly. "Cera, let's go."

"You're not going anywhere." Gray plants a hand on Maddox's chest and pushes him away. "Do you have any idea how much trouble you're in? I had to risk lives by sending in a team to protect your little group in that trash hole because you refuse to train—and have them trained. Art doesn't win a war. Training does. Now people are injured—"

"I messed up, I know," Maddox says, as Gray's shadow casts over him. "I made a mistake."

"That's not a mistake. That's being irresponsible. But *this*?" He looks at me. The hard lines on his face transform with disgust. "Bringing *that* into the Garden and putting the Well at risk isn't an innocent mistake. It's a serious infraction. How many times do you have to mess up before you'll get it through your thick head? You and I, we're not like everyone else. We have obligations. Responsibilities. A duty to our line."

"I said, I know." Maddox's voice is tight.

I squirm. He shouldn't get chewed out on account of me. "It wasn't his idea to bring me here," I say as an achy throb wakes in my leg. The serum must be wearing off.

Gray points a hard finger at me. "You've got no right to speak."

I open my mouth to snap back, but Maddox taps the back of his hand to mine. It's his way of telling me to stay quiet. I know because his focus is locked on Gray with the same intensity we had when fleeing from the Cormorants. I hate backing down, but I trust Maddox. I shut my mouth and swallow my acidic words.

Gray refocuses on Maddox. "You're lucky Albrecht isn't here. I'll work this out with Foster and tell him you're turning her in. Now get inside. And get a haircut. You look ridiculous."

Without warning, Gray seizes my wrist and jerks me forward. I land on my injured leg and cry out as sharp pain shoots from my wound, sending daggers into my eyeballs.

"Back off!" Maddox throws a fist at Gray.

Gray releases me, but only to thrust a backhanded punch

into Maddox's face, knocking him back. "You really want to do this right here? Over a Blight?"

Maddox staggers and wipes blood from his nose. Fire rages in his eyes.

Gray circles around Maddox, his hard boots echoing in this cramped cage. "Go on. Show this Blight what you're made of. Then let's see what she thinks of you." Gray taunts Maddox with a quick slap on the ear.

Maddox tenses. "Cera, it's time to go." He places a firm hand on my back.

"Oh, come on, Maddox. You started this fight. Finish it. Or maybe I'll tell her about you. About how—"

"Shut up," Maddox growls.

"Why? Maybe if she knew how you couldn't—"

"I said, shut up!" Maddox flies at Gray.

Gray dodges the hit, only to strike fast and knock Maddox to the ground. "That all you got?" Gray rolls Maddox to his side using the tip of his boot.

Sunlight hides behind the clouds, darkening the arbor as Maddox shoves Gray's foot aside. "Back off."

"I'll back off when you finally learn to fight. Now, get up. We're not done."

Blades instinctively know when something is about to strike and can anticipate a hit. But not Guardians. There's no way Maddox will win this. Not only is Gray a Blade, but he's too fluid. Too quick. And has way more muscle.

Maddox pushes off the ground. The side of his face, the side with the scar, is scraped and bleeding. Blood is smeared in his hair and dripping from his nose. Raging heat surges inside me. I can't stay silent. "Stop!" I rush between them.

"Not a threat, huh?" Gray twists my arm. I yelp in pain. "You have a thing for my kid brother?"

Maddox jumps to his feet. "Look, I'm here. I'll train. I'll fight, okay? Just leave her alone."

"Blights don't get left alone. Blights die. You of all people should know they're nothing but worthless rats trying to taint our line. Weaken us."

I know I'm worthless, that's nothing new. Gray can call me whatever name he wants, beat me, threaten to kill me—but family or not, if he ever hurts Maddox again, I'll call on Moloch to claw his heart out. I struggle to get away as Gray wrenches my arm behind my back. When I take a hard step, I feel the wound tear open under the bandage.

"Gray, don't." Maddox's eyes are trained on the brass knife with the opal handle Gray now holds, the one with the signature vine-etched pattern. The one I'm certain is Paradise Steel. "She doesn't want to destroy us. Let her talk to—"

"All Blights want to destroy us, whether they know it or not." Gray points the blade at Maddox. "Maybe it's time I stopped cleaning up after you. Maybe then you'd grow up and start caring about your obligation as an Elite—about what Mom and Dad sacrificed for us—about what *I* did for you. Maybe you'd stop being such a pathetic runt who screws up all the time. Like getting lured by this disease." Gray tips the knife near my cheek. A heated vibration radiates from the metal.

"I do care about being a Legacy. And about what Mom and Dad did, about what *you* did," Maddox says, the hurt in his eyes evident. "But I'm not you." He wipes the dirt from his arms. "Life is more than ranking up in Alliance Council. Making the world a better place is what matters. It's what we were taught, and I'm living it out, whether you like it or not."

Gray's grip on my arm slackens, but I don't dare move. I barely breathe. "We both know that's useless thinking that won't keep you alive."

"I'll do whatever you want. Just let her go." Maddox glances at me. "I never wanted her to come here. Lassiter did."

Gray lowers the knife. "Devon?"

"Pop."

Gray scoffs. "Lassiter might be senile, but he knows better."

"Ask him. He's inside." Maddox gestures toward the house. "Probably talking to Foster about her now."

Gray assesses Maddox for a moment. After a long silence, he releases my arm, only to land a jarring shove into my spine.

"Move it, Blight." Gray pushes me forward. "Time to see how long you'll live."

3
MAD MARTIN

Gray steers me through the front door and into a hallway filtered with scant light from a narrow stained glass window. The smell of baked bread might be comforting if his steel-toed boots weren't stomping on the earthy tile. Maddox's footsteps follow behind, out of sync with Gray's heavy stride.

Gray stops me just short of a grand archway on my left. "Not a word." His unwelcome breath steams hot against my ear. Then he pushes me into the room.

My entrance is far from graceful. I trip on the corner of an antique rug, stumbling into a ballroom with an intricate twenty-foot ceiling and ornate chandeliers. The vast room feels like an antiquated museum, a tomb of relics that smells of aged lacquer. Giant canvases and faded tapestries decorate the walls. Thick upholstered chairs in a variety of muted colors cluster in every corner, and a hand-carved conference table dominates the middle of the room where Pop is seated. Devon stands behind him deep in conversation with a middle-aged man sporting a pencil-thin mustache and a green sweater-vest. They stop talking and look in my direction.

"Lieutenant Foster, a Blight breached the gate." Gray's arrogant echo ricochets behind me. "She was searching the arbor."

Maddox comes to my side, blood smearing his lip. "She wasn't searching, Lieutenant. She—"

"Attacked me," Gray shoots Maddox a hard look. "Cast some sort of spell on my brother." He wrenches my arm behind my back, guiding me away from Maddox and deeper into the room, closer to the crackling fire that has no effect on me because angry heat has already invaded my veins.

"I can't cast spells," I spit at him. "I can only command a Legion to burn your skin off."

"Cera!" Devon is quickly at my side. His voice is steeped with warning as he whispers, "That's not helping."

Cooperate and stay alive, I know. But, not only is Gray making it next to impossible, the serum has worn off, and now a throbbing burn chews inside my leg.

"There's the proof." Gray stabs a hard finger in my direction.

"She can command Legions?" Lieutenant Foster asks. His perfect consonants are tinted by a slight British accent that totally suits his look.

"Sure as she can command a Cormorant to stay in a storm." Pop rises from the chair with a grunt and the help of his cane. "Thought it best for her to stay here. Keep her out of Sage's hands."

Yeah, well, I'm not doing so great in Gray's hands at the moment, Pop.

"Blights are known enemies to the Alliance, Edward." I bristle at the condescending way Gray talks to Pop. "Luring Awakened, divulging secrets, potentially giving Sage access to our power. How did you get this one in the Garden?"

"She ain't no enemy, Grayson James. The girl's just feisty, untrained, and careless."

While it's probably true, that's not the glowing support I was hoping for. I can't stay quiet any longer. "Then train me," I say. "All I want is to save lives. I'll do whatever it takes to help you destroy Sage and win the war. Unless he's stopped, more innocent people will die." My horrifying visions will continue, and Mom and I will never be safe.

"Hmph." Pop flares his nostrils, probably unhappy that I used the word "destroy," but it's the truth. "And the gate let this one through 'cause she's underage—not yet seventeen. Awakened at age seven."

Lieutenant Foster perks at the news of my unusual Awakening. He walks my way with the poised stride of a swordsman stepping out of an old-time movie. Every hair on his head is plastered down in proper submission. He smells of starched linen—and looks just as uptight. Other than a small quirk of his eyebrow, I can't read anything from his blank expression. "Is she a seeing child?"

"She is a Seer, yes," Devon says.

Pop feels his way along the back of the chairs and around the table. "There's only been one other Blight born with her peculiar combination of Bents. Seer and Guardian."

Gray inspects his Paradise Steel. Blood from the fight smears his fist. "And that one Blight caused extensive damage," he quickly points out as he walks to a drink cart in the far corner of the room.

"Did some harm to the gate, that's known." Pop stops near a set of wingback chairs not far from the fire. "Sage took a hit himself in that battle."

"But the blast didn't destroy him." Gray picks up a cloth napkin and polishes the Steel, with a death glare pinned on me. "Because of that incident, Council *requires* eliminations of all Blights for our safety. We can't risk a recurrence."

"Panicked thinking can create a greater hell than what we want to avoid," Pop says.

Gray stands in front of a vast painting and spins the weapon the same way Maddox does a pencil. The taunting blade glistens with each rotation. "That one Blight almost destroyed us. What guarantee do we have that this one won't finish the job?"

I protest, "I only want to destroy the Legions, Cormorants, and Sage." And at this moment, possibly Gray.

Gray tucks his weapon away. "Sage is indestructible."

No. That can't be true.

Gray notices my expression. "You heard me right. The Alliance has *one* responsibility: to keep Sage from annihilating us and our source of power." He dips the cloth into a water glass and meticulously wipes Maddox's blood from his hands. "Doesn't matter if you consciously choose to help Sage or not, dissension is in your blood. A Blight can give Sage the power to wipe us out. One almost did."

Maddox steps forward, shielding me from the heat of Gray's glare. "Everyone claims Sage is indestructible because of what happened in the Renaissance. But if a Blight could help Sage, why couldn't one help us?"

"I can't believe we're having this discussion." Gray turns to Lieutenant Foster and tosses the blood-smeared napkin on the cart. "Our code requires termination. Blights have always been a threat to our power and our people."

Maddox is relentless. "Sage hasn't had any influence on her."

"That's right," Devon vouches for me. "Her mother kept her hidden all these years. Maddox found her before Sage did—before she turned seventeen."

"She lure you too, Lassiter?" Gray scowls. "What do you think will happen after we've trained her, told her Alliance secrets? She'll turn against us. That's what."

"Outside these walls," Devon warns him, "Sage will get a hold of her. That is guaranteed. His getting a hold of her seems more of a threat than her being in the Garden."

Gray's eyes flash. "Our *only* responsibility is protecting our power. What proof do we have that Sage hasn't been influencing her? You think it's a coincidence that she was found *before* she's fully manifested all her powers? She may not tell you Sage is behind this, but I'm certain he is."

"Maddox Alexander." Lieutenant Foster's voice, stripped of

emotion, cuts through the rising tension. "I understand you were responsible for acquiring the Blight."

Acquiring. What an impersonal word, as if I'm not even human. Despite the tense words swirling in the air and the mauling pain in my leg, I gently take Pop's elbow to guide him to the chair he seems to be searching for with his cane.

Gray glares at me and doesn't let Maddox respond to the lieutenant. "He was turning her in so I can arrange proper termination."

"Ain't no need for termination!" Pop pounds his cane on the wood floor with a hard *thunk*. Even the small crystals on the giant chandelier tremble. "The boy's done right, keeping her out of Sage's hands. She ain't had no influence from the enemy. Talk to her, you'll see. She wants nothing more than to help the Alliance. Ain't that right, Honey?"

Once again, all eyes fall on me. Heat crawls under my skin. Whether it's from being put on the spot or the lapping flames in the nearby fire, I don't know. All I know is that this is my one chance to prove I'm not a threat. And stay alive.

I tuck my hair behind my ear and glance around at everything in the room, focusing on nothing in particular. "I only came here because I want to help end the battle with Sage. For good." I try to stand tall. "The Legions travel in a mist only I can see. They attack by sound and hiss like bees when they approach. And the Cormorants? I'm not sure how many, but I've seen at least three. They hunt by sight and smell, and I can detect their shriek before any Awakened can. Equip me. I won't turn against you. All I want is to make sure that no one else dies because of Sage and his horrible creatures."

Honestly, I really don't know if I have any ability to help the Alliance destroy Sage. But if I do, then all the running, the fear, and maybe even the excruciating visions, might finally end. "And I'd like to call my mom. Please."

The final syllable of my strained plea bounces back as the room turns uncomfortably quiet. I fix my stare on the desperate flames as they reach for an escape they'll never find.

Too many seconds pass. No one says a word. My breath turns shaky as a grandfather clock ticks away the silence. What more can I say?

Finally, Lieutenant Foster speaks. "Do you believe you are strong enough to suppress any Dissenting powers and avoid the fate of the last Blight?"

I stand perfectly still, hoping my knees won't crumble. "Besides commanding creatures, I'm not really sure what Dissenting powers are. But I won't be anything like my father. I don't want to be. I guess I was hoping that, with your help, maybe for the first time ever, my curse—my visions—could become a gift."

"Much better seems this vision, and more hope." Milton's verse whispers inside my head, a welcome affirmation that I'm on the right path.

As the sun breaks through the clouds, brightening the room, I find the strength to look up. "I only want to help you stop—" My gaze lands on the colossal painting across the room. With Gray out of the way, I have a clear shot of the whole canvas.

The tiny figure at the bottom of the painting . . .

I've seen this piece before. A man clambers over a ledge, struggling to find a foothold on the side of a craggy cliff, straining with all his might to find the source of a sacred waterfall. My breath is like charged air before a storm. "Is that a Mad Martin?"

Lieutenant Foster's one eyebrow almost reaches the ceiling. "A John Martin, yes," his tone corrective. "Are you familiar with *Sadak in Search of the Waters of Oblivion*?" His deep-set eyes probe for answers: processing, deliberating, and searching all at once. "How is it that you know this painting?"

Why can't I keep my mouth shut the way Devon told me to? Lieutenant Foster isn't physically intimidating, but it's clear he's a Caretaker, and he already knows the answer. He's just testing me for the truth.

I choose my words carefully. Honestly. "My mom had art books on Romantic painters."

"Were you instructed to study paintings in those books?"

"Not study. She'd have me look through pictures and make up stories about what I saw." My gaze returns to the reddish hues in the painting. "This piece stood out because of the glowing water in the wellspring. Or maybe it's a lake. I told her the light poured out from underneath, from another world, and flowed into the abyss."

"From underneath?" Foster questions. "Explain why you thought so."

My childish story suddenly feels inadequate. I'm not an art expert like Mom. I don't have a good answer, only an honest one. "Since the sky was red with flames, or molten lava, the cream-colored light in the water couldn't be a reflection. The bright light had to come from somewhere else."

"*Look into the clear / Smooth lake that to me seemed another sky,*" Milton prompts me. By "another sky," Milton do you mean . . .

"Maybe even another realm?" I say, taking Milton's lead. "I've always felt there was something hopeful, maybe even powerful, about the quiet water and how it streams into the world."

Milton must have been right because Foster motions to the artwork, inviting me closer. "Tell me the rest of the story and what you saw."

I hobble across the room, ignoring Gray's watchful glare as I pass the conference table. The daunting canvas looms right in front of me, highlighting how small I am, not unlike the tiny man in the painting.

I take in the angry shadows fighting the wispy strokes of light. "In my story, the man was sneaking to the water source while war raged all around him. In the distance misty shadows of monsters surround him, but he was determined. And the reddish rocks, the ones jutting around the water, those were the skull of a fallen beast. A sign of his victory and—" I stand frozen, seeing the painting clearly for the first time. It's as if my eyes have sharpened. Colors turn brighter. Lines cleaner. "The shadows are Legions. And the fallen beast is a bird with giant shoulders. That's a Cormorant."

Lieutenant Foster is watching me closely. "Not rocks?"

"Martin painted them to look like rocks, but they're not. Look." I point them out, shaking inside. "It's not the gorilla-like creature. Martin painted that beast, on the right side of the canvas. Over here."

"Show me." Maddox's encouraging tone helps settle my nerves. At least one person believes me. I find him standing behind me, Devon at his side. Pop is still seated in the chair, and Gray stands across the room alone, while someone quickly slips past the screen door, patrolling the outside.

"Yes, look." I return to the painting. "The cheekbones, the nose and that beady eye—that's the horrible beast. He doesn't see the man reaching the waters because he's too focused on the fallen creature in the background. And that gorilla-like thing? It's the worst of all." My pulse breaks into an all-out gallop as the message becomes clear. "This isn't a lone trek to find sacred waters. Martin painted a battle scene for that water source."

Another canvas hanging on the wall near the doorway catches my eye. One of a girl wearing a blue dress. Before I can pull any details, Lieutenant Foster steps in front of me. "Sergeant Carver," he commands evenly, "escort Miss Marlowe to my library. Have her wait there until further notice and then return immediately."

"I'll arrange a more secure location," Gray says.

"My library will do for now, thank you." Foster's face is unreadable. No glint in his eyes, no warmth in his expression, but no hate or anger either. His deadpan expression is just that, blank. Stoic.

"Am I wrong?"

Before I can read Maddox for the answer, Gray grabs my arm. "Move it."

I tear away. "I swear, if you touch me again—"

"You'll what?" Gray reaches for the pocket where his knife probably hides.

Pop clears his throat, sending me a signal, one I know. *Don't get hotheaded.* I back away before I say something I'll regret. As I do, Maddox shields me from Gray.

Gray shoots him a weighted look. "Don't be a traitor."

"She needs a Guardian."

"Blights don't get Guardians."

"That is quite enough," Lieutenant Foster snaps at them.

"Grayson James," Pop calls from the chair. "Leave the boy be. There's no threat of him breakin' code. I've been teaching him to intercept her visions. That's the only connection between those two. Nothing more."

Leave it to Pop to call things out like a slap in the face. But at least it explains Maddox's overprotective attitude.

Pop points a boney finger in my direction. "And don't you worry about her, neither. She's smart and won't do anything to detract from her own preparation." Pop is only half right, but I get his message loud and clear.

Gray walks me out of the room, keeping his hands to himself, thankfully.

As soon as we turn a corner, he gets in my face. "Nice try. But reading one painting won't save a monster disguised in skin." Cold hate drips off every word.

He shoves me into a room and slams the wooden door.

4

OUT OF THE SHADOWS

I'm locked behind a set of thick library doors, waiting for a verdict on my life. As muffled voices carry from the other side, I take in my holding cell. It's a dank room that smells of expensive leather and musky paper. An imposing desk swallows the nook in front of bay windows, while all around me shelved walls are crammed with old copies of art history, poetry, physics, botany, and archeology—caged voices shouting to be heard.

Coming here is proving to be a mistake. I had hoped that the Alliance would give me a chance to show that I'm on their side. But clearly luck isn't tipping in my direction.

What now? Make a run for it?

I can't escape out the library doors, but there's a glass door that leads to a courtyard. If I found my way out I could . . . go where? Back to Mom? She's healing at Hesperian with Gladys. And she needs to heal. Whatever Blades are with her will simply drag me back here—or worse. Not to mention the possibility of Sage finding me first. And he'd most likely torture me into doing his malicious will.

No, running doesn't do any good. It never has. Not that I'd get very far with a wounded leg screaming at me.

As difficult as it is for me to trust others, my best option is to stay put and hope that Devon, Pop, and Maddox will win Lieutenant Foster over somehow. Then I can prove there's not a drop of my father's blood luring me toward Sage. If not . . .

I lower myself on the couch near the hollow fireplace and rub my hands over my face. When I close my eyes, the image of the Legion resurrects in my mind. Its vile sallow skin and stench of sulfur. Those cavernous holes for eyes, and the raspy sounds pushing through its neck as if trying to speak. I can almost feel the tendril of smoke tracing an outline around my collarbone . . . I shudder.

Despite Gray's comment, *that* beast is the monster. Not me.

A soft *thunk* comes from the window behind the desk. That warning flare sizzles through me. The same one I had before I met Gray. The first time I ignored it and was caught off guard. That won't happen again.

The glass rattles as it slides open. I sneak into a crevice not far from the fireplace where two angled bookshelves meet. Whoever chooses to come in through a window can't be up to any good. I press my back into the bookcase, hiding in the shadow of a colossal globe perched on a stand. The African continent points to the ceiling, while my side of the world is shadowed in darkness.

In case it's another belligerent Blade like Gray, I slide a fireplace poker from the carrel and stare at the window. I don't dare blink. Or breathe.

A guy with disheveled hair the same color as his jet-black boots slips through the window, landing somewhere behind the desk. Silent. I force my breath steady.

After a thousand frantic heartbeats, the guy rises. He's dressed in all black. Tall. Lanky. He puts on a fedora the shade of rich mocha and then walks around the desk, dusting off his button-down with refined precision. He trips right in front of me. Nervous laughter bubbles into my throat. I choke it down.

"Stupid rug." He kicks the culprit and then stills. He's either listening, or he sees me out of the corner of his eye. But maybe not.

He quickly rummages through a stack of messy papers on the coffee table, carefully watching the doors.

If he's stealing, maybe I could prove my loyalty by confronting him and turning him in. He might be stronger than me, but if he tries anything, I can call out for Maddox and Devon, who are across the hall.

I step out of the shadows, weapon in hand. "Stop right there."

He spins around. "Whoa, easy there." Unruly locks poke out from under the hat, which he lowers even more. I can't read the Current in his eyes to tell if he's Awakened; they're shaded under the rim. He isn't as tall as Maddox but is around the same age. "Where'd you come from?" His baritone voice drips with a smile.

The warning flare subsides, but I keep the pointed weapon steady between us anyhow. "Not through a window."

"What's fun about busting through a door and letting Foster find me?" He runs a finger along the globe, spinning the world so quickly the colors blur.

"So you climbed through the window of his library? That's brilliant." I shouldn't be so sarcastic when I'm not sure what this guy is capable of, but I'm exhausted, starving, and my wounded leg is throbbing. Plus, he doesn't read as a threat.

This fedora guy stops the globe with a tattooed ring finger. "You must not know the guy. Be warned: he's always telling you what you should and shouldn't do, talks about triggers, and tries stuffing your head with things you don't care to know." When he steps closer, I get a whiff of smoky wildfire and hair gel, although I still can't get a good look at his eyes. "What's your name?" He flicks the collar of my shirt. He's either really bad at flirting, or he's checking for a Dissenter mark.

"Back off." I raise the poker an inch away from his chest. A risky move, I know. He's most likely a Blade, although he's nowhere near as intimidating as Gray. Especially when his hands fly up in immediate surrender.

An odd burn mark shaped like a jagged line tags his left wrist. I don't recall that mark on any Awakened, Blade or otherwise.

"Chill. I didn't mean to cross a line." He rests a mud-crusted boot on the couch and tightens his laces. "Just thought you'd want company instead of reading boring stuff like"—he picks a thin, red leather book off the coffee table—"*The Prince*." He tosses it back in the pile.

"Machiavelli?" I had that same book at home. I step closer to confirm the title.

"Just pretend to read that sixteenth-century garbage." He waves a dismissive hand in front of me while, in one smooth move, he simultaneously slides the weapon from my slack grip. It takes a split second too long for me to realize what he's done. When I whip around, he's already returned the poker to the stand. "Foster makes all Awakened study Machiavelli."

He might have disarmed me, but it doesn't mean I'm defenseless. I stare him down and wield the words that seem to shake everyone else. "Yeah, well, I'm a Blight."

He smirks. "Sounds hot."

The library door swings open. "Cera," Devon calls from the hall.

"Nice to meet you, *Cera*." The guy slinks around me with catlike reflexes and swiftly slides something out from under the cushions before Devon enters. I only get a quick glance, but it's enough for me to see the glistening, vine-etched blade.

Paradise Steel.

"Time to go." Devon, in full military mode, studies Fedora Guy straightening the hem of his jeans. The knife is nowhere in sight. "The lieutenant made a decision."

"Go . . . where?" I hobble over to Devon.

"The War Room." He eyes my leg. "I'll have Harper look at

that wound again. She's working on more serum with Lina."

"Forget about my leg, Devon. What did the lieutenant say?" He won't look at me. "You've got my back, right?" I follow him across the hall. "You won't let Gray, you know, get rid of me or anything, will you? I mean, he can't. That's murder. The Alliance can't get away with that. Someone will know—"

"The Alliance is everywhere. Including places you'd never imagine." Devon's hushed tone is thick with warning. "So remember what I said. Control your outbursts."

I swallow hard and enter the vast room.

5

EXTRAORDINARY ADVANTAGE

The lieutenant stands in front of the conference table, waiting. Pop is seated in one of the upholstered chairs. Maddox is nowhere in sight. Neither is Gray, though I can hear him. His berating lecture on Alliance protocol echoes near the entry hall. Devon nudges me closer to Lieutenant Foster, whose expression is unreadable. No surprise.

"Miss Marlowe." Foster motions to a chair in front of him.

Tension winds inside my chest, curling tighter and tighter. I carefully lower myself on the edge of the upholstered seat, remembering to sit upright. When I do, the itchy bandage pulls away from the skin. Maybe I shouldn't have been so quick to pass on getting more serum.

Foster folds his hands neatly in front of him, covering a silver wedding ring, and waits for me to settle before he begins. "As you know, the Alliance has uncovered countless messages embedded in classical works from Awakened artists over the centuries. However, some pieces contain indecipherable or incomplete messages crafted by artists we believe may have been undetected Blights, such as yourself."

Blights like me have stayed alive long enough to create famous works of art? I quickly take inventory of the room. A large tapestry with a gruesome battle hangs over the crackling fire, but nothing in particular stands out. Tiny artifacts are lit in a glass display case near the entry hall but are too far away for me to really see. Then there's the painting of the girl in the blue dress . . .

Foster regains my attention. "I believe your unique ability to interpret these messages could prove a tremendous benefit to Alliance intelligence. It is for this reason, until the admiral returns and states otherwise, I agree to offer sanctuary within the Garden in exchange for your cooperation."

I exhale in relief. They won't terminate me. Yet.

Lieutenant Foster continues. "During your stay, you will have limited access to the grounds and shall be provided with an escort, as well as monitored with a Cord, or traceable wristband, to ensure you remain within close proximity to this building."

A stealthy shadow slinks into the room, lingering somewhere behind me. "Welcome to the club, Blighty." Fedora Guy stands at the archway and lifts his sleeve. I study the thread wrapped across the jagged burn on his wrist. I'd seen the mark but don't recall the thread. At least I don't think.

"Mr. Hendrick Colton Tripton III. Your timing is impeccably . . . late." Lieutenant Foster's tone sours.

"Cole." The guy lifts his chin in my direction and then collapses into a chair near the archway. "Mr. Tripton makes me sound like an old man, Lieutenant Errol Ernest Foster."

"Lieutenant, who is this kid?" Devon asks, looking both bewildered and annoyed by the guy's presence.

"*Mr. Tripton* is a new member of the Alliance, a Blade with firsthand knowledge of Sage and his practices, which makes him rather indispensable. He was fortunate enough to escape, although he came quite close to dissenting."

Cole sits up. "Only because I woke up on my seventeenth birthday all tripped out and couldn't come down. Started seeing things no one else could. None of you *compadres* were around to explain what was happening. Sage was the only one."

Cole has met Sage? My skin prickles as a million questions form in my mind.

"You're a new bloodline." Devon pierces him with the same intimidating stare he gave me when I first met him. "Makes sense. Most Dissenters are."

"I didn't dissent." Cole yanks back the collar of his shirt. His neck is void of the flaky red mark. "If I did, I wouldn't be behind the Wall, would I? I was just hanging with the guy. Had no clue what he was after."

I face Cole, hoping to get a better read on him, but his eyes are still shaded under the hat. I forget I'm not supposed to speak. "I was told anyone coming face-to-face with Sage dissents." I quickly shut my mouth.

Luckily, Lieutenant Foster responds without seeming bothered. "In most cases, yes. Which is what makes Colton another integral part of Alliance intelligence. His time with Sage has given us an extraordinary advantage."

"And now I've got to stay behind this Wall like I'm under freakin' house arrest." I marvel at how Cole wanders to the drink cart with such causal nonchalance in Foster's presence. Maybe having firsthand knowledge of Sage gives him special status somehow.

"Only until it is safe for you to venture outside the perimeter." Foster's tone is firm but also sounds a little paternal. "Until then, you shall take part in Miss Marlowe's training."

Fedora Guy shoots me a lazy smirk. "I'm down with that." Ugh. I wish he'd take off that stupid hat so I could see his eyes.

I'm suddenly struck by Foster's words. "I get training? With the Paradise Steel?"

Pop clears his throat, and his disapproving lips flatline.

Foster doesn't look annoyed. But then again, it's hard to tell with him. All he says is, "Any assault training will most likely be withheld."

"Then what's my part in the battle? I can control the creatures, maybe even hold them off but—"

"Miss Marlowe," Foster says dryly. "Our desire is preservation, *not* destruction." I'm not following. The lieutenant must see the confusion on my face. "Our sole responsibility is to *defend* our power—or the source of that power, rather. We do not engage in offensive tactical strategies."

It takes a moment for what he's saying to sink in. "Wait. You *don't* attack? But you have all the weapons"—my voice rises—"the training, and second-realm knowledge to take down Sage. People are dying because of him—his creatures. He has to be stopped. If the Alliance doesn't do it, who will?"

"The Alliance has its ways, Honey." Pop's warning is clear.

Foster lifts his left brow with a micro-shift, but it's enough for me to read his dissatisfaction. "Is your desire to comply with the Alliance, Miss Marlowe?"

I get the feeling the only right answer is yes.

"Sir." I imply the "yes." I don't want to lie. I'm determined to cooperate and do what's right, but letting people die? How can I go along with something so wrong?

Devon speaks up. "Cera has proven her loyalty."

Pop nods in agreement.

"We can only hope," Foster says. I may not have won him over completely, but at least he's giving me a chance. "The more disconcerting issue is whether her connection to Sage will be greater than we anticipate. For that reason, a Blight's power is unquestionably incalculable and perilous. If she shows any aggression toward the Alliance, or utilizes any powers that may aid Sage in any manner, eradication orders will be issued. Her mother will be tried for treason against the Alliance, and any aid currently provided shall be withdrawn."

He says all that without a change in inflection or expression. I'm nauseated. I hadn't thought about what coming to Council would cost Mom. If I mess up in any way, not only will they kill me, but they won't heal her. And I'm not sure what punishment Council gives for treason, but judging by Gray's comments to Maddox, it can't be good.

Cole inspects fruit in a wooden bowl and selects a black plum. "You've got it rough, Blighty."

My life is on the line, so is my mother's, and he acts like it's a joke? I suddenly want to chuck the fruit bowl at his head.

"Our decision to harbor an emerging Blight behind the Wall is unprecedented," Foster says, keeping his unwavering eyes on me. "For that reason you will be removed from the Garden on the eve of your seventeenth birthday. If you fail to show signs of dissension and the admiral agrees, then your training may continue in a less fortified location." Less fortified? I thought this was the only location secure from Sage. "The unpredictability of what may happen when a Blight acquires full Dissenting powers puts the Garden—and our power source—at considerable risk."

"Why is that?" Cole takes a bite of the plum. Juice runs down his chin, which he wipes away with the back of his sleeve.

Surprisingly, it's Pop who answers. "He believes that if Honey gains full Dissenting powers while locked in the Garden, it might sense her as a threat, and the Circuit Wall could spark from the inside."

"We can only surmise that conclusion, since we are uncertain of her effect on the Garden," Foster adds.

Great, the one place that's supposed to be secure, and I'm a ticking time bomb inside it, threatening the lives of everyone around me. Again.

"How much time we got 'til you blow the whole place apart, Blighty?" Cole looks down, inspecting a stain on his shirt. "Two, three weeks 'til you turn seventeen?"

I hesitate and glance up at Devon, standing beside me. "Three days."

Cole lets out a long, low whistle. "That's not much time to train in any Bent."

"Miss Marlowe's training will focus solely on strengthening her Bent as a Seer. Doing so will allow her to accurately decipher the embedded messages in the encoded artwork," Foster tells us.

"That's it?" Cole frowns.

So do I.

What good could that training possibly do? I try to hide my frustration. They only want me to look at artwork and tell them what I see? And after the third day, I'll be kicked out of the Garden so I don't blow the place apart; and as long as I don't act out, I'll get to live in a "fortified" location, which is probably jail. I'm not seeing much of an upside here.

It's clear I'm their prisoner, and my cooperation is the only thing that will keep me alive. And Mom safe.

"Tripton!" Gray's assaulting voice shoots through the room. Every nerve bristles at the sight of him standing in the archway with his broad shoulders pulled taut and hard lips locked with a scowl. Lips I want to permanently glue shut. But this time his glare isn't aimed at me. "Where have you been?"

"Around," Cole says casually.

"Your Cord wasn't reading."

"Not my problem. It's still on me." Cole lifts his sleeve as proof. "Must be a weak transmitter." Somehow I doubt that.

"Sergeant Carver, please secure Miss Marlowe with a Cord and assign her an escort." You mean a prison guard, Lieutenant.

"I'll do it," Maddox enters the room. His expression is flushed with the anger of someone rising from a fight. The flames from the fire burn brighter as he walks my way, the heat warming my skin even from this distance. Through those tangled bangs, his eyes greet mine with a promise. One my heart races to remember.

Gray blocks his path. "I'm assigning Cole."

"Then tell Global Council I'm done training so I can have a weapon." Cole tosses the fruit pit at a nearby trashcan, missing by a foot. "Can't guard a Blight without Steel."

Doesn't he have a weapon? I sneak a quick glance at the hem of his jeans.

"Let's see how you do with the Blight." Gray's tone is almost a challenge. "Then I'll talk to the admiral about assigning you one. If you're lucky."

Cole's knife is stolen? No wonder he wears that hat. The truth must be obvious in his eyes. He catches me looking him over. So does Maddox.

Cole smirks, amused. "Sure. Whatever." He picks up the pit and tosses it at the trashcan. This time he makes it.

If I call out Cole about the hidden weapon, maybe it will help prove that I'm on the Alliance's side. They'll see I'm not a threat. And maybe it will wipe that cocky grin off Cole's face. The confession comes to my lips, but one look at Gray and I smother the words.

Despite Foster's promise of keeping me safe inside the Garden for the next three days, an icy chill courses through my veins as Gray studies me with soulless indifference, a vacant glare that says, no matter what I say or do, I'm dead.

It's simply a matter of when.

6
UNTIL NOW

After having a Cord fastened around my left wrist, which is nothing but a thin wire bracelet that monitors my location during my stay, Lina assesses my leg. Once that's done, I'm forced to sit on the leather couch in the library while Lieutenant Foster steadily grills me with a bazillion questions to determine if I'm truly worth the risk.

When was I Awakened? *Age seven.*

How did I grow up? *Moved every year.*

Extended family? *None alive, that I know of.*

Past friends? *Dead.*

Past boyfriends? *Nonexistent.*

Pets? *Never.*

It's a wonder he doesn't take a blood sample. Every now and then, Pop, sitting in a wingback chair to my right, makes an affirming sound of encouragement, while Cole reclines in a chair across the room. His feet are propped on the window ledge, and his hat is pulled down over his eyes. He's obviously asleep. At least I hope so, with the slew of embarrassing answers I'm forced to give.

I endure the interrogation, doing my best to cooperate, even though it's way past lunch, probably close to dinner, and my stomach is caving in. At least when Devon grilled me at Hesperian, he offered me a burger and a milkshake.

After exhausting the list, the only big "trigger" Foster identifies is my mother, which is no surprise. And the stream of bodies I've left behind from my visions—particularly Jess. Then Foster puts down the notepad and asks a question I knew would eventually come, but I'm still not prepared to answer.

"What about your father?"

I run my fingers over the raised cords of a decorative pillow in my lap. "He was a Dissenter, I guess. But you already know that."

"What do you recall about your time with him?"

I bring the pillow to my chest. "Not much."

Only that he smelled of beer and campfire. That he'd pat my head as he stumbled to the couch where he'd pass out, only to wake up screaming. That he'd grip his hair and writhe on the floor until he puked dinner and beer. That I'd get the bucket and rags from under the sink. Scrub the worn carpet and scoop out empty beer bottles from under the couch while Mom would walk him to bed. Then there was the night he left . . .

"Did he ever talk about or mention Sage?" With absolutely no emotion, Foster might as well be asking the time of day.

The seat turns uncomfortably hard. "I first learned about Sage from Gladys only a few days ago."

"Did your father ever mention anything you now believe could have been a reference to Sage, even though he may not have used his name?"

I weave my finger through a loose thread in the pillow and twist until it chokes purple. Dad talked about a monster . . . but he wasn't referring to Sage. "No." I release the thread and push the pillow aside.

Pop grunts and rubs out his knee. "I think it's 'bout time we stop. Let Honey get something to eat."

I'm thankful for the break. "Can I call my mother?" I ask. "I haven't spoken to her since . . ." Since I ran out to save Jess and left her in a coughing fit. "Devon told me they transported her to Hesperian. I'd like to know if her fever's come down." And warn her about what I've gotten us into.

"I will arrange an opportunity. In the meantime, Lina should have the ointment ready to heal your wound." Foster removes several stout hardbacks from the shelf. "And I suggest you eat, Miss Marlowe. Hunger has a way of making us rather cross."

I'm not cross. Okay, maybe a little. But I am starving.

"Colton." Foster's voice is stern.

Cole drops his feet to the floor, dazed. "What?"

"Escort Miss Marlowe to the kitchen."

He stretches. "Then am I free to go?"

Foster neatly aligns a stack of books on the coffee table. "Attend to your training and return this evening."

Cole opens the library door and waits for me to walk through. As soon as I pass him, he mumbles, "No boyfriends? Not even a pet, huh?"

"You were *pretending* to be asleep?"

My face burns as my mind whips through every detail I gave Foster. I storm through the hallway, only to find Maddox waiting by the archway to the War Room. His face is cleaned of blood from the fight, but the scrapes remain.

"How'd it go?" he asks me, his wary glance flickering to Cole.

"Foster wants me to sit around and do nothing but look at artwork for the next three days. They won't train me. They won't fight Sage." I fling out a hand. "If I even show an ounce of rebellion, I'm dead and Mom will be labeled a traitor. You know I can't sit still. What if I have another vision?"

"We'll figure it out." Maddox places his hand on my back guiding me away from Cole.

He really shouldn't touch me. "Figure what out?" I widen the distance between us. "How to get me trained? How to convince

Council to fight? I don't understand why everyone is so paranoid that I'll recreate something that happened way back in the Renaissance. Something I don't even know about."

Maddox walks through the War Room with a comfortable familiarity, even though he seems so out of place. It's hard to imagine this museum being his home. "It's because a Blight almost gave Sage access to the Empyrean Well," he says. "The portal was near a villa in Florence. Sage almost got through the gate but was splintered. Burst into sparks but didn't die. The rest of the world, the Commons, had no clue. Since the fight took place in the second realm, they only felt a minor earthquake."

Maddox glances at the gruesome tapestry. "It's taken Sage centuries to reform. But now that he knows the power of the gate, everyone's worried he'll find a way of getting through."

Cole follows surprisingly silent behind us, probably listening to every word and mapping it to what he knows about Sage.

I'll grill him about it later. Right now, I'm more interested in what Maddox can share. Something tells me I won't get this chance again. "When I was changing, I overheard you mention the Well was your power source—or at least where the Current comes from, but—"

Maddox comes to a hard stop as we reach the entry hall. "How much did you hear?"

"I kinda heard everything."

Maddox rubs his forehead. "About that. I wanted to, I mean, I tried to—"

"Forget it, seriously. That's over and done between us. You're Elite. I know what I am. I get it. Mistakes happen. Let's just move on." With those platitudes, I go into the dining room, following the scent of warm bread.

Maddox turns to Cole. "Hey man, you can go, if you want. I've got her."

"Not sure you do." Cole walks off and out the front door.

I overlook Maddox's expression and continue on. "I can't sit back and do nothing while those creatures roam around, picking off Awakened like a"—I catch sight of the dining table set buffet-style—"like a dessert bar. I only agreed to come here because I wanted training. I know that taking on Sage is way bigger than me. I wanted to join the Alliance so I could save lives. But now I learn they won't fight. Why?"

"Council will preserve what they have at all costs, but they won't initiate a fight they don't think they can win."

"But they have all the weapons, the training, the knowledge," I argue. "Even a global army. Don't they have what it takes?"

"I don't think they did, until now." I'm caught in the rising hope of Maddox's eyes that gleam brighter than a sunrise. An electric charge hums in the thin space between us, a connection that's so much more than the Current. I look down at the table set with pristine silver and white china. At the delicate patterns in the linen. I will myself to stay calm. He's not—it's not possible. But I wish it were.

A door to the back patio opens. A grumpy Blade with a patchy beard and pocked cheeks steps inside. Maddox pays him no attention, even as he side-eyes us not so discreetly.

My voice is a decibel above a whisper. "Maddox, I want to train. I want to fight, but they won't let me. What am I supposed to do now?"

"Trust Foster," he tells me. "Do what he asks."

The grumpy Blade walks out. Clearly spying.

"But he only wants me to stare at classical artwork for the next three days. Unless . . ." The flames in the wall sconces send fluid shadows over a Florentine urn in the middle of the table. The design suddenly feels alive. "Do you think he believes there's a solution embedded in the artwork that they haven't been able to decipher?"

"Maybe," Maddox says as we approach the entryway of a cozy terra-cotta kitchen.

"If I discover the answer, do you think Council will change their mind and fight?"

"Maybe not."

I stop. "Then what's the point? If there's a way to defeat Sage, shouldn't someone try?"

"Look, a lot of us feel the way you do. It's kinda why I created Hesperian." He lowers his voice, even though we're alone. His gaze lands on a stained glass frame hanging on the wall. The vivid colors remind me of Hesperian's ceiling. His words come quickly. "I've been thinking about something for a while now. About how to create art as an effective way to fight, you know, combine our talents and Bents for battle. We'll still need training, but art could give us an advantage Sage and the creatures wouldn't expect. If you could cooperate with Foster and find the answer, find something that might show how to bring Sage or those beasts down, then we might have a shot at convincing the Alliance."

"Really?"

"If they won't listen, then at least we'll have a strong group ready to protect Awakened. We can start something new. You find an answer. I'll gather support."

I want to brand his optimism into my heart.

Before I can ask him anything more, Lina comes in the back door with Harper at her heels. "So this flower will—" Harper frowns when she sees us. Then she notices the scrapes on Maddox's face. "What did you do? Was it Gray?" She drags him toward the small nook in the back of the kitchen and quickly washes her hands before whipping out supplies from her kit. "How are your ribs?" She prods his side.

He jumps a little. "Fine."

It never occurred to me that Harper's been the one bandaging his wounds and putting him back together after his brawls with Gray. It makes sense why she was so protective—possessive—of him when we first met. I shrink onto a wooden barstool, suddenly feeling out of place. Especially as Harper dabs the corner of Maddox's lip with clean gauze. Her face bears a skeptical look as he says something I can't hear over the exhaust fan. Not like it's any of my business. I turn away.

Lina scoops out a thick broth loaded with corn, chicken, and potato that's been bubbling on the stove. She sets the clay bowl in front of me and then slides over a plate filled with rice, chopped avocado, puffy cheese bread, and a few other foods I don't know. "*Gracias*, Lina." I swirl my spoon in the broth, watching wispy steam flit away.

Familiar but unwelcome steel-toed boots appear at the threshold. "Maddox. Get to training. We had a deal." Gray's voice grates under my skin and spreads like venom across the pit of my stomach. I don't dare look at him or else my fingers may accidentally chuck my steaming bowl in his direction.

Maddox stands without a word. Doesn't put up a fight. I'm not sure what deal was made, but he looks determined. Stronger. Taller. As he passes me, he whispers, "Later," and leaves.

Gray doesn't.

His hard footsteps shatter the solace. One. Two. Three steps in my direction, and he's standing beside me as Harper separates her cuttings on the counter. She doesn't acknowledge his presence. No, I take that back. She's refusing to.

"Harper." His tone is flatter than the herb she smashes on the counter.

"Gray." Her glower could chill the fires of hell.

I sit still, flicking my gaze back and forth between them as Lina stirs the bubbling pot. I'm trying not to squirm in the seething silence of their two-word exchange.

As if I'm invisible, Gray says, "Tell the Blight she'll be harnessed to someone else. All ties to my brother are now severed. If I find her near him again, she'll know what that means."

He walks out.

Harper picks up a knife and chops the flowers with hard, quick beats. "Elitist jerk."

I smile on the inside. I'm glad I'm not the only one who thinks so.

After I've finished eating and Lina has patched my leg with a waxy ointment that has the burn of fire ants chewing their way to the bone, Harper escorts me to the library.

I'm determined to stay focused. If I can find the solution to defeat Sage, then with Maddox's help, Council might agree to fight.

I stand outside the library doors, not sure what waits on the other side. But I'll cooperate and do what's required. I'll work hard to be who they want. Push aside what they don't. Show that I can be part of their community. Do my best to fit in and find a place in Maddox's world.

As I open the door, hope sprouts wings. My pulse charges faster than stormy lightning seeking solid ground.

My training is about to begin.

7
BROKEN GOBLET

Training is torture. Mental torture of the cruelest kind.

"Try again." Pop leans forward in the wingback chair as I sit in the corner of the couch for what seems like hours and try to interpret past visions from memory. "Pick another vision. We'll start over." Pop eases back in the chair.

Dusk chokes the library with purple hues as natural light fades.

He has no idea what he's asking, having me pull up images from the deep subconscious graves of my mind, cracking open nightmares I've spent my life trying to forget. Still, I bury my frustration because he's never taught a Blight, and I know he's teaching me to interpret visions the way normal Seers do—the only way he knows how.

Any vision training I should have received early on would have come from Dad, if he hadn't walked out on us. But as a Dissenter, Dad's teaching would have only skewed me toward helping Sage.

I refocus and work hard to give him what he wants. Foster, who has been at his desk observing, taking notes, and assessing, gets up to turn on the lights.

"Let the vision have control," Pop says. "Now don't go wrestling the images. Let the Current guide. Seers, we get a whole image. Art complete. We take that image and transcribe what's there. I know it ain't the same for you, but starting in the same place we do might help you see."

I study him talking to the air instead of looking in my direction. The amber lights soften his round face, aged with wrinkles of pain, wisdom, and loss. The dark glasses shield his delicate eyes. I can't imagine giving my life to the Alliance, only to be cast aside, blind, and walled up inside an apartment, counting down each sunset only by the heat withdrawing from my skin.

"You hearing me?" Pop points his shaky finger in my direction.

I pat his hand in both of mine. "Yes, Pop. I'm listening."

"Good." He sits upright. "Your visions are broken because both sides war within you, wantin' control. To interpret, you need to connect the lines. I'm guessin' that like you, Blight artists pulled one or two main elements from a vision and embedded those in the message. You'll be searching for the connection between 'em."

At this rate, my limited time to find an answer is going to quickly run out. "Should I look at the art now?" I pick up a book.

"Visions first." Pop taps his forehead. "Hold one element still in your mind. The Current will present itself, and slowly reveal the others, pulling 'em together until the pieces tell a whole story. Watch 'em come together from your periphery if you have to. Don't try 'n' grab one too fast. They'll scatter away like rabbits in a hawk field." He adjusts a blanket over his lap. "Let's give it another try. What do you remember from your last vision? First thing that comes to mind."

I set the book aside. "The broken goblet," I say, unequivocally.

"Close your eyes, and use that image."

I place my hands on my knees, yoga-style, and close my eyes. I work hard to shut out Foster shuffling papers and voices drifting from the courtyard. I visualize the goblet, but the only image that forms in my mind is the one Maddox drew—the careful strokes, the perfect details in the stem, the severed basin. Every detail foretelling Harper's impending death.

Pop's voice slices through the hazy memory. "Careful not to think on what the boy drew. That's a common problem. Think on what the Current gave you."

"Once it's on paper, I can't see anything else."

"'Cause your sight gets in the way," Pop tells me. "No worry. You'll be having another vision soon and can work on it then. Before you see the drawing."

"How do you know I will?" I sit up. "And if that's the case, I won't have time to wait around and figure things out. Someone's life will be on the line."

"I reckon it'll be different this time."

"Every vision I've had meant someone was about to die."

Pop's dark glasses focus on me. "Outside these Walls your visions were warnings about Sage finding you first. Now that you're here, things are different. I reckon the visions will be too. All depends on what the Current shows you the Well is tryin' to do." Pop is quiet for a moment. "The Well, it's up to something. I can feel it. When the time's right, it'll send you another message. In the meantime, practice lettin' the images form in your mind."

That's easy for him to say. He doesn't have years of carnage choking his memories. I slump in the couch, feeling like an epic failure.

Someone beats on the door, hard. Insistent. I jump. Foster gives the command to enter.

"Lieutenant." Devon rushes in, his voice urgent and his expression strikes fear within me. "We've received reports of an attack by Legions at a training location we thought was secure and unknown to the enemy."

Foster turns rigid. "Fatalities?"

"Unknown."

I spring off the couch. I have only one thought. "My mom?"

"It wasn't Hesperian." Devon's face is wrung tight.

My heart slows a millisecond. "Can you bring her here,

behind the Circuit Wall, so she's safe?" It's a bold request and probably out of line.

"Calm yourself, Honey."

I can't be calm. I've caused my mother so much pain over the last ten years. Her failing health is my fault. Taking on the pain of my visions, not using a Healer's help because she was hiding me from the Alliance and Sage. Now she's the one exposed while I'm locked inside the Garden.

"Edward is correct in his assertion that there has been a battle to acquire you. Now that you are here, Miss Marlowe, I expect this will be one of several attacks." Foster straightens a paperweight of Atlas holding the world on his shoulders. "I have no doubt that Sage will utilize whatever triggers possible to lure you. Securing your mother within the Garden for safekeeping may minimize those attacks." He adjusts a silver picture frame. "Call Sergeant Carver," he instructs Devon. "We will coordinate a plan for Delia Marlowe's transfer and outline a strategy to defend further attacks. I will notify the admiral."

Foster is agreeing to get my mother? I search him for any ulterior motives, but only worry shadows the crease between his slender brows.

He glances somewhere behind me. "Colton, escort Miss Marlowe to room three on the east corridor."

Cole? I look over my shoulder. Sure enough, Cole has slipped into the room without a sound, studying the chess table, playing a game against himself. His wavy locks poke out from under the hat, curling along the back of his neck where tension is binding his shoulders.

"Would it help if I stayed?" I ask. If they're making plans that include my mother, I want in on it.

"Not at this time." The lieutenant is firm. "Rest. We will convene after breakfast."

Cole opens the glass door to a pebbled courtyard lit with weak light from gas lanterns. "Come on, Blighty."

Our footsteps crunch over the rocks, echoing as we walk along the side of house where night greets the roofline. Despite the sweet nectar scent dousing the air, there's an unsettling chill that ripples under my skin. Or maybe it's the incessant thrum coursing through the Garden that drowns my pulse.

My feet grind into the gravel. I shouldn't be escorted off to bed. Not when I have only three days inside the Garden. Resting is a waste of time. But Maddox told me to trust Foster. So I will, if only for Mom's sake.

We turn the corner near the entrance of the arbor. I want to ask Cole about his weapon—or even about Sage—but several Blades dressed in black combat gear with glistening knives tucked in their belts linger within earshot. Who knows which one Foster might send to retrieve my mother? I scan their hard faces for any trace of kindness but find none.

We pass the water fountain and head toward the far side of the house, down a corridor covered by a wisteria canopy. Scarce light from flickering lamps casts distorting shadows. Cole stops and leans his shoulder on the wall. "Room three." He lingers as I open the door. "Hungry?"

Sage is out there terrorizing people. My mom isn't safe. Food is the last thing on my mind. "No, but . . ."

His flirty smile returns. "Yeah?"

"What can you tell me about Sage? Does he have a weakness?"

Cole gives a wry grimace. "Way to kill a mood. Hang with a guy first, maybe get to know him a little before grilling him for information like that."

"Cole, I was—"

"Too late, Blighty. Time's up." Cole glances behind me. Someone's dark shadow patrols the corridor. "See you tomorrow." He walks away.

I step into the room, turn the lock, and slump into the

closed door.

Alone.

I can't believe they've given me my own space. I look for cameras, sure that someone is watching me. The space isn't much different from a small hotel room. With a private bathroom, it's decorated with antique furniture that smells of polished lacquer and is nicer than any place I've ever had. Cotton pajamas and a neat pile of fresh clothes sit on the full-sized bed: a beige sweater and Blade-like cargo pants.

I fidget with the wire thread on my left wrist. I don't wear jewelry. Besides the hairpin Gladys gave me, I've never had any.

I take the silver pin out of my pocket and run my finger over the white flower. The petals curve inward, similar to the ones in the arbor. The metal heats my fingers. I could be imagining the warmth, but regardless, the feeling kicks up an ache for Hesperian, Gladys, and how safe life felt inside those walls.

I prep for bed in the bathroom and then tuck the wastebasket near the nightstand in case Pop is right and another vision strikes. Then I wiggle under the covers and turn off the lamp.

Strange sounds swing through the dark. A pipe gurgles with running water. Voices murmur, followed by a burst of harsh laughter.

The coils squeak as I roll to face the door. This is supposed to be a haven, but feels nothing of the kind. My mind is restless, far from sleep. I want to sneak out, find Maddox and ask him the ocean of questions crashing inside my brain.

As I get up, steady footsteps stop outside my door. I quietly jam a chair under the doorknob before crawling back under the blanket. I lie still, listening for the slightest click of the lock. It never comes.

I let my body sink into the mattress as a solemn cello sings through the walls. Alone, a prisoner in the dark, my thoughts turn to Mom. Hoping her fever broke and she's conscious again.

That she'll be with me soon. I try closing my eyes but the Legions' gaunt faces are all I can see. Beasts once human. Dissenters, like my father.

I flip on my back. I can't believe the Alliance won't fight, and I know I can't do it on my own, even though I can control both Cormorants and Legions. Except now the Alliance says I can't.

I stare at the dark ceiling as a relentless gnawing chews the lining of my stomach. Maybe it's hunger. Or maybe it's because what I thought was a gift that saved lives is really a forbidden power, a Dissenting one. One that confirms my connection to Sage.

But I'm nothing like him.

No matter what it takes, I'll find a way to fit in with the Alliance and overcome the odds against me. I have to.

I can't let more people die.

8

EMPYREAN WELL

I'm back on the library couch the next morning with my leg almost fully healed. Pop is seated in the same chair as yesterday. A tray of flaky croissants sits on the coffee table where Foster pours himself a steaming tea into a delicate cup.

A cloudy sky looms through the hazy bay windows. Flowers droop with wet petals waiting for the sun. No one speaks about yesterday's attack, but tension hides in the harsh whispers and alert glances.

I'm told a plan to bring Mom to the Garden is underway, but reports of Legions drifting nearby and others hovering too close to Hesperian will cause a delay. I'm unsettled, frustrated, and panicked at the news, but I cram the emotions down.

Foster, wearing a similar outfit with a navy sweater instead of green, sits down. "Miss Marlowe, the information I am about to present is sensitive in nature. Revealing this knowledge to someone such as yourself poses a great risk to the Alliance. However, after yesterday's attack, I believe this knowledge could prove a greater benefit than the potential risk. Additionally, Edward attests to your allegiance and openly declares complete faith in your alignment with the Alliance. He willingly agrees to shoulder the responsibility for any infraction. Do you understand?" He takes a long sip of tea, as if letting the weight of his words sink in.

Pop put himself on the line for me? The reflection of the window dances on his dark glasses. The tremor in his hands is lessened as they rest on his lap. I don't understand why he has so much faith in me. I almost wish he didn't. But something in me wants to prove him right to the Alliance. Prove that he's not senile the way Gray said, and that he still has value even though he no longer has visions.

I knit my fingers together. "I understand."

"Very well." Foster gives a curt nod and sets down his teacup. "The Current, as you know, powers our Bents and comes from a source we call the Empyrean Well. However, the source is somewhat of a mystery. To date, all information we possess about the Well is derived solely from visions transcribed into writings and artwork gathered over hundreds of years, similar to the way you deciphered the battle in John Martin's painting. However no one has ever seen the Well outright."

As he takes another sip of tea, I ask a careful question. "If no one has seen it, then how did Martin know what to paint?"

"Martin's depiction most likely came from a vision. No one can see the Well clearly because it exists in a realm of its own. A third realm. In the same way Commons cannot see the Legions or Cormorants, neither can we see the true nature of the Well. It reveals itself though visions, but only in snippets, as a means of protection. Only select individuals, Seers, are given insight, which we carefully piece together, hoping to form a complete picture."

"Like broken pieces of a mosaic." The same way visions appear in my head.

"Perhaps," Foster agrees. "We believe the Well to be a portal of sorts, a puncture in the universe created when Sage was evicted from another world. The portal is one-way only and has no reentry, but it allows an essence of that world to flow into ours. We also surmise that Sage is after the Well's total destruction. As long as the doorway is open, and the Well supplies our power, his control over this world is limited."

"Milton wrote about it," I say, savoring the thrill of so much information. "It had something to do with the archfiend hating the constant reminder of what he lost." I scan the shelves. "Do you have a copy of *Paradise Lost*?" It's been so long since I've held the words. Part of me feels missing. "There's a verse about how he fell . . ."

I must have woken Milton from hibernation because he decides to bust in and help me out:

> How I hate thy beams
> That bring to my remembrance from what state
> I fell, how glorious once above thy sphere,
> Till pride and worse ambition threw me down.

That's the exact verse I was thinking of. My pulse is charging. "I think the Well reminds Sage of this other place. Now that I know this war between Sage and the Awakened exists, maybe I can read through the poem again for information about the battle."

"Each generation passes on what they've discovered," Foster says, "including the inspection of every line of the poem, as well as commentaries and scholars. We haven't gleaned adequate insight that pertains to the protection of the Well, or an effective strategy to end the war, for that matter, but I shall provide you with a copy to review." Foster's emphasis on the word protection isn't lost on me.

"But what if I could find an answer that shows how?"

Pop clears his throat. I'm going to find him a throat lozenge so he'll cut that out. I know what he means, but still.

"The *answer* we are asking you to find pertains to the Well." Lieutenant Foster is adamant. "Over the course of history, the Well has transferred several times. Some postulate the location changes when threatened, but that theory has not been proven. A more likely conclusion is that the Well is seasonal, shifting whenever it has reached maturation for a particular location. We believe this to be true by monitoring sparks of creative energy in various places around the world, historically: Greek theater, Egyptian architecture, Italian Renaissance. Creative epicenters tend to be one trend showing where the Well has previously dwelt. However, to date, there is no knowledge regarding future shifts."

"You think it's about to change location?"

"Whether it be a day away or several years is uncertain. However, when in transfer, the Circuit Wall may become more susceptible to attack since most of the energy is used for transfer, rather than complete protection." Foster leans forward. "Global leaders will be returning tomorrow. Providing them with knowledge of an impending transfer would prove a tremendous value to the Alliance and our duty of protection."

"I see." Reading the artwork and finding the information they need about the transfer is what will keep me alive. But if the Well is about to shift and it's more vulnerable when it does, that also means the Alliance will never agree to fight. They'll let Sage terrorize the Awakened for who knows how long, all in the name of preservation. The book-crammed walls close in on me, and the air turns too thick to breathe. I sit back, sickened.

The library door bursts open, hitting the wall near the chess table.

"Hey, Pops." Cole saunters in the room. He's wearing the same dark clothes and sweat-stained fedora as yesterday.

Pop shakes a finger at him. "Don't you be waltzing in here late like you don't care nothing about being a Blade."

Cole lifts his hands in defense. "Whoa. And a good morning to you too. I only came in to spring Blighty outta here. Gray's request." He swipes a chocolate-filled croissant off of the table. "She good to go, or what?"

"Go where, exactly?" Foster asks.

"Training room," Cole replies with his mouth full. "Gray wants to work with her."

Foster considers the request, expressionless. Then he nods. "Remain with her at all times."

I jump off the couch. "Do I get to use weapons?"

"Yep," Cole says. "Time to put your hands on some sweet metal, Blighty."

Pop frowns and fidgets in his seat. "Have respect. Those weapons ain't regular knives." I'm not sure if Pop was talking to Cole or the both of us.

"Don't worry, Pops." Cole hangs his arm around my neck. "I'll have Blighty back in an hour." He flashes a wicked grin and whispers in my ear, "Unless you want to make out."

Ugh. I push him away.

"Mr. Tripton." Foster's corrective tone slaps across the room. "Rules apply to you, as well."

"Yeah, sure," Cole mumbles, but he lets go of me anyway.

The last thing I want is to be near Gray, but if it means training with a knife and learning how to fight, then I'll do it.

9

TRAINING GAME

Cole leads me on a rocky path through tangled woods until we come to a cinderblock building hidden deep within the Garden. He heaves open the solid metal door and steps inside. I enter right behind, squinting at the fluorescent light, hoping to find Maddox.

The space is lined with cedar walls. No windows. A black gym mat covers the floor. The air is filled with a strong woodsy scent that most likely comes from the splintery crates stacked to the twenty-foot ceiling along the sidewall. Maddox is nowhere in sight. Gray, however, is shirtless, hanging near the back wall. He's literally hanging in the air, holding himself six feet off the ground with arms outstretched between two metal poles. A large purple bruise is stamped on his side. I hope that was payback from Maddox.

Gray flicks a glance at us. Instead of letting go, he holds longer, counting the seconds through gritted teeth. His arms tremble but don't give way. "Thirty-eight . . . and thirty-nine." He springs effortlessly onto the mat and rolls his shoulders, massaging them out. He swaggers our way as if his body, shining with sweat and completely ripped, should impress me. Nothing crammed with that much arrogance ever could.

I look around, setting my sight on the knife marks that nick small painted circles on the wall. Probably targets of some sort.

Over my shoulder, the wall by the door is laden with an assortment of antique weapons: thin curved swords, clubs, and strange sticks with menacing spiked balls on chains.

"Your turn, Tripton."

"No, thanks." Cole wanders over to the table sorted with glistening knives. "But I'll toss a few of these babies." I bet he will. It's probably how he stole one in the first place.

Gray stands too close in front of me, taunting me to look at him. "Tripton, get out and leave us alone."

Cole picks up a knife, inspecting the thin blade. "Foster gave me orders to stay."

"Then put that down and make yourself invisible while I play a game with the Blight." Gray's voice is a dangerous calm. A metallic scent mixed with sweat radiates from his skin. Standing less than an arm's length away, he makes it impossible for me to look at anything but him—or the floor. But I'm not a coward.

"I'm here to train. Not play games." Currents collide as we lock eyes. Bucking. Wrestling. Fighting for control. But I hold steady.

So does Gray. "You're not doing a thing until I see how much you know."

Clinking metal chimes through the smothering air. "Hey, did you forge a new weapon?" Cole asks. "Haven't seen this one before."

Gray charges at him. "I said hands off the Steel!" He grabs Cole's wrist, then takes the weapon out of his hand. "Now disappear."

Cole backs away, lifting his hands in defense. "Chill. I'm out of your way."

Gray snatches a strip of fabric from the wall and wads it in his fist. "Put this on." He tosses it at me. I unravel the fabric. Binding? Or a blindfold? Heated panic replaces every drop of my blood. I search for Cole out of the corner of my eye, hoping to read his expression the way I can with Maddox, but he's abandoned me.

"What's this for?" My casual tone belies the terror pulsing under my skin.

Gray twirls a knife. His mouth curves with an offhanded grin. "Tie that over your eyes, and stand in the middle of the room."

This can't be good.

I steady my breath and grow roots on the wobbly mat. "Then what?"

"I toss a weapon anywhere in the room. You tell me where it lands." His unnerving smile flickers, then fades.

My palms feel spongy. Simultaneously hot and cold. And the beige sweater is suddenly too warm. "I just stand here, blindfolded, and tell you what you've hit?" I take a quick inventory of the colored circles on the cedar wall and memorize the pattern.

The hearty knife in Gray's hand glistens as he tilts the blade. "That's right."

"Then I train with a knife."

He mocks me with a hard laugh. "Is that what you think?"

"If she gets more than half right," Cole's voice drifts down, "why not let her toss a few, see her potential?" Cole is sitting on the highest crate near the ceiling, legs dangling over the side. How did he scale up so fast—and quiet?

"She'd have to get a hundred percent right," Gray sneers. "Tripton, get down here. Make sure she can't see."

Cole navigates his descent down the rickety crates with intense concentration and perfect balance. It's only when Gray barks, "Faster!" that Cole missteps but still manages to gracefully leap to the ground in perfect silence.

Cole comes behind me and ties the blindfold. "Whatever you do, don't move." His whisper tangles in my hair.

I swallow and nod slightly.

The black fabric holds my eyes shut. I hate not seeing. I hated it when Mom played a similar game with me when I was ten.

She'd make me close my eyes while she tossed things around the room. Car keys, coasters, pencils. I quickly learned it was anything within arm's reach. Before I could open my eyes, I'd have to call out where it landed and what she threw. I always thought she made up that game because we couldn't afford toys. Now I know it was her way of training me without my knowing. But this is a completely different game.

Letting Gray toss knives while I stand blindfolded is a horrible idea. My feet twitch, urging me to run. But I lock myself in place, determined.

Cole's stealthy footsteps move away from me. He stops near the weapons table. I exhale and keep my hands loose at my side. Stay calm. Listen close.

Gray paces with light footsteps. Left then right.

Metal slides off the table, followed by a quiet thud. He's changed knives. Now he's pacing again. Left, then right again. The air whirls where he stands. Might be him spinning the knife. Then everything's eerily quiet. He's standing across the room, somewhere in front of me. Sweat beads on my forehead, dripping into the blindfold. I force myself not to sway on this unstable mat.

Angry air whips past my right ear. My pulse pounds as heat flares through me. Then a hard *thunk* stabs the wall behind me. Cole's gulp is audible.

I'm certain Gray pulled the knife from the corner of the table, the one with the thin blade, and threw it past my right ear, and it landed in the circle. I have the answer ready, but uneasiness stops me. If I let on too much, Gray will know I've been trained. And he'll probably use it against me somehow.

"I think whatever you threw landed on the wall behind me . . . maybe about level with my head?" The circle is faded green, but I withhold that fact as well.

I pull off the blindfold. Gray stands frowning a good distance away, where I thought he'd be. Cole leans against the table, gnawing his nails. The knife from the corner of the table is missing. I glance at the wall. I'm right.

Gray prowls suspiciously. "Lucky guess." I stifle a shiver as he pulls the knife from the wall and walks back to the table. "Do it again."

"Maybe you should do something else." Cole rubs his fingers over his lips. "Have her stab the punching bag. Test her the way you do with us. That toss was a little too close."

"Shut it, Tripton. If you can't handle the training, then get out."

"It's fine." I'm not fine. I'm trembling inside. But I hope he can't tell. "We made a deal. Let's keep going."

Cole folds his arms and plants himself by the door. I'm relieved. Who knows what Gray might try if we were left alone?

Gray reties the cloth, way too tight, but I don't flinch.

Six times I get it right. Each time Gray barks at me to do it again. Each time the knife carves closer to my skin. Gray circles all the way around me, barefoot and quiet. Fabric puddles on the mat with a soft tumble. It's landed somewhere on my right. Gray might be trying to throw me off by tossing things on the ground, but his footsteps stick to the foam floor, stopping somewhere in front of me.

He hurls another knife—no, he's tossed two. They whir, slicing through the oppressive air with livid speed. My heartbeat punches inside my throat. Don't flinch. Don't move. Don't—

A quiet heat slides across my left shoulder. The sting roars to life. I yank off the blindfold and clamp my hand over the burning wound.

"You cut her!" Cole is at my side in a flash.

A spreading red stain leaks through the tan sweater and onto my fingers. The knife should have only grazed me. Why is there so much blood?

Gray leans against the table, casually spinning a knife. "The Blight moved."

We both know that's a lie. Trembles snake up my arms. The knives are less than ten feet away. My drumming pulse roars in my ears, blocking all sound. One solid cut. That's all it will take to inflict pain and erase that haughty glint in his eye. I lean forward ready to strike.

That's when I see his lip quirk with a stifled smirk. He's prodding me. Wanting me to lash out so I'll give him a reason to kill me. His taunting brows lift slightly.

"Gray is too good to have missed—even with two knives. I must have moved." I speak every syllable into the hollow cavern of his eyes. "It's stopped bleeding," I lie. The wound throbs, ten times worse than before. Blood, now cold, wets my fingers. "You only grazed the skin. Keep going."

"Don't," Cole mumbles with a warning undertone.

Gray stabs the knife into the table. "You're done."

"Thought so." I take the blindfold from Cole, wadding it in my fist, and march over to the weapons.

I turn to Gray. "Oh, on that last throw, one knife landed on the wall and hit the bottom red circle on my right. The brass blade that cut me, the one with the opal handle, is on the left side of the mat, about two feet from where I was standing." Maybe I shouldn't have spilled everything I know, but I couldn't help myself, and Gray's shocked expression is so worth it. "Lucky guess." I shrug and toss the blindfold at him.

The weapons glisten before me. Some knives are smaller than the palm of my hand, others are paper-thin swords, but each blade is Paradise Steel, perfectly polished and engraved with the ivy pattern. I reach for a knife with a curved blade.

Gray grabs my injured shoulder. "You're not touching a weapon."

Volcanic fire explodes through me, but I wrestle the urge to strike back. "We made a deal."

"That's right," Cole says. "You said—"

"I said she's done."

My breath is shallow and quick. "I kept my part."

"Paradise Steel can't cut the Awakened. It only harms Sage's army." Gray's words grind into a slow powder against my ear. "If it senses the Current, it repels from Awakened like a polarized magnet." He squeezes my shoulder and spins me around. A breath's span lies between us. Pupils blacker than tar. "It's now crystal clear what you are."

"Cool it, Gray." Cole's voice is low.

Gray shoves me hard. My back and my head slam into the metal door, knocking the wind out of me. I suck in a quick breath, preparing for another attack.

But Gray turns on Cole instead. "Who do you think you are?"

"Come on man, I'm just saying, be cool—"

Gray spins him into a chokehold. But not for long.

I blink, and somehow Cole has slipped free, only to sweep Gray's leg and bring him flat on his backside, right in front of me.

I'm stunned. So is Gray.

Before Gray springs to his feet, Cole has my hand and is dragging me out of the training room. My feet scramble to stay beneath me as I stumble onto the dirt path. The door slams behind us, followed by the hard click of a lock.

I clamp pressure on my pulsing wound.

Cole eyes my shoulder. "Have Lina look at that cut."

"It's fine," I brush off his concern. "But I need to work with a weapon. Can you get me back in there?"

"After what just happened?" Cole leads me away from the building. "No way! I'm already gonna pay for that move I pulled."

I shove a low-hanging branch out of my face. Yellow leaves fall to the ground. "I don't mean now."

"Still can't happen. Gray's got the place under lockdown twenty-four seven."

I pin Cole against a nearby tree. He'll probably use one of those crazy martial arts moves on me, but that's a chance I'll take. "Then take me somewhere else. Let me practice with the knife you stole, the one tucked in the hem of your pants, or I'll tell Foster about it."

His mouth gapes. "How'd you know about—"

"You're not as sly as you think."

"If you tell on me, I swear . . ."

I grip a fistful of his shirt. Inches separate the balmy air between us. "Train me, and I won't say a word."

Cole swallows but doesn't fight me off. "If you rat on me—"

"Despite what Gray thinks of me, I'm not a rat." I loosen my grip.

Cole hesitates and then says with a faint smirk, "You're more like a fox."

I let go and punch his shoulder. "Shut up."

He grins, then it evaporates. "You didn't move. He was testing the Steel on you."

"I know." I lift my elbow. The crimson splotch burns with the ferocity of a thousand hornet stings. "Could've been worse." At least I still have an arm.

"Yeah, well, I hate blood." Cole shoves his hat down low. "And you need a Healer."

"Healers only cause more pain." Blood drips down my arm, pooling into a fat drop on my knuckle and then plops into the dirt.

"Gray cut you with *his* Steel."

"Yeah, so?"

"Cuts from his knife don't heal on their own. Without a Healer's help, you'll bleed out, no matter how small the cut. Keep pressure on it." Cole puts his hand over my blood-speckled one and escorts me through the woods.

With every step, the wound burns deeper in my skin. So does my conviction that no matter how well I follow Alliance rules, Gray will surely find a way to kill me.

The slash on my arm is determined proof.

10

A BLIGHT LIKE ME

We arrive at the kitchen. My fingers are seeping with blood as I continue to smother the pulsing cut with steady pressure. Harper is mashing up herbs on the counter, releasing a pungent vapor cloud that smells worse than rotting potatoes.

"What now?" She fans out the air.

"Training." Cole chokes on a cough. "It was Gray's knife."

Harper glances at me sharply and purses her lips. She guides me to the barstool, even though I'm perfectly capable of walking on my own.

I wait for Cole to toss a flirty comment at Harper while she washes her hands, but he's looking at the back door. "Where's Lina?"

"I've got this." Harper pulls out a spray bottle from her kit.

"You sure? 'Cause it won't heal—"

"On its own. I'm aware." Harper shoots him an irritated glare. "Now wait outside."

Cole's eyes linger on me, on the cut, but with the shade of that hat, I can't read what he's thinking. "Yeah, sure . . ." His silhouette turns fuzzy.

"Go." She points to the dining room.

"Sure thing, Miss Bossy Pants." Cole walks out but doesn't

go far. Instead, he leans his back against the dining room threshold, waiting.

My helium-head floats, too light for my body. I'm tired of getting cut, burned, bruised, and knocked down. Tired of all this pain mimicking my visions, reminding me of the unrelenting torture waiting to resurface.

Harper pulls my sweater over my head, peeling away the bloodied fabric that sticks to my skin, and studies the wound with focused concentration. "I can't believe that jerk cut you."

"It was Gray." Blood slowly streams from the wound, zigzagging down my arm.

"I know." She douses a cloth in antiseptic. "He might be totally gorgeous, but he's a complete dirtbag."

I manage a weak smile.

After applying her torture spray and flattening a large gauze strip to my shoulder that makes the wound appear worse than it is, Harper makes me guzzle a tepid glass of green juice that tastes of fizzy bananas.

"Here." She takes off her navy sweater, leaving her in a tank top. "Wear this to keep warm. I'll find a way to fix yours."

"Thanks." I feel like an invalid as she guides my arms through the sleeves. Her sweater is snug and much warmer than mine.

As she cleans up the supplies, Devon walks through the back door holding a bushel of wildflowers and greenery. "Lina kept up with my garden while I was gone. Look at this. I brought you—" His pleased expression falls. "Did something happen?"

"Everything's fine." Harper touches his arm as she takes the cuttings. "Devon, these are amazing. Oh, wait, you've got something . . ." She wipes a smudge of dirt from his face with her thumb.

"I'm leaving." I slink off the barstool, suddenly feeling like I'm intruding. "Thanks, Harper." She's so focused on Devon I doubt she heard me.

I walk into the dining room, adjusting the sweater as I go. Cole waits by a basket of wrapped sandwiches. The way he looks me over shoots flushing warmth across my face. I walk off before he can notice.

The floor creaks as I cross through the quiet War Room. The painting of the girl in the blue dress is tucked in the corner. No one is around. I inch closer. The girl, about my age, is bathed in soft light as she sits on a burgundy stool. She's taking dictation from an older man sitting in a chair with a blanket draped over his lap. He's wearing a white shirt and black tunic, looking a lot like a Puritan.

"You into Delacroix?" Cole asks from behind me.

I'm almost afraid to ask. "Into what?"

"The artist." Cole gestures at the painting with a wrapped sandwich. "I've seen better." He rips the sandwich in half, wax paper and all, and offers me some.

"Thanks." I take a bite of the warm baguette, pressed with some kind of thin meat, mustard, pickles, and melted Swiss. Flavors I never put together, but somehow they make my stomach happy. "What do you know about this painting?"

Cole has already downed his entire sandwich. He wads the paper in a tight ball and aims for the wastebasket. "I'd get with her." The trash bounces off the rim.

"Can you be serious for once?" I take another bite, starved.

Cole swipes the wadded paper off the floor and chucks it in the trash. "Maybe I'm not the problem. Maybe you need to learn how to lighten up."

The savory bite lands hard as I swallow. I know he stood up for me against Gray. And he brought me food, but I've just had a knife thrown at me. Not only that, I've got less than two days to stay behind the Wall, and I haven't found anything to offer the Alliance. I don't have time to lighten up. I stare at the sandwich now squashed in my fist, proof that he's partly right. "Thanks." I hold up the sandwich. "I haven't eaten and think I'm just cranky."

"Yeah, you are." His expression softens. "I get it. You're into the serious type. Fine, I can do serious." He stands to his full height, folds his hands in front of him a lot like Foster, and says with a precise accent, "It's a neoclassical piece by the French artist, Ferdinand-Eugène-Victor Delacroix, better known for his Romantic paintings. Tell me what you see."

Is he messing with me again?

"Go on." He gestures at the painting.

I suppress a smile and examine the artwork, absorbing every detail. "The man is blind, because he's painted with his eyes closed. And the girl . . . she's figured something out. Something only she knows, because the older girl in the shadows is oblivious, bored, or both. But the girl in blue . . ." Bathed in a caramel light, she should be the focus, but there's something else. The girl leans forward, eager to capture the man's every word. "The girl has a connection to the blind man because the way light falls between them. I think he's transferring something." I straighten my spine. "He's a Seer, isn't he?"

Cole elbows me. "Bingo, Blighty. The painting is called *Milton Dictating* Paradise Lost *to His Daughters*."

I look again. Wrestling darkness looms behind the girl and collides with the light. "She's a Blight, a half-breed. The look on her face, she's discovering it for the first time. And maybe . . ." I study Milton. The light. The shadows. Every brush stroke clarifies the truth.

Milton is a Blight.

Certainty surges through me. Why didn't you reveal this to me earlier, Milton? Why wait until now?

His answer is a whisper in my head.

> *For how shall I relate*
> *To human sense the invisible exploits*
> *Of warring spirits . . .*

How last unfold
The secrets of another world perhaps
Not lawful to reveal?

Not lawful because you're an outlaw to the Alliance, just like me. Except you've done a better job of hiding it. It's taken Delacroix for me to see the shamed look on your face as you turn away from the girl, knowing what she is. Knowing what you are too.

No wonder Foster said no one could detect any insight about the war in your poem. Only a Blight like me can read what you've hidden in the verses.

Cole lifts his hat. "She's a Blight? Huh. Didn't notice that before." He studies the painting, scanning back and forth as though mapping it to something else.

"Come on." I take his hand and drag him to the library. Excitement charges each step. "I've got work to do."

11

DESTROYER

"That's the latest one." Maddox places a drawing from his sketchbook on Foster's desk as I burst through the open doors with Cole in tow.

"Foster." I cringe at my casualness. "I mean, Lieutenant."

Maddox's magnetic smile falls as soon as he sees my hand in Cole's.

"Miss Marlowe." Foster's voice lilts as he straightens an unruly stack of papers, tapping them on his desk until aligned. "Is there a viable explanation for your delayed return?"

I quickly drop Cole's hand. "It's Milton. I need to read through *Paradise Lost*. Please."

Maddox's eyes question me as I approach.

"I'm positive there's an answer in the poem," I say, answering Maddox more than Foster.

"You shall begin by reviewing artwork and providing insights on what you discover, as originally agreed." Foster walks to the coffee table and motions to five perfect towers of books that will take anyone an eternity to review. "Begin here."

Foster mentioned the poem didn't reveal anything, but maybe he doesn't know Milton is a Blight. "But—"

His lips twitch with irritation. "I applaud your zeal, however with less than twenty-four hours until your departure, the six hours and twelve minutes it will take to read over ten thousand lines of blank verse, previously scrutinized, does not constitute the most effective use of time."

"Milton is a Blight," I blurt. "It's written in the painting. The Delacroix."

Foster raises his brow a millimeter. Thoughts churn deep inside his eyes as he considers and processes my statement. He's probably cross-referencing my discovery against the library of facts crammed inside his perfectly groomed head.

Without a word, he walks to the fireplace and removes a black hardback book from the shelf and hands it to me. "Advise me on anything you glean. In the meantime . . ." He picks up a heavy book and gives it to Cole. "Sort works for her analysis. Begin with neoclassical and Romantic selections, please."

Cole groans quietly as he skims the pages. I thought Foster would be pleased, maybe even a little excited at my news, but then again, it's hard to tell.

Regardless, I finally have a copy of the poem. Electricity buzzes through me as I settle into the corner of the couch with Milton, a welcomed weight in my hands. Cole plops down next to me.

As Maddox sorts through his sketchbook, I tune everyone out and open to the first line, determined to find Milton's message.

> *Of man's first disobedience and the fruit*
> *Of that forbidden tree, whose mortal taste*
> *Brought death into the world and all our woe,*
> *With loss of Eden . . .*

"What about this one?" Cole wags a book in my face. "Cot's *The Storm*."

The picture kicks up thoughts of Mark, the Dissenter, back at the gallery, and how he watched me read the painting, luring me to bring Mom's drawings. Drawings I had no clue would point to this other world. I take in the glossy picture. Without the wispy brushstrokes, the image doesn't translate the same.

I try anyway.

The girl glances over her shoulder with that determined look on her face, ready to face what pursues her head on. The irony of what I'm reading isn't lost on me. But I don't look anything like the girl. The boy, however, with his disheveled black hair, smitten grin, completely entranced by the girl . . . I glance at Cole. My face flushes. Maddox notices.

"Nothing." I shove the book away and lift Milton in front of my face.

Cole studies the picture. "Really?"

"Lieutenant." Devon enters with phone in hand. "I've got Gladys on the line. Lines are spotty, and it's hard to hear, but Cera can speak with her mom."

I dump Milton and leap to my feet. I fumble for the phone, pressing it tight against my ear. "Gladys?" My voice echoes back. I pace the three steps behind the couch. Turn. Pace again.

A silent delay and then, "Darling?" Her voice is muffled and sounds caged in a tin can. "Your mama's here . . . better . . ."

Echoing silence.

Then a faint, broken, "Go on and . . . I'll hold it . . ."

Static fuzz drowns her out.

"Gladys?" My question ricochets back at me. "Mom? Can you hear me?" My desperate echo mocks me.

"Cera?" Noise rumbles in the background.

"Mom?"

A high-pitched static cuts the line. Then silence.

Gravity binds my lungs and lodges in my throat. That was Mom. It was her voice. I heard her say my name. I blink back tears of frustration. "Can we try again?"

Devon redials but can't get through. "Storms have been taking down some of the lines in East Ridge. And cells are spotty inside the Garden. I'll try later."

"Storms? Or Legions?" I can't hide the panic. My voice rises. "I've seen the way Legions travel in a cloud. She's not safe until she's here, with me."

Maddox touches my arm. "Kellan. Tanji," he reminds me. "They'll keep her safe. Gladys will make sure of it." I wish his confidence could dismantle the fear wreaking havoc in my heart.

"Maddox Alexander, you are excused." Foster's tone is clipped.

Devon puts a hand on Maddox's shoulder. "Come on."

"I'll find a way," Maddox assures me. His eyes are sealed with a promise as Devon ushers him out of the room.

"Sure thing, surfer boy." Cole throws a dismissive wave over his head as he reclines on the couch.

"Colton." Foster hands him another book. "Continue."

"Sir." Cole grumbles but sits up and fans the pages.

Mom is with Gladys. They're safe. It sounded as if Gladys said she was better. But that noise . . . What if Devon can't get through? What if—

"Miss Marlowe." Foster's tone is a gentle but stern reminder to focus. "Your mother is protected and cared for. However, our time is limited." His words bring some comfort but don't erase the unsettling feeling. As he starts a fire to warm the chill taking over the room, I force myself to return to the poem, hoping that Mom is getting better. Stronger.

I lean over the back of the couch to pick up the poem, and glance over Cole's shoulder as he sifts through a book. "Wait." I put a hand out. "Go back."

He flips a page. "This one?" Cole holds up *Sadak in Search of the Waters of Oblivion*, the same painting hanging in the War Room.

"Yes. That's the Well—or at least a hint of it." The glowing water is like a lake, that much is clear, but . . . "How can you destroy a lake?"

"Find the source and damage or pollute it." Cole tips his head back and briefly looks at me from under the rim of his hat. Seeing his eyes in the light for the first time catches me off guard. They're striking emerald green with sleepy black lashes. A million fizzy bubbles flit inside my stomach. He looks back at the book. "If the source is tainted, the whole stream goes bad."

I force the fluttery feeling aside and take the book to study the picture more closely. "What's the source? In the painting the light in the water looks as if it comes from underneath, but the way Martin painted those two rocks, it's as if they're pointing to something over the water. Look." I show Cole the picture.

"There's nothing there," he says.

"Lieutenant," I say as Foster adjusts the logs in the fire. "Is it possible Martin didn't transcribe the entire vision? Pop said Blights would only have a piece or two, not the whole picture." A thought occurs to me. "Would I see anything? I mean, as a Blight, could I see the source if I went and looked at the Well?"

Foster halts for a moment. "It's highly unlikely. The only way to fully see the Well is by unlocking the third realm where it dwells."

Cole sits up. "If it's unlocked, then you'd have your answer."

Foster bristles. "While opening the realm would provide the answers we seek, doing so would no longer keep the portal secure. If Sage and his army were to obtain access, they could eradicate our power. Unlocking the third realm, Mr. Tripton, is strictly forbidden."

"But wouldn't direct access to the source strengthen our powers?" Cole asks. "Maybe even give us what we need to defeat Sage?"

"While it is possible that a mainline infusion of the Current would significantly strengthen our abilities, the risk of whether that power will be enough to overtake the enemy remains uncertain. It is a risk the Alliance will never take." Foster stokes the fire. "Miss Marlowe has the capacity to connect the realms once her powers are fully manifested. The last one, the one we call a Destroyer—a Blight with her particular combination of

Bents—nearly did."

Milton taps inside my head: *"Destroyers rightlier called and plagues of men."* Then he adds, *"Made to destroy."*

I'm a plague to the Alliance, that's for sure. Which is why they want me out of the Garden the sunset before my birthday. I pick up the copy of the poem, searching for the verse, hoping to read a less daunting meaning than what Milton is suggesting.

Cole stands with a stretch. "Maybe so, but it's still not clear how she can connect the realms."

Foster hesitates but then says, "By utilizing fully manifested powers from both sides, Awakened and Dissenting, within close proximity of the Well." Our eyes meet with mutual understanding. He's equipping me with this knowledge, trusting I won't betray him.

I won't. But something doesn't sit right. "If I'm that much of a threat, and in the Garden nonetheless, then why keep me alive?"

Foster's eyes soften as he looks at me, even though, as usual, his face is empty of emotion. "Every life has equal value, Miss Marlowe. Even Blights. Perhaps one day we can all agree."

Cole messes with the chess table. "The way I see it. You can probably solve what no one else has been able to. For the first time, the Alliance will have a chance to control the game, and Sage won't know what hit him." He uncovers the black king in his palm. "Am I right?" Cole asks Foster. "If she finds the answer that can take down Sage, then we can all exhale, and I can spring outta here."

"Destruction is not our objective. However . . ." I swear there's a glimmer of hope in Foster's eyes as he says, "If there is evidence supporting a clear plan for Sage's demise, Global Council would be terribly remiss to not consider it as an option when they return."

Cole reaches out and picks up another book, quickly flipping through the pages. "Come on, Blighty. Get to work."

12

THE NIGHTMARE

Cole, Foster, and I are up well into the night. Lina brings in dinner as we barricade ourselves in the library. Pop comes in to listen as Cole sifts through art books, holding up pictures for me to read while I continue to scour the poem. All while Foster takes notes.

"What about this one?" Cole holds Fuseli's *The Nightmare* in front of me.

That picture gives me the creeps. The woman seems soulless, sprawled on the bed in her white gown while an ape-like demon perches on top of her, scowling at his intruding audience—me. Those bulging eyes . . . I'm sure it's the gorilla-like creature from my visions.

An icy chill snakes through me. "This is Sage." I point to the demon. "He's siphoning the Current." The woman's face, the listless hands, that delicate nose, something about it reminds me of . . . "Can I call my mom again?" I know it's not her in the picture. Looks nothing like her, but for some reason, an anxious fear suddenly takes over.

Pop tucks his blanket around his knees. "Devon's workin' on getting through. He'll let you know when he does. Now focus." He waves a finger in my direction. "Try readin' that one again."

Cole holds out the book. Despite the brooding weight pinned on my chest, I look again. The sneering creature is taunting the viewer to stop him. "The red curtains are a stage, a setup, and the horse peeking through with eyes of white fire could be another creature," I say. "Or maybe Sage's accomplice. Or something else entirely. It's not clear on the page, maybe if I saw it firsthand."

Foster takes furious notes. Outside the bay window, night descends. Tiny lights of what looks to be fireflies, dance in the underbrush, igniting the forest with the same flickers of beckoning light I saw in the treetops.

A thousand marbles feel dropped inside my stomach. I trust Foster. And Devon. I believe they're telling the truth about Mom's safety. So why can't I shake this unsettled feeling? I work hard to squelch the sensation and scour more artwork.

Hours pass.

The fire dies.

We're down to the last pile of books. Harper escorted Pop out of the room hours ago. Only Foster, Cole, and I remain.

Foster rubs his hand from all the note-taking. But as far as I can tell, nothing shouts out a conclusive answer. Either about the Well's transfer or Sage. Still, I keep going, skimming *Paradise Lost* while glancing at artwork: Blake, Girodet-Trioson, Doré, Martin, Delacroix, Gericault.

My eyes burn, and my head is foggy, but I'm determined to find a solution that will help defeat Sage—or protect the Alliance. And maybe absolve my mother and me.

Foster rubs the space between his eyebrows and checks his watch. "I think it best if we stop here for tonight."

I sit up. "No," I argue, "I can keep going."

Cole is sprawled on the couch next to me, asleep.

"Providing our mind and our bodies with proper rest is imperative for clarity." Foster removes Milton from my listless hands, setting it aside. "You've interpreted a remarkable amount of classical work in a short period of time. More than I anticipated. Quite exceptional, in fact." His gentle eyes hold the same expression my father had the first time I read a book aloud. "I suggest you rest."

"I don't need rest. I'm out by sunset tomorrow, and I haven't found the answer."

"If left unchecked, unbridled tenacity can destroy you in the process." Foster's words sound born from experience. "We shall resume in the morning." A deep sadness shadows his eyes as he looks at Cole, hat covering his face. "Hendrick Colton," he says with a gentle nudge.

"I'm up." Cole stretches. "I was just thinking with my eyes closed."

Foster's stoic expression returns. "Escort Miss Marlowe to her room."

"Sure thing." But I doubt Cole is fully awake.

I tuck Milton under my arm and head to the door. "Good night, Lieutenant."

Foster, seeming indifferent to his own need for sleep, nods as he cleans up his desk and adjusts the silver picture frame.

I step into the cool night. Blades walk the grounds. Crumbling gravel grinds under their steel-toed boots, disturbing the quiet as Cole and I walk to the east corridor in tired silence. He stops at my door and leans against the stucco wall under the gas lamp. The soft glow accents his jawline and full lips. "See you in the morning, unless . . ."

"Go." I point down the walkway.

He shrugs with that signature smirk. I doubt he means it. He didn't try anything on our way to the training room. In fact, he brought Gray to the ground right in front of me.

"Cole?"

He turns to go. "I know. I know. I'm leaving."

"Thank you."

He looks over his shoulder. "Yeah, whatever, Blighty." Through the unsteady flickers of light, I catch his smile. Not that expected smirk, but a genuine, boyish smile that wakes a rowdy whirlwind inside my stomach. Cole pulls his hat down and walks away, still grinning. "And get some rest. You look like crap."

After shutting the door, I check the room to be sure I'm alone. I don't bother undressing. I plop onto bed, and despite Foster's advice, I settle in to read *Paradise Lost.*

"Like those Hesperian gardens famed of old, / Fortunate fields, and groves, and flowery vales, / Thrice happy isles, but who dwelt happy there . . ."

Hesperian. The name brings up a hollow ache for Gladys. Juniper. Tanji. Kellan. And Rhys. Maybe one day I'll return. A buoyant hope lifts the weighted feeling about my mother. I imagine her resting in Harper's room at Hesperian with Gladys watching over her. The sounds of the frothing milk and chatty voices lulling her to sleep, knowing we'll see each other soon.

I flop my head on the pillow. Paper crinkles. It carries a scent of rain. Like Maddox. He left me a note? No. It's a drawing. The five cords knotted together, the same one that was tacked on his wall in Hesperian when I first met him. The one he kept trying to hide. At the bottom he's neatly written *"Together."*

The twisted cords are braided tight, stronger than the single strand straining to pull free. This might be his way of telling me what he couldn't say earlier—that he has a team ready. Maybe the group from Hesperian. My spirit rises. But I still have to do my part and find a solid answer, a clear solution that will help win the war. And I have less than a day to do it.

Footsteps sound outside my door again. I bolster the chair under the knob and then quickly crawl back into bed. I tuck the drawing next to my pillow and listen for anyone still lurking near my room. Hearing nothing, I settle in to read.

Then my fingers clench.

Tremors coil through my arms.

Stabbing heat streaks down my legs.

Oh no. I drop the book. That familiar but unwelcome wrenching pain from an oncoming vision spirals down my back. I grip the sheets. Crushing pressure rips down my spine. I lie on my back with eyes closed and exhale slow and deep. Don't fight it. Don't grasp the images. Do what Pop said. Let them come.

Heated pain slashes down my back. I writhe and smother my face in the suffocating pillow. The paper crinkles. Maddox's scent lingers. I inhale and focus on him and not the unbearable spinal contraction. On his turbulent cerulean eyes. On the way his hand feels in mine. On the way he smiles when I walk into the room.

I exhale.

The pain subsides.

Silver fog swirls, clouding my sight. The hazy vision lies just behind the frosty veil. I don't wrestle to see. I wait.

Wrenching pressure kneads down my back. Hot tears drip down my cheek, wetting my ear. Another pang compresses each vertebra, every nerve screaming for release, but deep twisting pain kicks me into silence. Then the wispy fog billows.

A handheld lantern shines

A ray of caramel light beams

A narrow path illuminates through the dark

The taunting fog dances in front of the vision. My body shakes. Don't fight it.

White smoke billows

Strong hands press on an exposed spine

Lips drip with burning fire

Fading bodies writhe

I'm seized with an overwhelming sense to hide. Not fear. Not panic. But terrifying relentless shame. Consuming guilt.

A streak of red light flashes

A heart-shaped stone

Everything fades black.

Intense grief radiates, a deep regret. Not with impending death, but something else entirely. Pop was right. This one vision is different. And the vivid images were sharper, the feelings more intense. I close my eyes and try to interpret, recalling the first thing that comes to mind: lips. They dripped with fire. Luring. Dangerous.

Maddox's stormy eyes are all I see.

And the exposed spine? Heat invades my face. I melted under his kiss. Then he called it a mistake. Maybe it was, because now a horrible thought overtakes me: what if this time, I'm the threat in the vision, the creature luring Maddox away? If that's so, then this nightmare vision confirms Gray's suspicion. And now he'll have a solid case against me.

Something softly *thunks* outside the door. Panic seizes me as I blindly search for the wastebasket by the bed. My fingers grasp the edge. I pull it close, lean over, and wretch. But no one enters.

I flop on the bed, blinded by the silver haze, lie still, and wait. Shame creeps along my skin, wrapping tight around my throat as I think on the vision—on Maddox. Then Cole's dangling smirk gets in the way. I push thoughts of him aside and try to focus on the vision.

After who knows how long, the wispy haze disappears. I sit up, finally able to see with an insatiable drive to find Maddox. A desperate draw to be near him, which must be an effect of the vision because, according to Gray, Maddox isn't harnessed to me anymore. I'll be assigned someone new. They'll draw out the vision. Then everyone will see.

And know the truth.

13

WINTER

A lingering headache ebbs and flows as morning light brightens the cloudy window above the threshold. Someone beats my door with an impatient knock.

"Coming." I stagger through the room, brushing my teeth, throwing on clean clothes. I twist my hair in a flimsy knot. I would slide Gladys's hairpin behind my ear, but last time I did that, I lost it. Instead, I safely tuck it in my pocket. After several more savage beatings that rattle the glass, I emerge with Milton in hand.

The grumpy Blade that spied on Maddox and me in the dining room escorts me to the library in suspicious silence. He's bound to report my delay to Gray. Guilty heat covers me despite the crisp morning air. Regardless of the shame, I'll confess the vision to Foster first.

Grumpy dumps me at the library, even though no one is there when I arrive. He must not know because he leaves me at the courtyard door and walks away. Art books sprawl on the coffee table the same way we left them during our late-night marathon session. Foster's desk is neatly straightened. Only the picture frame is out of line.

I adjust it for him, taking a quick peek. A woman with shiny strawberry hair draped over her left shoulder crinkles her nose with a modest grin. Her forehead rests by the ear of a frowning toddler with his arms crossed over a crumpled school uniform. The boy looks like a mini-Foster, minus the mustache. But the plastered hair is the same.

It's hard to imagine Foster with a family. Or maybe he doesn't have one anymore.

Voices collide with clanking breakfast dishes. I tuck Milton under my arm and, despite Gray's threat on my life, search for Maddox. As I cut through the War Room, I glance out the screen door. Pop sits alone, rocking in a chair. A few gray birds with spotted wings flutter at his feet.

"Had another one, Honey?" He rolls a seed between his fingers. "Come, sit with me."

I'm still amazed at how Pop knows it's me. But I don't have time to sit around. It's my final morning in the Garden. I'm saddled with the crushing weight of deciphering messages, finding answers, and staying alive. But if Pop can help . . .

"I did." I walk out and sit in the chair next to him, tucking Milton beside me. "The first part was exactly the same as before, with the lantern. But then . . . it wasn't like the others." I feel the heat climb up my neck. "The danger felt . . ."

"Different?" Pop tosses a seed into the grass, and then turns as if he can see my face. "Thought it might."

"I interpreted the vision the way you taught me." I hesitate with the truth, but keeping secrets has only led to more harm. "The vision is a warning about being lured. A warning about me. A tempting." I lean away. "It started with a lantern like the last one, but it had burning lips. An exposed spine. And writhing bodies. Maybe in pain . . ." My face warms. "And a stone heart."

Pop rolls another seed between his long fingers, considering my words for a moment. "I think you might be right. When the lieutenant's through lookin' at the drawing, then you'll get a chance to find the gaps."

"Wait. Foster has a drawing of it?"

"The lieutenant," Pop corrects me. "And yes. The boy drew it out."

A crisp morning breeze whips around me. I shiver. "Do you mean Maddox? Gray had him unharnessed." I suddenly feel the need to justify myself. "And he wasn't anywhere near me."

Pop tosses another seed. Feathers ruffle as the spotted birds frantically search for the kernel. "Ain't no unharnessing. The bond's too strong. And behind the Wall, proximity don't matter, since there ain't no threat of interception."

I'm not quite sure what to think about Pop's comment about my bond with Maddox. But I'm more unsettled by everyone seeing what's in my head.

"Pop, this vision confirms I'm a threat." My voice falters. "I haven't done anything to help the Alliance, and Global Council leaders are on their way. I want to do what's right, but I'm scared I won't be strong enough when it counts." A question is burning inside me, and I desperately need to hear his answer. "Do you think I'll ever belong, or is there too much of my father in me?"

Pop counts seeds in his palm, rubbing a soft finger over each one. "I believe in what you can do, Honey. It's all there, in the seed."

Not sure about the seed part, but . . . "Foster said I have the potential to connect the realms and help Sage destroy the Well. Is that what you believe?"

"I'm saying I believe in you. Sure, you're a Blight, maybe even a Destroyer, like the last one. That might be what you are, but it ain't *who* you are." Pop tosses the last seed into the wind. "Who are you, Honey?"

I stare at the wooden slats, waiting for some miraculous answer to appear that won't confirm my deepest fear.

But even Milton stays silent.

Pop reaches out and finds my hand. "Every choice reveals

who you are. Creates what you'll become. Who's that going to be?"

"I don't know."

"Yes, you do. But you're too afraid to take a good look. It's easier to spend your time running around, saving everyone's life, 'cept your own. Sit still too long, and you've got to deal with that monster lurking inside."

I snap my head up. "I'm not a monster."

"Didn't say you were. But we'd be fools to think we're not all wrestling with something dark inside." He scoots to the edge of the seat and motions for me to come closer. I lean in. His smooth hands touch my face. I sit still and let his fingers trace along my eyebrows, my nose, my chin, mapping me somehow. "Spring will come. Can you feel it in the wind?"

As if orchestrated, a fiery sunrise breaks over the lush treetops. A nectar breeze whips a loose strand of hair in my face. My distorted reflection elongates on his dark glasses.

I look at the vibrant treetops. "They say it's always spring in the Garden. But outside the Wall it's fall, almost winter."

Pop sits back. "You fancy yourself a winter?"

His question makes no sense. "I don't *fancy* anything except trying to save lives."

He braces one hand on the cane to stand. I take his frail arm, helping him out of the chair. "Winter hides what spring brings to life. But spring *will* rise." His hand finds my cheek, patting it gently.

I have no idea what that means.

The dining room door creaks open. "Ready, Pop?" Harper steps out wearing almost no makeup. Why is it that the less makeup she wears, the more she glows? Maybe it's a Healer's gift but probably just a Harper thing. "How's your shoulder?" she asks me.

I'd completely forgotten about the compress under the sweater since it doesn't hurt. I lift my arm. No pain. "Fine. Thanks."

"Come inside. I'll check the cut."

I rub the hidden wound. "Thanks, but I've got work to do." A message to find, and a monster to deal with.

"Later then." She guides Pop inside.

The dining room door bangs closed just as Cole jogs up the porch steps. "Mornin', gorgeous."

"Harper's inside, so I doubt she heard you."

"Hey, Blindy, I wasn't talking about Harper."

A waking flutter sprawls across my stomach. "I'm not blind. I'm a Blight."

"Makes no difference to me." Cole tips his hat, dangling that dangerous smile on his lips.

"Cut it out." I head to the porch rail for distance.

"Come on, you know you love me." Cole drapes his arm around my neck and whispers against my ear, "Probably dream about me."

"Oh, you mean a nightmare?" I elbow him in the ribs and duck out of his headlock. As he rubs his side, I quickly take off his stupid hat so I can finally read him. Now I've got a clear look at his face. He scrubs out his jet-black hair, messing it up even more.

His high cheekbones are kissed with windburn, and behind those long black lashes, his mischievous eyes are striking emeralds caught by surprise. The color darkens as the blazing Current splits every neuron wide open.

I'm melted frozen.

"Give me that." He swipes the hat back. He shouldn't cover his face. Not with hypnotic eyes that gorgeous.

But Cole shoves the hat on my head, pressing it low. It carries a faint smell of him, smoky wildfire and hair gel. "Looks good on you, Blighty." His muffled voice sounds shaky.

I look up from under the rim of the hat and press my back into the wooden rail. Through the window, Maddox turns his head and moves away, or at least I think it's him. The meshed screen and warped glass make it hard to tell. Cole leans his shoulder into mine as he faces the lawn. "Listen. Foster's in a briefing about how things are going down at sunset. I'm supposed to watch over you for an hour or so. There's a place inside the Garden by the lake's edge. Five-minute drive. If we go now, I can train you with the Steel. In private."

"Seriously?" Excitement bubbles in my voice.

"Plus, I hate the flowers around here. Looks like my mom's couch puked all over the place."

I try to imagine him sprawled on a floral couch, asleep. "Was it pink?"

"The couch?" He exaggerates a shudder. "Yeah."

When I laugh out loud, a wide grin spreads across his full lips. "Keep the hat on, and let's go before someone drags you inside."

He takes my hand and leads me down the patio steps and around the side of the house. With incredible stealth and perfect timing, Cole sneaks us past a cluster of Blades patrolling the yard.

When we get to the woods, I let go of his hand. "I forgot." I hold out my arm with the tracker wrapped snug against my skin. "Gray will know."

Cole takes the knife from the hem of his jeans. "Give me your wrist."

I hesitate.

"Look." Cole slides the knife against his own Cord, placing it just under the thread and over the jagged burn on his wrist. Sparks and smoke kick off the wire when the Steel makes contact. He plucks at the string until it loosens enough to slide over his hand. "The Cord will show you're in the area, but exact location won't register for an hour or so." He stuffs his tracker in his pocket and then holds my wrist. "Take a deep breath. And try not to move."

The knife sizzles. I grit my teeth. If this burning is what it takes to get some training, then I'll gladly endure it.

After placing my tracker in his pocket, Cole effortlessly weaves through the shadows in the woods. I stick right behind, even though my stomach twists a little. He pushes a branch aside and steps onto the end of the sloped drive.

"Where's this ride of yours?" I ask.

He carefully plucks back a blanket of overgrown shrubs, sparking with something silver underneath. "It's technically not my ride, but Gray won't mind."

"We're stealing Gray's motorcycle? Are you insane?" I yank the hat off.

Cole smirks. "Yeah, kinda." Pulling the keys from his pocket, he straddles the seat and kicks the pedal. When he revs the engine, my bones rattle. "Get on. We're running out of time."

I straddle the bike behind Cole without question, because once I leave this Garden, everything changes. And I really need to know how to wield a weapon.

I feel awkward on the bike. I'm not sure what to do with my hands. Should I let them hang? Put them on his shoulder or . . .

He takes his hat, tossing it in the brush. Then he brings my hands to his waist. "Hang on, princess."

"I'm not a prin—"

As soon as he guns the engine, I swallow the word and grip him tight. *No helmet? What am I thinking?* This is bound to end badly. But as soon as Cole peels out and the wind kisses my cheeks, I forget everything.

In this moment, I feel like I've been kicked alive.

14

WILDERNESS

Cole parks the bike near the matted brushwood by the road. I follow him through a worn path in the winding woods until we reach a small clearing by the lake, a picnic spot of smooth grass engulfed by wilderness. Charred wood from a blackened campfire sits near the lake. Morning sun sparkles on the placid water and the soggy air smells of mud and pine. With each step, my running shoes sink into the wet earth.

Cole squats to remove the knife from the hem of his jeans, or sock, or wherever he has it hidden. "Let's get you trained, Blighty."

"I'm so ready." I reach out, eager to hold the weapon.

He pulls it back. "Don't put your greasy fingerprints on the blade. That's seventeenth-century metal, for crying out loud."

I frown. "I'm not exactly a knife expert."

"Yeah, well this one's a relic, so treat it with respect."

"You get that lecture from Foster or Pop?"

"No. Pretentious overseas boarding schools." As he starts hacking at low-hanging vines on the perimeter, the knife glistens, even in the shade.

"How'd you swipe the Paradise Steel from Gray?"

"Let's just say distractions work in my favor." He slices another vine, tossing it aside.

My fingers are itching to hold the knife. "Can you get me one?"

Cole looks at me, incredulous. "Do you have any idea what it took to get this? I couldn't do it again without Gray catching on. And the problem with having one is stashing it, moving the weapon around so they won't find it on me. If they find one on you . . . ?" His expression shadows. "Just hurry and clear the trunks. We'll use them as targets." He turns away to cut another knot of tangled vines.

They'd kill me, I know. I'm already on the termination short list. I push up my sleeves. The clunky bandage sticks to my shoulder. I take a fistful of the vine. "If I accidentally get cut, will this knife make me bleed out too?" My palm scorches as the waxy leaves turn yellow and the branch wilts with time-lapse speed. I let go, startled. Did I do that?

I glance at Cole's vines. They stayed green.

He doesn't seem to notice my shriveled ones. "No. Just Gray's Steel," he says, walking to the center of the clearing while counting under his breath. I follow after him, not wanting to touch another branch. "It's a unique composite. His weapon has been handed down through their family for generations. There's talk that the metal is actually a piece of the gate that broke off during an attack with Sage back in the Renaissance. I highly doubt that. The gate is indestructible and transfers with the Well. My guess? It's been forged differently and probably has a higher concentration of whatever special alloy is in ours." Cole stops. So do I. "That's about fifteen paces. Memorize this distance, Blighty. You don't want to get any closer to a Legion than this. Gives you time to duck if they come your way."

He doesn't know how close I've already been to one. I shudder thinking about it. No less than fifteen paces seems a safe distance to me.

"You ever throw knives?" He spins me around to face the tree line.

"Never." Unless tossing pencils into foam blocks that Mom would bring home from work counts.

"Watch how I do it." He flings the blade with one swift motion. It sticks perfectly in the tree. He plucks the weapon free, inspecting the tip. "Most knives can't be used for throwing and slicing. But these babies play by their own rules."

"Why knives? Why not make bullets out of that special alloy?"

"It's something about what happens when the edge of the blade makes contact. Don't know that bullets would have the same effect." Cole puts his arm around my waist. "Now stand like this." He leans into my back, positioning my arms, the same way Maddox did when teaching me guitar. "It's in the release. Keep your wrist and arm straight. Don't flick it, that'll cause too much rotation. Just let go when it's about eye level." Cole gently moves my hand to demonstrate the motion and looks down my arm to make sure my wrist is straight. My flittering stomach tingles as his wildfire scent intensifies. "These knives are lighter, so when applying force, account for the weight. And don't forget to factor in wind. Got it?"

I nod even though I'm not a physics genius. Honestly, my brain tuned out about half of what he just said. Not only is he too close, but I want to test the knife out for myself. Then I'll make adjustments.

"Good." Cole releases my hand. "Now aim for the center." The hilt pulses in my fist, bucking against my palm. I grip tighter.

"Go for it." Cole crosses his arms, waiting.

I lift the blade and concentrate on a smooth release. The tumbling knife trips through the air and lands at the base of the trunk. Yeah, I was bad at tossing pencils too. Maybe I should have paid more attention in physics.

"Try again." I'm impressed that Cole doesn't laugh at my horrible attempt. He picks up the weapon and wipes away the mud with the hem of his shirt. "Release sooner. Toss harder."

He watches me throw the blade again. When it gets caught in the vines, he ducks his head, swallowing a laugh, I'm sure.

All told, I must have tried thirty times. Each time, I miss or it bounces off the bark, despite Cole moving me closer or farther away from the target. Nothing seems to help.

Cole scrubs out his hair. "Let's try something else."

After collecting the loose vines, he wraps them into a winding ball. "Let's see how hard you can stab into this sucker." He fastens the knotted vines to the tree. "Imagine, if you will, a Legion or Cormorant—or Sage." He takes my wrist and walks me to the tree. "One handed. See how far you can get through."

"Seriously? It would be like stabbing the tree."

"Consider it more like a punching bag wrapped in chains."

"That's worse." I clutch the knife with both hands.

"Nope. One handed." Cole removes my left hand. "And shank up."

"Just stab it?" Judging by what happened when I touched the leaves, these vines might turn yellow and wither just the same. What will Cole do if he sees how my touch destroys the Garden? On top of that, I'll probably end up digging the knife into the tree or breaking my hand. "Can we do something else?"

"One hit, Blighty. Let's see what you've got. Strike deep. Upward thrust. Come on."

Kellan used that same phrase when we were on the streets. He said the way to kill the creatures was to aim for the heart, strike deep, and pray I don't die. Maybe this is how he trained. If it is, I can do this. I *have* to learn this.

I take a deep breath and strike hard. On impact, the hilt sizzles my palm. I let go. The knife is caught in the vines. But barely.

Cole plucks the weapon free. "Was that all you've got?"

I wrap my arms around myself. My sweater is damp from the soppy air. "Let me see you try," I snap. For some reason, I can't bring myself to pierce the vines—or the tree. So I cross the short distance to the shore, hoping the sun will warm me.

"Actually, it'd probably be the same for me." Cole walks along the lake's edge. "I only wanted to see if you could. Gray has us all try something similar, but no one's been able to, as far as I know." His voice drops low. "Except for Gray."

In the sunlight, Cole's skin looks ashen, and with those dark circles under his eyes, I wonder if he ever sleeps. Maybe being with Sage does that to you.

The ground is slippery near the shore. I step gently beside Cole. "What can you tell me about Sage?"

Cole halts, then walks off. I hurry after him, slipping across the mud, but quickly regain my balance. I catch up to him. "Please."

Cole's eyes bore into me. When the fiery Current swells, he shifts his gaze to the horizon. "The problem with Sage is that when you think you're going against him, you find you're right where he's wanted you to be all along."

"But that's not the case with me. Being here, helping the Alliance by searching for a way to defeat him . . . He wouldn't want that. Would he?"

"I sure hope not." Cole abandons the sun, ducking into the shadows. Fresh pine invades the air as he clips a thin branch from a nearby tree. "But Sage has been around forever and experienced things firsthand. Probably even manipulates situations to keep Blights alive, since they work in his favor." He picks up a vine. "He knows more than the Alliance, that's for sure. He's slick and can get anyone to do anything he wants. Might be mind control, poisonous air, who knows."

"Is that how he gets Awakened to give up their Bents and become Dissenters?" I could understand being tricked, but the idea of someone like my dad willingly siding with someone so evil is beyond me.

"Maybe. But he only keeps Dissenters alive if they can help him get to the Well. Once they're no longer useful, he sucks out their power and turns them into Legions." Cole's expression turns grim. "I'd rather die and let him take all my power at once."

"I'd rather not give him any power."

"Yeah, well, if you're dead, you don't have much of a choice." Cole hands me a thick branch and fastens the vine to the end with a tight knot.

"Wait, I thought Sage could only siphon a Dissenter's power?"

"He can siphon any Awakened's power if he's nearby when they die. The same way Legions surround you and suck out the power so they can get stronger. Speaking of which . . ." Cole inspects his makeshift fishing pole. "Let's pretend this is a Legion. I'll swing it around. You swipe at the leaves. Don't cut the vine, though. This is about precision." He hands me the knife. It heats my palm.

Cole dangles the line over my head, baiting me with the vine. "Ready?"

The leaf twirls, an arm's length from my nose. "Ready." I hold the weapon steady despite the odd vibration from the hilt. I follow the leaf out the corner of my eye, and then swipe hard. The vine leaps into the air as Cole tugs with quicker reflexes.

The vine is now somewhere behind me. Without warning, I spin around ready to slice at—

A button on Cole's chest. I gasp and fling the knife away. Cole jumps at the same moment, wide-eyed.

"Holy—yeah, okay. Bad idea." He exhales, running a nervous hand through his hair. "That wasn't supposed to happen. The Steel should have deflected, unless . . ." He studies me. "A Blight's power throws it off, interferes, somehow."

Tears wrestle to the surface. "I didn't mean to—"

"Don't cry." Cole retrieves the knife from the mud. "I hate crying." He straightens his shirt, inspecting the clipped button. "It's fine. We'll just be more careful."

I roughly wipe my eyes with the back of my wrist. "I'm sorry. I had no idea."

"Don't apologize. That's why it is called training." He wipes the blade clean. "I should probably have trained you with a wooden stick first, but it wouldn't help you get a sense for the Steel. In any case, we're going to do something different." He glances at the rustling trees. "You seem to work better when you can't see. I've got an idea."

I pluck my sweater free from the bandage underneath. "You're not going to make me wear a blindfold too, are you?"

Cole scowls. "I'm not Gray." He hands me the knife with slight hesitation. I don't blame him. I hold the weapon with careful respect, away from him. The knife sits calmly against my skin. No bucking or kickback, only a meditative hum.

Cole swiftly climbs a tree with the makeshift pole in hand. Not only is he nimble and navigates the branches with ease, but his every movement blends with the wind. With perfect balance, he sprawls, belly down, on a thick bough and lowers the vine. "I'm going to swing this around. Shut your eyes and listen the same way you did with Gray. Then try again, and let's see what happens."

With Cole out of harm's way, I close my eyes. Jostling leaves mimic tapping rain. Not far, a gurgling stream splashes into the lake. Quiet ripples lap at the water's edge.

Air flitters near my face. I duck and cut.

"That's a falling leaf. Not the vine." His voice smiles. "Focus."

A wayward strand of my hair tickles my nose. I blow it out of the way. Focus. Right. My very touch seems to be destroying the Garden. I can't toss a knife. I can't stab through vines. Yeah, super easy to focus with all these things mounting evidence against me.

"Blighty." Cole interrupts my mental rant. "You taking a nap or what?"

"I'm ready."

"Good. Now imagine a Legion."

Spots dance inside my eyes from the vibrant sun. It takes

incredible willpower not to peek through my lashes. I squeeze my eyes tight and think of the Legion's vacant eyes. Of the black mist hissing around its knees. The humming knife squirms, the hilt growing hot. I loosen my fingers.

A quiet swish of air flies near my right ear. I freeze. Now the flutter blows in front of me, lower this time. I cut the air, the tip of the blade making contact.

I open my eyes. "Did I get it?"

"Almost," Cole encourages me. "Whatever you were doing was working. Do it again. And go for a single leaf."

My eyelids feel heavy as I stand blind. This time I imagine the Legion that attacked Maddox, recalling the panic seizing my blood as I stood there helpless, watching it strike. I freeze-frame the greedy look of death in his eyes as Maddox writhed on the floor. A faint breeze tickles the back of my hair. I spin around. The weapon scorches my palms. I should let go. I need to let go. But I spin around again, feet steady beneath me, and track the sound of the mocking breeze. Deep-seated vengeance charges each labored breath. I raise the blade and slash into the vile Legion formed in my mind, sparking the monster into a burst of angry cinder.

The hilt sizzles with icy heat and sticks to my skin. I quickly let go.

Cole leaps down from the tree with perfect grace.

My palms are cherry red and pulsing, but not blistered. Thankfully. Regardless, I hide them so he won't demand I go see a Healer. The slashed vine lies at my feet, lifeless and withered in a serpent's coil. Leaves left intact.

"Not bad, Blighty."

Glad he thinks so, because failure is all I see. How can I have this unrelenting desire to fight, identify weapons as they strike, but can't use one to save my life? "How will I ever be good enough to fight Sage?"

"Maybe you aren't supposed to," Cole says, picking up the knife. "Maybe defeating him isn't about stabbing him with the Steel. For all I know, the tactic doesn't work."

Heavy footsteps crunch in the woods. Cole stands perfectly still and scans the area.

"Time to go," he whispers and leads me through the forest, pushing branches aside as we head back. When we reach the road, Cole swiftly mounts the bike. His eyes are colored with the same intensity that every Blade wears.

I straddle in behind him with a crazy thought. I lean forward, my chin near his shoulder, so he can hear me. "I need to find an answer and don't have much time. Can you take me to see the Well?"

"No way." Cole snaps his head around. His hushed voice growls, "Look, Blighty. Do you have any idea how many rules I'm breaking right now?"

He's right. If anyone found out, they'll tag him a traitor for helping me. I drop my hands to my side. "Then why are you?"

"Because you need to know how to fight. Don't think for a second that Sage won't be waiting when they take you outside that Wall. When they do, the stuff they're teaching you will be completely useless." Cole kickstarts the engine. He guides my right hand to his stomach, drawing me closer.

This training felt like a complete failure and probably won't help me outside the Wall either, but Cole trusted me to work with the Steel. That says a lot.

"Thank you." I rest my cheek against his back, the roaring engine trembling through me. He holds me tight, and together we race onto the dirt road, leaving nothing but a dust cloud in our wake.

15

THE ANSWER

We arrive just under the hour. Cole returns the bike to brushwood and then retrieves my tracking Cord from his front pocket. As he takes my hand to replace the bracelet, his fingers brush across my skin with a feather-light touch. He turns my palm, exposing my wrist.

"This part hurts." He keeps the knife steady. When the tip touches the wire, dancing sparks of white fire land on my skin. A ribbon of sharp incense rises from the thread. The pain sizzles. I tense up, but don't dare move as the wire shrivels back to size. A thin red line tags my skin, nothing more than a scratch. He refits his tracker on his own, which can't be easy.

"Need help?"

He stifles a grunt. "No."

I back away and wait until he's done. Golden light flickers through the shaded forest like coins scattered on the ground. I blink and it's gone. That's not sunlight. And it's too early for fireflies.

Cole places his hat on my head. "Keep your head down, Blighty."

Wearing his fedora won't disguise me. The Blades know who I am. Regardless, I follow after him as we navigate an unmarked path in the woods back to the Estate. When we reach a waxy hedge, Cole moves an armful of branches. A path opens to the east corridor. He climbs through first and then waits for me.

White steam, smelling of Lina's bread, pipes from the kitchen vent. My grouchy stomach complains as Cole makes his way to the front door. I keep up with his brisk pace. "We can get back inside the house faster through the kitchen."

He leans closer, lips barely moving, and whispers, "We need them to see us."

Sure enough, two Blades stand guard near the arbor not far from Devon's beat-up sedan and the spitting water fountain. I lower my head and concentrate on every muddy step as we speed-walk the drive.

"Tripton, where've you been?" one of them calls out.

"Training," Cole says as he jogs up the front steps. That's the total truth. I suppress a smile as we enter the house. Cole and I might not be so different after all.

"Now we can eat," Cole says. The house is quiet. Everyone must still be in the briefing.

"I need to get Milton. I left him on the porch and haven't finished searching through the poem."

"You expecting me to bring you lunch again?" Cole meticulously straightens his cuffs. "That was a one-time deal."

I hand his hat back. "Go." I point to the kitchen. "I'll be right there."

I dart off in the opposite direction, through the vacant War Room and out the patio door. The stiff copy of *Paradise Lost* waits for me on the chair right where I left it.

Maybe if this were my torn-up copy with all my highlights and notes, I'd be able to find what Milton's hiding much quicker. Not that my scribbles would give any insight. I knew nothing about this world and its war back then. It's just that Foster's black leather copy is so stiff and the thick fancy pages are so sterile, every time I read, the words regard me blankly.

I could really use the help of a fellow Blight right now, Milton. I've burned all my time. I only have a few more hours inside the

Garden. Global Council leaders are on their way, and I don't have an answer on how to protect the Well or defeat Sage. I have no doubt Gray saw the sketch of my vision. He'll convince Council I'm a threat. So please, guide me with something, or else you might be left talking to yourself.

I close my eyes, hoping for a verse to pop inside my head. I get nothing but a nudging wind that smells of the arbor. I teeter to the left and open my eyes. So much for any guidance.

I start for the kitchen, fanning through the book as I go. When I do, one verse seems to rise off the page. *"But hard be hardened, blind be blinded more, / That they may stumble on and deeper fall."*

Electricity charges through my fingertips. This is you, Milton, isn't it? But what do you mean by "blinded" and "deeper fall?" The whole poem is about the fall of humankind.

I pace, flipping through another few pages. Again, the same thing happens: *"I feel / The link of nature draw me: flesh of flesh, / Bone of my bone thou art."*

I stop. "Link of nature?" This is Adam's speech to Eve after she ate from the tree and ruined everything. I don't see the connection, unless you're referring to the Well and how its power is linked to the Awakened. But what can you show me about Sage?

"What might lead / To happier life: knowledge of good and evil?"

Yes! A "happier life" would exist without Sage. Not just for me, but for everyone. Or do you mean *me* knowing good and evil? I already know I'm both good and bad. I'm dualistic. And so are you, Milton, by the way. I flip another page.

> *In the day*
> *Ye eat thereof your eyes, that seem so clear*
> *Yet are but dim, shall perfectly be then*
> *Opened and cleared, and ye shall be as gods,*
> *Knowing both good and evil as they know.*

In the day I eat? Like, literally? My vision had lips dripping with fire. Are you talking about my vision? The images I see are never literal. You mean a different type of consumption, right? Unless eyes being "opened and cleared" means this *is* the answer. Get Sage to eat something poisonous. Maybe one of Harper's elixirs?

That's the answer isn't it? My fingers tremble as I turn a shaky page.

"O much deceived, much failing, hapless Eve."

The floor feels ripped out from under me. My stomach sinks with the sensation of plummeting ten stories deep. "Oh, shut up, Milton." I chuck the book across the patio. That was downright cruel. Calling me "deceived" when you're not being clear. I glower at the gap in the weathered planks where one of Pop's seeds is caught. I'll be removed from the Garden by sunset tonight. I haven't come up with any solutions to offer Council. My knife skills are horrible. And now I can't even read Milton clearly.

I've failed in every way. The only thing I haven't been able to do is see the Well for myself. I might be risking everything to do it. But what option is left?

I pick up the seed and toss it in the nectar breeze. Besides, Foster never said I couldn't, just that I wouldn't see anything if I did. But what if he's wrong?

The kitchen door squeaks open. It's probably Cole, wondering where I am. I don't want him to stop me, so I race down the porch steps.

"Cera, wait." It's not Cole. It's Maddox. He quickly jogs over to where I've stopped. My heart skips a beat . . . actually, three. He's washed up. Wearing a snug white T-shirt, new jeans, and those same black Converse with the frayed laces. He looks good. Somehow older. Stronger.

"What's wrong?" Through tangled bangs, his eyes search mine. "I saw you go off with Cole. Did something happen?" His tone is layered with deeper questions underneath. Is he jealous?

"Or is it about the vision? If someone is in trouble, I could—"

"No!" I throw my hands out in front as a barrier. "I'm running out of time. I'm out by sunset, and I haven't found anything to help Council. I thought that maybe if . . ." I hesitate with the truth, but I know Maddox will help me see what I can't. Talk sense into me. Somehow with him, the truth always comes easy. "I want to see the Well. It's the only thing I haven't tried."

Maddox is silent, studying me.

I look down. "I shouldn't, I know. I need to stay put and wait for Foster to get out of the briefing. Do what's right. Cooperate. Stay alive. Wait until Council—"

"C'mon." He takes my hand.

"What? What are—"

"You should see it." He leads me around the house, straight to the arbor.

"You're taking me?" I whisper even though the Blades patrolling the front have gone inside and our path is clear. Cole refused. Maybe Maddox should too. "You'll get in trouble—I don't want—I shouldn't, right? I mean, my Cord." I lift my hand. "Gray will know."

"He won't check until he's out of the briefing. And if he does, I'll take the heat for it."

"They'll say I lured you. My vision—"

"Your instincts aren't wrong. I trust you. If the answer is there, you'll find it. You read things about our world that we can't see. You deserve the right to experience it. But we better go now." There's a boldness, a mature confidence, about him that leaves me speechless.

When he enters the maze, I quickly follow.

Tiny lights, similar to the arbor flowers, dot the hedge. The deeper we go, the thicker the nectar scent becomes, the taste sweeter on my tongue.

We walk in silence, turning right and then left. I'm careful not to touch the hedge and drop a trail of yellow leaves. The glowing lights bounce along with my giddy pulse. But I tell myself not to get hopeful.

Finally, we come to the end. "Here it is." Maddox steps onto the lawn, making room for me to join him. "We don't have much time."

I look out.

Two majestic trees tower at the bottom of a sloped clearing surrounded by a thick forest. One tree is a stalwart oak. The other, a weeping willow with branches so low they sweep the ground like a soulful dancer. Both are so imposing, I feel small in their presence.

The expansive lawn is about three acres, maybe more. The leaves on both trees are painted with every shade of vibrant green. The space pulses with the sacred quiet of a resting heartbeat.

For some reason, I have an inexplicable desire to wrap myself in the branches of the willow and spin like I'm seven again, cocooned in the canopy where no one can find me.

As soon as I step onto the lawn, faint light ignites across the field like cracks over a pond. Each strand flows like live wires with the same creamy color as the arbor flowers and the flickering light in the woods.

The lines ebb and flow slowly, transforming into a pattern. Circles ring around the entire field, one inside the other. Parallelograms intersect with the circles. The center rests between both trees, where short reeds sprout in a circle around the muddy ground. Then it hits me: the lights have formed the Alliance symbol, the one Devon drew on a napkin at Hesperian.

The marshy watering hole between the trees must be what the Alliance is fighting to protect. What Sage wants to demolish. What everyone believes I could hand over for complete destruction.

How can something so murky, so ordinary, and unassuming be what feeds creative powers to the world?

The glowing symbol fades, transforming back into hundreds of hairline cracks of light zipping through the soil and disappearing into the woods. A strand of thick golden light races underneath the grass, heading in our direction. It stops and pools under Maddox's feet, radiating as if he were standing on a sunbeam.

"Can you see that?" I ask, stepping back. The light recedes, disappearing into the ground.

He looks down, confused. "It's not much to look at, but . . . do you see something?"

I glance between the trees. I do. A faint shadow lies behind warping air that rises from the tips of the reeds.

I don't answer Maddox. But I don't need to. Somehow he knows what I'm thinking. He gives me a nod. "Go on. I'll wait here," he says, standing guard at the entrance.

I move a few steps closer. When I do, an unquenchable joy washes over me. Hopeful memories I buried long ago spin through my dizzy mind like a merry-go-round. When I stop, so does a memory. It's one where I'm seven years old, squealing with laughter in my grandmother's garden. Escaping under the canopy of honeysuckle. Hidden from the world in the shelter of my imagination, where love came through hugs, warm cookies, and summer clothes soaked by a cool garden hose.

Where I was a princess, and outside the canopy of vines was my kingdom.

Where I made a difference in the world, and fear had no roots.

Where I drank the nectar of the flower that shares my name, and the scent permeated my skin.

Where I believed the sweet drops could transform me into something beautiful like my mother.

Something worthy.

Something wanted.

Something loved.

A gentle wind rustles the branches of the willow tree. The

glowing lights fade with the memory and so does the sense of joy. I tremble in the cloudy afternoon and wipe my face dry.

I take a second look at the warping air. A shadow lingers, but from this distance, it's hard to know what it is. It's not a person, as far as I can tell. Whatever it is hides behind a warping, protective Wall, much like the one at the gate. Maybe if I'm close enough, I can steal one quick look into this realm and have the answer.

But I can't.

Not because my feet won't move. Believe me, they bounce, wanting more than anything to impulsively run and peer inside. But something about the feel of that lingering memory stops me. If the Well has been revealing itself through visions for centuries, what right do I have to barge in and see, firsthand, what's hidden? What damage could that choice do?

From afar the Well may not be beautiful, but in its presence, anything feels possible.

Belonging.

Love.

Peace.

Beauty.

A thriving hopefulness circles around me. Through me. Embeds itself somewhere deep inside me. I suddenly understand why the Alliance wants to protect the Well. Why they won't fight if there's a chance they could lose all creativity, belonging, and breath of hope.

I step back. I might have the power to reveal the mystery of this third realm, but it doesn't mean I should. Going back to the house, listening and complying, accepting my fate—doing anything that will keep me from aligning with Sage—*that's* what I should do.

Hard footsteps and curt voices sound through the graveled maze. Panic sticks in my throat. We can't be found. Not together.

Not here. Maddox quickly takes my hand. He doesn't need words to tell me what to do.

I do the one thing I've had to do so many times before.

I run.

16

SCARS

Together we run along the edge of the clearing, following the hedge of the maze. Maddox aims for a narrow path in the woods ahead. My legs burn as I pump them faster, hoping to duck into the shadows before we're caught.

We race at full speed in unison, flying over the soft grass, the creamy light bursting under every step until Maddox ducks into the woods. I'm quick to follow. Luckily, no one else does.

The air is cool and damp. I'm panting as we venture along a trail teeming with bright wildflowers and thick undergrowth. Rustling trees and a songbird's melody fill the strained silence of each hurried step. Maddox glances at me every now and then. But neither of us speaks.

We come to a camping spot in the woods where the dirt is cleared of vines and shrubs. The placid lake sits a few yards away. Broken and decaying pieces of a hand-built fort, or a fallen tree house, are scattered against the tree trunks. I sidestep him and go to the rocky shore.

"You okay?" Maddox stands in the middle of the childhood wreckage. "Did you get a read on anything that might give us the answers we need?"

I gaze across the lake, thinking about the Well. "Something

in me couldn't do it. It didn't feel right. It was like I'd be stealing something sacred and private. Something belonging to the Alliance. Not me." I turn around and glance at Maddox. He's watching me.

I quickly turn back and concentrate on the muddy stones half-buried under the water and not how Maddox glows as the sunlight streaks taught ribbons of hazy light onto his shoulders. Or how close he stands. Or how his bright eyes stay pinned on me.

"The vision I had," I say, speaking to the stones, "the one you drew, it's a warning to the Alliance. I should have never asked you to take me there. In fact, I shouldn't be near you." I stride into the damp woods.

"Cera, you didn't ask me to take you." Maddox is right behind me. "I took you because, I mean, didn't you feel it? Standing there, the way something about it makes anything feel possible? Like there's a world that should be but isn't." He's quiet for a moment. "It's where I got the idea for Hesperian. I wanted to take what I feel when I'm standing at the Well and let others feel it too." He steps closer. "We're in this together. Maybe we can't change the world by fighting Sage the way the Alliance can, but I think I might have found a different way."

"Really?"

His eyes spark. "Sage expects a traditional fight, but if we put together a Ghost Army, then we won't need a full one."

Ghost Army? "That sounds oddly cryptic."

He doesn't hide his enthusiasm. "They used a Ghost Army in the Second World War. It was a group of unseen artists that used their talents to throw off the enemy. They'd stage battles, set up fake camps. We could do the same, use our talents and art to somehow outwit Sage."

I want to latch on to his optimism, but my heart sinks. The fight is too big, and there's not enough time. "Even if we could, I'll be escorted out of the Garden by sunset with nothing to offer

Global Council when they arrive except a vision that confirms I'm a threat as a Blight. And on top of that, I'm destroying the Garden. Leaves are changing color, dying everywhere I go." I touch the leaf of a low-hanging branch for proof. The bold green fades to sickly yellow and falls off. "My mere presence is hurting this place." I hand him the evidence. "Forget fighting. I was naïve to think Sage could be destroyed. He's unstoppable."

Maddox tosses the dead leaf aside. "*You're* the one who's unstoppable. Why do you think Gray feels so threatened?" He shrinks the narrow space between us. Not only does he smell as if he's showered with a scent that could be appropriately called Warrior Storm, but he draws so close, I'm drowning in the warmth radiating between us. "Look, if there isn't a clear way to take down Sage, then we'll convince Council to let us use the Ghost Army to keep you and your mother hidden and safe. We'll go back to Hesperian. Or find a new place if we have to. We'll save Awakened. Create something new." His eyes lock into mine. "Together."

Something about his confidence, how he believes so much in what he says, as if his words were a song that could change the world, sends my heart racing through my blood, crashing into my spinning mind.

I should run.

But I don't want to.

I look down at my grimy shoes. "Maddox, I can't. I'm too impulsive, even though I'm trying to be levelheaded. I want to do the right thing the way Pop says I should. But . . ." I hesitate. "I'm terrified." And I am. Terrified about getting close to him. About losing Mom. About Gray and the Alliance. But I only say, "I'm terrified that I'll side with Sage and not even know it. That I'll give him the chance to destroy the creative life that pours out of the Well and put everyone in danger. The vision it . . ."

"It can be stopped. You've proven that. Together we saved

Harper." Maddox rests his hand on my arm. Electricity courses through me. I keep my head down. He shouldn't touch me. He shouldn't be anywhere near me. For his sake. And my own.

But I don't want to pull away. Ever.

"Cera." He speaks my name as if sacred, urging me to look at him, but I don't. "Maybe I can't read the vision the way you can, but I know what I felt when I drew it out—that we can save Awakened." Passion rises in his voice. "Maybe that means changing the Alliance so they'll fight. Maybe it means something different. But I think you've got the power to change everything for the better." His fingers curl with a slow restraint, as if wanting to hold something he can't. "Believe it."

I find the strength to look at him. In that moment, a gusty wind rushes over the lake and into the woods, finding us. It brushes back his hair, exposing the scar, as my own hair whips in my face. He quickly shakes out his bangs, covering the gash.

I want to believe what he says, I really do. But there's just one thing. "Why do you hide it?"

"Hide what?"

"You have this amazing conviction. You see things in others and believe in them more than they can believe in themselves. But then you hide part of who you are. If you would let people see—"

"Then that's all they see." His voice is hard, and as clouds block the sun, his expression shadows. "They wonder about it. Wonder when and how and why."

"Let them wonder. Besides, being mysterious is hot." I grin, hoping to lighten the weighty air, because I suddenly feel like I've made a mistake.

It does the trick because Maddox shakes his head, returning a faint smile. He should definitely smile more. A lot more.

"Right. It freaks girls out."

"The wrong girls, maybe."

Another intruding gust blows his hair away from his face

again. He glances at me. I'm betting more than anything he wants to cover his scar, but he doesn't. He lets me get a good look. I've seen the wound before, but never this close.

The scar is unsettling. The red ridge puckers the skin and curves all the way down in front of his ear, disfiguring his cheek. His face must have been cut open to the bone. A twinge knots my stomach. I stifle it as Maddox watches me study the deep rippling. A mark like that couldn't have come from a knife. It had to be something much worse. The air turns heavy. I force myself to breathe normally. I don't want him thinking I'm grossed out. If anything, I want to trace the depth of his wound as he stands in front of me, vulnerable. Trusting. As if I'm the first person he's ever let fully see. Maybe I am.

My hand reaches up slowly.

He swallows hard.

I run my fingers over my lips instead. "Seriously, Maddox." My heart won't slow down. "A scar says you know how to live through the fight. Anyone with a scar like that is a hero in my book." I try another lighthearted grin. "Like I said, it amps up the hotness factor."

When my eyes meet his, I forget to breathe. Daring, impossible thoughts churn behind those stormy eyes. Thoughts I desperately want to know. Thoughts that hold the same look he had in the alcove before he kissed me.

His glance falls to my lips.

"I should go." I don't want to. But I step back anyhow, knocking into the tree. Am I luring him right now? I don't mean to . . . I feel my way around the tree. Words tumble from my mouth. "I haven't had lunch. I left Milton. I mean, Cole was—we were—"

Maddox's turbulent eyes shade a troubled blue. "Cole might not be the best person for you to hang around."

So, he *is* jealous. "I don't get a choice." I fidget with the Cord on my wrist, twisting the irritating tracker, and head for the trail.

"He was assigned to guard me."

Maddox stays close. "That's what bothers me. Gray is intentional about everything. He chose Cole for a reason."

"Because you volunteered, remember?" I forge up a sloped path similar to the one near Gray's training room.

"It's more than that. What if Cole's time with Sage will trigger something? Influence you somehow."

"Meaning?"

"I don't know what being around Sage does to an Awakened if they don't dissent. What if Sage has influenced Cole somehow without his knowing? And what if some part of you senses it, making your dissenting pull stronger and blurring what you think is right?"

I'm sure he means well, but I can't help but feel insulted. He has no idea what Cole's done to help me. Maybe it's me he doesn't really trust. "Is that your way of saying you don't believe I'll make the right choice when it counts?"

He intercepts me before I step onto the backyard lawn. "I believe in you, Cera." Frustration cracks through every word. "I'm saying, be careful."

"What makes you think I haven't been?"

"I'm only say—" He reaches for my hand but stops. "How did your Cord get loose?"

Sure enough the loopy thread hangs just above my knuckles. "I was only twisting it."

"Maddox?" Gray's voice cracks through the woods behind us.

"Go. Now." Maddox urges me, shielding me from Gray's sight. I don't wait. I sprint fast and hard across the lawn heading straight for the kitchen.

I need to find Cole.

17
PLANNING FOR WAR

Cole isn't in the kitchen.

"He went that way." Harper points me to the back door, leading to the east corridor. I clutch the Cord tight against my wrist. He has to fix it so Gray won't know it's been messed with. My heart stills a moment. Maybe Gray already knows.

I rush out the back door and into the corridor. Rich notes from a brooding cello seep through the walkway, changing the tempo of my stride. It's the same melody that sings me to sleep. I follow the weeping bass tones as they glide into a yearning tenor. I stop at the second door. It's cracked slightly open enough for me to see Cole. Fluid notes flow from his gentle hands. His body leans in, swaying with each stroke, playing so unguarded; it feels wrong to barge in.

He glances my way.

The music stops.

I push the door open, stunned. I shouldn't be. Probably another prodigy boarding school requirement, but still.

"What do you want?" He delicately rests the cello on its side and then reaches for the fedora on his rumpled bedsheets.

"Just . . . I was . . ." For some reason I can only focus on one thing. "Cole, you're amazing."

"Bach's amazing." He sets the bow on a dresser piled with books.

"You didn't have to stop playing."

"I don't play in front of people. In fact . . ." He holds the door open. "Unless you have something worth telling me, then get going." Why is he so cranky? Is he embarrassed that I caught him?

Cole tries to usher me into the corridor, but I dig my heels. "The Cord." I hold out my wrist. The thread droops low.

Cole spins me back into his room. He quickly shuts the door and then glides around clothes and books pig-piled on the floor to slip his knife out from behind the bed's headboard. I don't dare step anywhere near the cello. Knowing me, I'll accidentally stumble and knock it over.

He takes my hand, turning my wrist over. I brace for the pain.

Cole runs his thumb over the thread, studying my wrist. "Surfer boy know you're skulking around my door like a groupie?"

"I'm not a groupie. Don't flatter yourself," I snap as Cole works the thread. "Why do you have to twist everything around?"

Cole shrugs, but his focus is laser locked on my wrist. "You're cute when you get mad."

"I'm not mad." I narrow my eyes, hoping he can feel the heat from my glare, because he's not looking at me.

An unbelieving smile brightens his face. "Embarrassed I called you out?"

"No!"

Sparks fly. The knife sizzles. Sharp incense tickles my nose.

"There. It's done." His smile falls as he drops my wrist. He's back to being annoyed.

What? I glance down. Sure enough, the thread fits snug against my skin. "I didn't feel a thing."

"Told you, distractions work in my favor." He ushers me into the hall where the damp air sticks to my skin.

"Cera." Devon appears at the end of the corridor. The

knotted vines that canopy the ceiling shade his expression, but it's clear he's frowning. "We need you."

A car door slams. "Is it my mom?"

"Not yet." Devon walks to the front drive, and I follow. A line of cars and motorcycles are parked along the fountain. "There's been another attack. Your mom's in a temporary location until it's safe to move again. Gray has the details." He walks up the front steps.

"But she's fine, right?"

"As far as I know, yes." There is a slight crack in his strong voice. "But Cera . . . It was Hesperian. We don't know who survived."

A crushing weight presses in my chest, nearly buckling my knees. Juniper. Tanji. Kellan. Amide. Claire. And Gladys. Along with other nameless faces . . .

My feet twitch, wanting to sprint down the drive and not stop until I reach Hesperian and . . . then what? "I could have commanded the Legions or Cormorants to flee." My voice is a strangled whisper. "I should have stayed."

"And Sage would have found you." Devon takes me into the house. "We have a plan against Sage, but we need your help."

Voices rumble through the entryway. The War Room is filled with tense-jawed Blades who greet one another with hard slaps on the back and what looks to be crushing hugs. Fresh pine replaces the smell of antique lacquer as Blades carry crate after crate into the room. Devon leads me through the crowd as we make our way to the library, passing Lina and her food-filled cart along the way. Despite the buzzing chaos, time stops around her. There's something beautiful about the way she cups each person's hands with a gentle squeeze, passing a blessing as they receive the meal. Harper works in tandem beside her.

Devon enters the library first. I stay at the door and peer in from behind him.

The room is packed. Gray paces by the fireplace, giving a lecture to a group of people I don't know. Most of them are older. All of them are dressed in dark denim or black fatigues. Several occupy both couches, while others stand along the back wall behind Pop, who sits in his wingback chair. I find Lieutenant Foster near his desk. Maddox is right beside him.

He subtly touches the back of his wrist and looks at me, questioning.

I nod, but I'm unsure how to tell him the truth without ratting on Cole.

Gray glances at Devon before addressing the crowd. "The Blight is scheduled for removal before sunset. With Global Council arriving soon, we plan on executing an effective strike in two hours, ensuring plenty of daylight."

"Strike?" I whisper to Devon.

"Stay quiet and listen."

"Sage's attacks have increased since we acquired the Blight, hitting all of our locations, weakening our surrounding army. We believe he is planning an ambush attack similar to the one in the Renaissance when the Well was in transfer. He knows we won't have enough time to assemble the troops needed for war. He'll be ready, knowing we can't be. If history is any indication, he'll surround the Circuit Wall, keeping us locked inside with limited supplies until we're forced to open the gate. Except this time we plan on launching an offensive attack. We've got one chance to get it right. And that's it. Lance will hand out additional weapons and shields to protect from the blast." An older Blade with a buzz cut and sword tattoos running the length of his arms steps beside Gray.

"Blast?" Harper gasps from behind me. Her shock echoes through the room. I step aside to let her and Lina through.

Gray frowns at her.

Devon comes to her side and whispers in her ear. Her face blanches.

"We believe we have a way to destroy Sage," Gray says.

"What?" The word falls out before I can stop it.

Cole enters from the courtyard as Pop grunts with disapproval and pushes himself taller in his chair. I'm not sure if Pop's grunt was aimed at my outburst, Gray's comment, or Cole's late arrival, but what does it matter? There's a way to destroy Sage? I'm not sure how Gray came across it. Maybe there was a solution in the notes Foster took while I was reading the paintings. Or maybe the answer is in my latest vision that I haven't seen drawn out.

Gray's arrogant face hardens. "We believe we can lure Sage to the Garden—"

"Whoa. You want to do *what?*" Cole halts midstride. "Are you insane?"

Gray ignores Cole's interruption. He pins his callous stare on me. I force myself not to squirm as all eyes follow. "We bait him. Get him to use his powers and deflect the hit to the Circuit Wall."

"Powers, like the red lightning from my visions?" I ask, trying to keep my voice steady despite the gawking expressions and Gray's obvious hatred.

"Hold up, *amigo*," Cole comes to my side, shifting the attention away from me. "Do you even know what that power does?"

"We know that you do." Gray's tight jaw grinds his words. "So unless you're withholding information—"

"I told you everything I know. I even gave you a detailed layout of his place, and how to get in and out undetected. But having him use his power?" Cole shakes his head. "It's a bad idea, man."

"What does it do?" I ask Cole, quietly. "The red lightning appears as a flash in my visions, but I never see the effects."

"And it's better if we keep it that way," Gray snaps.

Lieutenant Foster steps away from his desk. "Partial knowledge will most certainly result in defeat. I think it best for Mr. Tripton to inform the entire team of the implications of Sage's power." He motions to Cole. "Proceed."

Gray keeps his scowling mouth shut as Cole straightens and pushes his hat back. "Sage's power comes right from his fingertips. It's a red current. Looks like lightning. He uses it to siphon Dissenters' powers and turn them into Legions. He also uses it to blast through all kinds of walls, gates—anywhere he wants to gain access. When he wants, the bolt can vaporize anything into black cinder. I even saw him use it on a girl . . ."

Cole's voice drops. "I thought Sage was going to siphon her powers the way he does with the Awakened when they die. She wasn't a Dissenter, so he couldn't turn her into a Legion. She was a Common who wouldn't do what he wanted. He struck her. Kept the bolt on her until she was nothing but a pile of ash. When he was done, the suck-faced Legions rolled around in her remains like rabid dogs rolling on a carcass."

The room goes quiet.

Cole's voice firms. "All I know is that getting Sage to come anywhere near the Garden is a horrible idea. Our tiny weapons won't stand a chance against him."

"But a blast from the Circuit Wall will." Gray is unmoved. No surprise. "That's why we're turning it into a weapon," he says. "Use Sage's own power against himself. We'll get him to strike, deflecting the hit to the Circuit Wall with the shields. The hit will set off a blast, and if he's close enough, it will destroy him and his army."

"Won't he expect that?" Maddox asks. "What if we tried a different tactic? Surprise him. Throw him off instead. I could get artists to—"

"Artists won't help the fight," Gray barks. "And we know Sage won't strike the Circuit Wall directly. But I can get him to strike at me. The team of Blades will cover me, deflecting the hit."

Why is Gray so sure Sage will strike him? Regardless, I side with Maddox. Gray's slight change to an old tactic doesn't seem drastic enough to throw Sage off. Even Pop shifts in his seat, uneasy.

"Have we enough weaponry to ensure everyone's safety?" Foster asks.

"Lance will distribute what we have. We've counted enough for Blades and Caretakers. Everyone else stays inside the Garden. We anticipate a few losses, but nothing to the degree of recent attacks." There isn't a hint of cockiness in his voice. He actually sounds . . . not like a jerk. I'm shocked.

"Won't they get hurt by the blast?" Harper asks Devon, but everyone hears.

"The shields come from the same guild as the Paradise Steel. That metal will protect them as long as they follow Gray's command," Devon assures her, and the rest of the room, as grave silence settles over each face.

"Sage is gonna know something's up as soon as he sees the shields," Cole says. "It'll be a matter of seconds before he figures out your plan."

"That's inconsequential." Gray stares him down. "He'll strike anyway."

Cole lifts an eyebrow. "How are you so sure?"

Gray looks at me. "We'll use her as bait."

Cole points in my direction with wide-eyed shock. "You want to use her to get Sage to strike the Wall? Gray, are you freakin' *high*?"

"She's out before sunset anyway—"

"No!" Maddox starts in on Gray, but Lance intercepts him.

"Do you have any idea who you're dealing with?" Cole descends on Gray, but Devon sprints over in time to plant a firm hand on his chest, backing him away.

"It's our best chance." Devon's tone is calm. "If she agrees, we'll be sure she's protected."

Pop clears his throat. "Protected from who?"

"From Sage," Devon answers. "She'll be shielded along with Gray."

Pop leans forward. "What I'm sayin' is that once she's outside that Wall, what happens to her? I reckon she ain't just walkin' out 'n' standing there, is she?"

Gray's icy stare flickers in my direction. "The Blades will be in attack positions as I take her outside the gate. I'll stage an altercation with the Blight, and as soon as we know Sage is near, I'll convincingly attempt her execution. But as long as she's compliant and the Steel senses her Current, no harm will come to her."

We both know that's a lie. Gray's been searching for a way to kill me ever since I've set foot in the Garden. He's even tested the knife to be sure it would cut me. There's no way I'll walk out of this plan alive. But it's also clear no place is secure outside these borders. Not for me, or anyone else. Not if Sage is alive. I glance at the tense faces peppering the room. If this is the only chance . . .

Cole frowns. "Gray, you know your Steel—"

"I'll do it." I step forward with a confidence that isn't my own. "If Gray is putting himself, and others, on the line because there's a chance the plan will work, then I have to." I'm certain I'll die in the process, but if killing me will destroy that monster so no one else has to die, then it's worth it.

"Cera, don't!" Maddox grapples with Lance and another Blade who holds him back. "Gray, we had a deal." His voice is fueled with anger. "If you do anything to her, I swear I'll—"

"Get him out," Gray commands.

It takes three Blades to drag Maddox to the door. He's shouting, wrestling, and struggling to break free to reach me. "Cera, please don't," he begs, trying to look at me. "We'll find a—"

The door slams shut.

Part of me desperately wants to fight to stay alive and build a world with Maddox—the naïve part, the one that believes I can run the way Mom and I have done all these years. But the darker side knows the truth. Life is no longer a viable option. Once I turn seventeen, Sage will sense my Dissenting power, and no one around me will be safe because he'll hunt me down forever. Yet life wars inside me, screaming for me to run.

But if I've learned anything, it's that running only leads to greater destruction.

"I'll do whatever you ask," I say. "But in return, please keep my mother safe. Heal her. Absolve her of any wrongdoing."

I ready myself with a plea about how they wouldn't have this chance if Mom hadn't kept me alive, but Gray surprisingly agrees. "You can call her before we leave."

"Very well." Lieutenant Foster shifts. Maybe he's uneasy, or maybe it's something else entirely, I can't tell. But for the first time, his expression is clear: worry creases his forehead.

Pop wrings his hands together and sighs deeply.

"You are all dismissed," Foster says. "Everyone, prepare for assignments in the War Room."

"Does nothing I say about Sage matter?" Cole marches over to Foster as the crowd disperses. "If he sees anyone put a knife to her throat—I'm telling you, I *know* the guy. There's got to be another way."

"This is the only way," Gray cuts in.

"What if it's not? Let's rethink this. What if it's a combination of power that does the trick? Something about her Blight powers and"—Cole glances at Gray's knife tucked in his belt—"the strength of your Steel. She can turn the weapon against—"

"Nobody touches my knife." Gray's eyes blaze. "That's the plan, Tripton. We lost twelve Guardians and seven Blades in yesterday's attack. Sage isn't going to stop until he gets what he wants. I won't lose any more lives." His heavy footsteps pound through the suffocating air as he walks out of the room.

Pop works his way to the edge of the chair, frowning. I don't want Pop disappointed in me. Can't he see I'm finally doing something right?

I help him stand. "Pop. Spring will rise." I'm still not sure what that means, but I know it means something to Pop. I want him to know I'm trying to do the right thing. Devon and Harper take over walking him to the door.

"That so?" Pop rests his hand on his cane, but won't face me. "Then be warned. Spring brings the fiercest storms."

What does *that* mean?

"Lina, prepare accordingly," Lieutenant Foster tells her. "We need all available Healers on site, ready to tend our wounded."

"*Si.*" Her shoulders slump. There's a heavy weight clouding every face. This decision to attack changes their defensive position and brings troubling uncertainty. For some reason, I feel somewhat responsible.

As the space clears, Lieutenant Foster invites me to his desk. "Miss Marlowe. We have a few matters to discuss in preparation."

Cole leaps around the couch. "This is a bad idea, Lieutenant. You know it is—"

"Mr. Tripton. You are excused."

"But—"

"You are to spend the next hour assisting the other Blades."

Cole plants his feet. "I'm staying here."

"Mr. Tripton, as of this moment, you are to share your knowledge of enemy practices with the Blades. Are we clear?"

Cole shoots Foster a defiant glare and then shoves his hat low on his head. Without saying another word, he storms out, slamming the door behind him. The small table quivers, shaking the chessmen, but none fall.

Everyone's gone. I'm left with Foster who takes an even breath. "Now, Miss Marlowe, I believe we have a vision to discuss."

18

CAPTURED

Foster's desk is wiped clean except for the Atlas paperweight and silver frame. My throat swells as I sit on the edge of the chair and watch him spread the visual carnage of the last ten years of my visions in perfect rows.

I squirm, feeling uneasy. "Does my mom know you have these?"

"They were retrieved prior to the attack." Foster lowers himself into the chair behind the desk. There is a strange melancholy in his eyes that I can't place. Disappointment? Regret? "It is imperative that you review your previous visions and determine if there is anything that may guide or warn us."

I immediately spot the sketch of the Cormorant and the small mouse I know to be Jess. The unwanted memory of smashing glass and her tiny scream rushes back, drowning out clanging metal sounds that now come from the living room. She bled out on the street, her body limp and cold . . . I vowed never to let that happen again. I wipe my eyes dry with my sleeve.

Foster clears his throat and straightens the edge of the paper. "I know this may be difficult, but we have only a few hours. We shall review the images in order. I believe there is a cohesive reasoning in the way the visions were granted to you. Start at the beginning. Push aside the emotion. Focus the same way you have been reviewing the classical works."

Push aside emotion? Does he have any idea what he's asking of me? There isn't a single piece of classical artwork that holds as much blood as these ten sheets of paper.

I twist my hands in my lap. Rushed strokes and unsteady marks smear where Mom's pencil barely kissed the paper. For some reason, I can't shake my uneasiness.

Foster must see me struggling because his voice turns quiet. "I was certain an alternative solution would arise from your research and quell the admiral's impatience. Perhaps I was too hopeful." His defeated, apologetic eyes meet mine. "What you are being asked to do, participating in this perilous attack, it comes at a great cost."

I straighten the sketch of Jess. "I know. Gray will kill me once I'm outside the Garden. That's always been his plan."

"We will take every precaution to ensure that is not the case." Foster believes what he says, although I know it's not possible. He must know it too because he shifts, uncomfortable. "But there is something more you should—"

"Lieutenant," an urgent voice interrupts from the door. It's Grumpy, the Blade who walked me here this morning. "A message from the admiral, sir."

Through the open door, I spot Cole lingering near the hall, pretending to inspect an intricate shield, but when he glances my way, I know he's there listening.

"Please decode what you can until my return." Foster excuses himself before making a hasty exit with Grumpy.

Cole is in the room as soon as they leave. "Listen, Blighty." His voice is a rough whisper. "They won't let me fight. If this is gonna go down the way Gray wants it to, then you need to know how to slip out of his grip if he really tries to . . ."

"Kill me."

Cole frowns. Ringing metal echoes from the War Room. "I can't pull you out now with everyone watching. I'll arrange it after I go back to my room and get my Steel. If I can swing it, I'll get you one too."

My heart leaps. "Seriously?"

"But you've got to keep it hidden. I'll show you how."

I jump up and throw my arms around his neck with an impulsive hug. "Thank you."

When I let go, he adjusts his hat. "Sure." He suppresses a smile. "Whatever."

In a blink, he's blended in with the Blades swarming across the hall. I walk over and close the door to block out the noise, but a draft that smells of the arbor pushes the courtyard door open. Voices carry from outside. I peer out.

"The admiral will arrive within the hour." Lance crosses his tattooed arms. He's standing near the arbor talking to . . . Foster.

"Has the rescue been approved?" the lieutenant asks.

"Denied," Lance says. "The admiral disapproves of sending troops into Sage's compound, stating all resources should be available for the strike."

"If that be so, then I cannot, in good conscience, allow Miss Marlowe to execute this plan without knowing the full extent of this situation."

Situation? I hide beside the door and strain to listen over the rustling trees as Foster continues. "Sage is sure to inform her of her mother's capture once she is removed from the Estate. Withholding this information may turn her against the Alliance, as he desires. She has proven faithful in her task. It is unconscionable for us to allow Miss Marlowe to proceed without knowing the sacrifice."

My blood turns to ice. Capture? But they said—

"The admiral forbids the Blight's knowledge of it," Gray's smug voice cuts in. "Reports from the attack on Hesperian say the creatures were searching for the sketches we retrieved. When the renderings couldn't be found, the Legions took Delia Marlowe.

The admiral believes Sage will siphon the visions himself but doesn't want the Blight to know. It might interfere with the plan."

Sage has my mother. Gray looked me straight in the eyes and lied. My heart feels like he's flung a hundred daggers into my chest. That's why he agreed to my request so quickly. Even suggested I call her to calm me down, knowing I wouldn't get through. I clutch a nearby bookcase to support my trembling legs.

"The admiral believes this abduction is the luring shown in her vision. A warning," Gray adds. "Under no circumstances is she to know."

"Withholding information of this nature is negligent for an attack of this magnitude. Miss Marlowe is a young girl. Her mother has been captured. She has a right to know. I will speak to the admiral." Foster's clipped tone is the last thing I hear.

My pulse explodes, battering my eardrums, drowning everything out. The Alliance couldn't protect my mother. Sage will torture her to extract my visions. She'll die. Sage will be right by her side when she does. He'll strike her with that current, sucking all her strength. She'll be abandoned, helpless, and alone. Or worse. He'll siphon her power, taking the last bit of her for himself. I shift away from the door, unable to breathe.

I can't let that happen.

I won't.

But how can I save her?

Gray's grinding footsteps approach the library. "Where is she now?"

"Reviewing sketches," comes Foster's reply.

"The admiral wants a close watch on her."

Violent heat charges my blood. I pace the worn carpet near Foster's desk. What do I do? Stay here and help the Alliance, knowing I'll die? Knowing Sage has my mother? Knowing what he'll do to her?

Light flickers in the grass outside the window as if taunting me to choose. My mother? Or the Alliance?

As soon as the door cracks open, I make my choice. I jump out the bay window.

And I run.

Hard. Fast.

Golden light flickers in the grass as I fly around the house, over the back lawn. My feet know exactly where I'm headed. I'll cut through the hedge, the way Cole showed me, and follow the path through the woods. I know how to use the lanterns and open the gate. I want to find Maddox and tell him what I'm about to do, but I don't have the time.

I'll find a way to get to Mom. Maybe I can't save her, but at least I can say goodbye. I skid around the corner and duck into the wisteria grove. The hedge beckons me from the other side. I pick up speed. My breath is labored, hard—I collide right into Cole as he steps out of his room.

"Whoa. What's going on? What's wrong?"

"My mother. Sage." I can't choke out the words. Air strangles my throat. "Gray lied." Tears flow freely now. I try to wipe them back, but it does no good. "I have to see her." My words are fueled by passion that has no weight. No logic or plan.

Cole takes hold of my shoulders and shakes me lightly. "Were you trying to run through that gate with your Cord? Your freakin' arm will blow off!"

I lift my wrist. "Take it off."

"No."

"Then I'll crawl out of here with one arm!" I push him away. "I can't let Sage siphon her powers to get to my visions. It will kill her!" I dash to the hedge, pushing the tangled branches aside. I step through and trip over the vines.

Cole catches me as I fall. "Come here." He takes me by the wrist, leading me into my room. He shuts the door and points a finger at me, so close that if I speak the tip of his finger will brush my lips. "Stop and think. If you leave, you're throwing away any chance the Alliance has to destroy Sage. You'll never be free. Sage will find you."

I step back. "What can Sage do to me? If he needs me in order to gain access to the Well, he won't kill me. You and I both know Gray won't let me live. If I stay and help the Alliance, rescuing my mother won't even be a possibility because I'll be dead. And so will she. Sage will be there when she dies, taking the last bit of her for himself. She'll be alone. Abandoned. And I'll never get the chance to tell her I love her." My pent-up remorse overflows. "That I'm sorry for all the pain I've caused her over the years. That I forgive her and understand why she hid me."

My lips tremble. "Dad abandoned us when I was seven. I won't abandon her too." Tears streak down my face. "She's the only family I have. If I let her die, I'll be no different from my father." I grip his shirt. "Cole, please help me. Tell me how to get into his place. Where Sage will be keeping her. I know I can't do this alone."

Cole swallows. "Did you ask surfer boy and he said no?"

I quickly release him. "Maddox has nothing to do with this. You're the one with a knife. You're the one who knows Sage better than anyone else. And I'm not asking you to come, just to help."

Cole's expression turns hard. "It's a trap."

"Even if it is, what choice do I have? All my life I've played in the shadows. I've hidden, stayed out of trouble, and lived unseen, blending in, trying to be normal. Even here I've been trying to fit in. But I'm not like everyone else. I'm not an Awakened. I'm not a Dissenter. I'm a Blight, and my mother is dying in Sage's hands." I beat his chest. "Nothing is more important to me than her." He takes each hit, holding me until my fight wanes. "If I can't save her or at least say good bye, then what good am I?"

"Listen, Blighty." His voice is thick. He says the nickname with true affection, no mocking now. He rubs his hand over his mouth. Conflict blazes behind his eyes. "What you're asking of me . . . I can't."

My stomach turns hollow. Of course he can't. Helping me will make him a traitor or worse—a Dissenter. I move away. "I wasn't thinking about what this would mean for you. I shouldn't have asked. But . . ." I'm unsure of what this next request might cost him, but I'll ask anyway. "Can you let me use your knife so I can take off the Cord, and don't tell anyone I've left—at least until I'm well outside the gate? I know it ruins Gray's plans, but at least I'll be outside the Garden. I'll no longer be a threat to the Well."

"There has to be another way."

"Obviously, there isn't."

He spins me around, staring with those emerald eyes, searching, almost desperate. "Tell me the truth about you and surfer boy."

My face flushes. "Where did that come from? We're not—he's only. My interceptor." I don't know what Cole is up to, but this has nothing to do with saving my mother.

"You're a liar," he says.

"You're the one who doesn't tell the truth."

"I may be a lot of things, but a liar isn't one of them."

"We've been through a lot together. That's all."

"That's not all." He's inches from me. "I'm not blind to the way he never takes his eyes off you, always watching how you tuck that one loose strand behind your ear, or the way you nervously twist your ring finger when you're around him, or how he glances at your lips when he thinks no one's looking. Friends don't look at each other like that. And they certainly don't sleep outside your door at night."

Maddox does all that?

"Talking about Maddox has nothing to do with saving my mother. And I'm running out of time."

He takes my wrist. My pulse is frantic under his thumb.

"Until you acknowledge the truth, you'll be blind to whatever is standing right in front of you."

"What's that supposed to mean?" His accusations are messing with my head. He's stalling me. He must be.

"You know exactly what it means." Cole's eyes blaze with anger, hurt, or maybe it's something else entirely.

"No, Cole, I don't. So why don't you enlight—" He presses his lips to mine with a heated kiss, so fierce and deep, I'm broken.

He releases my hand and steps away. Fluttering heat rolls under my skin. My bones are liquid fire. I stagger for words, but none find the surface.

He tosses something on the bed.

My Cord.

Waking thoughts, too fluid to grasp, drip from my mind. He can't feel anything for me. Why would he? But that's not the real problem.

The question I wrestle with is . . . do I?

Cole adjusts his hat the same way he always does. "I'm taking you," he says, "only because you'll die otherwise. Do exactly what I tell you. Cut through the hedge and wait for me at the end of the drive. I'll be there in ten minutes. I need to pull some things together."

He opens the door and walks out.

19

INTO MY HANDS

His kiss won't affect me. It was merely another one of his distractions. A way to take off my Cord without feeling the pain. That's all it was. At least I think it was. But maybe not. I can't think straight. I have to think straight. Focus. Gray will be hunting me down any minute now, demanding to know where I've gone.

I want to leave Maddox a note, but I know it would only waste time. I quickly take Gladys's hairpin from the dresser, the gift she gave when she said I'd always belong. That I'd always have a family. She handed me the hairpin and said her days in the field were over, and now she protects hearts. But that was before she knew what I really was.

My finger brushes over the white flower. I wish she could see the silver pin in my hair and know how badly I want to belong. That I tried. But more than anything, I want to see my mother. I want to place this token in her hair to let her know she is loved.

I tuck it in my pocket and then unfold Maddox's note. The knotted twine. *Together.* I hold the sketch longer than I should and let the scent soak into my fingers. I want to take it with me. But I can't risk Sage finding the drawing and connecting it to Maddox somehow. I glance at the beautiful, perfect strokes of each line one last time. Then tuck it under the pillow. With nothing more that belongs to me, I leave.

The corridor is shaded with inky light from the setting sun ducking behind the trees. When I reach the hedge, I hesitate. Maybe the right choice is to find Maddox and have him talk me out of this. Follow the plan and fight in the war. Give up my life. Too many thoughts muddle together at the same time.

"Hold it right there." Heavy boots clomp behind me.

I freeze.

It's Gray. The glint in his lying eyes and the arrogant curve of his cruel lips destroy any self-restraint. "You knew about my mother. You knew Sage took her, and you lied!" I charge at him, fueled with nothing but raw emotion. I claw at his neck and manage one good swipe before he twists my arm behind my back.

"Your time is up." He jerks me around and drags me down the pathway. Around the building. Toward another door.

I dig my heels, kicking, fighting to break free. I punch, wiggle, even bite, for crying out loud. Gray tries to shove me down a stone staircase, but his strength can't break my fight. It's only when he tries to kick me and I dodge his boot that I lose my balance and end up falling down the uneven stairs. My back hits the cold ground of a dark cellar. My breath is knocked to the ceiling. Gray is masked by daylight as he descends the stairs. I scurry backward, deeper into the damp air. Into swallowing darkness. I try to scream, but the sound gets caught in my throat.

Gray's walk is deliberate and slow. The smell of blood intensifies. I crawl backward until my fingers meet a wall. I slide up along the bumpy stone. I rise to my feet. But the cellar is too narrow. I can't dart around him to escape up the stairs.

I'm trapped.

I can't see his face. Or even if his knife is in his hands. Only his black silhouette standing in front of me with one hand against the wall, hemming me in.

A metal gate squeaks open near me. Gray forces me inside.

My heels find the back wall. I turn my cheek, blindly waiting, waiting, and waiting to feel what he'll do to me down in the damp pit where no one will hear me scream.

He slams the door.

A lock clicks shut.

I search for the scent of blood. Listen for his footsteps. Wait for the feel of his breath.

But his receding boots pound each stone step. Fifteen total. The wooden door bangs shut. Lights black out.

I collapse in a puddle on the floor, trembling. The Cormorants were terrible, but Gray's loathsome hate, treating me like I'm the monster I always feared I was, caging me in a cellar, is so much worse.

My fingers grope the dark. Gritty shelves line the wall. A nagging leak drips with no rhythm. There's a chill in the humid air that rubbing my arms won't quell. Something skitters.

I scramble to my feet. My fingers fumble, searching for a doorknob on the gate. There isn't one. Just a hole smaller than my pinky in the center of a rough metal plate. I shake the door. Clanging iron reverberates through the dark but won't give way. I reach through the slats and brush my fingers over the slick stone, hoping for a nearby key. Something crawls over my knuckles with a soft tickle. I scream and shake out my hand—shake my whole body free of spiders, scorpions, or who knows what else is locked in here with me.

There's no way out. No way to save my mother. No way to survive. I hang my head against the iron slat.

Maybe this is what Milton meant when he said, *"Blind be blinded more, / That they may stumble on and deeper fall."* I've reached that. I'm blinded, fallen, and waiting for execution along with the death of whatever fantasy I had about fitting in, changing the world, and protecting Mom. She will die before sunlight ever touches my skin. I'll never see her face or smell the lavender in her hair. I'll never hear her laugh or feel her fingers tuck my hair behind my ear and tell me to stand up straight. She'll die alone. She'll never know that I've died too, left to bleed on the ground in some dismal prison where the sun can't find me.

I wipe my eyes. The scent of Maddox's drawing lingers on my hands. How could he believe that I could make a difference in the world?

As an endless leak counts the time, Milton's verse whispers in my head. *"This powerful key / Into my hands was given."*

There is no key, Milton. I've searched. And Sin's lines about guarding the gates so no one leaves hell isn't the encouragement I need right now.

I sink to the floor.

Something pokes my leg from inside my pocket. Gladys's hairpin. As my fingers blindly trace the flower, the metal warms in my hand with a similar hum as the Paradise Steel.

"Then in the keyhole turns / The intricate wards, and every bolt and bar / Of massy iron or solid rock with ease / Unfastens."

I doubt the hairpin will turn the lock. The hole is too big. But I'm desperate. I search the metal plate with one hand and guide the hairpin to the lock with the other. The metal scorches my fingers. Instinctively, I let go, dropping the pin. Stupid! I reach through the bar, scouring the ground, searching over the slimy stone. My shoulder digs into the slats as I strain, stretching until my fingers find the slim metal.

I try again. This time I hold the pin loosely—with the same respect I gave the Steel. I place the pin in the lock, wiggling it around, and breathe through the burning. A tiny flash of golden light sparks inside the lock. Then a faint click snaps. The door springs open.

I'm shocked, but somehow not. Thank you, Milton. I secure the pin back in my pocket and reach out, feeling for the stairs. I once thought heights and I weren't compatible. But I'll take hanging ten stories high in a freezing cell tower over being trapped in the dark any day. I kick into the bottom step and trip, my shins digging into the stone. I'll have a nasty bruise for sure.

From somewhere outside a voice says, "The admiral arrived. Sergeant Carver wants us all in the War Room."

I hold my breath and listen. Two sets of footsteps walk away. With everyone busy, and Gray believing I'm locked up, I've got time to escape. I hope.

I carefully slip outside. A daunting brigade of gunmetal-gray vehicles pack the drive, but no one is around. As quietly as I can, I duck into the hedge and navigate through the woods, leaving a trail of yellow leaves with every touch.

I blast through the forest following the path Cole showed me. Finally, I push aside the curtain of shrubs at the end of the drive. White flowers from the crepe myrtles fall like snowflake blossoms. Cole is waiting for me. My breath quickens at the sight of him without his hat. He carries a sling bag over his shoulder and dangles the straps of two thin helmets on his index finger.

"You're late," he says with the same tense expression Maddox has when he's angry. "Thought you changed your mind."

Being trapped in a cellar has only solidified my decision to leave. "I got held up," I say. I hesitate sharing the rest of the story, afraid he might change his mind now that I'm a fugitive. But then again, maybe Cole should stay. I wouldn't want the same treatment for him if he gets caught. "It was Gray," I confess. "He thinks I'm still locked in his dungeon. I don't know how long I have before he knows I've escaped."

Cole looks me over, searching for the bruising evidence of my truth. "Was it the cellar?"

"Maybe it's better if you don't come," I say. "You've already taken off my Cord. Just close the gate after I'm gone. And, just in case, can I have the Paradise Steel?" I hold out my palm.

Cole hands me a helmet as if he didn't hear my question. His eyes narrow with determined focus, undaunted by my confession. "I've been thinking of a plan to get your mother out." He takes Gray's bike from the thicket and walks it down the drive at a brisk pace. "It's basically a suicide mission, but it will work if Sage or his army aren't waiting for us."

I jog after him. "Really?"

He checks over his shoulder, but it's clear. "Sage's place is several stories high. The cars are parked in a garage underneath with keys in the ignition. Your mom is most likely on the second floor in one of the guest suites at the top of the stairs. Reports say Sage and his army are headed this way. If we can dodge him, I'll go up, get your mom, and bring her down. If she's not there, then there's no telling where Sage has her. And we'll need to get out before we're caught."

"I'm not—"

"Cera." His use of my name stops me from arguing. "If we hit that point, we won't be able to get out. Sage will use his entire army to keep you. Destroying a Legion is one thing, but killing Cormorants . . . that's a different story. As far as I know, the only person who's ever killed one is Gray. He's legendary on both sides of the Wall."

A branch cracks under my feet when I stop. "He's killed one?"

Cole keeps walking. "Rumor has it he saved a young kid by shoving his Steel so hard in the Cormorant's chest, he hit the beast's heart, and the sucker died instantly. Don't know if it was the knife, his own strength, or both, but Gray walked away with nothing but a small scratch on his left shoulder."

I've been close enough to a Cormorant to know being that near and not dying is impossible enough, but to stab one deep in the heart? "His whole arm would have been inside the beast." I shiver.

"Yeah, Pretty nasty, huh?"

I doubt that story is true. "Who was the kid?"

Cole ducks under a low-hanging branch. "Don't know. Gray doesn't talk about it. Neither does anyone else."

Maybe I can't stab a Cormorant but . . . "If the beasts are around, I can command them to leave us alone."

"That will only tip off Sage that you're outside the Wall. No. I can get us in. I'll just need to know where Sage is first. He's always working on a few Dissenters at a time. If we're lucky, he'll be occupied and not waiting at the gate, but I'm not counting on it."

Can Cole's plan really work? "If my mom is as weak as they say she is, how can we get her out that quickly?"

Cole pulls something from a small side pocket of the bag. "Harper's gonna hate me." He holds up a vial with deep violet liquid. "But I swiped this from her stash in the kitchen. The potency of this serum should strengthen your mom enough so we can walk her out of the room and downstairs to the car."

He's brilliant. I shake my head, speechless. He tucks the serum into his front pocket as we pick up the pace.

A car engine rumbles around the bend in the road. Cole quickly ducks into the woods with the bike. I'm at his heels. "Get down." He shoves my head below the thick brush, so low, I can taste the gritty scent of wet dirt.

I peek through a break in the leaves. A slow-moving SUV with dark windows, the same gunmetal gray as the others, crawls up the drive toward the Estate. A zooming groundskeeping cart follows right behind. "Council," Cole mumbles. "Glad we're getting you out now." We crouch in the woods and wait in silence until it's clear.

Cole rises and quickly guides the bike back onto the road. "Once we're close to Sage's place, we'll have to park the bike and walk the rest of the way. You don't want to make a sound and tip off the Legions, so you need to listen as you walk. There's a rhythm to the world, but we're always out of sync. If you want to get into places and not be heard, you've got to open yourself to the Current. Feel the rhythm pulsing though the world, and let your movements respond. It's like dancing. When you do, then you can blend with the sounds around you."

I think of Gladys. She mentioned something similar about the Current. "Someone once told me it's an ebb and flow that we don't stop to listen to. A slight hum." I check over my shoulder, but we're alone. No other cars head in our direction.

"Yeah, like that, I guess."

"But I'm not a dancer." I trip over an overgrown root. "I doubt I can pull it off."

"Don't overthink it. Just listen. Be in the moment, then watch what happens."

I follow behind, listening for the hum, and not searching for voices that might signal Gray knows I've escaped. Or for any other oncoming cars. I try walking in step with Cole. Our footsteps blend with a nearby stream. He's right. As the treetops rustle, I leap over a log. My landing was a little loud. I try again, listening for sounds around me. I keep my steps light. The hum underscores scraping branches as a strong wind pushes through the woods. My senses sharpen. My mind feels alert. I take a step with the beat. A fish splashes in the rowdy stream. I am surprised at how simple it is to not be heard.

We stride silently in tune with the Garden until we reach Uriel and Gabriel and the twisted gate gnarled between them. The lantern hangs on a wooden post. On the other side, autumn leaves cover the ground. The trees are stripped bare. Only a few fat evergreens dot the road. I won't know for sure until I open the gate and detect ash in the wind, but for now, I don't see any evidence of Sage or his army.

Cole straddles the bike and puts his helmet on. "If you see anything, tell me." He tucks the knife in a holder at his waist.

He shouldn't come with me. Leaving will make him a traitor— or worse. "Cole, please don't come."

"I'm the best chance you've got of saving your mom. And I'm not sending you out there alone. Now lose the sweater."

"What?"

"Warmth intensifies scent. I don't want the Cormorants detecting you once that gate opens."

I do what he says. I have a tank top on underneath but try to ignore the way his glance drifts over me as I fasten my helmet. "Cole, if something happens while we're there . . . don't let me betray the Alliance. If I have a vision or help Sage in any way. I want you to promise me that you'll use your knife on me."

"I won't." Cole scowls.

"Please."

"Just open the gate." He starts the engine.

He didn't say no. I'll take that as a promise. I wave the lantern behind Uriel. Up and down, left and right. The ground rumbles under my feet in sync with the roaring engine of Gray's bike and the opening gate. Icy air whips through the gap. I gasp. Behind the Circuit Wall, it's easy to forget how cold the world is.

"Close it. Then get on. Quick," Cole shouts over the roaring sound.

I run to the other statue and wave the lantern behind Gabriel. Reversing the order. The gate creaks, churning as the vines twist. "Now!" Cole yells.

I abandon the lantern and jump into place behind Cole. Despite the sling bag resting between us, I wrap my arms around him and lean in as close as possible to stay warm enough but not give myself away.

"If you see any of those suck-face Legions on the way, let me know." Cole revs the engine and kicks the bike into action.

I grip tight, wincing as he peels out, deftly maneuvering through the narrow exit. As the gate closes behind us, frigid air lashes across my face. Uneasiness washes over me as I look to the sky.

Something isn't right.

20

ENEMY GROUNDS

Sage isn't around.

In the distance a Cormorant cries out. Another one answers in response, and then another, announcing my presence. Their piercing shrieks crawl through my skin. I'd forgotten how horrible they sound.

We take the corners of the barren woods much faster than Devon did in getting here. Turning left, weaving right, we fly down the narrow dirt route as the sun hangs low in the west. I scour the gnarled brush for mist. Surely a creature is watching. Waiting. Reporting every move back to Sage.

When we clear a bend in the road, Cole hits the brakes. My sight is limited because of the helmet. I can't see around his shoulder. I crane my body left, then right. If we've run into a creature, despite what Cole said about tipping Sage off, I'll command it to leave Cole alone. I'll even go with it, willingly. If it means Cole can go free.

We skid to a hard stop, avoiding a near collision with a shiny red sports car. White steam rises from the tailpipe as the convertible top lowers, exposing someone in the front seat.

Cole mutters something under his breath that I can't hear clearly.

A lanky guy steps out of the car. Late twenties, pushing thirty.

With black-framed glasses and scaly red skin climbing up the base of his neck, it's a face I recognize. A face from the gallery Elysium's Edge.

Mark.

Mark who pursued me with a job, luring me to bring my mother's drawings. Mark, the Dissenter who tried bringing me into Sage's hands before I ever knew this world existed.

Any hope of rescuing my mother evaporates along with the wispy air steaming from my rapid breath.

"Good to see you again, Cera." Only half of Mark's face smiles. The other half droops when he talks, as though his jaw has melted. He wasn't this way at the gallery. "Are you ready?" He opens a car door. "And Sage will be thrilled to have you back, Hendrick," he says to Cole.

"He's not coming." My words slur between frozen lips as I awkwardly dismount from the bike. My body shivers, whether from cold or fear of knowing this is a trap, I don't know.

"Cera, don't," Cole mutters.

Voices shout from somewhere up the hill. The Alliance must know I've escaped.

I wrestle with the helmet, yanking it off. "Cole, go back. Tell them I ran off and you tried to catch me." As I look at the conflict piercing his eyes, the Current wobbles between us. "Go. Now."

Cole doesn't move. "I won't lie."

A Cormorant screeches in the distance. "Time to go." Mark checks the sky. "My backup is moving in." I don't hesitate. I bolt to the car. "Sit in the back," he tells me.

Five canvases with assaulting neon colors that are wrapped in clear plastic occupy the front seat. Mark's paintings from the gallery. Five trees with black fog hovering at the roots. I shiver and crawl into the cramped back seat. He called them different personalities, but I know better now. "Those are the five Bents, aren't they?"

Healer. Guardian. Blade. Caretaker. And Seer.

Mark gets in and shuts the door. "I thought you would have picked that up sooner."

His chemical scent still overwhelms me. I slowly scoot behind the passenger seat and take one last look at Cole, etching his face in my mind.

Mark backs the car out of the tight space. "Last chance, Hendrick," he calls out.

Next thing I know, Cole jumps in next to me. My insides turn hollow as Mark smiles and lowers the convertible top like a coffin lid.

We drive for at least half an hour while Mark blasts heavy bass music with spitting lyrics. Talking isn't possible. I want to tell Cole he shouldn't have come. I'm angry that he did. And I'm angry with myself for being selfishly relieved that I'm not alone.

Dusk descends on a long stretch of highway lit by the unnatural blue glow of the headlights. Cole takes his fedora from the sling bag and straightens out the edges before setting it low on his head. He sits cramped with arms crossed and knees high against the back of Mark's seat. Every reverberating beat of the music burrows deeper into my bones, rattling my core. Willingly going with Mark to meet Sage without putting up a fight has to be wrong. My mind tells me it is, but an inner pull I can't explain, assures me that this is exactly what I should do.

As we drive, I catalog what I know: Sage is a shapeshifter. He'll use his red current to torture Awakened and siphon powers from Dissenters. He'll know my triggers—Mom—and will spin the truth to get me to side with him. He'll want me to use my Dissenting powers to join the realms and give him access to destroy the Well. That's about all I know. But I'm sure there's more I don't. Maybe even something that might explain this relentless inner pull I can't seem to shake.

We turn off and drive through a dark county road lined with imposing evergreens. As we cruise up a hill and turn onto a sloping drive, Mark turns down the music.

"Sage bought a new car after your last joy ride." Mark speaks to Cole with unsettling familiarity. "But I wouldn't try that stunt again. He's less patient now."

Cole only stares out the window. I check him for the Dissenter's mark. But in the weak light from the dashboard, I can't tell.

As Mark lowers the convertible top, floodlights from the garage turn on, lighting the perimeter as if it were daylight. Sage's house is gorgeous. The entire place is made from glass, outlined by white rectangular beams. Stunning, but empty of human life. Clean light shines from every room, casting a soft shadow onto the perfectly manicured lawn. Swirling black clouds hover above the house with the quiet droning sound of resting bees. The thin air smells of ash. I inspect Cole's neck again. No red marks appear as far as I can see. Cole catches me looking.

I switch my attention to Mark. "Where is my mother?"

A girl's cackling laughter drifts down the hill. Contained flames from a fire pit flicker on the far end of the house. "You'll get to see her after you visit with Sage." Mark takes his artwork from the front seat. "He's on the east veranda. He's got company." My stomach twists at the way he smiles at Cole when he adds, "Two girls."

From this distance, I can't get a good view of any girls, but I can tell there is someone else up there. A man wearing white.

"Wait in the downstairs lounge. I'll tell him you're here," Mark says.

A Cormorant's shriek cuts through the night. The creature

lands on the roof with its razor-sharp claws. With that gluttonous look of death in its eye and puffed out chest, I know it's Moloch. "It's only me." Mark waves his hand at the beast before entering the garage, disappearing in the dark. Moloch watches Cole with thirsty greed. The beast had that same look before killing Jess. Before attacking Maddox in the alley.

Belial, the smaller Cormorant, joins Moloch on the roof. Both creatures, as big as grizzlies, jut their necks forward, bickering in staccato squawks as we walk toward the garage.

Moloch glides off the roof, landing on the driveway. Cole freezes. If I had his knife, I'd stab it deep into Moloch's chest, wedging it up into his heart until he died. I must have taken a step forward because Cole holds me back. "Don't. They might be under Sage's control, but they have a mind of their own."

"They're under my control too," I remind him.

Moloch squawks and clicks his serpent tongue. The trees rustle all around us. The pit of my stomach deepens. Moloch has called others. At least four dozen younger Cormorants the size of mountain lions perch in the trees. All around, the air smells of rotting flesh.

Moloch, with his beady yellow eyes, backs up but stares right at Cole. For a moment I think he may fly away, but he retracts his wings, lowers his gruesome head, and crouches, ready to strike.

And he does. Moloch leaps into the air, launching right at Cole. I throw my hands out. "Stay back!" The words break free with a hungry power. A surging, euphoric and greedy force rises in me, desperate to take control. Moloch bucks, fighting my command, but doesn't make contact with Cole.

I quickly drag him into the relative safety of the expansive garage as the floodlights black out. The air smells of new tires and expensive leather. Beyond a row of imported cars, a gentle light drapes down a spiral staircase.

Instead of being thankful, Cole sounds irritated. "Careful,

Blighty," he says as we climb the metal stairs. "You might . . ."

"Connect the realms? Not until I'm seventeen. And what will it matter if I'm not behind the Wall?"

"The more you use the power, the more you'll want to. Then you might not be able to stop. Think of it like an insect bite. Once you scratch it—"

"I get it," I snap. That would have been useful information for the Alliance to warn me about. I climb the rest of the way in silence. Cole's light footsteps harmonize with mine until I'm standing on a marble floor.

The room is sparse and everything is white: Floors. Interior walls. Gauzy silk curtains flanking the terrarium windows. The only color comes from silver accents on various side tables, red pillows, and black picture frames.

On the surface, everything seems so normal. A gentle water wall separates us from a glass dining room table with ten chairs. All white, naturally. Mark climbs stairs of glass jutting out from the wall. He reaches the second story with a wraparound balcony. A set of black doors creates an entry at the top, just the way Cole described.

"Wait there," Mark says and then walks around the corner with his paintings. He must feel certain that I won't run.

"Cole, get out now," I whisper. "I'll hold off Moloch again. Take the car. Go."

"I'm not leaving you here. With Sage on the patio and Mark out of the way, I can find your mom, give her the serum, and bring her down. Be out in five. Wait here."

Cole doesn't give me the chance to protest. He flies up the stairs two at a time and disappears around the corner. But something about him going off alone doesn't feel right. I race up the stairs after him, but I'm not nearly as swift. Without a handrail, I have to be careful to keep my balance. As soon as I reach the top step, a glass door on the first floor rumbles open.

I stand frozen.

The trickling waterfall muffles the sound of bare feet on the marble. Then I smell a sickeningly sweet ashy aroma. A deepening chill coils through me as a strong presence invades the room. I've been caught.

Sage is here.

21

SAGE MARROCK LASALLE

I stand exposed on the marble balcony. My whole life I've been moved, hidden, and dragged around to the farthest corners of the country to keep Sage from finding me; yet here I am, inside his house at night. That hideous, taunting monster from Fuseli's *Nightmare* stands in the shadows below, preying on Awakened, mutilating Dissenter's bodies, transforming them into Legions, and enslaving them. The presence of pure evil is so strong it permeates my skin.

A voice tinted with a French accent, as smooth as it is mellow, floats up to my ears. *"She walks in darkness, like the night . . ."* Sage greets me with Lord Byron's poem on the beautiful harmony of blending of dark and light. I suppress a shiver. The message isn't lost on me. I'm a Blight—both light and darkness. But the words don't sound right.

"Of cloudless climes and starry skies . . ."

His voice drifts from all directions. I try but can't find him in the lounge below.

"And all that's best of dark and bright / Meet in her aspect and her eyes . . ."

The rhythmic cadence of his speech sets off a longing twinge. I squint at the dark. And that's when I see him. A mauve light from the outdoor pool outlines the eerie shadow of a man casually leaning against a chair. He's not a troll-like beast the way Fuseli painted him, but a man.

"Thus mellowed to that tender light . . ." He glides barefoot into the soft light near the leather couch. *"Which heaven to gaudy day denies."*

With the slender build of a retired athlete, wavy hair, and a Roman nose, he looks to be about fifty with tanned skin that makes his white pants and half buttoned shirt glow. He is simultaneously dangerous and beautiful. Like hypnotic flames dancing in a fire, I'm mesmerized and can't pull my eyes away.

Then something nudges me from inside, drawing me back to the poem. He's misquoted Byron. The right words slap inside my head as if my English teacher was calling me out for not paying attention in class.

"It's beauty." I force my voice to be strong. "She walks in beauty . . . not darkness."

"That is a matter of opinion." Sage moves closer but stays in the supple shadows as he trails a long finger along the back of the couch. "Some would say that darkness is beautiful." Gold flecks flicker in his eyes. "Byron's poetry is deliciously Romantic. It's such a shame he died of a fever and not something more . . . heroic, as he desired. Don't you agree, Lonicera?"

I grip the balcony rail. I expected Sage to know my name. But not my real one. Hard as I try, I can't stifle a shiver.

Sage notices. "How blatantly inconsiderate of the Alliance not to care for you the way you deserve, dressing you in unsuitable rags in this weather. It is rather unconscionable." He waves his hand, igniting a row of smooth river rocks tucked in a recessed part of the wall. "Come down and warm yourself by the fire."

He didn't use his red lightning source to do that. This is a different power. One Cole didn't mention.

Two sets of footsteps clomp and shuffle around the corner

from where I'm standing.

"Look who's back." Mark shoves Cole toward the metal handrail. His hat is missing, his face fully exposed as he stares at the polished floor. His hands hang empty and limp at his side. I stare at him. Why isn't he fighting? Use the knife, Cole. Get away. My eyes plead with him, but he won't look at me.

"Hendrick Colton." Sage smiles. His perfect teeth gleam. "Such a charming, pretty boy, and one of my favorites." He glides around the couch. "Your preferred gifts are waiting for you."

Cole yanks his head up with fire in his eyes. "I'm clean now."

"Don't refuse." Mark shakes Cole back into submission.

"Come now, Hendrick." Sage pours a clear drink in a crystal tumbler. "We both know that ten days with the Alliance has not cleansed your palate. No doubt you were counting the days until you could return."

Cole drops his head, stare returning to the floor.

"I have acquired a few ancillary treasures for you as well. They came in this morning." Sage sips his drink. "I assure you— these two will be eager and nothing like the last one."

Finally, Cole's drags his eyes up to meet mine, the fire gone.

"Marcus, allow him to indulge." Sage waves him away.

What's going on? Why doesn't Cole put up a fight? He has the knife. He could easily pull off some distraction, use one of those martial arts moves to get him out of this mess. But then again, Cole knows firsthand what Sage will do if someone defies his command. Mark drags him off, out of my sight.

"Let him go." I can't hide the desperation.

Sage laughs, amused. "No one stays against their will. I only request that before my guests leave they partake of my generosity."

"Cole doesn't want anything from you."

"Oh, I believe he does." Sage thoughtfully rubs the neck of the liquor bottle. "You may join him later if you prefer, as I believe he would love nothing more." His volcanic eyes bore into me.

I look away. My mind whirls with frantic uncertainty. Did Cole betray me? No. He couldn't have. I was the one who asked him to help me. Instead of turning back to the Alliance when he had the chance . . . he came with me. And he tried to rescue my mother when I told him to run.

My mother. "Where is she?" My voice trembles. "Where is my mother?"

Sage reclines on the couch with legs crossed, fluffing a pillow at his side. "Resting at the moment. She was far from well when we found her, so I brought her here for refuge." Sage swirls his glass, watching the clear liquid dance along the edge.

"I'm here now, so you can let her go." The words sound bolder than I feel.

Sage catches me off guard with a lighthearted laugh. "You are delightfully spunky. I like that about you." He tips the glass up in my direction.

Confusion mounts inside of me. Why isn't he evil and ruthless the way the Alliance painted him? And why does something about the way his mouth curves when he smiles set off a longing ache for my father? Sage looks nothing like him.

"Your mother is not here against her will, just as you and Hendrick are not. I suggest you relax. After all, no place in the world is safer for the both of you than right here with me."

"I'm not—" I bite the words down. I'm not safe anywhere. But I won't give that away.

Sage sighs, disappointed. "Lonicera. *Know ye not me?*"

Now he's messing with me by quoting Milton. The archfiend's line when two angels find him in the garden disguised as a toad, whispering in Eve's ear as she sleeps. With one touch of the angel's sword, the demon returns to his true form, igniting the air—*as when a spark lights.*

A disturbing heaviness settles between my lungs. Has my connection to the poem been with Sage this whole time and not

Milton? Or maybe Milton has been luring me to Sage instead of warning me . . .

No. That can't be right. Milton wasn't a Dissenter. He's a Blight. We're a breed all our own.

The only clear truth is that Sage wants to confuse me. As Maddox feared, Sage is trying to blur right from wrong. I collect myself, breathing slow and steady. "I know who you are."

He takes a final sip, relishing the burn. "I don't believe you do. You only know what others have said about me, which is often askew. I'm not at all what they paint me to be. I assume they have adorned me as a horrid creature with a desire to gain control of their prized possession—that Empyrean Well, the obscure container for their power. They believe I wish to destroy the world. Am I correct?"

I open my mouth and quickly shut it. I won't give him the satisfaction of knowing he's right.

He sets his glass aside and leans back to look at me. "You and I, we have the same desire."

"I doubt that."

"I'm not a monster, and neither are you. You want your mother healed and to be free from the visions that haunt you. You wish to preserve those you love. *Oui?*"

I blink. I expected him to know details of my life but not my heart.

He rises from the couch with silky elegance. "As do I." He walks to the base of the steps with regal strides. "Perhaps you have heard my tragic story, although I am certain it was tainted for you to hate me. I understand, you may be fearful and anxious, or perhaps you worry that I will hurt the ones you love. But you are dualistic, and one side of the story does not befit you. How could it?"

Reason and desire war within me. I shouldn't stand here and willingly listen to Sage's lies. But he's speaking truths that won't let me turn away.

As he ascends the stairs with perfect balance, I back into the corner. "Lonicera, you have nothing to fear. I would simply like to share my story, if you will indulge me. I feel it only fair."

He runs the palm of his hand over his perfect waves, smoothing them out as he begins. "I was in love, and Ayala loved me too. Perhaps too much. She knew my desires would cause nothing but my own destruction, yet I was determined to reach the highest pinnacle and prove myself worthy of her love. She pleaded for me not to seek the greater things, but I was not created for the ordinary. As a tragic tale often goes, though I loved her, I failed to listen."

Remorse shades his expression as he reaches the top step. Part of me demands I run, but another part feels a deeper longing at his scent—steam tinged with liquor and sweet ash, one similar to my father—and demands I stay.

"I didn't know how much I loved her until my quest destroyed her. I had ripped a seam in the realms as we fell into this kingdom, unseen. Me, now a horrid creature, marred by my choice, and she, splintered into the dust of a thousand tiny feathers in flight."

He stands on the balcony, not ten feet away, and sighs. "My one desire is to restore her." His voice drips with regret. "The Alliance conceals the truth of how my heart longs to put back what my pride destroyed. You see, as my power grows, Ayala reforms as well. The misguided Alliance so cruelly withholds my full story to deceive you into hating me. They hoard the only power that will heal Ayala and grant her back the beauty she sacrificed for me. All I desire is to save my beloved from a life of endless torment and shame."

Sage's eyes glisten as he looks beyond the thick window. Outside, Cormorants dance in circles around a stray light pinned to a pine tree. Their flapping wings brush over my warped reflection.

"Do I hate the Alliance?" he continues. "How could I not,

when in the name of preservation, they withhold the only power that can restore my love?" He studies my reflection.

I look away. "What does this have to do with me?"

"You, like me, understand the power of love and how it sacrifices everything for the one it adores. It is in your heart, the glint your eyes can't hide."

"We're nothing alike. I'm not willing to kill and destroy anyone who gets in my way."

Sage smiles, sadly. "The deeper your love, the easier to tear even the strongest moral fiber, I assure you."

"Is that a threat?"

"A promise, but not by me. It is what will be." He retreats to the polished doors. "You don't trust me; I understand. However, allow me to ask one question. How do you know what the Alliance seeks is good? Your realm believes in a binary world. Right, wrong. Black, white. Shadow, light. But you are the prevailing gray line dancing between."

He is silent for a moment, watching me. I stand as stoic as Lieutenant Foster. I know I'm outmatched, but I try to be strong anyhow.

"Tell me," his voice eases. "What have they done for you? Have they healed your mother? Protected her? Protected you? Or have they used and imprisoned you, kept you under surveillance, called you a threat, denied you the power you seek. Yet you see them as good?" He clicks his tongue, shaking his head. "What a shame. That is a captive mindset, *mon amour*. You are brighter than that."

He might be partly right about the Alliance but not about everyone who is Awakened. And he's absolutely wrong about one thing. "I don't want power."

Sage laughs. "Of course you do. You want the power to save those you love. You want the power to end your plight. You want the power to create a place where you can be free of the bondage and destruction that haunts you. Tell me, if you could, at this very moment, save those you love, heal yourself from the visions, and find a place where you can begin anew, would you?"

Yes. A thousand times yes. But . . . "Not if it means harming others."

"A noble mindset, but ignorant." Sage waves nonchalantly at the double doors, the same way he did with the fire. Nothing happens. "What if your actions will not destroy others but free them? Imagine a world where everyone could do as they please. No orders. No Alliance. No protocol. A place where Blights and Awakened mingle freely. A new earth would arise, released from the tyranny of the Well's oppressive control, as now guarded by an archaic mindset."

Those are the words I was expecting. "So, you admit you want me to give you access to the Well. Doesn't that make you the same as the Alliance?"

Sage waves at the doors a second time. Again, nothing happens. He frowns. "The Alliance will fight so as to not lose control. I seek not to control, but to, as Milton speaks, '*set free / From out this dark and dismal house of pain.*' And just like you, I would do it for love." A tiny bird lands on his hand. Sage runs his thumb down the bird's back. But it's not a bird. It's a Cormorant the size of a finch. Not solid black like the others, but ghost white with a thin black line running down its chest. "She's waited long enough."

Realization dawns. "The Cormorants . . . ?"

"*Oui.* Broken fragments of a cursed Ayala, hoping to one day rejoin and transform back into the beauty she once was."

I'm speechless, as something within his words digs deep into the wound I've tried to hide. Am I not also searching to restore what I was before the visions hit? Before my dad left and I had to move every year? When anything seemed possible? No shadows, no pain.

I shake it off. I can't side with him and betray the Alliance. I can't turn my back on Maddox. And I can't forget what Sage has done.

Sage sets the Cormorant on a glass perch near the doors. "For the Alliance, retaining power is more important than love. They're afraid of what the world will be if they don't have control. I don't want control. I only want a way to bring Ayala back."

I step closer, drawn in by the tiny Cormorant. "But doing so will destroy—"

"That is the lie. Not destroy. Restore." Sage lifts his sleeve and taps at a sleek onyx band around his wrist. He waves his hand a third time. With a quiet thunder, the doors slide open to a dark room. At the sound, the tiny Cormorant, Ayala, flies away.

"Technology is such a temperamental monstrosity." Sage pulls down his sleeve, hiding the wristband once again. Not supernatural powers at all. "*Cela passera aussi*—this too shall pass," he says, rubbing his hands together. "But now, *mon amour*, welcome home." Sage swoops the air with his fingers. An assaulting white light bursts inside the room.

Although this isn't my home, a yearning familiarity is lulling me to stay.

"Come. I know how much you've longed to see your mother. It is time the two of you reconcile. She's just beyond my gallery— and you can enjoy the collection along the way. There are a few exquisite pieces I desire to show you." He gestures for me to follow.

"I'm not some 'temperamental monstrosity' you can push around with your fancy wristband," I tell him.

Sage laughs, warm, inviting. "Well said." His eyes soften as he tips his head with a graceful nod. "My apologies. It is just that I have waited so long for you to view my collection—I hope you will indulge me, even for a few moments."

He strides into the room, leaving me on the balcony in the dark of night. My blurred reflection stares back at me. I'm positive this is all some sort of trap, but I won't run. I won't leave without my mother and Cole.

And I'm certain Sage knows it.

22

THE GALLERY

"Did the Alliance tell you how the Empyrean Well moves every century or so?" Sage's voice carries from inside the gallery.

The natural wood floors, twenty-foot ceiling, and artificial lighting copies that of Elysium Edge, his gallery in Wakefield. Except here, art covers every inch of the expansive walls, mimicking Hesperian. But in the safe house Maddox created, the art felt vibrant and alive. Here, every piece seems caged and terrified. I quickly skim the paintings, printing plates, and sculptures decorating the room. There are so many, my head spins trying to take them all in from the doorway. It's as if the Met was collapsing in on itself. I step over the threshold for a better look.

Sage saunters around a marble statue over thirteen feet tall that's prominently displayed in the middle of the room. "Did you also know the Well uses its power for transfer and not protection when it shifts? I discovered that fact when I acquired this piece, *Abduction of the Sabine Women,* in the Renaissance." When he flicks his finger in the air, the base spins. The three figures twirl in an orchestrated dance. The terrified woman stretches her hands to the sky, seeking release. A muscular man grabs her waist while crushing a horror-struck suitor underfoot. Sage smiles adoringly. "Beautiful, don't you agree?"

The sculpture is beautiful. But I'm not about to reveal more than I should. "It's disturbing," are the only words I offer.

"That too." Sage shrugs. "Were you aware that the Well is housed within the Garden?" He wanders to a giant canvas, each question prodding me to speak. "And that you alone can connect the realms by using the fullness of powers I have made available to you?" Sage stands with his hands behind his back, taking in the painting. "It is quite simple in fact, although it took me centuries to discover the secret. A Dissenting Seer"—he holds out one palm—"and a Guardian with strong lineage"—he holds out the other hand—"join together to create a rare beauty who offers the perfect balance needed to unlock the realms by utilizing both sides of your power at once in its presence. Doing so 'confuses' the realms, thereby granting access for both sides to see what only you can."

The Alliance barely fed me anything compared to the bounty of information that freely flows from Sage's mouth. Regardless, I weave around another set of glass cases and a bronze sculpture. According to Sage, my mother lies somewhere behind the next set of double doors.

"Are you aware of all the powers you possess? I have no doubt the Alliance has withheld that revelation from you."

I stop, hidden behind the twirling sculpture. I know I can control the creatures and see how they travel in black mist when no one else could. But I didn't think I could do more.

"Not only do you possess the means to wield the Alliance's weapons against them—weapons that would never strike their flesh otherwise—but you also hold the unique power of seeing the Current move in the world, and can taste of its richness."

I think on how I almost stabbed Cole with the Paradise Steel while we trained. And how I could see the Current at the Well but Maddox couldn't. And Milton did mention something about tasting, or consuming.

Even if these aren't lies, I can't let my guard down. I'm positive Sage is trying hard to lure me; perhaps it was written into the vision that I didn't take time to read. I ease past a bronze statue of a boy with a wide hat leaning on a sword and try to stay focused on the door ahead.

"Perhaps Delacroix is more to your liking, *ma belle?*"

I halt, midstride. *Ma belle*—my beautiful. The lilt in his voice. Dad said it the same way. A surprising surge of grief punches me. Sage isn't my father. I'm certain of that. But what is it about him that keeps resurrecting this yearning?

"*The Barque of Dante.*" Sage feasts on every inch of a large canvas as though reading it the way I can.

My pulse quickens the same way it did when I read the Delacroix back at the Estate, the one that told me Milton was a Blight.

I quickly scan over the painting, drinking up every detail. Two men. One older in a red cloak shields a younger man in a rose tunic. Both travel on a flimsy raft across a raging black sea. Ashen demons clamor to get aboard. Dead bodies float in the foaming water. In the background, a city burns like a lantern in the night. A city that for some reason reminds me of East Ridge where Hesperian once hid.

"I thought you might connect with this one," Sage remarks. "I consider this Delacroix's conversion painting—the moment he turned away from the tedious restraints of neoclassicism and embraced the exotic, adventurous freedom of Romanticism. With so much movement and passion, it is a thrilling story, don't you think? The uncertain anticipation of whether they will make their destination or fall victim to the raging sea."

I do connect with the piece, but I won't say so. Something in the portrait about the older man's face reminds me of Foster. His raised hand should be holding a light, but it's empty. The city burns in the distance where a lantern would be. The boy wrapped in a sienna-colored cloak shares the same black hair as Cole. Demons clamor underfoot, but they're not succeeding. They won't win because another figure, a muscular oarsmen, is surefooted and knows the waters. The three men. *Three.* There's something about the number three.

"All those years you thought you were alone, I was there keeping you safe. Unlike your father, I have never abandoned you." He moves on, running his finger along a glass case housing William Blake's handwritten poem and illustration of *A Poison Tree.* In the drawing a blond boy lies dead at the foot of a gnarled tree. Maddox immediately leaps to mind, but I push the thought away.

"Then you ran off with that scarred boy." Sage's piercing glance flickers at Blake's drawing before turning to me again.

I pretend to study the other prints in the case, a series from Blake's *The Marriage of Heaven and Hell.* I clear my mind by focusing on whether they're original or copies.

"It was my intention to have him eliminated, but you, oh, you knew better." Sage moves to a set of prints near the back doors. "You directed things so beautifully–manipulating the boy by feigning fear of my dear Cormorants from the start, and then announcing your presence to my army so the Alliance would shelter you inside the Garden, which allowed you to discover secrets of their hidden world." He claps. "Lonicera, it was simply brilliant! You followed every step as planned."

He thinks that? I didn't follow a plan or manipulate Maddox. At least not intentionally. My stomach churns.

"And I must thank you for bringing back my darling boy." He tips his head. "He was a joy to have. I hated giving him back, even for a short while, but it was necessary to provide you with a sufficient escort. I asked myself concerning you: '*Whom shall we send / . . . whom shall we find / Sufficient? Who shall tempt with wandering feet?*'" I'm sickened every time he quotes Milton.

"Hendrick is a young man I approve of. He would do anything for you. It was all there, written in the painting of *The Storm*."

The double doors fling open. It's Mark.

Sage turns. "He accepted, did he not?"

"He knew better than to refuse."

"Good." Sage's slow smile disturbs me to no end.

"Where is he?" I demand. "And where is my mother?"

Sage glances at me out of the corner of his eye. "Marcus, prepare Lonicera my finest meal. An evening feast will be such a celebration, and I would hate for her to become unpleasantly petulant."

Mark frowns. "That's what the servant girl is for. I'm—"

"You will do what I ask!" Sage's voice booms, shaking the room. The paintings shudder. He whips around, stretching his long fingers in Mark's direction. Warping air hisses as it twists from his fingers.

Mark's eyes widen. "Please don't." He backs away, shielding his face. "I'm sorry. I'll go. I'll do it."

The red current seeps from Sage's hands, snaking across the room like a narrow thread. The warped light finds Mark's neck and wraps around his throat. Mark struggles to breathe. His eyes bulge.

Sage pulls his left hand back, extracting Mark's powers with the thread. Thin wisps of golden light, similar to the flickering light in the Garden, tumble along the ribbon.

Shock holds me still.

Mark contorts in agony. Gurgling. Choking. Foamy black saliva oozes from the corner of his mouth. His glasses crash to the floor.

Something bursts within me and I rush toward him. "Stop! Stop it!"

Sage whips his hand back, breaking the current before I run into the scarlet thread. Mark staggers, gasping for air. His skin molts onto the floor in ashen gray flakes, leaving an inky mist in its place.

"Lonicera, *ma belle,*" Sage reprimands me as steam lingers on his fingertips.

I shield Mark, standing in a cloud that smells of burning hair. "He didn't do anything wrong. Leave him alone."

"He disrespected you," Sage says. He motions to Mark. *"Au plus vite.* Now go. Quickly." Mark stumbles into the dark hallway, swaying one elongated arm.

Sage inhales deep and tastes his lips. Not only has he grown an inch or two taller, but he glows with a hazy aura. My throat heaves. I might throw up.

"I'm leaving."

"*Ma belle,* please. I didn't mean to frighten you."

"Frighten?" That's a gross understatement. "You're sick. I'm getting my mother and Cole, and we're leaving."

"Without first viewing John Martin's *Bridge over Chaos?*"

"After what I just saw, I couldn't care less about any more artwork."

Sage waves at the doors, slamming them shut.

Terror climbs through my veins. What was I thinking? "You said you never keep anyone against their will." I try to sound strong. Angry. But my insides are a trembling mess.

"Not without partaking of my generosity first," he corrects me. "The door isn't locked. I'm simply asking you to view my collection. Lovely, isn't it?" He straightens the small black-and-white print on the wall. "'*Thou wilt bring me soon / To that new world of light and bliss . . . / Where I shall reign . . . / Thy daughter and thy darling, without end.*'"

I hate how Sage wields Milton like a taunting play toy. This time he uses the verse where the archfiend meets his daughter, Sin, at hell's gate, and he convinces her to let him cross. A bridge over chaos.

I spin around. The art pieces Sage has collected . . .

Delacroix's boat in raging waters.

Martin's bridge to a world of light.

The capture of the woman seeking release . . .

He's been reading messages that will ensure his passage to the Well. And here I am in the center of it all, the bridge that will give him exactly what he wants.

Only I won't.

I fling the door open and forge into the hallway, desperate to find my mother. But as soon as I step into the hall, a warning pang kicks inside me.

Sage follows right behind. "*Ma belle.* You aren't really searching for your mother, *oui?*" His smooth voice is too gentle and luring. "You desire an end to the visions, the destruction, and wish to save those around you, perhaps? But those answers cannot give you what you truly desire."

I have to shut him out. Concentrate on nothing but getting out. The dark corridor is a velvet maze. Once I turn the first corner, Sage slams the gallery doors shut. I'm surrounded in complete darkness.

"Do you even know what it is that you desire?" Sage's voice creeps closer. I widen my eyes, searching for any pinhole of light, but find none. Still, I don't stop searching. I reach out, running my fingers over the plush wallpaper, feeling for the next corner.

"Mom?" I cry out, hoping she's near.

"I know what you desire." Sage's voice is too gentle. His scent of liquor and ash grows stronger.

"Cole!" I shout. There has to be a door somewhere close. I don't know if Sage can see in the dark, but I'm positive he has the path memorized. I keep my steps light the way Cole taught me, hoping to blend with the surroundings, but everything in the hall is a vacant quiet. The silky air is hard to breathe. My quickened breath gives me away.

"I've always known." Sage is right behind me once again. His fingers graze my neck, brushing aside my hair. I swat his hand, or at least where his hand should be, but my fingers glide through a slick mist.

Like a Legion.

I hold my breath to listen. No footsteps. No breathing. He is a voice closer than my own skin, echoing in the dark, burrowing into my head. I push on, hands following the wall, searching for a way through.

"What you want more than anything in the world is *not* my destruction, nor the safety of your mother, or even the protection of the Well or the Alliance." His scent engulfs me. I continue to take shallow breaths and press my back against the wall, inching deeper into the dark.

"No," Sage croons. "Your deepest desire, the one thing you treasure over all the rest is to be . . . wanted." His whisper is so close his breath brushes my cheek.

My throat tightens. I slide along the wall, fighting back tears as a nagging wound is punctured inside my heart. Don't listen. Get out.

"You think by saving your mother, you may prove yourself worthy of being wanted. How could she want something as appalling as the monster you believe yourself to be? And the Alliance, they only want what you can give them. They don't want *you*."

My hand slips into the open air. I've found another corner. I force myself to fill my head with a melody, humming the song Maddox played that night at Hesperian, at the final farewell, when his eyes met mine through the crowd. He sang about belonging. About finding a home.

Another wall meets my fingers. Sage remains near. No longer mist, but flesh. His bare footsteps slap along the stone. His hand joins mine as if trying to lead me through the dark. I flatten my palm against the wall. There is a break in the continuous panel. A door. I fumble, searching for a handle that doesn't seem to exist.

Sage sighs. "Lonicera, we should be celebrating rather than loitering in the dark. This is a glorious moment, having you here with me. All these years your mother has kept you hidden, but I have always been near. She knew it was only a matter of time before I found you. And now, I have. And now you can free her from the burden."

I press a hand over one ear. These are lies. All lies. But it's too late. The words have already coiled too deep inside my heart.

I tremble. "Stop!"

A slight wind brushes my wet cheeks. Midway down the hall, a burgundy sconce flickers, lighting the way.

"Your mother is right through there." Sage, back in human form, motions to a frosted door at the end of the maze. "Ask her if these are lies. But before I open the door, tell me the name the Alliance has for children like you."

The word immediately rises in my mind, but I refuse to give him the satisfaction.

"Come, Lonicera. What is it they call you?" He wipes a hair from my forehead. I cringe. His ebony eyes stare, deep and probing. Then he says slowly, enunciating every excruciating sound of that one syllable, "Blight. A disease. An unwanted plight to be eliminated."

Tears well in my eyes. My lip quivers. Why do the words he speaks sound so much like my father? I'm back to being a trembling seven-year-old, standing barefoot in the kitchen. Beer bottle fragments shattered on the floor as the back door slams and he walks out in pouring rain.

"Lonicera." Sage's voice softens, and the ache, the longing inside me, leaps up again. "They don't see you. They don't want you. They don't value the beautiful creature you are." He wipes my tears. I turn away. "You are not a disease. You are glorious. A dualistic *reine*—a queen without boundaries. The Destroyer, with powers beyond measure. All I have longed to do is give you the one thing your heart desires more than anything in this world." His words are a sweet poison, a balm soothing the ache in my heart. "Yet I can only do so if you show me the Well."

I back into the wall and lock my knees to keep standing. I won't tell him anything. I refuse.

"Has your innocent mind so easily believed their deception?" Sage asks. "They withhold truth. Forbid you to use your powers. Urgently warn you to suppress your true nature for fear that something catastrophic will happen. They lie." Sage brushes the back of his hand against my cheek. I tense and close my eyes. I wait for a shiver to crawl through me, but instead I lean into his hand. A tremble rises. His touch feels like my father's.

"Your powers are not evil. Your powers are the fullness of who you were always meant to be." He lifts my chin. "The Alliance lies because they are afraid."

My fingers clench.

Tremors coil through my arms.

Stabbing heat streaks down my legs.

The unwanted but familiar feeling of pain from an oncoming vision returns.

No. No. Please, no. Not with Sage. Hot tears race down my cheeks.

My knees buckle, and I crumple to the floor. The hallway spins upside down, and then everything turns black.

"That's my girl." Sage kneels beside me. "I believe you have what I've been waiting for, *mon petit trésor.*"

His voice drips into my soul, setting my blood on fire. Wrenching pain, worse than any before, sears my spine. Sage cradles me in his lap, hugging me against his chest that has no heartbeat. I kick, buck, and struggle to break free, but pain claws down my back. Sage clutches tighter than humanly possible, holding down my flailing arms. "Don't fight."

As the silver fog floods my mind, he runs an icy finger across my forehead, stopping at the temple. "There it is." His touch is burning acid against my skin. "That's right, *ma belle*. Show me. Show me what you see."

My eyes throb. They feel bound. Tethered. Something tugs inside my skull as if trying to rip my eyes out through my temples. I writhe. Sage holds me tighter. I taste his scent of ash and liquor as I scream my throat raw.

Cole, please, wherever you are, come find me. Use the knife. Kill me, now.

23

ABOUT MY FATHER

"You should eat something." A familiar soprano voice glides through pale light.

Silky white sheets stroke my cheek. They're scented like nectar, like the arbor, except for one sour note. My mind is hazy, drifting like the chiffon curtains that drape from the midnight-black ceiling, surrounding the plush bed I'm on. My body feels too heavy, every touch too sensitive. I feel as translucent and exposed as a message read and extracted from a painted canvas. Then my memory launches into warp speed: I'm with Sage. I had a vision. But I can't recall a single detail.

"I did the best I could to clean you up," a girl says.

I know that voice. Harper? No. Claire?

The corner of a black tray pushes the silky fabric aside. Then comes a familiar pixie-nosed face with curly hair corralled by a yellow headband. She's the shy girl with the severe limp from Hesperian, the one I rescued.

Juniper? I blink to be sure. Her once-round cheeks are gaunt. She looks older than when I found her hiding from the Legions less than a week ago. Only a week? I rub my eyes clear.

She sets the tray of breakfast on the bed. "Sage has clean clothes for you."

I glance at my puke-crusted tank top and then manage to sit up. "How did you survive the attack on Hesperian? And what are you doing *here*? You need to get out."

She lowers herself on the bed near my feet. "Sage isn't at all how they said. Look what he's done for me." She stretches with perfectly pointed toes.

"Juniper. Please tell me you didn't."

"The branding hurts a little, but it's not horrible." She tugs at her sweater. A red mark claws up her neck.

No. Oh please, no.

I rip back the sheets. "Why didn't anyone stop you?"

"They tried, but when Sage said I could be the one to heal your mom, that he'd leave the others at Hesperian alone, I just had to. I wanted to pay you back for, you know"—she absentmindedly rearranges the plates on the tray—"saving me."

"Juniper. No." I drop my head in my hands. In the back of my mind, there is a faint awareness a headache should be forming any minute now. They always do after a vision, but it's slow this time.

"But Sage said I'd be able to help your mother if I just . . ."

"Give him your power."

She nods brightly. "He'd heal me in return. Cera, I can walk normal. For the first time ever, I can dance!" Why didn't anyone stop her? Had I been there, I certainly would have. Her lip quivers as she looks at me. "You're not mad at me, are you?"

"Not at you." I take hold of her arm. There isn't any black mist seeping around her, which means Sage hasn't taken any of her powers. Yet. "Juniper, you need to leave this place. Get out of here before Sage siphons your powers."

Juniper rocks back, laughing as she sits crisscross style on the bed. "Sage won't to do that to me. He'll restore me once you help him. He's shared so much about the Alliance." Her expression turns sour. "About how they were holding you captive and using you. Turning you against him. Can you believe they wanted to harm him with the power from some gate, or maybe it was a wall? I can't remember. Anyway, he was expecting it."

Juniper leans forward with just as much excitement as she did in the girls' room at Hesperian. "He talks so much about you. Said he couldn't stand the way the Alliance was treating you. That if you hadn't found a way to escape, and if they tried their plan, that he would have . . . I know it sounds bad, but he would have killed everyone." She throws her hands out wide. "Just to protect you. He really cares about you. He has it out for a cocky Blade that killed one of his Cormorants. He was worried that Blade would try and hurt you. But I told Sage you were smart and how you went against the rules and found me. I told him that you'd find a way to escape."

I'm deflated with defiling shame. Not just with everything Juniper is saying, but because I don't know what information I've leaked to Sage when he intercepted the vision. I'm so glad that I didn't peer inside the third realm when I had the chance.

"Once you help Sage, I'll be healed." Juniper plucks her collar away from her neck.

"Juniper, I'll never agree to help Sage."

Her hopeful expression falls. "But I did this all for you. So I could help your mother . . ."

"I'm thankful, really I am, but . . ."

"But what?" Juniper stands, her eyes hard. "You'll leave me like this?" She scratches the red ring on her neck. Steam rises from her flesh. She winces. "I thought it would stop hurting by now."

A lump jams inside my throat. "I can't fix it. You turned against the Alliance. What you've done, it's irrevocable."

"But it's not! When Sage has the power to restore, he'll heal me."

How could she be so naïve? "Sage wants my help to destroy all Awakened, and I can't. I won't."

"He only wants you to tell him what you see. What's the harm of that? Cera, if you side with the Alliance and they harm Sage, I'll never be restored. I'll die too."

I take her hand. It's cold. "You're not going to die," I tell her. "I'm getting you out of here. What time is it?"

"Close to sunrise."

I push off the bed. "Where are my mother and Cole?"

The door slides open. I stiffen at the sound.

"They're in the guest suites," says Mark's raspy voice. Not Sage, thankfully. "It would have been a lot easier if you had brought the drawings in the day I asked you to. We could have avoided this mess." He touches his lopsided face. "All the attacks, the death of your father, that never had to happen."

The death of who? "My father?" I barely breathe. "That happened years ago."

"That's easy to believe," Mark says wryly. "Truth is, your father thought coming back to Sage would keep you safer than if he stayed around. Sage had him protected here until recently."

My chest hurts. This has to be another lie. A way to get information about the Well. I scrutinize Mark, but he looks sincere as he staggers into the room. "When Sage decided he no longer needed him, and believed your father had plans to warn you, he siphoned all his power to get information about you. You sensed it, didn't you? Something about your father in Sage? That's what siphoning does. Gives Sage all your memories, your knowledge, and your essence so he can use that to his advantage."

I teeter as the black walls close in on me. My father has been alive all this time. My father was working with Sage. My father was . . . protecting me? That has to be another lie. My father called me a monster. He walked out and left Mom and me on our own, struggling to survive.

Numbness takes hold as Mark's words sink in. Sage siphoned my father's powers so I would yearn for him. My father's essence is why Sage's voice, his touch, was so familiar. I bite my lip to keep it from quivering. To keep from throwing up.

Black steam billows around Mark's feet. "Sage left to prepare a surprise for you. He will be back in an hour or so and wants you to be ready when the sun comes up. Says it's a big day."

Sage would think so. Born at seven in the morning, I turn seventeen by sunrise. My Dissenting powers will be fully manifested by then, and I will be able to unlock the realms.

"Look," Mark's tone changes. "I could distract the Legions for a while. Cormorants too. If you chose to—"

"She's not leaving." Juniper marches toward Mark. "She's going to restore me."

"There is no restoring, kid. That's all a lie," Mark hisses at her.

"No, it's not," she insists. "Look how Sage—"

"That's what he does to get you to agree. It only lasts until he needs more for himself. You're not special, or needed, or whatever lie he used to fool you. Get out while you're still whole enough."

I narrow my eyes at him. This has to be a trick. A setup of some sort. "Why would you help me?" My leaving could be precisely what Sage wants. But even if I left, where would I go?

Half of Mark's face is smoking as it droops. "You don't believe me, I get it. I wouldn't believe me either. But nobody does what you did—stopping Sage from siphoning me like that."

Juniper gasps.

"So thank you." Steam rises from his throat. "Listen, I know what he plans on doing to your mother to get you to agree. It's painted in Fuseli's *Nightmare*." My heart seizes. I can't let my mother become like the woman sprawled on the bed in an alabaster gown, nearly dead, as the beast siphons her powers away.

"If I were you, I'd run and hide out as long as possible," Mark tells me. "But know that Sage is patient. If he doesn't get what he's after this time, he'll try again, taking centuries if he has to. Each battle brings him more knowledge and one step closer until, eventually, he wins the war." Mark coughs, steam rises from the skin around his throat. "I can give you thirty minutes, forty tops. Keys are in the car."

I'm still not convinced—not sure who to trust.

Getting out seems too easy.

But then Milton nudges me. *"Thou mayst believe and be confirmed / Ere thou from hence depart, know I am sent / To show thee what shall come in future days."*

This verse, where the angel Michael speaks to Adam, erases my skepticism. Not only has Milton guided me every step of the way, but there's an unmistakable kindness in Mark's single eye.

"But what will this cost you?"

He shrugs his one solid shoulder. "Nothing more than he's already taken."

I have one burning question. "Mark? My father, was he a . . ." I can't bring myself to say it.

"A Legion? No." Mark walks away, black mist trailing each step.

"I'll help any way I can," Juniper says, wiping her eyes. Any reservation she's had about leaving has vanished. She opens a closet stocked with designer clothes. "Change first. You don't want anything that might make your mom, you know, more ill." She crinkles her nose as I approach.

Wearing clothes picked out by Sage makes my skin crawl, but I can't have Mom sickened at the stench. The expensive outfits are warm and look as if they would fit disturbingly well. Juniper picks out crushed velvet pants and a top that's as close to a T-shirt as she can find. I draw the line with the shoes and keep my worn-out running ones instead. I tuck Gladys's pin in my new pocket, glad I didn't lose it again.

Without any details from last night's vision, I'm wandering blind, unsure of what Sage knows. Why did he leave me alone? Where will I go next? Even if this is part of Sage's plan, one thing is certain: Staying here won't do Cole or my mother any good.

Juniper leads me to the farthest corner of the hall. "This is it."

I hesitate. How does Juniper know the person in the room is really my mom? What if it's another elaborate ruse to lure me? She opens the door. The room is identical to the one I woke up in, with its black walls, gauzy curtains, and that caged portrait feeling. The curtains have been pushed aside and left open. She's there.

My mom is on the bed in an ivory gown, pale and unmoving. I collapse next to her. "Mama?" Her hands are burning hot. Her lips are slightly parted, her chest barely rising. But her lavender scent remains.

I take her hand. "I'm so sorry. I didn't know. I'm sorry I left you." I curl up beside her, not letting go. She doesn't respond. I stifle a sob. I can't break down. Not now. I sit up.

Be brave and stay focused, the way Pop said I should. Time is running out fast. I try lifting her, but I'm not strong enough.

"She's sedated," Juniper says. "It's better for her healing. I traded knowledge of Harper's elixir, the Gloss, in exchange for . . ." Her voice falters. "But it didn't do much to take away the fever. I tried." She digs in her pocket. "You might want to have this. I found it pinned inside her shirt when they brought her to Hesperian. I only kept it because I was trying to match Harper's flowers to the one on the locket. Gladys said that flower is rare and has a strong healing power." She hands me a small charm that is hooked through a safety pin. The flower, the style, the humming metal, are the exact same as Gladys's hairpin that I have tucked in my pocket. Both pieces match the tiny flower that glows in the arbor.

I inspect the locket I never knew Mom owned. "It's Lonicera," Juniper tells me, "the Winter Beauty honeysuckle but modified somehow, maybe even crossed with the Goldflame variety." She touches my mom's cheek with the back of her hand. "Harper didn't leave any of her serum for me to copy, or else I would have matched the ingredients and made some to heal your mom."

"You could make more?"

"It would take me a bit of time, and I'd need a vial to sample."

I stand. "Where is Cole?"

Juniper blushes. "Down the hall."

I check ahead as we rush through the corridor. Mark has been true to his word about keeping the creatures away—so far.

"I'll handle Cole. You pack anything you think we'll need."

I mentally map the path back to Mom's room. I'm not sure how much time has gone by, but Mark only gave me forty minutes, tops.

"And go where? This is the only safe place."

"It's not safe for any of us. I'll find somewhere we can hide until I can figure things out."

"Hesperian might work. Everyone's gone, but most of the building is standing. If Harper left her ingredients and I had the vial, I could make the serum a lot faster."

It's not a great plan, but it's the only one we have, and our window to escape is closing fast.

Juniper stops at a cloudy door. "He's in here."

"Go on. I'll get Cole to help us." Especially since I don't know how to drive and I doubt Juniper can.

As I slide the door open, Juniper touches my arm, stopping me. "I have to let you know, there's no chance for him. Sage made it clear he needs him and won't let him leave. He's probably dissented by now."

My heart drops.

Please don't let that be true.

24
THE FALL

The room is steeped in grim darkness. Sloppy notes from a drunken cello mingle in the cloudy air. The sticky haze tastes of bitter sugar and a tangy herb I can't place.

"Cole?" I accidentally kick something glass across the floor as I frantically search for the light switch.

"Lights up," Cole slurs with the waking flicker. He's playing a flirty melody, but the sound is choppy and broken.

A spinning bottle slows, then stops, pointing at the sleek curtain. I fling the fabric aside.

The music stops. The raspy strings cringe under the sliding bow of Cole's slack hand. He slouches in a chair with a white cello between his knees, shirtless, wearing a pink scarf. No, it's a sweater that probably belongs to one of the two girls surrounding him. A blonde girl lies passed out at his feet. A brunette with a bearcat tattoo running under her low-riding tank top kneels on the bed. Both have red marks around their necks.

Cole's glassy eyes rise to meet mine. "Hey, gorgeous." He pokes the bow in my direction.

"Cole. It's time to go." I hope my voice doesn't sound as shaky as my insides.

"Watch this." Cole mocks a serious expression as he runs the bow across one string, playing a deep, sustained note. Bearcat cranes her neck, her face recoiling at the noise, disoriented somehow. The scrawny blonde stays passed out. Cole releases the bow with a high-pitched laugh as Bearcat returns to her kneeling position. "Crazy."

I'm not sure what's he's doing or why, but we don't have time. "Cole. Let's go. Now."

Bearcat climbs off the bed to massage his shoulders. The tattoo of the cat's tail tracks down her right arm. "He's staying with me." She runs a hand through his hair, pulling his head back, and kisses him, upside down. Disjointed notes stumble as Cole drops the cello. It falls to the floor, snapping off the bridge. The loose strings wobble. Broken.

My stomach hardens.

"Cole, stop." I will my voice to be strong. The bitter air tastes thicker. "We need to leave."

"You promised something," Bearcat says, whispering in his ear, but her glassy eyes are fixed on me.

Cole stares beyond the ceiling with a lazy smile. "I did." Not a question.

"Uh-huh," she says. The sweater loosens from around his neck. There isn't a Dissenter's mark. Thankfully.

"It doesn't hurt," she nibbles his ear. "Just a vow. A single breath. Then one secret. After that, you get whatever you want."

Cole leans into her advances.

"No!" I shout, leaping over the scrawny girl to take Cole's hand. Scrawny wakes up and claws my ankles, keeping me back. I kick at her. "Cole, get up."

Cole's eyes barely open. What kind of cocktail did he take? There's got to be a way to get him clearheaded. "Cole, where's the serum?" There's not enough for both him and my mother, but I won't let him dissent. And unless he's lucid, I'm not sure how I'll get everyone out and escape in time.

"In my pocket." His laugh is so light it's alarming. Bearcat kisses his neck, stealing his attention.

I rub away a headache forming at my temples. "Cole. Come on. We need to go. Please."

Bearcat growls at me. An actual growl. Like a dog. Stringy saliva drips from the corner of her red lips. What has Sage done to her? It's like she's not human anymore. There's no way I'll let Sage do the same to Cole. She takes a cigarette burning on a table nearby. "He's not leaving. Right, babe?" She takes one long drag, then blows it into his mouth with another kiss.

"Back off and leave him alone!" That greedy power leaps up within me as I release the booming words. I reach for his arm, hanging limp at his side. Bearcat swipes my wrist but is about three inches from contact.

Cole coughs. Scrawny, lying on the floor, stumbles to her feet, holding onto to the wall and any furniture she can find, as she walks out of the room. Bearcat's face contorts. Her hands shake, fighting to stay locked on Cole.

I can control Dissenters? I knew about Legions, but . . .

I'm seized with momentary panic. If this is another one of Sage's powers, this close to my birthday, I just tapped into it. My six-word command might have joined the realms. But does it matter? I'm nowhere near the Well. And I have to do whatever it takes to keep Cole from dissenting. "Get your hands off of him, and get out!" The release feels incredible, a surging adrenaline coursing through me, making me feel invincible.

Bearcat jerks back, hissing. Fighting. Mauling the air. But she lets go. Insatiable strength rises in me with every command. "Now get out!"

Her hands swing the air, fighting to break free of my control. Her rabid eyes are locked on me as she backs away against her will. But somehow, she breaks from whatever control my words had on her and launches at me with a guttural roar, claws extended.

I shift. Thick air swooshes across my throat. She hits the wall, recovers, and claws at me again. This time she catches my shirt.

"A girl fight?" Cole wilts onto the bed. His knife, the one with the handle carved like twine falls out from inside the hem of his pant leg.

Bearcat springs at me with unnatural speed. We collide. My elbow to her temple. Her fist punching a sharp blow to my ribs, knocking me on the bed. The pain shocks me. I want to cry, but raging fire detonates in my core instead. I lift my knees and kick my heels into her stomach as she attacks again.

She's driven backward as her head hits the wall. She slides to the ground, knocked out. I'm shaking. I didn't mean to hurt her. I only wanted her to leave Cole alone. He's half on the bed, half on the floor, eyes closed. I shake him awake. The room warps. "Cole, wake up. We have to leave now." My tongue feels swollen.

I need the serum. Cole needs the serum. Where is it? I tug at his pocket.

Cole paws at my face, laughing.

"Stop." I dodge his touch and fish out the vial. "What did you take?"

"Nothing."

"Don't lie to me. How much, Cole, an entire bottle? Two? And what else?"

His fierce eyes turn a deep basil-green. "I don't lie, Blighty. I didn't take any of it."

In this state, how can I believe him? I shove the serum in his hand. "You need this."

Cole pushes himself upright. "You know the one thing I need?" He wrestles away the sheets and somehow gets to his feet. I stand, ready to help him. I'm not sure how much good the serum will do if he falls, hits his head, and passes out.

Cole staggers. "The Alliance kept me behind the Wall, locked up like a prisoner, when all I wanted was to see my family.

I want"—he holds up a tattooed finger—"one visit to tell them I am sorry for being such a screwup and making their life hell. That was it. One chance to do something right for a change. Be worth something. Belong somewhere. Maybe even make them proud, so they'd no longer be ashamed of me." He drops his head. "But I even messed up with you. Couldn't stand up to fight when it counted."

"You can still get that chance if we leave now. We'll hide at Hesperian. But I need your help—"

"I'm not a hero, Blighty. I'm a freakin' letdown. Always have been. Always will be. It's the only thing I do well. So why mess with people's expectations?" He sinks onto the bed.

I lower myself beside him. Cole needs to snap out of this. Our time is running out. "You're not a letdown, and you know it. You helped me when no one else would. You just settle for less and won't let anyone see your true heart. Don't give up. You're worth the fight. You just don't believe it." I don't know if any of my slushy words are making it through his stupor, but I have to try.

Cole's smirk mocks me. "I'm good at jacking with people, Blighty. Take your serum. Go."

Instead, I take his face in my hands and burn a laser stare into his eyes. "You're better than this."

He runs a clumsy finger over my lips. "Your optimism is cute."

"My optimism is getting us out of this place." Now my words sound slurred too. Wow, I'm lightheaded. I cough. The walls turn sideways. "Cole?"

"Yeah." His wildfire scent magnifies as he leans in. His forehead meets mine. Why am I not shying away? I should. But I like the way he nuzzles my ear. The way his wanting lips find their way to mine. He's nothing like that other guy . . .

I suck in a deep breath of air.

Air.

Something's in the air.

I lean back. Cole's glossy eyes beam. Hopeful. Expectant.

His face warps. The sparkling lights overhead glisten like giant diamonds ready to fall from the sky. This isn't right. I'm not right.

I force my rubbery hand to slap his face away. "Get it together, and don't breathe." I hold my breath.

Cole rubs his cheek, stunned. Then spits out a loud laugh. "You slapped me."

"Yeah, and I'll do it again. We need to get out."

His eyes widen at something looming behind me. "Cera, look—"

Something slams into the back of my head. I collapse onto Cole, taking him down with me. His head *thunks* into the nightstand as we crash between it and the bed.

My head throbs. I blink. A blurry Bearcat stands over me. She growls with bloodstained lips and raises a broken lamp over her head one more time.

Someone calls my name. A distant voice, firm and confident, tugging me back to consciousness. Light shines too brightly. I wince as a splitting headache ignites. I'm lying on the floor. Someone's heavy arm drapes over me. He's facedown, shirtless, and passed out.

"Cera?" they call out again. My heart pumps faster. I know that voice. I slowly roll my head to the side, toward the tilted doorway. And he's there. Standing with gorgeous, raging blue eyes in that fitted T-shirt and black denim jacket. My pulse riots through my veins.

"California?" My throat cracks. That's his name, right? Doesn't sound right, but it's the only name I remember.

He sees me on the floor with . . . I lift my head. Ouch. That hurts. I lower it.

California flings the guy's arm away from me. The heavy weight releases my lungs. I cough. California kneels beside me. His fingers slide through my tangled hair and lift my head, gently. "Drink this."

He touches a tiny glass vial to my lips. The sweet liquid drains into my mouth, washing out the bitterness, and burns down my sore throat. I swallow. Cough. The top of my head throbs. I reach up, but California stops me. "Don't touch it. You'll only feel worse." He rocks me forward so I'm sitting upright. "You okay?"

I nod. Wince. Ouch, that hurts. No, I'm not okay.

He slides his arms around me, helping my feet find the floor. I think I'm standing. The swaying room dances without music. Or maybe I'm the one swaying. I slump into his chest and close my eyes, but the world won't stop spinning. Faces blur in my whirling memory. The only image I grasp is . . . "My mom."

"They're getting her." He urges me to take a step. "C'mon."

"But . . . him." My hand is too heavy to point at the guy on the floor.

"Someone else will get Cole. But you and me, we need to go."

"Maddox!" A sharp voice cuts through my haze. His name is Maddox? Oh, that's right. Why'd I call him California? I laugh lightly.

"We need to get you out now." He whispers into the curve of my ear. I smile.

"Who did you find?" The harsh voice belongs to the serious guy I hate. The one that smells like metal. I frown.

"Leave her with me. Get back to the car with the others." Metal guy scowls. I scowl back.

"I'll get her downstairs." Maddox tightens his arm around

me. "Foster said I needed to stay within range in case she has any visions. You get Cole."

Metal guy hesitates, then says, "Fine. Take her downstairs. But wait for me." He doesn't look happy about it. Then he sees Cole on the floor and a knife nearby. "Take this just in case." He tosses the weapon on the bed for Maddox and then mutters to Cole. "This is the second time I've rescued you from Sage, buddy." He inspects Cole's neck. "If it weren't for the note you left Maddox, you'd be dead." In one swoop he flings Cole over his shoulder. A thought sluggishly forces its way through my brain. Cole left a note for *Maddox*?

"Cera, let's go." Maddox tucks the knife in his belt. My eyelids suddenly weigh too much. I rest my cheek against his chest. The world spins so fast, I feel like I'm free-falling, but Maddox feels safe.

Next thing I know, Maddox scoops me up. I nestle my nose against his neck and breathe his ocean scent—no, he smells like rain. Like a wild storm.

"Maddox? I'm sorry." I'm not sure what for, but the words feel right.

My head rises and falls in sync with his deep breath. After what seems like forever, he says, "Let's get you back." His soft voice doesn't rumble the way it does when he's mad. I'm glad. I float as he carries me through the murky hall, the long corridor, and down the stairs.

Everything is quiet except for the waterfall where the water flows . . . red? I lift my head. Juniper is sprawled on the floor, facedown and unmoving. Her curly hair is wet with blood. Dead. Another body drowns in the bottom of the fountain beside her. A cattail tattoo runs up the lifeless arm.

"Maddox!" Gray's voice shoots up from the garage stairwell.

Maddox rests his forehead against my temple and murmurs, "Stay quiet. I'm taking you home."

"Hesperian?"

He doesn't answer as he opens the glass door with his fingers, holding me secure. The image of a lifeless Juniper is all I can see. Any remaining strength evaporates. I huddle in Maddox's arms and close my eyes as he carries me into the dawn.

25

REENTRY

I jolt awake as the motorcycle's underbelly scrapes the concrete with a hard bounce. The sun is still asleep and the air smells like snow. My nose nuzzles the back of . . . I lift my head. Maddox? I don't remember getting on the bike, and I certainly don't remember putting on his jacket or being tethered to his waist with a thick vine. In fact, I don't remember much at all.

A single headlight illuminates our path through the soggy forest. I lean back. Maddox entwines his fingers with mine, holding them against his stomach to keep me close. I nestle behind him, staying warm as our bodies vibrate with the roaring engine.

"We've been lucky so far, but watch for Legions," Maddox shouts.

Legions. Cormorants.

Icy wind slashes my hair in my face. Foggy memories swirl, trickling in with a splitting headache: Mom lying in a bed. Then there was Cole. We kissed. I fell to the ground.

I lean and peer over Maddox's shoulder. Blurry taillights glow through the dim road ahead. Two? Maybe three cars? It's hard to tell. And so is any evidence of black mist possibly creeping between the inky treetops. The air, however, is tinted with ash, but it's so faint it could be burnt engine oil.

"What did—" I can't form the rest of the question. My lips are too frozen, and my mind's not fully awake.

"We're almost back. Devon has your mom in the car up ahead. Lina will heal her. Don't worry."

Cole's expectant expression whips through my hazy mind. His face so close. His glassy eyes, hopeful. "And Cole?"

Maddox's body tenses. After a brief silence he says, "He's also in the car." His tone is flat. I lean my forehead onto his back. I know I messed up. Believe me, I know. And to make matters worse, Milton jabs me with Adam's lament on the fall.

Good lost, and evil got . . .
Cover me ye pines,
Ye cedars; with innumerable boughs
Hide me—

I know. I *know.* If I could hide away forever, I would.

Bruising dawn peers through the barren treetops as we rocket down the dirt path. Something wet splatters on my legs, sinking through the designer velvet. Probably mud.

So far, the forest appears clear of mist. Clear of creatures. My mind rises from the fog of the drugs. Our getaway seems too easy. Sage probably wants me to go back to the Estate. He said he orchestrated every part of my being with the Alliance, and how I fell right into his plans. He most likely gave Mark the window to let us go, knowing I'd save my mother at any cost.

Panic roars through my veins. Sage wants me back in the Garden. He needs me close to the Well.

"Maddox—stop!" I pound my hand into his stomach. "I can't go back."

"Don't listen to the lies." Maddox keeps a tight grip on my hand. "Sage wants to confuse you. Make you doubt." Another bike engine roars up from behind. Maddox lets go and grabs both handlebars. "Hang on. It's Gray." I wrap both arms around him as we pick up speed.

Sure enough, a stone-faced Gray pulls up beside us and stabs the air with his finger, signaling for Maddox to pull over.

Maddox leans forward and guns the engine. I hold onto him with my life. In the distance, two amber lights hang like fallen stars. We're approaching the gate at terrifying speed.

Gray signals again, his shout drowned out by the dueling engines. We fly faster toward the gate. Gray veers off road, cutting through the underbrush, racing as though he's done this a thousand times.

Cars line up waiting to enter the Estate. Maddox has to slow down. Better yet, he needs to turn around and get me as far from the Garden as possible. I tug on his arm, but I'm sapped of strength from whatever drugs Sage had piped through the vents. "Maddox, please." My weak words get lost in the belligerent wind.

Right then, Gray shoots out in front, cutting us off. Maddox swerves. The engine grinds and then sputters. The back wheel locks, and Maddox wrestles the bike upright as we skid across the graveled road. Heading straight for the Circuit Wall.

Dust flies. Rocks sling.

I squeeze Maddox and bury my head to swallow a scream. He swerves into the bushes and somehow stops the bike inches from a thick tree.

I'm shaking as Maddox frantically unties the vine at his waist, with me still gripping him tight. As the cord slackens, he leans the bike so I can bail off. "You okay?"

"I'm good." A bold-faced lie. My legs are wobbly, and any minute now I'll burst into tears. Despite all that, I manage to get off on my own. Black oil is splattered on my trembling legs.

Devon's car rolls through the gate. So do the others, a parade of glowing taillights slowly disappearing over the hill of the misty gray light from the predawn sky. Mom and Cole are now safe inside the Garden.

As Maddox dismounts, Gray marches over. His scowl is

washed in the menacing blue hues of morning shadows. "You deliberately disobeyed me! I told you to take her to the car. Instead you steal my—" When he glances at the oil covering the back wheel, his face shades a deep scarlet. "You trashed my bike?"

"Cera, get inside the Garden." Maddox holds his hands to the side, shielding me from Gray. "Go now."

The gate lies thirty feet away. An easy sprint to safety where Pop waits, lantern in hand. But this is exactly what Sage wants. "I can't—"

Gray shoves Maddox's arm aside. "She's not going back. I have orders."

"So do I." Maddox is firm.

"I can't go back!" I start down the road, frantic to get as far from the open gate as possible, but Gray lunges for me.

"Back off!" Maddox punches Gray square in the jaw.

Gray stumbles, shocked. Maddox launches at Gray again, landing an uppercut to his chin. Another to his head. Then his gut. Side. Ribs. Spleen. He strikes so fast, unleashing with such fury, Gray can't strike back.

I choke at every hit as Milton whispers, *"Waked by the circling hours, with rosy hand / Unbarred the gates of light . . . with such impetuous fury smote, / That, whom they hit, none on their feet might stand."*

Lines from the war in Heaven, tearing the world apart.

Gray finally collects himself enough to deliver a solid drive to Maddox's stomach. Maddox staggers but stays upright, panting, pacing, knuckles bright red.

"Look what she's done to you." Gray spits blood on the ground. He pins his glare on me, his knife drawn. "Stop pretending she's Malee. She's not even close."

The sky flushes with a waking copper light. A distant shriek carries on the wind. I look up. So does Gray. And in that split second, Maddox jumps Gray, knocking the Steel from his hand.

They wrestle to the ground, fists flying.

I scream for them to stop. They don't hear me over their heated words, vicious hits, and stifled grunts.

The Cormorant grows closer. Louder.

I grab a broken tree branch, ready to bash Gray on the back, but Blades sprint out from behind the gate with knives drawn. One of them knocks me back, and I fall into a prickly bush. Each breath stabs with fierce pain.

But the brothers have stopped fighting. Both of them rest on the ground, bloody and spent. Gray wipes the blood from his nose. "Lance, get Maddox inside the gate. Now."

Maddox pushes off the ground. He manages to stand on his own, but he's scraped and bleeding. His eyes find me in the shadows.

Lance takes Maddox by the arm. "Let's get you inside." He checks the sky. "Something's on the way."

Fire burns in Maddox's eyes. "Get Cera inside first." He wrestles what little fight he has left, but Lance manages to drag him through the gate with the help of a red-bearded Blade.

Another shriek carries on the wind. They all need to get inside the gate, and fast.

I sit up. My side hurts. I can only take shallow breaths. "Gray." My voice is raspy and weak. "Get behind the gate."

Gray finds his knife in the dirt and dusts it off, not listening. He staggers my way.

I scramble to my feet with hands out in front of me. "Gray, listen to me, please." Something moves deep within the woods behind him. Not the Cormorant. A black shadow. Not misted. Something else entirely. "Please get inside the Garden and shut the gate right now."

Gray holds his knife out to the side, twisting it slowly as he approaches. "I've got a promise to keep."

Everyone else is safe behind the gate. Pop is in position, ready to close it.

Treetops rustle. Branches break.

"There's a creature behind you," I say, trying to stay upright. The shadow moves closer. Through the misted gray light of the forest, it looks to be the gorilla-like beast, the one in Martin's painting. His goat horns are pulled back, low against his elongated forehead, watching our every move. Milton whispers the description of the archfiend, *"With head uplift above the wave and eyes / That sparkling blazed."*

The beast's eyes widen as they meet mine. They are blazing. Flickering, in fact. Flickering with gold flecks, just like Sage's . . .

"Gray. Get inside now." I take too deep a breath and grab my side.

Gray pays me no mind. He steps closer. "You don't give orders around here."

I hold up a hand—stupid I know, but it's the only shield I have against him at the moment. "Sage is here. Get inside. Close the gate, quickly." I'm practically pleading with him. But he won't listen.

"You'd want me to think so, wouldn't you? Take one look over my shoulder so you can run back inside." He adjusts the knife in his hand.

Run? I can barely stand. "The last thing I want is to be inside the Garden. Not now." A caramel sunrise lights the sky as a Cormorant cries nearby. Maddox shouts from somewhere behind the gate. Lance and Red Beard must have him restrained. Good.

Gray spins the Steel, unconvinced.

Sage fixates on Gray—the cocky Blade who killed a Cormorant—the one Sage wants to destroy. The one standing here threatening me now.

The beast raises a black hand, twisting three fingers, aiming for Gray. For his knife. A red spark kicks off the beast's fingertips.

"Toss the knife!" I slam Gray's wrist.

The Steel flies out of his grip. Red lightning strikes the

tumbling weapon in midair. On impact, a roaring fireball ignites the forest.

We both hit the ground.

The Steel sizzles on the forest floor, not ten feet away. Sparks kick off the blade.

Seconds later, Moloch screeches through the forest. Branches harpoon the ground. The beast circles above the scant treetops, ripping apart thick boughs, launching them at me—no, at Gray. Gray is less than five feet from me. His determined expression is now ashen.

"Go!" I tell Gray as I push to my feet. I search the surrounding woods for Sage. He's gone? No, he wouldn't leave. Not when he's this close to the Well with the gate wide open, and me, standing so close that one command will give him what he wants. But where did he go?

A branch whirs near me. Gray rolls, dodging a hit, getting closer to the knife. The weapon isn't hard to spot. A circle of white dust surrounds the glowing Steel. Gray hesitates before taking the knife, then uses his jacket sleeve to pick up the smoking weapon.

By now Moloch has cleared enough branches to get through. I still can't find Sage. Maddox is shouting. Moloch is screeching. With a few swift steps, Gray can make it into the Garden before Moloch reaches the ground.

"Gray, please run!" I plead.

Gray crouches. For a split second, his eyes meet mine. Then Moloch sends down a thick bough, pinning Gray to the floor. As if that didn't secure him, the beast harpoons another thin branch into Gray's upper arm. Gray cries out in pain. Moloch leaps to the forest floor, blocking the gate. I spin around. Searching for Sage. For more beasts. For an army of Legions. But only Moloch, Gray, and I remain outside the gate.

I controlled Moloch just a few hours ago, but as sunrise bursts through treetops, an insatiable stirring awakes inside me. I'm brimming with an even greater consuming desire to command Moloch to back away. Three little words hang on my tongue with a familiar sweetness, begging me, urging me to speak. I'm wrought with an itch to use a power that I know can save Gray's life. But the consequences are too great.

Moloch's talons dig into the decomposing leaves. He takes one hop closer. His lion head juts forward, straining to find its prey as Gray writhes, working to push the branch off his chest.

Maddox shouts my name from inside the Garden. The Blades hold him back. Which is good because his brother isn't doing so well out here with me. Bright blood oozes on the ground, mixing with white ash. What can I do? Nothing but a knife will kill that beast.

Two Blades brave enough to leave the Garden dart out. Moloch takes them down, one by one, swiping a talon across their chests. He easily snaps their necks with his jaws and flings their lifeless bodies deep into the woods as if play toys. With each kill, he moves closer to Gray. No one else dares to leave the safety of the Garden.

Moloch hovers right above his target. Warring powers collide inside me. A sick, dark part of me enjoys how Gray writhes. But the stronger part knows I can't let him die. Even someone like Gray.

What do I do?

If I command Moloch to back away, this close to the Well, I'll connect the realms. And the gate is still open. The Legions have arrived, and they'll be sure to rush through. Sage's army inches closer, hiding in the black mist that now hovers in the ash-scented woods. Everything will be just as Sage planned.

Gray cries out, pitching his Steel at Moloch. Despite his trembling hand, the weapon whirs with arrow-like precision, landing in Moloch's chest. The beast stumbles back with a bloody cry, but only for a moment. It cranes its ghastly head, ripping the knife from the wound with its jagged teeth and spitting it out of sight. Black blood oozes from the cut. The beast's eyes narrow into slits. Hot breath steams between his curled lips and bared canines.

There's only one thing I know how to do. It's suicidal. But it's the only thing I do well.

I run.

With every ounce of strength in me I run straight for Moloch. I leap over Gray and throw all my weight into the beast, screaming as I dig my shoulder into his breastbone, a full tackle into the wound. His skin slimes against my cheek and oozes all over Maddox's jacket.

The beast hops back. How can this monster be a fragment of the splintered Ayala that Sage loves so much? Moloch stretches his—no, probably her—neck and releases a thunderous squawk, rattling the ground.

I stand my ground and choose each word carefully. "I'm not letting him die."

Moloch swats a talon, but doesn't come close to striking me. She won't kill me. Not as long as Sage needs me. But I'm still cautious, because that doesn't mean she won't hurt me in the process.

"I'll get you behind the Circuit Wall," I tell Gray from over my shoulder. "Help me get that branch off of you. Then get inside and close the gate." Gray's stoic expression gives no indication that he's listening. But as a frigid wind kicks up a dust cloud around us, Gray and I lift the bough off his chest, together. I'm careful to stay between him and Moloch.

The ground shakes as creaking, twisting metal signals the gate is closing.

"Stay behind me," I tell Gray. "I'll stay out here. You close the gate. And whatever happens, keep Maddox inside the Garden. Protect him. Please."

Gray's eyes meet mine. His haughty expression fades, then he scrambles to his feet without a word and stays behind me. Relief floods me. He's listening.

I face Moloch with arms spread wide. Gray probably has another knife hidden in his jacket and could stab me in the back any minute, but that's a chance I'll take. I circle around Moloch. Gravel crunches under Gray's footsteps, offbeat with mine as we inch closer to the gate.

A ridge of feathers rises on Moloch's back. Those yellow eyes narrow once again. I tune out all sound and lock eyes with Moloch, watching for any sudden moves while my peripheral vision scans for any sneak attack from another beast.

Gray's footsteps scuffle and then stop. "I'm in."

I won't turn to be sure, but out of the corner of my eye, the Circuit Wall throws sparks. Not enough to heat the air, but the same way Gray's knife sizzled with tiny pops. "Close the gate!" I shout. "Now!"

The gate creaks and grinds. I ignore Maddox as he yells for me to run. Moloch purrs and clicks. Teeth bared, the creature inches closer to the gate. But the opening should be too narrow for Moloch to enter by now. I risk a glance to be sure but quickly swing my attention back to the shrieking beast. I'm startled as Moloch springs into the air at that moment. Her talons are reaching out, coming right toward me.

There's no time to shift out of the way. Moloch will gouge out my heart, unless I leap backward. But if I do, I'll hit the gate and splinter into a dust cloud.

Moloch's wings beat the air. Fangs drip with black blood. The razor-sharp claws aim for my chest. Death by splintering dust cloud suits me just fine.

I jump back, close my eyes, and accept my fate.

26
THE THREAT

Death feels like two strong arms wrapped around me, holding so tight, air can't find my lungs. Like panting breath against my ear, and Maddox's strained voice saying, "I've got you."

I open my eyes. Chaos erupts. The gate stalls. Throws more sparks. Biting wind whips through the opening too small for Moloch, but not a Legion.

"No, no, no!" I wrestle out of Maddox's arms, slipping out of the jacket. This is a mistake.

"It's okay. Calm down." The idiot grabs my wrists, pulling me further into the Garden. "It's me. Maddox." He holds my face in his hands. "You're through the gate, safe." His eyes are fixed on mine. Frantic. Angry. Terrified. Afraid. His emotions are a storm I can't quite make out.

"But you're not!" I twist and pull, but he's much stronger. "I can't be inside the Garden. Sage wants me here." He dodges my kicks.

He spins me around, clamping both of his arms around me. His breath labors close by my ear, and his heart is pounding. "Stop fighting me."

"I had a vision. Sage siphoned it. I can't remember any details. But my presence puts everyone in terrible danger. I have to leave!"

In our wrestling, Maddox has managed to get me to the base of the hill, away from the gate that remains several feet open.

"It won't close!" The baby-faced Blade takes the lantern from Pop. He struggles to work the light, waving it up and down and back and forth, over and over again. Sparks kick off the gate, but it refuses to seal shut. Ash-scented wind whisks through the opening—and with it comes the sound of angry bees.

A dense fog rolls across the forest floor, swallowing everything in its path. A pitchy sandstorm of Legions creeps toward the gate. No one notices. But they wouldn't know because they can't see the beasts in mist form. Only I can.

I fight to break away. "Let me go! That gate won't close if I'm inside. And Legions are coming. This is exactly what Sage wants!"

Maddox holds tighter. "Pop says the Well wants you here. So do I."

A strand of black fog breaks from the cloud and rockets toward the gate. The buzzing mist corkscrews through the air. Gray paces near the opening, shouting commands as he ties his wound with a piece of torn fabric. Lance and Red Beard help the baby-faced Blade with the lantern, as Pop stands nearby.

The mist soars through the gate, a sideways tornado. "There's a Legion inside!" I shout. The misted beast swirls, aiming for its target: Gray. I break away from Maddox. "Gray, strike above your head!" He stops pacing but doesn't listen to me.

Luckily, Lance does. He raises a fist and cuts at the air above Gray. Red embers explode into a spark shower as Steel and Legion collide.

"Felipe, shut that gate. Now!" Gray commands the baby-faced Blade. Then he glances at me and looks away.

"The Garden senses a threat." Pop rests both fragile hands on his cane as the wind billows through his flannel shirt. He stands too close to Gabriel and the exposed entry. Another Legion breaks from the cloud. This one comes in faster.

Maddox holds me back. "Stay by my side. Tell me when and where to strike. We'll fight together." Maddox pulls a knife from his belt. The one with the black handle, carved like twine. Cole's blade. He faces the violent wind with the weapon drawn.

"More are on the way," Maddox tells the others, his hair blown back as he moves toward the opening. Gray joins his side. Lance and Red Beard flank the inside of the gate as Felipe works the lantern.

Pop stays right behind Gabriel. He tilts his head as though looking intently at the blurry shadows dancing on the Circuit Wall, but he can't possibly see the honey-colored light shifting images on the warping air. Maybe this light is an aftereffect of the swirling drugs in my system, maybe a trick of the light in the Garden, or maybe the Current itself.

Gray takes the lead. His face is pale. Blood soaks through the fabric on his bicep as he struggles to stand against the raging wind. Perhaps we can take down two or three together, but not the rolling thundercloud that approaches. There's no way they can fight that bubbling mass on their own and survive.

My being here is the problem. Despite what Pop says the Well wants, leaving is the solution.

But I've made my decision too late. A Legion slips through the gate. "Gray, strike now!"

Gray swipes the air with a smooth cut. The creature squeals, exploding into tiny embers. A bigger stream of black mist launches from the cloud. Then another. Then a throng of them. "Six. Maybe seven more. Three chest level, three overhead. One down low." I count down their arrival. Three. Two. "Strike!"

Gray hits three. Maddox gets two. Lance explodes another one, but Red Beard gets hit in the chest. Gray spins and cuts the air, exploding the Legion, but it's too late. The Blade falls several feet in front of me, eyes open and slack-jawed. I slap a hand over my mouth and muffle a scream.

I didn't even know his name.

"Are there more?" Gray demands to know.

Fiery sunrise burns through the clouds. There are more. Too many. "They're swaying, holding form, preparing for another attack, but there's no way we can hold this many off."

"Felipe!" Gray shouts. "The gate."

"I'm trying!" The Blade is frantic.

"It won't close on its own." Pop grimaces. "Can't breach its own law. Gonna need to force it closed, or else we'll all die."

"Cera, how many more?" Maddox stands exposed at the entry. Gray and Lance circle near him. The entire cloud of Legions lines up. My stomach is queasy. "Over a hundred."

Gray shields Maddox from the opening. "Go get backup. Now!"

Pop leans into the violent wind as he shuffles forward. "Listen here." The top of Pop's round head only comes to Gray's bleeding bicep. "Go on and back up. I'll take care of the gate. Just be ready." He turns his head in my direction. "And Honey?"

"Yes, Pop?" I'm ready to do whatever he tells me. To use whatever I can to save the Alliance. To run out that gate, like I know I should.

His lips broaden into a smile. "Time for spring to rise."

That's not a directive. "Pop?" His name is drowned out by the fierce wind kicking through the opening, blinding us in a dust storm. I rush in his direction, aiming for the gate. Through the howling wind comes the growing sound of bees.

The wind rages as I race toward the opening. A Legion knocks me in the chest, sending me to the ground. Everything swirls in slow motion. Gray, Lance, Felipe, and Maddox fight the Legions as they pour inside the Garden like serpents sliding through cracks in a wall. Pop pushes hard against the wind.

"Pop!" I shout as he raises his cane with both hands lifted high over his head. "Pop, stop!" I scramble to my feet. He connects each end of his cane with the gate at the same moment

Legions strike his body. The air turns still for one breath. Then a bright light explodes like the midday sun, silhouetting and then eclipsing Pop. The earth quakes as I hit the ground.

Then ringing silence. The wind settles. A yellow leaf lands in front of me as I lie in the dirt, afraid to move. Afraid of what I'll see.

I manage the strength to look. Maddox was tossed a few feet away from me. He groans, barely moving. But alive. Gray and Lance are facedown in the dirt near the base of the hill. Also alive. But baby-faced Felipe . . . I look away.

The gate is closed as if never disturbed. The trees overhead shudder, then sit still. The scent of ash is replaced by the sweet arbor smell. Vibrant green leaves uncurl, sprouting to life with warp speed. Outside the Circuit Wall, in the barren winter, the Legions slowly retract—a creeping mist reeling back into the forest before disappearing altogether, leaving no sign of battle.

Pop did it.

I push to my knees and stand. "Pop?" Earth and blood mix on my tongue. His name rebounds through the piercing silence. Where he stood, shimmering dust dances in warm sunlight before drifting to the ground.

"Pop?" I look around. Muted clouds hide the sun.

Gray and Lance stir. Both sit up to survey the quiet gate. Maddox pushes to his knees. Deep sadness shadows his eyes.

No, Maddox. Don't look at me like that. Pop is here. He *has* to be here. He needs to shake that boney finger at me, telling me I'm being hotheaded. He needs to clear his raspy throat when I'm out of line. Toss seeds into the wind and remind me to believe. Please, Pop. You need to be here.

It's only when a yellow leaf falls that the truth sinks in. I collapse to the ground.

Pop is gone.

27

WORLDS COLLIDE

Lieutenant Foster sits across from me as my breath hitches and tears linger. I've recounted everything that Sage and the others revealed, including the artwork I can remember being in Sage's collection. I also divulge all the dualistic powers Sage claims I have as Maddox leans on the back of the couch near me. Gray paces near the globe when he should be with a Healer, or at least sitting down to keep the blood from seeping through the wound.

I'm waiting for Foster to chew me out. But he doesn't. He hasn't said a word about punishment, or what lies ahead. He makes no mention of Pop. The only words he has spoken have been to Lance, instructing him to call Devon and then to find the admiral and Council leaders who are viewing the Well.

"So you have no recollection of any details in your vision?" Foster now says, his voice controlled and even, without a trace of anger. I squirm, nonetheless. Punishment has to be coming. I ruined their plans, even though doing so saved them from Sage's counterattack.

I lower my head. The only images that come to mind are from the rising death toll: Juniper. Bearcat. Two Blades strewn somewhere outside the gate. Red Beard. Felipe. And Pop.

Maddox lays a gentle hand on my back. "I can extract it."

Gray stops pacing. "Once it's siphoned—"

"She's not an ordinary Seer. It's still there. I can sense it." Maddox's confidence gives me a bit of hope that maybe all isn't lost. "It just might take me time."

Gray frowns. "No. I don't want you to be a target."

For once the two of us agree.

"For what it's worth," I tell Foster, "I don't think Sage wants to destroy the Well."

"Of course you don't," Gray says sharply. "You're under his spell."

"He's not a warlock," I snap back. "He just knew my triggers the way Lieutenant Foster thought he would. Sage siphoned my father's powers long before I arrived, which gave him knowledge about me, keeping him one step ahead. It wasn't a coincidence that Sage was gone when you came. He *let* you go in. He didn't put up a fight until we came back to the Garden gate. He was watching from the woods. Even then, he attacked only when you threatened me."

Gray's jaw tightens. "You said it was a creature."

"Sage *is* the gorilla creature, shapeshifted. His eyes were the same. His fingers lit with a red spark aimed at your knife. He wanted to be sure I'd go through the gate because he knew it wouldn't close. He sent his Legions so I'd use my powers and bridge the realms to save"—I glance at Maddox—"to save everyone. Sage had every detail planned, just how you feared. But I don't think he expected Pop to close the gate." I swallow and look at Lieutenant Foster. "I never meant to cause the Alliance harm. I'm sorry. I know I don't have the right to ask, and I'll take whatever punishment you want to give me, but please, heal my mother. And Cole."

"They're with Lina," Maddox reassures me.

Gray crosses his arms. "What happens now that the gate is closed and both sides of her powers are fully manifested?"

Harsh voices come from the courtyard, headed in our direction.

The lieutenant quickly stands. "Go to Lina," he directs me. There is an unsettling urgency in his tone as he says, "I will call for you when we are ready. I need a word with the admiral."

Maddox walks me to the door, but Foster stops him from leaving. "Maddox, remain here. Devon may require your support. Grayson, remain as well. The admiral will expect a detailed account of events."

Foster assigns Grumpy as my escort and shuts the library doors.

After Lina wipes a few scrapes and checks the bump Bearcat stamped on my forehead with the bed lamp, she has me chew on a bitter herb that tastes of salty water. She makes no mention of Pop and the incident with the Circuit Wall, but her eyes are somber and her movements are weighted with quiet reverence.

Convinced that I've masticated the herb enough to cleanse whatever poison Sage pumped through the air vents while I was with Cole, she finally lets me spit out the giant wad. It's gross, but the residual haze in my mind is gone.

"*Venga.*" She motions to the back door. Go where?

I follow her through the wisteria grove, around the building where Gray had me locked in the cellar, and then over to another suite of rooms. Behind the second door, in a room gently lit by a bedside lamp, my mother is resting. Healing.

She lies under a light blue blanket. Her arms are tucked at her sides. I tremble as I watch for signs that she's breathing. Her chest barely rises and falls, but it's enough.

Lina places a cool cloth to Mom's forehead. *"Regreso en cinco minutos."* She motions to the clock by the door and holds up five fingers. Then she gathers a few supplies and walks out, leaving the door open. Grumpy stays stationed somewhere outside.

"Mom?" I whisper and sit in the chair, taking her hand. It's warm, but not hot. An encouraging sign that her fever is coming down. "I'm sorry I've hurt you all these years. I'm sorry I ran out. I've made so many mistakes." I rest my head on the bed, my cheek against the back of her hand, and inhale her lavender scent. It smells like home.

"Please get better." My words float in the silence like a sacred wish. Clean light from the open door streams into the room and her eyes flutter under her eyelids, so pale and translucent. I sit up, hopeful that she can hear me. "We'll go somewhere warm when this is over. You and me. We'll start over." Tears blur my eyes. "People are dying because of me, because of what I have the power to do. I don't know how to stop it. If we could talk things through, I know you'd tell me what I should do." I swallow. "Mama, I still need you. Please don't leave me. We'll find a way to get through this and be okay."

Mom's fingers twitch. I take her charm and Gladys's matching hairpin from my pocket. I secure the pin in her hair and place the charm in her palm, closing her fingers around it. She coughs.

"No running." It's barely a whisper through her blue lips.

I lean closer. "Mom?"

"Stay," she wheezes, choking on her own breath.

Stay here? That's impossible, but I won't argue with her. There's so much I'd rather say. "Mom, I didn't understand before. But now I know what you sacrificed for me. I want to change things for us. For you." I take the cloth from her forehead and blot her lips. "I know what I am. But I don't know what to do with *who* I am." I hesitate. I want to ask if she knew Dad was alive all this time, but the mere mention of his name might set her off.

"Don't be afraid." She closes her eyes and winces. She musters a breath. "I was."

The dirty rag wadded in my fist is as inadequate in soothing her pain as I am.

Swallowing takes her great effort. "I want to show you . . ." Her fingers search for something on the bed.

I take her hand again. Her fingernails, once manicured and polished to perfection, are chipped and yellow.

She struggles to hold out a small paper that has been tucked nearby.

It's a small photograph, turned facedown. The line from Byron's poem, "*she walks in beauty,*" is written in blue ink. The handwriting is too neat to be Mom's.

I turn it over, and my heart stills. It's my father and me. I'm sitting on his shoulders wearing my favorite periwinkle T-shirt with a sunbeam streaming from the clouds. A rainbow of blurry flowers blooms in the background as he holds my wiry legs around his neck, hiding his Dissenter's mark. My ponytail was messy even then. I'm smiling, my two front teeth missing. I don't remember his hair being caramel in the sunset. Or the scruff on his square chin. Or how much we look alike. The shape, the hazel color, the glint in his eyes, and mine, are the same. Even our smiles as we both laugh are strikingly similar.

No wonder Mom was so afraid. Our resemblance can't be denied.

I run my finger over the photograph. Despite the fact that he dissented, there's good in him too. It's written in the way he looks up as I flatten my little hands on top of his head.

Maybe Mark's words about him protecting me all these years were true. But even if not, for this brief moment caught on film, he did love me.

"Is this what you wanted to show me the day I ran out?"

"I wanted you to know." Her fingers search for mine.

"Mom." I clasp her hand. "You have to get better. Please. You're all I have."

Sunlight from the open door brightens the room with a warm glow. A shadow too tall to be Lina appears. Probably Grumpy telling me my time is up. I wipe my face dry.

"How's she doing?" Maddox hovers at the door with bloodshot eyes that won't look at me.

I tuck the thin blanket around Mom. "Resting."

"How about you? Holding up okay?"

I shrug and place the photo on the nightstand. "How's Devon?"

"With Foster."

As Maddox comes to the foot of the bed, I straighten Mom's collar and brush her hair back.

"Your mom is amazing. Everyone's talking about how she guarded you for so long. It's unreal."

"All this time I was hurting her and I didn't know it. She endured all that pain year after year without a Healer, all on her own."

"You're a lot like her."

"I'm nothing like her. But I wish I was," I say quietly. "Apparently I'm more like my father." I hold up the photograph. "I've spent my life fighting, trying not to be like Dad or the monster he said I was. I didn't want to prove his words true." My chest tightens as I look at Dad's smile. I dig deep to remember the sound of his laugh and what I did that made him love me in this one moment. "Maybe if I embrace my past as part of who I am, and stop fighting it, then maybe I'll stop messing up and more people won't get hurt." I watch my mom breathe. "All I know is that I'm afraid of losing anyone else."

"So am I," Maddox says so softly, I'm not sure he's talking to me. As I walk to the bathroom and rinse the cloth under cool water, Maddox picks up the photograph. "You were cute."

I wring the cloth out the best I can and try to smile. "What do you mean by 'were'?" When I turn around, Maddox is seated in the chair, holding Mom's hand. I freeze, suddenly hit with the bizarre, stomach-spinning sensation of seeing my two worlds collide. Mom's lips are barely moving as she says something to Maddox. He leans in to listen.

"Mom?" I push Lina's medical cart aside to get to her.

"Him," is all she says.

"What's that?" I reapply the cool cloth on her forehead. But she only searches for my hand again. I take hers and sit on the bed. She closes her eyes, holding both our hands.

Maddox's eyes meet mine. The electric Current kicks stronger than ever between us.

"She must think I need a Guardian—or maybe she knows that you're my interceptor. Or that you're an Elite, and . . ." A thousand thoughts race across those stormy eyes that won't leave mine. I can't help but remember that it's not me he's drawn to. It's the power I have to lure others away. But even if that's wrong, what difference does it make? I'm a Blight. He's Elite. And his broken heart is tied to someone named Malee.

I'm not even sure what to do about Cole . . .

Lina walks in with a woven basket of vials and herbal water. "*Vaya. Camina.*" She points to the door.

My time is up. I hesitate leaving. I want to sit here until I'm convinced Mom will pull through.

Maddox stands and touches my shoulder. "Let's go."

Reluctantly, I kiss Mom on the cheek, inhaling her lavender scent once more. "I'll come back later. Trust Lina to heal you." I turn to Lina. "*Gracias. ¿Cómo está Cole?*"

Lina's eyes crease with a smile. "*Mejor.*"

Maddox nods. "So he's better? He must be healed." I'm glad he doesn't sound mad.

As we leave the room, a stray yellow leaf floats down and lands on the dusty trail. I'm still affecting the Garden. Figures.

"Let me guess. It's time I face Global Council?" I look around. "Where's Grumpy? Uh, I mean, my escort?"

"I took over for him. He knows where we'll be," Maddox tells me. "There's something I want you to see."

28

HAUNTING AND BEAUTIFUL

Gilded light flickers through the thick brush in the woods. Could be the flowers from the arbor, could be the Current, or even the morning sun, I'm not sure. Maddox and I go down the sloped path leading to the same tucked-away campground where broken pieces of wood are strewn throughout the trees.

He stands at the shore and cups his hands, lifting them to his lips as the midmorning sun shines overhead. He whispers to whatever he's holding, and then crouches down, releasing a white flower into the pond. A vibrant wind whisks the glowing flower away. The lake is filled with dozens of shining petals that turn the water a silky caramel.

Ivory flowers from the arbor—modified Lonicera—glide atop the water, collecting in the middle of the lake like lanterns of floating prayers. All around the shoreline, people I didn't know were on the grounds keep emerging from the forest to cast their petals. "It's for Pop," Maddox says. "Word got around. I thought you'd want to be a part."

I watch the tiny petals converge like dancing fireflies. A mournful trumpet from somewhere deep in the woods carries stalwart notes on the solemn wind.

Maddox holds out a tiny flower, but I know it will shrivel at my touch. "Hold it for me?" I cradle my hands under his. What could I possibly whisper that could honor Pop? He sacrificed himself to keep me safe inside the Garden. He saw more in me behind those dark glasses than I might ever know.

I whisper the only thing that feels right. "For rising spring and the coming storms, I'll believe."

Maddox sets my wish in the pond. The mesmerizing flower twirls but stays near the shore. I dip my fingers in the cool water, urging it, shooing it to join the others. Maddox takes a branch and guides it further into the lake, but without a swift breeze to carry it away, the lost flower spins in the murky water, alone.

I sit on a smooth log and twirl a short twig and stare at the petals. Maddox joins me. Together, we settle in the splintered ruins, sharing the silence.

Something rustles behind us. I glance over my shoulder, but it's just a spotted bird landing on a wooden platform near a muddy soccer ball. I'm thankful it's not someone coming to whisk me to Council. Yet. "What are all these broken wood pieces?"

"An old tree house," he says. "Gray and I used to hang out here when we were younger and talk about the future. I always thought it'd be cool to slay monsters with my brother." He picks up a small stone and dusts it off. "But I'm not a Blade."

Maddox studies the stone, deep in thought, rolling it between his fingers as if evaluating its worth. After a long while he says, "When I was in Belize, there was a girl . . ." He looks out at the water. He doesn't have to explain. I get it. Things are complicated.

"Malee was newly Awakened, and tough. A fighter, like you." He glances at me a brief moment. "I thought I could save her by destroying the beast. Then before I knew it, the Cormorant gashed my face. I hit the floor. That's when it got my shoulder. I couldn't move, so I couldn't protect her. The beast . . ."

He stares at the small pebble between his fingers. "I'll never forget the look in her eyes as she stared at me, bleeding out on the ground, knowing she would die. Knowing I would too. The beast came to finish me off, and that's when . . ." The pebble falls.

I touch his arm. He doesn't have to tell me.

"Gray killed the Cormorant." His tone is more dejected than bitter. "He's always been the hero. I've always been the runt who couldn't save the girl, or myself." He exhales. "Now you know."

I think I've always known. Maddox is the boy Gray saved.

But Maddox sees himself all wrong. He is a hero. More than Gray could ever be.

I do the only thing I can think of. I tuck his hair behind his ear, fully revealing the rough scar. Sunlight streams through the clouds as he glances at me as unguarded and exposed as his wound. My hand lingers by his ear. Maddox doesn't shy away, even as my fingertips lightly trace the scar outlining his jaw.

It's haunting and beautiful.

"You're more a hero than anyone I've ever known." My voice trembles. "You saved me. And I never said thank you." I softly kiss him on the cheek. Then I'm staring at his perfect lips, the curve of his smile.

Maddox lifts his hand and tilts my face up. His eyes search me, my thoughts, and my erratic broken heart that is beating way too fast. He leans in, drawing me close, brushing his soft lips over mine. Gentle, at first. Then as if it will never be enough. His kiss is a storm of electrifying fire, consuming my bones, disintegrating my fear.

The ground trembles. The vision flashes across my mind, too quick to grasp. I break away, breathless, elated, and terrified. The water ripples. The floating flowers shudder. Something happened, but Maddox doesn't seem to notice.

He wraps his arms around me and nudges his chin near my ear. His scent floods over me, and I'm drowning in him, in his arms, in the feel of his racing heart as he whispers, "Promise, when this is over, you'll write songs with me." And now I'm a mess of hope and fear, a collision of lightning and thunder, and he is the pouring rain, washing doubt away. For this one moment, I allow myself to believe being with him is possible. But I know I can't get used to the feel of his arms.

I know what's waiting for me. "I have to meet with Council. I'm not sure what that will mean. But I know I want to fight. I want things to change. But I don't know how." I place my hand on his chest, learning the rhythm of his heart, because I won't have this chance ever again.

"The group from Hesperian . . ." His nose, his lips, touch my cheek. I close my eyes convinced it's a dream. "Those who've survived the attack, they set up camp in a cabin not far from the training room. They've been working on a few things to fight Sage. Maybe, together, we can find a way."

"Really?" I lift my head to look at him. Sunlight dances on his lashes, sparking wonder in his eyes. He leans in.

"Maddox?" a familiar voice calls out from the woods.

"Hey, Amide." Maddox sits up, attempting to sound calm.

I tear out of his arms. "Amide?" I scan the woods and see him swatting briars and vines as he jogs down the trail. He hasn't noticed me yet.

"We need a few scrap pieces. Can we use—whoa, Cera?"

"Hi, Amide."

He flashes that bright smile. "We've missed your face."

"Yours too." I'm grinning. "Did you find that drummer?"

His eyes dance. "Tanji."

Good to know she's alive.

Amide surveys the campground and wiggles a wooden pallet away from the tree. "What's this?"

"It's part of an old tree house turned into a raft. Leave that piece, if you can." Maddox secures the pallet back in place and picks up the soccer ball, spinning it between his fingers. "Gray and I used it for raft battles. Devon's not bad either. But I always won."

"You beat Gray?" I ask a little surprised.

Maddox tosses the ball in the air, squinting at the sun breaking through the treetops. He catches the ball with his fingertips. "Who said he was any good?" He shoots me a sly smile, waking those dimples. "When this is over, I'll see how your skills stack up against mine."

Amide glances back and forth between us. "So, it's legit? You two are . . . ?"

"It's complicated," I say. "He's my interceptor. I'm a Blight."

Amide shrugs. "Not following the problem."

"It's forbidden." I dart a look at Maddox, reminding him of that fact.

"Ah, okay then." Amide seems amused. "But for the record, you two don't make it seem so." He picks up a few stray pieces of wood.

Thick voices carry through the forest and kick me back into reality. Someone will be coming for me soon. "Is there somewhere I can change before meeting Council?" I ask. "I don't want to face them wearing Sage's clothes." I motion to my outfit.

"I'm sure there's stuff at the cabin," Amide says.

"C'mon." Maddox boldly takes my hand, despite my previous comments about us being together. But I don't let go, either. I want to bottle this feeling and hold on for as long as I can. But as bubbling clouds darken the sky, I know it won't last.

My time with Council is coming soon.

29

GHOST ARMY

We trudge about twenty yards uphill through the damp
forest. A swelling sound of buzzsaws, hammers, and animated
conversation grows closer. Strangely no one is around. I glance
down for a brief moment so I don't trip over a root, and suddenly,
Amide, who's been walking a few paces in front of me, vanishes.

"Amide?"

"A little further." His voice comes from somewhere inside
the hazy afternoon light filtered by the overgrown canopy, but I
don't see him.

Maddox suppresses a grin. "Keep walking."

I take a tentative step through the narrow trees and blink
at a sudden rush of warm air. Then, as if I've entered through a
portal, Amide is standing in front of a quaint two-story cabin. Not
just Amide, but random faces from Hesperian are milling around
a sea of tents pitched near blackened campfires.

I spin around. "What was . . . ?"

"Projections that mirror the surroundings." Maddox walks
through the invisible screen. "Pretty cool, huh?"

My mouth gapes. "Amazing."

Amide waits at the bottom porch step. "The group has been
working on a way to cloak our hideouts." He hands the weathered

wood scraps to a girl with a red bandana protecting her curls. "Kellan is around back. Everyone else is inside."

Everyone who? Besides knowing Sage took my mother and Juniper from Hesperian, I never knew who made it out alive. I don't wait to find out. I zip up the steps two at a time.

Inside, the cabin is bustling. Familiar faces with names I don't know fill every inch of the cozy living room and galley kitchen. A few rush up and down the stairs as a pulsing beat with no lyrics vibrates air that smells of vanilla and coffee.

Like Hesperian.

Maddox is swarmed and swept away by a group bombarding him with questions and updates. I wait at the door, unsure of where to go.

Harper nearly bumps into me. "Hey, watch out." She stabilizes the pitcher of steaming blue liquid with both hands, keeping it away from her ivory pants. Then she realizes it's me. "Cera!" Her eyes grow wide. She hands off her latest concoction to a thin guy in a blue apron. "Will you take this to the kitchen?"

She takes my hands and squeezes them tight. "Don't go off without the rest of us. We're in this together, whether you like it or not. I already chewed out Cole." She gestures to a group settled around the couches. "We were able to clean out whatever toxins were in his system. I thought he might fit in with the group, so I brought him over while he waits to hear from . . . Council." She whispers the final word as if it's too heavy to speak.

Cole reclines on the edge of the navy couch, blending with the others around him. Amide greets him with a jovial laugh. Together they mess with keyboards, speakers, and a board peppered with intimidating knobs and buttons.

I hate that he'll be punished for what he did to help me. I want to run over and ask him a million questions. Punch him for having left with me, hug him for not letting me go alone. And tell him thank you, or I'm sorry, or both. I feel awkward and bashful, an emotional oxymoron not sure of what to say.

The glassy look in his eyes has worn off, thanks to Lina's herbs. But there's still a slight malaise about him. His hair is wet from a shower, the waves brushed to the side. Without his hat, he no longer hides his striking eyes. He places a headphone to his ear. "Lower," he says to the girl with the pretzel braid. "To throw off the Legions, the frequency has to be slightly lower."

"And add more bass. Pulse it like a heartbeat," someone else says. The voice cuts the air from my lungs. The crowd moves enough for me to see a guy in a wheelchair with his head wrapped in thick bandages and a scarf the color of silver moonlight draped around his neck.

In that moment, Tanji knocks a pounding beat on an electric drum. Her explosive dark curls bounce with the rhythm that echoes into my bones. "A lot softer." The guy winces. "And keep it steady." Then he points to Amide, who is tinkering with the knobby board. "Record it." His voice may sound raspier, but the skinny jeans and sharp boots haven't changed.

"Rhys." I choke on his name. He wheels around, searching for my voice. Half his face is draped with clean gauze. The one exposed eye, void of eyelashes or eyebrows, blinks at me.

How do you say sorry to the person you nearly destroyed? How can words be enough to erase the pain and scars grafted under those bandages?

The next thing I know, I'm at his side, falling to my knees, fighting to hold back tears. "Rhys, I'm so sorry. I never should have gone out that night. It was all my fault. You were selfless and brave. I was impulsive and naïve." I'm sobbing now. Stupid tears rush down my face as the whole room turns quiet. "If I could take it all back, I would. I'm so sorry."

"I know." He touches my wet cheek with the tip of his finger. "At least I nail the bandaged look. I totally miss my hair, but I'm kind of a legend now." He attempts a smile but winces when his blistered lip bleeds. "I keep forgetting." He blots it. "We all make mistakes. But we find a way to get up again." He rests his thick-bandaged hand on mine. "I can't be in the field, but that doesn't mean I can't help fight the war," he assures me. "This time we'll get it right. We'll blast those creatures back to dust. Deal?"

"Deal," I agree, wishing his buoyant optimism could unpin the weight clotting my lungs. I look around. "But I've got a Council to meet, first. Is there somewhere I can change clothes?"

"Everything you'll need is in the back room," Rhys says. He inspects my face. "Strengthen and highlight. Don't cover up." He winks, or blinks rather, and then resumes directing the group. "Where are we on the projections of the Wall?"

Harper has come over and helps me to my feet. "Why are they making images of the Circuit Wall?" I ask her, but my gaze is locked on Cole, who is so enmeshed with the group, he hasn't even glanced my way.

Harper walks me down a short hall. "There's talk that Council is planning an attack on Sage. To help the fight, they're developing fake explosions that mimic a sparking hit on the Circuit Wall. They're hoping to confuse the creatures so they can corner them for an ambush. I've come up with a few things too. I modified Gloss, the elixir that takes away the bruising. Now it emits a fragrance that will throw off the Cormorants and mask our scent. We're basically turning the creatures' strengths against them." She stops at a door. "Come take a look when you're done."

Rivulets of hot water run over my head, washing down my cheeks, arms, legs. I scrub away the feel of Sage's clothes, his touch, any trace of his scent, until my skin is red and burning. Harper is bringing me new clothes. I hope she burns the old ones, disintegrates them in the hottest flames possible.

Satisfied that I'm clean, I wipe a small circle in the foggy mirror. A tired-faced girl stares back at me. Golden eyes, circled with green, like my father's. Delicate nose and soft chin like my mother. But the low cheekbones and arched brows are my own.

I know I don't have much time, but I'm determined to make a statement. Now that I'm seventeen and both powers are fully manifested, it's time to change. Time to let Council see who I am as soon as I step into the room.

I quickly brush my tangled hair. No more messy ponytails. I braid and then twist my hair into a tight knot, securing it with a band. I sift through the bins of makeup, choosing striking eyeliner to highlight my Seer eyes and complementary eye shadow to make them glow. My cheeks I paint soft and natural to heighten my features. The lip gloss I keep blush pink.

Harper knocks lightly on the bathroom door. "I brought clothes. Let me know when you're ready."

I step out. "I'm ready."

Harper's mouth gapes. "You look . . . stunning." Well, that's never been a phrase used to describe me. "Forget these outfits." She tosses her pastel rainbow selections on the bed. "You need something bold."

"No jeans or T-shirts," I tell her. "I want to make a statement."

"I've got it. Give me a second." She returns in less than a minute with a neatly folded bundle. "This outfit was made by Gladys. Claire has been designing others for combat." The charcoal fabric is thin and hums with a slight warmth when I touch it. "The group brought these here, and Lina's been dying them in a vat mixed with metal shavings from the Paradise Steel."

I slip on the top. The tunic dress hangs just shy of my fingertips. Harper adds a flowing sleeveless vest. "The fabric is holographic and will reflect the surroundings, keeping you hidden. And with the fragments of the Paradise Steel coating the fabric, it's been tested to withstand a blast. Not like the shields, but better than street wear."

I run my fingers over the silken fabric that somehow still holds a trace of Gladys's scent: vanilla and peaches. "Is Gladys here? Or . . ." My voice trembles. "The attack—did she . . . ?"

Harper shakes her head. "From what I heard, she busted those Legions like nobody's business. Put Tanji and Kellan to shame, if you can believe it." Harper grins as she hands me a pair of matching leggings. "I would have liked to see that. I mean, I wouldn't want to be there with the Legions but, you know, to see Gladys fight."

I try to smile, imagining Gladys whipping around her rolled-up dishtowel with a simultaneous side-kick or maybe even a duck and roll.

Harper steadies me as I put on the pants. "She chose to stay behind. Said she wanted to pick up the pieces and rebuild. But I heard there's bad blood between her and the admiral and she was ordered not to come."

Someone pounds on the door. "What?" Harper demands. "We're busy."

"Council is ready," a girl's muffled voice answers. My stomach tightens at the news.

"Give us a minute." Harper fastens a leather belt around my waist. "This is for your weapon." She points to the divots. I doubt I'll get a weapon, but her optimism is kind. She rummages through a drawer, finding a few black nylon straps.

"And these"—she kneels beside me and fastens the straps around my thighs, just above the hem of the tunic—"are designed to fit with the leggings. They hold extra weapons and serum in the pouches. And this one"—she fastens a third band on my arm and drops a metal cube inside the sack—"will hold the frequency scrambler. They tested it when they went to rescue you, but they're modifying the tone for stronger effect." She fine-tunes the outfit, adjusting the cowl-neck and vest. "When you want to camouflage, pull this over your head."

I'm stunned. "I was only gone one day. How did everyone pull this off so quickly?"

"You mainly met new recruits to Hesperian." Her voice is muted while she digs in the closet and then hands me a pair of ebony riding boots. "But Maddox has been working on these pieces with some of the more advanced artists for a while. He contacted Hesperian as soon as we arrived in the Garden. Everyone was on board, pulling together whatever they had. When the attack happened, Maddox convinced Lieutenant Foster to let the group come here and finish the work." She straightens the band around my arm. "I think you're more than ready." She stands back, inspecting me. "You look killer."

"That's not exactly the word I was looking for."

"I mean, you're clearly not someone they want to mess with."

Then Council will get the message. Good.

I walk into the bustling common area. Despite the undercurrent of an impending fight, the room is filled with laughter, excited voices, and the dissonant sound of dueling notes and pulsing beats. We're on the edge of uncertainty, but somehow the creative energy pulses ten times stronger than it did at Hesperian.

Maddox sits on the steps, guitar in his lap, adding a chord to Rhys's soundtrack. He looks completely at home.

Cole has somehow taken center stage for a moment. He paces behind the couch. "That's it. That's the sound. Keep it long and sustained, and underscore it with a droning 'C' note, like this." He picks up his cello and plays the note. "Got it?" When he's done, he carefully sets the instrument aside. He scrubs out his hair, taking in the room, not looking for anything in particular as his mind whirls behind those bright eyes. His head suddenly jerks back in my direction with laser focus.

Claire comes up, blocking my view of him. "Foster says it's time."

"Hey, Claire." I smile, hoping she's forgiven me too.

"Your ride's out front."

My smile fades. I guess she hasn't. "Thanks." I make my way through the crowd.

Cole trips over the carpet as he dashes for the door, reaching it before me. There's something sweet about the way he says, "Hey," as he regains his balance.

"Hey." I try not to notice the quick bite of his bottom lip. I focus on his hands instead. "Nice to see you're back. Cord-free. Me too." I hold up my wrist. "For now, at least." I drop my hand, not sure what to do. "I was, um, really worried about you."

"Yeah, you too. I guess we, I mean . . ." He squints as if searching for the words. "You look amazing."

"Thanks." I blush and look away, catching a glimpse of Maddox setting down the guitar.

My heart collides at seeing the both of them at the same time. Maddox, in his white T-shirt with hair swept back, now focused my way. And Cole with hypnotic eyes sparking against his black button-down.

Claire again. "Devon's waiting for you. *Outside*." Her words strike me with grief.

Devon! I race out the front door and down the porch steps, leaving everyone behind. As he steps away from the car, I throw my arms around him. "Oh, Devon, I'm so sorry. I tried to stop Pop before he reached the gate."

"Pop was going to do what Pop needed to do," Devon says as he pats my back. "No one was going to stop him."

I'm terrified that an ocean of tears will burst out any minute. I let go of him and work hard to stay composed.

"Pop believed in you, Cera." He glances at me with swollen and bloodshot eyes. "More than he believed in anyone else." I glance down, knowing that can't be true. "I was next in line to be the Caretaker for the Estate, after my parents. I wasn't ready. I disappointed him."

"Everyone disappointed Pop, including me." I raise my head, realizing something for the first time. "Maybe you were never supposed to run this place because you were meant for something greater."

Devon looks unconvinced. "What's greater for a Caretaker than watching over the Empyrean Well?"

"Leading and caring for the Awakened in a new way, like you did at Hesperian?" My glance drifts to the cabin. Maddox and Cole are standing near the bottom step. "I think Pop could see that in you, too. Maybe he was waiting for you to see it yourself."

Devon is silent for a moment. "One question," he says as he opens the car door. "Do you know *why* Pop closed the gate to keep you inside?"

"Maddox told me that Pop said the Well wanted me here, but that doesn't make much sense, since I'm a threat. The last thing Pop said to me before touching the gate was: 'Time for spring to rise.'"

Devon shakes his head with a wry smile. "Then we go with that until we can figure out what he meant."

Maddox approaches. "Hey, uh . . . I can take her. We can walk back."

Devon, back in full military mode, doesn't even entertain the idea. "Get in." He motions to Cole, too. "Council wants all three of you."

As I climb in the back seat, Tanji shouts from the door. "Hey, toddler!" With hands on her hips in that sleek performance wear, she zeroes in on me. "Stay tough."

Thanks, Tanji. That's about the only choice I have when

facing Global Council. I imagine things will unfold in only one of two ways: I'll live and get to join in the fight, or they say it's time for me to die.

30

THE TRANSFER

I ride in the back seat between Maddox and Cole as Devon drives up the sloping hill to the Estate. Thick afternoon clouds sprawl across the sky like a rumpled gray blanket, trapping us underneath. Here I am again. Seemingly on replay, but with each run, spiraling deeper. I'm not the same girl who rode up this drive days ago. There's no more running or hiding from Global Council.

They know I've been with Sage.

They know I've had a vision in his presence.

They know I'm seventeen and my dualistic powers are fully manifested, and with that power comes the ability to join the realms.

What they don't know is how hard I fight.

Devon parks the car a good distance from the water fountain because a line of expensive cars and shiny motorcycles clots the driveway. I stride with confident strength as the warm fabric hums over my skin. Maddox and Cole linger a few steps behind.

I'm thankful that the thick soles of the boots hold steady beneath me instead of sliding over the uneven gravel as I walk beside Devon. "What can I expect when I go in there?"

"The same thing I said before. Lay low, and stay in line.

The admiral's family was on the front lines fighting Sage in the Renaissance. Borgia Albrecht is an Elite Caretaker and a Blade with no patience for emotion."

"Good to know."

"Now go in there and show them who you are." Devon has me walk up the steps first. "You look fierce, by the way."

My eyes widen. "Threatening?"

"In a good way."

I don't know how looking threatening in front of Council can be a good thing. But I'm glad I don't appear weak.

Before I walk through the front door, the ground trembles with violent force. Devon quickly pushes me inside the foyer. Terra-cotta shingles crash on the ground where I stood. Cracks break across tile floor and crawl up interior walls. Maddox swiftly dodges the falling shingles, rushing in behind us.

My pulse is roaring. "Was that an earthquake?"

"No. Sage has been using Legions to attack the Circuit Wall," Devon says. "That's the second hit today. And much stronger. The last one happened not too long ago."

I glance at Maddox as he runs a hand through his hair. So the ground *did* tremble when we, uh—it wasn't just because of . . .

Maddox dusts debris from his shoulders. "Why would Sage expend his army by splintering them against the Circuit Wall?"

"We're about to find out." Devon walks into the clanging sound of metal invading the War Room. I follow, stealing a brief glance over my shoulder. Maddox is close behind, but Cole hasn't come in yet.

The War Room is filled with Blades and Caretakers, most of whom I don't know. I recognize only two: one wearing a denim jacket with crossing swords on the back and another with a goatee and brass knuckles. Both I remember from Hesperian. They're hunting through the crates lined near the Martin painting. Crates I remember seeing in the training room. Along with other members of the Alliance army, they take out weapons and archaic shields in a frenzied rush. A team of five Blades blitz around us and out the front door. Soon after, the sound of buzzing motorcycles zips down the drive.

"Wait here until Foster calls for you," Devon says. He leaves me at the archway and cuts through the swarm of bodies until he reaches Lieutenant Foster, who is sliding the gruesome war tapestry aside, uncovering what looks to be a large map underneath. He's talking to a stout man in a decorated military suit with silver hair and a rugged face. It's the face of a man that's clearly taken a life or two—or a hundred. Foster appears dwarfed compared to the silver assassin Blade, who might be the admiral, since there is a distinguished bald man in a suit and suspenders standing diplomatically nearby.

Gray is over by the drink cart talking to another cluster of Blades. He seems a gnat compared to the men with Foster. But it's when I spot a regal woman with crimson lips and a posture of absolute control that I suddenly get nervous.

Her head is crowned with spiky, burnt-orange hair. In her high-collar pantsuit and single-strand necklace holding a flower pendant at her chest, she stands in the middle of the room, speaking to no one, but thoughts churn on her face, as if she's listening to every conversation at once. And deciding their fates.

When Foster notices me, both eyebrows rise. That's a new expression. I tug at the tunic dress and reposition the straps as he waves me over.

Quiet whispers trail behind me as I cross the room. I glance out the window. Yellow leaves continue to fall. The Garden is supposed to be in spring all year round, but now the treetops are aflame in gold, red, and orange hues, changing at a much faster rate than when I was last inside the Wall. Either it's me being inside the Garden or this is what happens when the Well transfers.

As I reach Foster, the steel-framed woman turns with

sniper's timing. She delivers a trained and elegant smile. "You are seventeen." It's not a question.

"Yes. Since sunrise . . . ma'am." I hope my voice sounds as firm as I stand because her voice carries the unnerving trill of a preying hawk. I clear my throat. "That's why I believe the gate wouldn't shut and now the Garden is—"

"Has she received full gifting, Lieutenant?" She asks Foster. I get that she's centuries older than me, or whatever, but she should really hear me out.

"In her capacity as a Seer and Guardian, yes, Admiral," the lieutenant answers.

She's the admiral? I'm not sure why I'm surprised. There's an unsettling way she speaks control over something inside you, rather than to you, that's way more intimidating than any Awakened I've ever met.

I swallow my discomfort. "Lieutenant, does the Garden change before a transfer? Because if not—"

"Sit down," Foster says to me as he glances at the admiral out of the corner of his eye.

"But, Lieutenant—"

"Miss Marlowe." The sharp edge to Foster's tone sends the whole room silent. "You *will* be seated. And speak only when spoken to. Admiral Albrecht has been gracious in her leniency. I have explained that, despite your unauthorized leave from the Estate, your cooperation has been essential in discovering pertinent facts about the Well and pending transfer."

It has? For all I knew, I found nothing worthwhile in what I read.

"I know your cooperation will continue." Foster motions to a chair pulled away from the conference table. He's not angry, although his voice sounds so. Concern creases the edge of his eyes. The woman is watching my every move. No, she's not watching me. She's looking for something beyond what's in front of her, reading it in my face, hair, eyes, and the tightening of my lips.

"Yes, sir." I perch on the edge of the chair, stoic and willing to be read.

Foster nods. "I assure you, Admiral, Miss Marlowe's visions and interpretations will prove essential to the Well's security despite these attacks to the Wall."

She raises a slim, disbelieving eyebrow and wears a deceptively sweet smile. "Is this assumption based on conscious reasoning or careless intuition?"

"Factual evidence," Foster replies. He lifts his voice. "Her readings saved the lives of key members of the Alliance," he informs the whole room. I appreciate his confidence, but I disagree. More people have died than I've been able to save.

"Has she activated any Dissenting powers?" Of course, the admiral would want to know. Now that I'm seventeen and this close to the Well, I'm definitely not a threat to be considered lightly.

"No." Foster is emphatic.

He sets another chair beside me, motioning for Maddox to approach.

"Mr. Carver." Albrecht eyes Maddox with disfavor. "Your parents would be disappointed by your apathy toward achieving a notable rank within the Alliance. As am I. However, I have been assured that your ability to extract and transcribe visions is beyond compare. I have been given the impression that you believe the vision remains intact, despite the siphoning from the enemy. Is that so?"

"Yes, Admiral." Maddox glances at my lips for a brief moment.

So the vision *did* flash through me even though I couldn't gather any details. If he felt it too, why didn't he tell me?

"Do you believe you are capable of enduring its extraction?"

"Yes." Even though Maddox is firm, my heart sinks a little. I know what transferring the vision will do to him.

"Proceed." Albrecht startles me by standing back as if expecting a show, and I'm the spectacle on whom Maddox will test his powers.

He looks over the swarming room buzzing with voices. "It's better if I'm somewhere quiet."

Albrecht's face tightens.

"Privacy is a luxury we can no longer afford." Foster's eyes seem troubled as he places a hand on Maddox's shoulder. "I have complete confidence that you will retrieve what is necessary. Our course of action will be determined by your findings."

No pressure there. I'm not sure what "action" Council is planning to take. Maybe if I had a detail or two from the vision, I'd be less nervous of what they might find.

Admiral Albrecht impatiently switches her attention to Gray. "Sergeant Carver," she barks, and then waits until she has everyone's attention before adding, "Provide the report."

"Admiral." Gray tips his head, standing straighter than usual. It's strange to hear discomfort in his voice, but I don't blame him. "We've experienced two attacks on the Garden in less than an hour. The initial impact was caused by at least six Legions making simultaneous contact with the gate. Additionally, Cormorants have been spotted in surrounding trees, spread in five key points outside the Circuit Wall. A reconnaissance team is surveying the damage from inside the Garden. We are awaiting that report now."

In that moment, Milton nudges me with the verse about the archfiend and his immortal spirits: *Doubled ranks they bend / From wing to wing and half enclose him round / With all his peers.* I hear you Milton. Sage is surrounding the Garden. But why?

Maddox reaches for my hand and whispers, "I'm not getting anything. Replay what happened leading up to the vision. Where were you?"

"I was in a dark hall," I whisper back, as Cole quietly enters from the library hall, spinning a chess piece between his fingers. He quickly blends into the crowd. I thought he followed us in, but he must have come in through the courtyard.

"Close your eyes and try again." Maddox is trying to keep me focused, but Gray's voice is like an earwig to my brain.

"We have forces on the outside that can launch an attack," Gray is saying. "But not enough weapons. Even if we pooled the Alliance army from around the globe, it would take days, if not weeks, to gather equipment and develop tactics necessary to combat what's surrounding us. We believe Sage is attempting an encirclement similar to the attack in the Renaissance; surrounding us from all sides, trapping us inside, cutting off our only entrance and exit, to place us under siege. He wants us to open the gate, knowing we will die from lack of supplies."

I squirm. For some reason I don't think that's what Sage wants. Outside, a forceful wind swirls yellow leaves across the lawn. Sage doesn't need us to open the gate. Not as long as I'm in here weakening the Garden. And possibly its defenses.

Albrecht stops pacing and intentionally blocks my view of the window. I'm sure of it. Even though she's not looking directly at me, I can feel her watching me.

"And what is Sage's rationale behind his attacks on the Garden?" she asks Gray. Her mouth quirks as if she's testing him. I bounce my foot, desperately wanting to answer.

"Cera, please." Maddox squeezes my hands, regaining my attention. "Picture me beside you. That's how you let me see last time."

"Agitation." Gray is so matter-of-fact, but he's so completely wrong. "Sage can't get through the Circuit Wall but wants to create fear within."

Unable to contain myself any longer, I jump out of the chair, pulling away from Maddox. "Sage isn't waiting for you to open the gate. He is testing the strength of the Wall."

Gray narrows his eyes. But surprisingly not at me. He's contemplating my theory, at least I think. I endure the stares of the entire room without flinching, but Albrecht's simmering disdain makes my knees tremble.

"Was that information gleaned from the vision you freely provided the enemy?" Her question seeps with accusing condemnation. "The Circuit Wall does not weaken to the point of allowing the enemy entrance during transfer. That theory has been proven historically."

I force myself to stand tall. "Sage wasn't expecting Pop, I mean, Mr. Lassiter, Senior, to close the gate and keep me inside the way he did. And with my powers fully engaged, the Garden didn't splinter or explode the way everyone anticipated. But now my presence is weakening the Garden." I speak quickly, hoping to prove my case before Albrecht can cut me off. "Look at the leaves, the grass, the trees. It's turning to winter. With every passing second, the Wall is weakening. And Sage is expending forces to test it. When he determines how much longer they'll stand, it will only be a matter of time before he breaks through. What will be the plan then?"

"Execution," Albrecht says as if it were a command.

I take a breath and step forward. "If that's what it takes to keep the Well secure, then go ahead." I hold out my wrists and look her in the eyes. Her Current is searing, slashing through every cell in my body. But I stay strong. "From what I've been told, Sage is patient. He's been waiting for this moment for centuries. If he can't get to the Well this time, he'll try again and again until he's figured out every detail that will ensure he gets what he wants."

I'm so certain, I address the whole room. "If there is a way to use this opportunity to our advantage, then shouldn't we try? This might be the very reason why Pop closed the gate with me inside. He was reading something on the Circuit Wall right before he did. He was blind, I know. It doesn't make sense, but somehow he saw something. He believed the Well had a personality of its own. I know this sounds crazy, but I think he was doing what the Well showed him." The words sound even crazier as soon as they leave my mouth, but I'm sure they're true.

"Yet you have no recollection of this siphoned vision, and we are left under siege in an ignorant huddle with no knowledge as to what information Sage received." Albrecht is too controlled, as if something vicious is simmering under the surface. She flicks her gaze at Maddox. "It seems your awareness as an interceptor is underwhelming, Mr. Carver."

"The vision is there." Maddox stands with a confidence that makes me believe it. "I promise you, she still has it."

"Then demonstrate your truth, Mr. Carver," the admiral demands.

I'm not the enemy. Lives are on the line, and if there is a way to save them through my vision, then it needs to be proved.

In front of the entire room Maddox traps my face in his hands, bringing me close, resting his forehead against mine, speaking as if we are the only ones there. His scent covers me. "You can do this, Cera. We can stop the vision from happening. Together." His lips are so close. Too close. And lingering with a promise I want to believe. I'm simultaneously consumed and wrecked by him. Softening to his touch, I close my eyes to give him unguarded access, letting him see everything.

A handheld lantern shines
A ray of caramel light beams
A narrow path illuminates through the dark

Power leaches out from me. My whole body turns weightless. I don't even know if I'm standing. A blinding light so bright blazes inside my closed eyes.

A bridge intact
Ravaging wildfire
A flash of red lightning
Rain wets the earth white.

An unspeakable, gripping loss cracks through me like an angry streak of white-hot lightning scorching the ground. I'm numb. Shaking. It's only when I feel Maddox pull away that I open my eyes. He collapses in a heap on the rug.

I throw myself onto him, but a swarm of Blades descends, pulling me away as the room erupts with chaos.

"Get the library door!" Gray shouts. Terror taints his eyes as he lifts Maddox from the floor with the help of another Blade.

Someone takes me by both elbows. My view of Maddox is blocked. I wrestle to break loose. I'm shouting, fighting, kicking. Crying out Maddox's name as they drag me from the War Room and carry his limp body to the library. Unbearable grief rips through my heart . . . *rain wets the earth white* . . . Maddox is the rain. An image flashes across my mind: Maddox, with his blond hair trampled in the mud.

Dead.

The library doors slam shut, and I scream my throat raw.

31

THE FOX AND THE LION

"Take a breath." Devon props me up on the wall in the shadowed entryway. I slump, my legs too weak to stand. Cole and two Blades I don't know crowd behind Devon. "What was it?"

I can't stop shaking. All I can do is press the heels of my palms into my eyes, hoping to push away the image.

"Spit it out," Cole says.

I grip Cole's shirt with both fists, leaning into him for support. The Blades advance but Devon signals them back.

"He dies." The words barely escape my lips.

Cole tenses. "Who, me?"

I shake my head because I'm terrified that speaking the words will make it true. Hot tears drip down my cheeks. Cole frowns. I know he hates crying.

"Who dies?" Devon peels me away from Cole and holds me by the shoulders.

I drop my head. I can't say it. So Cole does.

"Surfer boy."

"Maddox is only passed out," Devon says. "They'll get him conscious. He'll draw out the vision. Then we'll know for sure." He tries to sound reassuring, but it's not working. His own grief underscores his words. "And if anything, Gray won't let it happen.

He won't lose Maddox. He promised his parents, and himself, that he'd do whatever it takes to keep Maddox safe and alive."

They've bound my wrists together in front of me and tied my ankles to the chair. I'm forced to sit at the conference table and wait for news on Maddox, while every minute, the sun tips lower on the horizon, pouring sunset on the trees. They won't execute me yet. Not until they're sure the vision has been extracted and I'm no longer needed. Until then, I can only sit and wait. I hate waiting.

The room is packed with anxious Blades trading weapons. Tight whispers fuse with the incessant ticking of the grandfather clock. Foster has laid sketches of my previous visions on the conference table for all to see. Blades cast furtive glances at the images and then at me. I look away, a prisoner stripped of dignity, waiting for execution.

But it's not really me I'm worried about. I keep my eyes on the archway near the library, waiting for signs of Maddox.

"I wonder," Foster says, laying out several art books in front of me. He opens them to specific pieces I've viewed before, including several pieces I mentioned seeing in Sage's collection. "If now that both powers are fully manifested, you might read things differently than before. A bit clearer, perhaps."

I twist uncomfortably. "Lieutenant, the defenses are weakening. I *know* they are. Sage will attack again. He's probably waiting until the Circuit Wall is weak enough to break through, or at least until it's dark, when the creatures are harder to see." I can feel Sage's call in my bones—a promise that he'll come for me. He'll use me to connect the realms, so he can have control, altering the world as we know it. "Why won't the admiral listen to me?"

Foster opens a book to the picture of Cot's *The Storm*. "Use this time to your advantage, Miss Marlowe." He doesn't have to tell me each breath is numbered. I can read it in his solemn eyes. "Perhaps the answer we had been hoping for will arise."

Maybe Foster's right. Maybe I couldn't fully read the embedded messages because both sides of my powers weren't activated. Maybe that's why Pop insisted I come back and gave his life to keep me here.

I take in the artwork, cataloging every detail.

In *The Storm*, the message painted in the girl's expression tells me not to run. To face the coming storm. The feet running in unison says *work together.*

In Martin's *Sadak in Search of the Waters of Oblivion*, the message lies in the struggling man reaching the sacred water source . . . alone. I know this painting details the coming battle. The message says the victory lies in reaching the source. The question is whose victory? The Alliance or Sage's?

In the Delacroix, *Milton Dictating Paradise Lost to His Daughters*, the message is clear. Milton is a Blight, dictating the words the same way he guides me to see the events unfold each step of the way. It's what happens next that I haven't discovered. I look for a copy of the poem on the table. There isn't one.

Foster has gone across the room and is surrounded by Blades asking questions. I start to call out and ask him for a copy when the library door scrapes open. Voices carry from the hall.

"I suggest you remind your brother of his obligations." Albrecht's frigid tone makes me shiver. "Some might call his behavior treason."

With bound hands, I manage to push aside Blake's copy of *A Poison Tree*, the one with the blond boy lying dead on the ground. I know that message is showing something tainted will destroy Maddox. And that something is most likely me.

"My apologies, Admiral." Gray's formal tone sounds odd. "Maddox is aware of his position with the Blight. He was extracting the vision by whatever means possible. When he completes the sketch, you'll see his ability."

"*It is undoubtedly necessary for the ambassador occasionally to mask his game; but it should be done so as not to awaken suspicion,*" Albrecht responds. No, she quotes. I'm familiar with that line, but can't recall from where.

"Maddox has been taught Machiavelli," Gray is quick to answer.

Machiavelli sounds about right. I had a copy of *The Prince* in my drawer at home. Gray studied Renaissance philosophers? I don't know why I'm surprised. He does seem like an *Art of War* kind of guy. But not Maddox.

"My brother's tactics are unconventional," Gray continues. "But he abides by the law. He is her assigned interceptor and believes gaining her trust is essential for extraction. But I assure you, there is nothing more."

A crate slams shut. I wince.

Nothing more. It's the same phrase Pop used when assuring Gray I wasn't a threat. I felt slapped in the face then, but it feels more like Tanji's punch in the jaw this time. His insinuation that Maddox is only playing me, using Machiavellian tactics to gain my trust, might be necessary, but it still hurts.

Sage's words echo deep in the wound. "*They only want what you can give them.*"

Nothing more.

Albrecht enters the room. I focus on a book of Romantic apocalyptic landscapes, watching her in my peripheral vision. With the wall map as her backdrop, she stops at the opposite end of the table. A few others file into the room. I glance up. None of them are Maddox. Only Silver Assassin, Suspenders, and Gray.

Albrecht burrows her stare into me until I look at her. When

I finally do, she says, *"Quello che giova al nemico nuoce a te, e quel che giova a te nuoce al nemico,"* as if I should understand. Honestly, I don't have a clue what she said. But her penetrating stare stays fastened on me, regardless.

The room suddenly feels too big with nowhere to hide. Silence ripples as everyone waits for my response. I swallow, searching for a way out.

"That which is good for the enemy harms you," Cole says, from out of nowhere. "And that which is good for you harms the enemy." He leans on the entryway threshold with arms crossed, looking way too serious. "Machiavelli's *The Art of War.*"

I'm not surprised Cole knows Machiavelli, in Italian, nonetheless. He probably studied it in that overseas boarding school. He's certainly impressed Foster. This is the first time I've ever seen the lieutenant come close to a smile.

Albrecht, on the other hand, is less than enthusiastic. "Who is the enemy?" she questions me, with a tone that could cut diamonds.

"Sage," I say. But the moment the words come out, they feel as if they're a lie.

"You call him your enemy with such confidence, yet, as a Blight, you hold allegiance to both sides." She over-enunciates every syllable with unnerving precision. "You have proven your susceptibility to the enemy's power through your lack of emotional restraint and, in doing so, have influenced others toward dissenting behavior." When Albrecht glances at Cole, I tense. Her gaze trails through the room, holding the silence as if it were a soap bubble about to pop. "How is it that you believe you can discern your allegiance? How can we? You are merely a child."

Everything in me wants to snap back. I almost do until a cool breeze smelling of the arbor wafts through the screen door. Pop's words *don't get hotheaded* echo in my head.

I sit back. I need to walk this road carefully. She's testing me. The same way Gray did in the training room.

I take a breath to think. Albrecht navigates with historical academics and literary quotes. Milton isn't giving me anything to throw at her right now, but surprisingly, Machiavelli is.

A crisp sharpness surges through me. I keep my tone calm. "As a Blight, neither Awakened nor Dissenter, I know that a *'lion cannot protect himself from traps, and the fox cannot defend himself from wolves. One must therefore be a fox to recognize traps, and a lion to frighten wolves.'*" I quote Machiavelli's *The Prince*, hoping I got it right. Cole ducks his head, but not before I catch him grin.

"Carver!" Kellan bursts into the room. My heart leaps at his pale, freckled face. He rushes past Cole, looking just as intense as he did on the streets of East Ridge, wearing the same sleeveless jacket. He probably has that flask filled with Spike tucked in the lining. "The last hit wasn't at the gate."

"Where did they strike?" Gray's expression tightens.

I look at the map of the grounds. The entire outline of the Garden roughly matches the circled pattern I'd seen at the Well. The entry gate is far south. The Well is marked on the map by two trees, east of this building.

"Southwest part of the Wall," Kellan says.

"Assemble reinforcements in that quadrant," Albrecht commands. "If the Circuit Wall has weakened, the enemy will most certainly attempt another breach."

A bold awareness floods me, and I can't keep my mouth shut. "He won't enter there. Sage will break through in the top right quadrant of the Garden."

Albrecht's stare is piercing. "Is that because you shared a layout of the grounds with the enemy on your recent escapade?"

Foster approaches her. "With all due respect, Admiral. To our knowledge, the enemy has no awareness of the terrain inside the Garden. Nor has he siphoned any Alliance intelligence from

Miss Marlowe, save for one vision. What Miss Marlowe speaks, she gleans from messages embedded by Blight artists. Isn't that so?" The look he gives me is almost pleading.

"Yes," I say quickly. "Sage had these two paintings at his place." The entire room watches as I push Delacroix's *Barque of Dante* next to John Martin's *Bridge over Chaos*. "They both show light breaking through in the top left corner. And so does the one depicting the coming battle." My bound hands lift to point at the Martin painting on the wall. "Blights painted a dual message. The light is both a hope of success and a warning of what is to come. If Sage has figured it out, then he'll enter in the northwest quadrant, the spot closest to the Well."

Albrecht searches me as if weighing my truth. I let her read me, knowing I'm right. "How much damage has occurred to the Circuit Wall thus far?" she asks Kellan, while keeping her eyes on me.

"Part is emitting sparks. Still holdin' but the power's weakening."

"Weakening, how?" Gray asks.

Kellan, with his southern drawl, confirms my warning with his intel. "There's a small fissure where the Wall keeps sparkin'. Nothin' but cold air's coming through. But the last group of Legions . . . they didn't splinter completely."

Silence descends over room, amplifying the clock's ticking hand. My theory about the Circuit Wall weakening was right.

Another hit or two and Sage will break through.

32

RISE

The admiral and her entourage are clustered in a tight conversation with Gray. Questions blast across the War Room from all directions. I'm still bound to the chair, as Foster tries to settle the chaos.

"Enough!" He silences the crowd and then turns to one side of the room. "Terminating a Blight within the Circuit Wall brings great uncertainty to the fragile state of the Garden. It is not an option." He switches his attention to the other side. "Opening the gate to remove the Blight from the grounds so the Wall stays intact shall only expedite Sage's entry." To a small group hovering in the corner he adds, "And we are quite certain the enemy does not wish to negotiate."

"We'll set up decoys," Gray says, breaking from his discussion with Albrecht. "When Sage breaches the Wall, we'll send out four teams on motorcycles, three being decoys, one containing the Blight. Each will depart in different directions." It's not lost on me that Gray pointed to the northwest corner of the map; the very place where I believe Sage will enter. "I anticipate that Sage and his creatures will follow, separating his army, reducing the impact of the attack. With a skilled team, we can have the Blight outside the grounds in a matter of minutes."

Albrecht nods in agreement. "Excellent, Sergeant Carver. I agree that the quick and fatal execution of the Blight outside the grounds is essential to preserve the Empyrean Well until transfer is complete. Once the transfer occurs, the power and protection of the Well will renew, in full."

I'm all for this plan, minus the death part, if I can help it.

Cole, who's been quietly spinning a chess piece this whole time, has had enough and elbows his way through the room. "You think Sage is going to walk away from the fight because the Blight isn't around? What happens if your escape plan doesn't work and Sage brings her back to the Garden? You have a plan for that? Stop and think for a minute. Even if you terminate Cera, Sage isn't going to walk away from this fight. Not if he's cornered this many Awakened with Elite power *and* Alliance secrets. He'll terminate every last one of us and siphon our powers to make himself stronger while gaining our knowledge."

With my attention on Cole, I didn't see Devon come in, but somehow he's made his way to my side. "Maddox says to see what you can find," he whispers, handing me a book.

But it's not any book. It's *my* copy of Milton—with all my highlighted passages, notes, crazy thoughts and theories scribbled illegibly in the margins. "How did he—*when* did he get this?"

"It was with Sage."

The thought of Sage reading my thoughts, touching my stuff, sends fire through my veins.

"Ask yourself," Cole continues, "what information do you have inside your head that you'll hand over to the enemy when you die?" He stands near the sketches, where the last ten years of carnage from my life are displayed for all to see. "Think about how that information will make things easier for Sage to take over the Well and annihilate us, either this time or next, or however many times after that. Machiavelli says, *'There is no avoiding war; it can only be postponed to the advantage of others.'* And with your plan, the advantage will go to Sage."

"I agree." Devon joins Cole. "Better to plan an offensive attack. Maybe we can use Cera to help draw in Sage."

The admiral's voice is hard. "The Blight is no longer necessary and poses too great a risk. Now that the vision has been extracted, our priority is to ensure that under no circumstance is the third realm to be joined with the second."

As they argue, I fan through the pages of the poem searching for any hidden messages. Folded sheets of paper are tucked in random places throughout the book. I remove a note, sliding it under the table. The paper holds Maddox's scent, but it's not a note. Not with words, anyway. He's sketched a scene from *Paradise Lost*: Adam with tangled bangs, gazing at an innocent Eve as she stares at her reflection in a lake, seeing herself for the first time.

I quickly unfold another note. In this one, Eve is nestled in Adam's arms as they lounge under the cool shade of a majestic tree within a garden that looks a lot like this place. Longing flows from every stroke, every pencil mark, every curve and shadow. The way he's drawn Eve, she looks a lot like . . . The paper trembles as my heartbeat pulses in my fingertips.

I unfold another sheet. This one is worn, as if held a lot. Or it could be the one he's kept in his back pocket, because the frayed creases tell me it's been folded and refolded several times. I'm careful not to tear the edges as I open it.

Loose hair blows across a girl's face as she looks over her shoulder with a mix of concentration and fascination in her determined eyes. An army of butterflies takes flight in my stomach. He's captured . . . me.

In the bottom corner he's written, "You change everything."

"Termination is our only option." The admiral's callous words shatter my daydream.

Foster's lip twitches. "We may choose to disagree, but we cannot be divided. It will surely result in our demise. A unified plan is our only means for success, no matter how success may look."

I am searching for another note when Milton breaks in, freely flowing, as if a spigot has been busted open, simply by holding my old copy.

> *Among the constellations war were sprung,*
> *Two planets rushing from aspect malign*
> *Of fiercest opposition in mid-sky*
> *Should combat, and their jarring spheres confound.*

Yes, war between these two realms is imminent. In fact, Sage will break through the Circuit Wall any minute now. As far as I know, the only plan in place is my death. If there is something I'm missing, please let me see. I fumble through the pages until I hit this highlighted verse:

> *The sword of Satan with steep force to smite*
> *Descending and in half cut sheer, nor stayed,*
> *But with swift wheel reverse, deep entering sheared*
> *All his right side.*

Can this really be it? You're never literal, Milton.

Devon must notice my expression. "Cera, what did you find?" Cole looks just as curious.

I clutch the poem so I don't lose the page. I work hard to stand, despite the binding on my ankles. "This might be an answer. A swift cut to Sage's right side, perhaps with the Paradise Steel. Listen to the rest. *The griding sword with discontinuous wound / Passed through him.*"

Could this be the answer? "Stab Sage, probably the same way Gray killed the Cormorant. Maybe Gray's knife is the answer. If it is part of the gate broken off in the last battle, the power from his Steel must be the only thing strong enough to fatally wound Sage. That might be why Sage aimed to destroy it when we were outside of the gate."

There is a silent hush over the room. I keep reading, devouring the words for confirmation. *"But the ethereal substance closed / Not long divisible . . . / Yet soon he healed."* Wait, what? Blood drains from my face.

"Continue," Albrecht says, sounding . . . the opposite of encouraging.

I skim another few pages. The words choke with a strangled whisper. *"Incapable of mortal injury / Imperishable and, though pierced with wound, / Soon closing and by native vigor healed."*

My hands go limp. Not only is Sage a powerful ancient force and able to shapeshift . . .

"Sage is indestructible," Albrecht says. "Confirmed." The word echoes like a gavel on my soul.

But there is a message in those verses. Those lines mean something. I know they do. But what? I rub the itchy rope on my wrists, wishing someone would unbind me. Maybe then I could think clearer. I tug at the twine around my ankles, but can't break loose.

Gray watches me a moment, then turns his back. "We expect the Circuit Wall to stay intact another few hours, at most. We need to decide on our course of action and mobilize quickly."

"Use the Ghost Army." Devon boldly approaches the admiral. "They've been working on projections and explosions that mimic the Circuit Wall. When Sage breaks through, we'll launch an offensive attack. It's to our advantage, since Sage and his army are unfamiliar with our terrain. I'll have the team cloak the training room so we can keep the sick and wounded protected while we fight."

The Blades draw closer to Devon as he speaks with the confidence of a seasoned Caretaker that would make Pop proud. "We should also employ Gray's plan and use decoys to split Sage's army but lead them into ambush traps instead. If Sage remains near the Well, which Cole suspects he will, then we'll use projections to hide the Well's location, making it appear like the surrounding forest. We can lure Sage closer and get him to strike, using his power source. We'll deflect the hit to the Inner Wall and call out the code word: rise. The blast should splinter him enough to end the fight."

Leave it to Devon to tie everyone's ideas together. However, it's not lost on me that I've been left out of his strategy.

Albrecht looks somewhat pleased. "Have these projections been tested?"

"Yes," Devon affirms. "Along with the use of frequency scramblers to disorient the Legions and elixirs to mask scents from Cormorants. With these additions, there is a higher chance of success."

"Good plan." Cole spins the sketches of my visions upside down. "But I still think Sage will be expecting us to trick him somehow, and knowing him, he might be hesitant to strike. We need to think differently. Learn from what happened in the Renaissance, from Machiavelli: *There is nothing as likely to succeed as what the enemy believes you cannot attempt.*"

"Until we view Miss Marlowe's latest vision and understand what knowledge Sage has acquired," Foster says as he realigns the sketches, "an effective plan cannot be conceived."

"Is the rendering complete?" Albrecht asks.

"Almost," Devon replies.

"Until then we will prepare according to the plan outlined by Mr. Lassiter." She gives the command to Silver Assassin and Suspenders and then turns to Kellan. "Secure reinforcements in the northwest quadrant." At least she's heeding my advice about Sage's entrance. She hands out the rest of the assignments; Foster will lead a battalion to fight the front lines of Legions. Gray will mobilize an advanced team to battle Cormorants, while she and her entourage handle Sage.

"And the Blight?" Gray wants to know.

"Terminate at your discretion."

Daylight fades, darkening the room. Foster approaches the admiral. "Edward Lassiter secured Miss Marlowe in the Garden with intention. He would not have done so if not compelled by either a vision or knowledge beyond our understanding coming directly from the Well itself."

"Perhaps it was simply to allow us to retrieve the vision. And that task has been completed." Albrecht inspects Foster with scorn. "I expected greatness from you, Lieutenant, but it seems your personal loss has damaged your resolve. You have become disappointingly . . . adequate."

Foster's expression is no longer unreadable. His stoic features fall as if his heart has been squeezed in her steely fist. She pivots sharply and studies the map with hands behind her rigid spine that I suddenly want to crack with a solid kick of my boot.

Cole makes his way around the table to Gray. "The success of the plan is slim to none. It failed back in the Renaissance. Sage will catch on, and it will fail again."

"What do you suggest we do, Tripton?" Gray scowls, but he doesn't seem angry. Fear, hurt, or possibly both, outline his features. "You think we should run? Break our promises and abandon what we believe we're called to defend, leave it unguarded so Sage can test its strength and eventually find a way to destroy it? Maybe Cera isn't the only Blight he's bred, but she's the only one of age. This is the one chance we have to splinter him and secure the Well for centuries to come. We have to try."

I feel sickened by his insinuation that I was born as a product of Sage's planning, another creature created for his army. I don't belong to Sage. But bound to a chair, it's clear I don't belong to the Alliance either.

I'm the gray line in between. I always have been.

Machiavelli's quote, *"What the enemy believes you cannot*

attempt," sticks to my brain. As far as I know, the only thing Sage believes the Alliance can't attempt is harming the Well.

But I can.

Maybe Milton's message wasn't about striking Sage but something else entirely. Maybe the answer is about striking the Inner Wall, as Devon suggested, except not with Sage's power. With mine.

My pulse quickens, knowing we've wasted too much time. With the air turning dusky gray, Sage is sure to strike again soon. I know I'm no match for the years of knowledge and experience clustered in the room, or even what's waiting outside the Garden, but if there's a chance I'm right, a chance I can make a difference, then I can't stay quiet. "Admiral? What if I strike the Inner Wall with the Paradise Steel when Sage is within range? It's not as unpredictable as relying on Sage to create the blast." And I'd die in the process. "It's the one thing Sage won't expect."

She doesn't bother turning around. "The Current will not allow Paradise Steel to strike the protective Wall."

I have nothing to lose in making the case. "Except that I have the power to wield your weapons against you. Somehow I break the Current. I can do it." I avoid Cole's stare. "If I strike the Inner Wall when Sage is close enough, I'll give myself up in the process the same way Pop did with the Circuit Wall. Sage will be splintered and no longer able to fight, and I'll no longer be a threat." The Alliance will be saved.

Finally, a slight turn of her head in my direction. "Utilizing that power in such a manner may join the realms."

"If Sage is close enough when I strike—"

"It is out of the question." She turns her head away.

But the fervent gnawing won't relent. I clamp my mouth shut and stay quiet until I find a solid verse from Milton to convince her otherwise. It's somewhere in this cloudy mess. If I'm persistent, if I continue searching, the individual pieces will come together, and then I'll see. I quickly scan the pages as hazy shadows taint the room. Clouds churn. The steady thrum seeping into my veins grows stronger.

Maybe I'm searching for something I can never find. Maybe I was never supposed to fight this battle. Maybe—I stop on the highlighted verse: *"Perverts best things / To worse abuse or to their meanest use."*

This means something, Milton. But improper use? Are you speaking of the Well or me? I sift through several pages, stopping at a passage I circled in black ink. It's the archfiend's speech. *"Our labor must be to pervert that end / And out of good still to find means of evil."* There's that word again. Pervert. Why did I circle that? My notes in the margin say, "leading toward evil." Sage leading me toward evil is a given, and too easily spelled out. What am I missing?

Cole sits on the edge of the table. *"The greatest sign of an impending loss is when one does not believe one can win."*

I shut the poem, using my finger as a placeholder. "What's that?"

"It's from Machiavelli. And right now, everyone feels it." Cole drops his glance and finds the picture of Eve in Adam's arms. "You and surfer boy, huh?"

Oh. I didn't mean to leave it on the table. I awkwardly tuck the sketch in the book. "It's just a drawing. That's all." But the warmth rushing to my face betrays me.

"Thought so."

The hurt in his eyes burns more than the bindings on my wrists. "Cole, wait." Somehow my bound hands manage to clasp his elbow before he can walk away.

"Look, I don't blame you. I wouldn't choose me either. I don't belong here. Never did."

Despite Cole's nonchalant attitude, I know he wants more than anything to belong, to right his wrongs. And make his family proud. "You and me—we're not so different."

He looks through those intense lashes. "Yeah? How so?"

I'm keenly aware of my hands resting on him for too long, and how my pulse is sprinting faster. "We've been trying to deny what we really are." A line from Machiavelli snaps into my head. *"Everyone sees what you appear to be, few really know what you are."* The line couldn't be more fitting.

"The Prince." Cole's mouth quirks. Heat returns to my face as I suddenly remember the way his lips felt when we kissed. "Machiavelli and Milton, huh?" He shakes his head, shrugging away a thought. "Yeah, well, you've got me all wrong, Blighty. That handbook is for rulers and royals. I'm just an expendable pawn. And I'm pretty sure your line of prose was meant for someone else." He tips his head, gesturing to something across the room.

I look up to find Maddox at the archway, holding my drawn-out vision in his hands. His hair, although ragged, is tucked neatly behind his ear, showing off his scar. Dark circles shade his tired eyes that know exactly how to find me.

Foster takes the sketchbook, but the admiral snatches it away, setting the drawing on a table near the map.

Clouds darken. Thunder rolls. Sage is getting closer. I can feel it in my bones. It's a deep luring call, urging me to run. "My visions come to pass in less than twenty-four hours." I raise my voice, hoping Albrecht will listen. "If Sage is unfamiliar with the Garden, he will most likely attack at dusk when the air is gray and the Legions are hard to see. If I view the sketch, I can tell you how to stop him." I try stepping forward but trip, taking the chair with me.

Albrecht turns around with an expression that confirms my fate. After what feels like an eternity, she says, "Prepare as planned."

In that moment, deep thunder, a vibrating wave of moving earth, sends tremors through the wood floors. Chandeliers swing. One crashes to the ground.

"Check the perimeter!" Albrecht commands.

As the room erupts with frenzy, Cole quickly cuts the twine on my wrists and around my ankles and then slips away to join the crowd before anyone notices.

The tremor grows with a rhythmic push and pull. I imagine thirsty Legions rocking the Circuit Wall back and forth in tempo, wedging the invisible barrier loose. Once the Circuit Wall implodes, a tidal wave of Legions will come crashing into the Garden. And feast.

Our time is up.

33

BREAKING THROUGH

Slow, growling thunder shakes the Garden. Deep fissures crack along the stucco walls, fleeing up to the ceiling. Hard metal clashes with frantic voices as Gray and Devon quickly distribute weapons.

"Please, let me see the sketch!" I beg the admiral. I can't recall any specific detail, except Maddox's death. I have to read the sketch to know how to keep him—and everyone—alive.

I only take three steps toward Albrecht when someone clasps my elbows from behind, dragging me back on my heels.

I trample over broken glass from the chandelier and wrestle to break free. But I'm forced back over to the conference table.

Maddox intervenes. "I've got her." His grip is firm. He knows I'll make a second run at seeing the sketch if he lets go. And I will. "Don't fight." His whisper is a low warning in my ear.

"I have to read the vision." I try not to cry. The rising vibration pulses through me. I tug, but Maddox won't let go. "I need to know how to stop it from happening."

"Calm down." He guides me into the corner near the Martin painting. Brazen light from a nearby lamp strokes his face as he looks at me with that stormy expression, the one that makes me forget there's anyone else in the room.

But then I think of what Gray said about my powers, and I drop my gaze to the floor. "Maddox, please don't look at me that way. Whatever you think you feel—it's not me. It's whatever ability Blights have to lure Awakened away from the Alliance." I try to sidestep him, but he won't let me.

"The Alliance only claims you have that power so they can keep our lines pure, but it's not true. And I know what I feel."

"You don't know me."

He pulls me closer as the frantic room grows louder. "I know you want to do what's right. I've seen you put others above yourself every time. You want to make a difference. You want to belong but don't think you can. I heard it in the poem you wrote. I see it in your eyes. I know because we almost died together. Twice. Cera, I can sense what you're feeling the same way you read me. Like, your heart is racing right now. Your eyes want to look at me, but you're afraid. You think I'll turn away at what I find." His voice intensifies. "I won't leave you."

He's so right, but at the same time . . .

"You're wrong. I won't look at you because I'm afraid of believing in something that can't happen. That if I do, my heart will break beyond what I can bear. I'm not afraid that you'll leave me. I'm afraid that you won't. And somehow I'll end up destroying you in the process." I stare straight into his blustery eyes and try my hardest not to cry. "I can't have you die on account of me."

Maddox darts his eyes back and forth across mine. "I don't plan on dying soon, remember?"

"You don't understand. Sage knows how I feel about you. If Albrecht doesn't kill me first, Sage will do whatever he can to ensure I side with him. And that means harming you."

Maddox tenses. "Is that what you think the vision shows?"

"Yes." My heart fights not to confess the rest, to stay strong and believe that everything will work out, somehow. But I know the truth. "Don't say you won't leave me. Because unless that vision changes, then it's not true."

Tremors shake the walls, growing stronger each minute. Gray shouts commands. Paintings shift. Furniture shudders. So do I.

Foster strides over to us. "We will read the recent vision after the admiral's review. Be patient."

The world is crumbling down. How can I be patient? All I've ever known is how to run.

Foster sets two sketches on the table. Maddox backs away, as he should. "I suggest one final review of your previous visions. Ensure nothing was missed."

I'm not sure what good it will do. The events have already come to pass, but I've messed up enough to know I don't have all the answers. And Sage has us surrounded. He will break through at any moment, and there is nowhere to run.

I will myself to follow Foster's orders. The first sketch is the one Maddox drew, showing the broken goblet. Liquid spills on the ground as tendrils of black threads rise from a puddle, all foretelling Harper's death. It was the first vision of mine that didn't come to pass. We intervened in time and changed the outcome.

Harper rushes in from the dining room carrying a wooden crate. "Take these, quickly. The healing serum is purple." She starts handing out small vials as Devon takes the heavy crate off her hands. "The green one, we call Spike, and it will sharpen your senses and keep you alert. And this"—she doles out something that looks like royal-blue sugar cubes—"is called Gloss, and it will throw off your scent so the Cormorants can't track you."

"What more do you see?" Foster places another drawing in front of me, regaining my attention. It's the one I tried to interpret with Pop's help. The one I never had a chance to see.

As I read the image, intense shame creeps over me once again. I push aside the feeling and concentrate on the message. What I thought were hands pressing on a spine are sultry curves of a tree trunk. The bodies writhing are broken limbs, worming in pain on the ground. Probably Juniper and Bearcat. The wet lips are Sage's words luring me, tempting me to join him. And the heart-shaped stone is Cole's fedora.

A searing coldness descends on me. The vision was a warning about Cole's dissension and Sage's temptation of me—not about me luring Maddox. This vision was also thwarted, but only because Maddox and Gray intervened. If they hadn't, Cole wouldn't be here right now, and neither would I. Or my mom.

Albrecht tosses my latest vision to the floor, only to tread over the sketch and rip it in half with her heels. "Sergeant Carver, handle the Blight and then prepare as planned." She plucks the intricate Steel from Cole's hand and then walks out the door. Foster swiftly picks up the torn sketch before the pieces are entirely shredded.

The roaring hum swells. Dusk descends, spattering long shadows across tight faces. I'm certain the Wall won't hold much longer.

"Assume attack positions at twelve and six," Gray orders the remaining Awakened army while Cole searches through another crate, flinging out handfuls of straw. "Three-man configuration. Alert the others." Hard soles clatter on the hardwood, fleeing out of every doorway. If there was a time for me to run, it would be now, but I can't. I have to see the sketch first.

"Gather all Healers." Devon ushers Harper to the front hall. "Have them parcel out the remaining serum for Caretakers to hold in the field. I'll order Guardians to transport Cera's mother along with any sick and wounded to the training room. You'll be secure there."

I hadn't considered my mother's safety. I'm thankful Devon has. Before Harper leaves, she flings her arms around Devon, burying her face in his neck.

Foster steps in front of me and briskly smooths the drawing

on the table. "Quickly, Cera. I believe only you can accurately decipher the message." I'm taken aback by his use of my first name and the way his usually well-behaved hair hangs in his face. "If there is anything—anything at all—that suggests a change in our strategy, please advise." His voice is urgent, pleading. "The Alliance can protect the Well only in the limited ways given to us. You see with different eyes. Trust the solution that is made clear to you. The outcome may not be what is expected, but the path will be right, I assure you."

The drumming vibration grows louder. The Delacroix painting falls, catching on the corner of an open crate. The canvas rips, cutting Milton's daughter free.

"Come on, Blighty, whatcha got?" Cole leans on the corner of the table fidgeting with that chess piece.

I slide the flimsy sheets together and, as fast as possible, take in every beautiful, yet terrifying, stroke Maddox drew: Consuming flames lick the earth. A dark cloud rolls across a teetering bridge, a suspension bridge. Planks split and then fall under the weight.

I work hard to steady the image on the shaking table. I squint through the faint light. Half of the bridge was erased and then redrawn, as if the bridge had been broken right where the paper was torn. Rain falls to the ground, running across a field like strands of hair stretched in the mud. Wrenching grief snakes through me, confirming Maddox's death. There has to be something else—something more. But the only clear image is the bridge. A message that says I will give Sage exactly what he wants.

"Time's up," Gray announces.

Foster blocks him. "Do you see a solution?" His penetrating eyes look to mine.

I spill the whole truth, even though I know it will cost my life. "Sage uses his powers to spark a fire, here." I show them the fires that burn the Garden. "The realms are linked." I point to the bridge and the dark cloud rolling across. "And here . . ." I glance at Maddox. "Everyone dies." I swallow hard. If this is the vision Sage intercepted, he knows he'll win.

"There's got to be something more." Cole spins one half of the drawing upside down.

I turn the sketch back. "I'm telling you what the vision shows."

Cole spins the paper sideways. "Try looking at it from a different angle."

"That's not how it works, Cole." Anger seeps under my skin. A thunderous pulse shakes the room. The grand center chandelier wobbles, slipping from its hinges, but holds steady for now. "I'm telling you what it says. Sage is about to break through the Circuit Wall. He knows what the vision shows and will ensure every detail will come to pass. There's no way to stop it."

"Look harder." Cole pushes the drawing closer, badgering a hard finger at it.

"I told you, there's no—"

He slams the white queen on the table in front of me. "Look again!"

Heat boils through my veins. I knock the chess piece in his direction. "The *only* answer to stopping the vision is *me*! I'm the bridge that joins the realms. Take away the bridge, and you can stop the vision."

Chunks of plaster fall from the ceiling, and with it comes another chandelier. Glass shatters. Crates topple. Metal clanks across the floor. I throw my hands over my head as the room darkens. Maddox shelters me to his chest.

The steady vibration resumes, shaking the walls and the sketches. I slip out of Maddox's arms, but he stays rooted at my side.

Impatient motorcycles rev in the front drive. I'm shocked that Gray hasn't taken me out. "Decoys are ready. We need to get in place. Now." His voice rumbles offbeat with the roaring thunder. "Maddox, get to the training room. Stay hidden with the Healers."

Maddox shakes off Gray's hold. "I'm fighting this battle."

"You're a Guardian—"

"I'm also a Blade, and you know it." There's a shift in his stance, a power that radiates through the contour of his tight muscles. With those intense eyes and hair swept back, he's very much a Blade. I push to the table for one final look at my three visions before Gray carts me away.

Three.

There's something about the number three.

"*Prepare thee for another sight.*" Milton whispers in my head as I put two pieces of the torn sketch together where the paper thinned from so much erasing.

I hold out a hand. "Wait. There is something here."

"I'll gather more light." Foster rushes off, glass crunching under his hard soles.

"Why did you erase this part of the bridge?" I ask Maddox.

"It kept changing. The bridge would form, then break, but it wasn't clear why."

Foster returns with a trembling flame in a glass lantern. The soft light dances over the sketches, making them seem alive. In that moment, the rumbling recedes. Silence takes its place.

Something strikes me. Something I didn't notice until now. All three visions have a lantern in the corner. I glance at the far end of the table, at my other visions. None of those do.

"Quiet is never good," Cole says.

"Shh," I slide the images around. As soon as I move the picture of the tree up top, the hairs on the back of my neck rise. Something *is* here. Cole was right. I slide the one of the goblet to the middle. The spilled black liquid now appears to be an obsidian lake. I spin part of the torn bridge upside down and move it to the bottom. The other piece I turn sideways. When I do, the broken bridge becomes a ladder. My hands are shaking.

The three individual visions, like a mosaic, piece together

to make one picture. Yes. Three separate lanterns cast different points of light, illuminating one image.

"At this last sight, assured that man shall live," Milton whispers. My heart pumps faster.

Man shall live . . . This is the answer I've been searching for, isn't it? These three visions, when combined, tell me how to save the Awakened—and Maddox.

Throttling motorcycles shatter the silence. I read the sketches as fast as I can.

In the center, the tree rests over a black lake. The torn bridge is inverted, half of the ladder leads somewhere underneath where sparks light. Cole won't stop spinning that chess piece, distracting me. I close my eyes for a moment. Let the images show me what they want. Don't force it. Don't try to figure it out. I clear my mind and then open my eyes, doing what Pop believed I could do.

Flickering light refracts off the shattered glass across the room. From my periphery, the image comes into focus as if rising off the page. A gust of wind smelling of the arbor sweeps through the room, rustling the sketches.

The images shift but remain clear. Hands press on the tree, blackening the bark, sending adders through the grass. Then a strike of bright light explodes into white rain.

Striking is the answer. But strike what?

Foster sets the lantern on the table. "Do you, in fact, see something?"

"These three visions make one large image. The sketch with the goblet represents the Well. And this one"—I point to the vision with the tree—"I'm not quite sure what the black tree represents, but it sits on top of the Well. And here, the bridge that's formed sits under the water as an explosion turns it"—I move the last vision into position—"into a ladder leading to something underneath. Or new. Or . . . I'm not exactly sure." I step back so the others can see.

Foster gives a quick nod. "When the time comes, the answer will become clear. You'll know which path to choose."

Gray's patience has run out. "If you're going to fight, then let's go. You're ready." He tosses a shield to Maddox, who catches it without looking. "But stay at my side at all times. The plan—"

"I heard the plan," Maddox says. "This place echoes, remember?"

Gray slides Maddox a weapon from across the table. "Caretakers and lower-ranked Blades have the perimeter. You'll fight midfield alongside Lance and me. Albrecht handles Sage. And Tripton?" He slides another weapon over to Cole. It's Cole's Steel, the stolen knife with the woven handle. "You take care of the Blight."

He wants *Cole* to kill me? I search Gray's face for mercy, but he avoids my gaze. Cole stands next to me, looking about as shocked as I am. This has to be Gray's sick way of hazing Cole, making him prove his allegiance once and for all, or some type of punishment for helping me rescue my mother. Why else would Gray choose him? He has to know Cole won't kill me. At least I don't think Cole will.

The next thing I know, exploding thunder blasts the Garden with a violent jolt. The floor ripples. I'm knocked off my feet.

The ceiling groans. Then plummets, collapsing into the center of the room. I duck and cover my head. Commands shout though the cloudy air, but Maddox calling my name is the only one I hear. Flames from the broken lantern run free. Lightning flashes in the wintry air as an icy chill courses through me.

It's done. Sage has broken through.

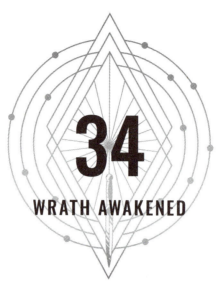

34

WRATH AWAKENED

"**M**ove it!" Cole finds me through the smoke and pulls me away from the fiery debris. Another support beam crashes down, devouring the books and the sketches. My copy of Milton evaporates into black ash as the fire licks everything in its path.

I'm coughing. Choking on the smoke. An arctic wind rushes down, clearing the haze enough for me to see Maddox fighting the rising flames, shouting my name with desperation. He can't reach me, and he knows it.

Frantic motorcycles roar and then peel down the drive. "Do it now, Tripton!" Gray drags Maddox to safety with the help of Foster.

Cole ignores Gray's command. He takes me by the elbow and hovers low, covering his face with the collar of his shirt. I do the same. Flames lap at our heels as we search for a way out, but we're trapped.

The heat is searing. Sweat beads on my temples. I look up, hoping to catch a clean breath of air from the night sky. At that moment a throng of hissing Legions with black vellum wings fervently chase the sound of buzzing motorcycles. Two monstrous beasts with cavernous holes for eyes break from the pack and dive into the flames. They're giddy, searching for life to devour.

Cole and I stay down low, hopefully unseen. Smoke mixes with the stench of sulfur. I wrestle a tickle in my chest, suppressing the urge to cough, but that only makes it worse.

I squeeze Cole's arm. I don't have a weapon. No one entrusted me with one. And I can't command the beasts away or else I'll connect the realms. Cole lifts his Steel with a slight tremble, and I wonder if he's ever killed a creature.

Luckily, these beasts hunt by sound alone. If we stay quiet, they might flee. But the persistent cough pounds inside my lungs, demanding release. My eyes water. I can't choke it back any longer. I release it into my sleeve.

The beasts let out a piercing shriek, the one that haunts my dreams. Their hollow eyes fix in our direction, creeping closer as they sway in unison, searching. I stay still. Please don't hear me. Please let the scrambler tucked in the pouch on my arm throw them off.

They twitch their elongated arms as they hang in midair over the flames that consume the broken table. Cole can't strike them without getting burned. The crawling fire hems us in the corner. Our only way out is to climb up the wall and escape through a broken section where the roof collapsed. We can't stay pinned here much longer. We have to make a move. And fast.

I look to Cole the same way I do with Maddox. But he stands frozen. The Steel is positioned out in front of him as he covers his face with his shirt collar. He stares at the beast with an expression accepting death. But I won't let us die.

I reach through searing heat and quietly pick up an apple from the toppled cart nearby. I'm just about to chuck it across the room as a distraction, hopefully giving us time to make our way out when, without warning, both Legions spin into black tornados and launch up into the night sky, disappearing in the same direction as the others.

The scramblers must have worked. Thank goodness. If

I had tossed the apple, they would have known we were here and searched until they found us. Maybe even alerted others. Now that they're gone, I quickly work at stacking empty crates the best I can.

Cole coughs. "What are you doing?"

"Getting us out." I heave the Martin painting on top, propping it up as a ramp. Then I climb. My boots stay steady beneath me as I reach up, my fingers grasping the ledge. I'm an inch shy of getting a good grip to pull myself up and over.

Cole scales my makeshift stairs, nimble and light. He holds my waist, lifting me up. "Go."

With his help, I pull myself up and swing one leg over the wall, much like I did with the metal fence on my outing in East Ridge. I try not to breathe the billowing smoke as I search for a way down. It's a twelve-foot jump. At least.

The crumbling wall teeters. Oh no. I swing my other leg around as fast as possible. I feel myself falling forward as Cole appears beside me.

"Jump!" He vaults over the wall. I follow.

The wall chases me to the ground, crashing at my heels. Cole drags me away with a fierce grip that solidifies his Bent as a Blade. He doesn't let go until we're well past the water fountain, hidden in the shadow of the woods.

Fire lights the sky, a raging dawn at night. Cole removes the Steel from the strap on his belt. His mouth is set in a determined line. "I'm taking you out of here. We'll find a place to hide."

"I'm not hiding anymore. If I run, then my vision comes true." The word "confirmed," scrawled in my mom's handwriting, flashes across my mind. "Only two visions in my life have changed. And only because I—we—ran into the fight. If I had more time, I could've changed a third. I can't let time steal more lives."

"You think the Alliance will let you step foot anywhere near the Well? They'll kill you at first sight. Maybe Gray was showing mercy when he assigned me to take you out, but that will change if you go out there and try to fight."

"If I run away, somehow Sage will win. I may not have the special gifts or powers you have, but what I have is a chance. One chance to do what only I can do—strike the Inner Wall to make it spark enough to splinter Sage. Because you know as well as I do that otherwise, no one will make it out alive."

Cole's frown confirms that truth. "Don't you think Sage wants you there so he can lure you to activate your power?"

"Of course he does. It's written in the vision. But you don't change anything by avoiding it. You stand in the face of that terrifying reality and then find a way to overcome."

"What if the temptation to join him is too great?" Cole persists. "You can't be both a fox and a lion—not with Sage. He plays the game better than anyone else. He always gets what he wants."

Cole's collarbone is smudged with soot but not a Dissenter's mark. "Not always."

A Cormorant screeches in the distance. Cole makes the mistake of looking over his shoulder. In that moment, I do the one thing I do best.

I run.

The boots don't make it easy, but I sprint up the drive toward the blistering flames and skid around the corner, ducking into the arbor. The growing fire gives me enough light to navigate the buckled floor. The scent of ash thickens the air. Cole's footsteps aren't far behind.

I hopscotch through the canopy. The ceiling caves in as I reach the other side. I'm unscathed, but Cole's path is blocked. I look back at him. The shadows from the fire highlight his tense features.

"Go find your family," I urge him. "Now's your chance. Do what you've always wanted." I take one final look, etching his troubled face and those brilliant eyes in my mind. Then, knowing he's safe, I leave him behind and sprint full force through the maze. I race with one hand along the leaves to guide me through the inky dark. I don't need light to know the leaves are turning yellow in my wake.

A raindrop pelts my head, and then another. The biting air turns to winter and tastes of nectar wrestling ash. A vicious hunger leaps inside me, leading me deeper into the maze.

I run faster. Getting closer. The Well is the last place I should be. But I know it's the very place I need to be. Ash snuffs out the nectar scent. The Legions' piercing shrieks override the agonizing cries of the Awakened army as battle sounds grow louder.

Then the maze ends.

I spill onto the edge of war. The ground smolders. The air smells of sulfur, ash, and burning pine. Milton's verse of hell spins in my mind:

> *Clouds began*
> *To darken and all the hill, and smoke to roll*
> *In dusky wreaths, reluctant flames, the sign*
> *Of wrath awaked.*

Wrath is awakened for sure. The barren treetops surrounding the clearing are in flames, lighting the battle below. Pockets of small fires ignite the field.

Legions invade the sloping meadow with gleeful shrieks. Cormorants circle like vultures, claiming the marshy basin as their own. Lights and laser projections fill the space with the energy of an outdoor concert as a deep vibration invades the air with the thrumming soundtrack designed by the Ghost Army.

The front line of the Awakened army fight along the perimeter with shields too small to do them any good as Legions rocket down, luckily missing by a foot or two.

In the *anarchy of chaos* I can't make out the distinct silhouettes of anyone I know. But somewhere in the sea of people, Devon, Kellan, Tanji, and all the others are fighting for their lives.

I shove back the desire to command the beasts away. With the Ghost Army's projections, the disabling beat pulsing through the Garden, plus the scramblers, the Awakened army is holding their own for now.

My job is to get my hands on the Paradise Steel and somehow slip through the battle unnoticed until I reach the cloaked Well. I'll wait, hidden behind the projection until Sage is in position. Then I'll strike—Steel to Wall—and blast him to dust, knowing the cost will be my life.

Bubbling black clouds shroud the sky. Thunder growls and the shrill cries of the Cormorants pierce my ears. The beasts swoop down through the middle of the field, attacking pockets of Blades fighting closer to the Well, but the creatures miss their targets by several feet. It looks as if the scramblers and scents Harper created are working. I touch the pouch on my shoulder, feeling the tiny square. The scrambler is still there. I might be protected from the Legions, but I don't have the potion to throw off my scent from the Cormorants. Hopefully draping the cowl-neck over my head will be enough to cloak me from the beasts' sight.

I pull the fabric over my head. As soon as I step onto the lawn, caramel threads illuminate the ground with the Alliance symbol and a flicker of hope warms me.

Lightning flashes. From what I can tell, a group of the Awakened army is fighting around the outer rings of the symbol near the woods. Another army that looks to be geared-up Blades fights halfway down the sloping field where several more glowing rings pulse under the grass. The Well, with its marshy reeds and warping protective Inner Wall, hides between the two trees, but right now it's cloaked behind a reflective screen, mirroring pockets of fire and the fighting army. In each of the four quadrants of the field, additional projections have been set up as decoys, mimicking the Inner Wall. They're so vivid the creatures can't tell which location is real. And if I didn't know better, neither could I. I go further into the fight and search for a clear path. Roaring thunder drowns bloody cries. Bodies fall along the perimeter to the east. I can't tell who is fighting and who has fallen.

The itch to command the creatures away grows stronger. I press my lips together, swallowing the taste of ash. I'm sure Sage is here, somewhere. I can feel the arctic coil winding inside me, but I can't find him through the rising smoke.

A loud hiss sweeps in my direction as a Legion whips near me. Adrenaline jolts my reflexes. I duck and roll just in time. The Legion isn't so lucky. It catches the tip of a towering Blade's Steel and explodes into a shower of red embers. Tanji emerges from the ashes.

I rise with her help. "Thanks."

The fire highlights her frown as she notices that I'm weaponless. "Take this." She thrusts her Steel in my palm. The humming metal burns with icy heat, not unlike the way it did when I trained with Cole. "Keep your chin up. Listen for the wind." She removes another weapon from her belt strap. "It's time these cowards get their payback." Her pouch is missing from her arm.

"Where's your scrambler?" I ask.

"Lost it in a hit."

"Take mine." I quickly remove my strap and fasten it around her thick bicep.

As soon as I'm done, an angry buzz whips through the sulfur wind. I spin around and cut the air with the Steel. The beast explodes on impact, the hilt sizzling my palm.

"Good stuff." Tanji nods as if pleased with my skill. But I'm shaking with fear, betrayal, satisfaction—a million clashing emotions. I can't sort out which side of me has control. A wounded cry cuts through the night. "Go." Tanji races toward the sound, disappearing into the smoke cloud.

I'm not a fighter, but something about having the weapon brings comfort as I navigate the field, aiming for the Well. Without a scrambler, I keep my steps light, listening as they blend with the clanking metal and groans of war. I head east around the top of the hill, staying out of the main battle. I sneak closer to the decoy projection, cloaking a thirty-foot area. The beasts stay a good distance away from the sparking image.

The further down I go, the softer the ground. This far down, it's easier to see the rivers of golden Current racing through the grass, pooling under the Awakened army's feet.

A Current no one can see but me.

Some threads shine brighter than others. I glance at my own feet. The hollow ground is black beneath me, but my fabric glows with the dust of a thousand stars.

As I make my way around the screen, a group of Blades fights Legions twice their size. Kellan is stabbing, slicing, ducking, and defending with fluid speed. The grass glows beneath them as they battle. My hand twitches as the weapon warms my palm, wanting to join their fight. But I'm not a Blade. My knife skills don't come close to theirs, and I could end up doing more damage than good. I need to stick to my part, despite the temptation to play a different one.

I'm halfway down the hill. This deep inside the basin, wounded cries echo louder. The ground is muddier. The smoky air thickens as war smothers the field from all sides. But the Ghost Army's strategy is working. And the holographic fabric is doing a fine job of masking me as I race down the lawn to the willow tree.

Thunder roars. Louder. Closer. I slide my sleeve over my palm so the Steel won't burn my skin. I'm close to the Well. I can feel the tug, a deep pulse through my blood fueling me with the same hope, same quiet confidence, I felt before. I inch closer, knowing I can get into position without anyone seeing me. The closer I get, the more I tremble, knowing what I'm about to lose.

And I'm not sure if I'll be strong enough to go through with it when the time comes.

That's when I realize there's one other problem.

No one in the field knows what I'm about to do. If I strike the Inner Wall while Sage is near, he will splinter, but I may end up killing everyone in the blast. Someone needs to warn the Awakened army as I strike so they can protect themselves from the explosion.

I survey the field for someone I trust. A group of Blades fights on the northeast side of the hill, not far from another decoy projection. They're battling a swarm of young Cormorants. The glowing light under their coordinated steps is way brighter than any Awakened lining the perimeter. They are probably more advanced Blades, or maybe Maddox and Gray. I start in their direction. But stop as soon as the smoke clears. Through the dancing flames, I make out Albrecht's graceful silhouette as she executes each kill with precise choreography. Behind her, Silver Assassin and Suspenders shadow the rhythmic cadence of the fight.

If they're attacking Cormorants, then where is Sage?

He's here, somewhere. I can feel the coil deepening inside me, luring with the restless, gnawing ache of destruction. But I can't find him. Then a flash of lightning illuminates the sky. That's when I spot Maddox not far from the oak tree. But he's way across the lawn.

Maddox is holding off Cormorants the size of bulldogs. Even from this distance it's easy to see the radiant light shining under his feet like a sunbeam. Gray's Current shines brightly too. The brothers battle Cormorants, dodging hits and slinging the Steel with synchronized ease. Gray fends off the creatures using two knives while Maddox isolates a smaller one, striking the black beast. Slaying monsters.

The ground rumbles with shuddering thunder. Louder. Closer.

A buzzing Legion breaks from the hilltop and swoops into the valley, heading straight for Maddox. On impulse, I run, Steel in hand, chasing down the vile beast. The Legion torpedoes faster, spinning tighter as if controlled by something other than itself. Maddox's back is turned. He won't see it. Gray is too occupied to notice. No one else is around.

I pump my legs faster. I can't reach him in time, but I can protect him with one word. The Legion rockets faster. Screeching louder.

I can't hold back.

The cry explodes as I shout. "Maddox!"

Then I slap my hand over my mouth, stifling the overwhelming desire to command the Legion.

Maddox glances up, then ducks seconds before impact. He raises his Steel, piercing the beast. The creature explodes.

My knees sink into the mud.

Maddox lives.

But I'm painfully aware that I've given myself away, the same way I did on the streets of East Ridge. Because a smooth, melodic voice echoing from the woods confirms it.

It's a voice I know all too well.

35

A PLACE FORETOLD

"*I come no enemy.*" The storm clouds churn and growl overhead as Sage's voice, tinted with that light accent, creeps like a haunting shadow in the midnight woods. I hate how the strangled longing for my father leaps up as he quotes Milton. "*But to set free / From out this dark and dismal house of pain . . . / To search, with wandering quest, a place foretold.*"

My heart won't slow down. I know he's speaking to me as he quotes the archfiend's speech luring his daughter, Sin, to unlock the gates of hell. But in the presence of the Well, his deceptively gentle words don't wield the power on my heart the way they did at his place. I stay rooted in the mud, not twenty feet from the Well, as wisps of hope stir deep inside me.

Wearing his white linen suit, Sage is easy to find in the blackened woods. As I suspected, he enters from the northwest corner of the hill, walking through billowing smoke in his human form.

As soon as he steps onto the field, the ground shakes with a violent tremble. He releases an excruciating growl as a black cloud erupts, transforming his handsome features into those of the monstrous gorilla beast and no longer a man.

Lightning cracks across the sky for all to see his goat horns lying flat against his oblong head. Another flash reveals his oil-slick tail slithering behind him. His obsidian snake-like eyes shimmer in the tawny light of the forest fire. Fighting slows as the Awakened army takes in the gruesome sight at the top of the hill.

I'm seized by panic. Paralyzed. He's much bigger than I imagined, even from my brief encounter in the woods.

Legions swell with pride. Cormorants, the fractured form of Ayala—Sage's fiancé, beloved, or whatever twisted relationship they have—shriek and flock behind him, their wings pulsing like a cape adorning their king. The tiny white Cormorant, Ayala herself, is nothing but a tiny speck perched on his shoulder.

The Steel feels too small in my fist. This encounter is nothing like fighting the Legions on the streets of East Ridge. My once-confident plan to strike the Inner Wall suddenly feels grossly inadequate. But I have no choice. I have to stay strong and do my part. It might be the only chance the Alliance has to survive. But Albrecht has to get Sage close enough to the Well. And not kill me first.

She's marching toward Sage with Silver Assassin and Suspenders at her side. I lower my head to stay disguised by the holographic fabric. I can't strike the Inner Wall now; Sage is too far away for the blast to do any good. And someone needs to know of my plan. Maddox isn't far from the oak tree. If he could turn around and catch my expression as I lift the Steel, maybe through the firelight, he'll read me and know what I'm about to do. Or maybe he won't.

When Albrecht stands her ground and faces Sage, undaunted, I move to find Maddox, dodging Blades as they sling swords and defend with dented shields.

Albrecht's voice cuts through the clamor as she faces Sage. *"The constellations this year seem unfavorable to rebels.* It seems your true identity, and those of your army, cannot be hidden in this place."

"Greeting me with the words spoken by your family long ago? Quite charming, Borgia." Sage shifts his volcanic eyes in my direction. I lower my head further. I must be blending in with the fire, because Sage doesn't call me out. Instead he focuses on Albrecht. "I believe my patience has rewarded me a success beyond a simple skirmish at the gate. Your forefather's death was delectably essential in bringing me one step closer. I look forward to what hidden treasures you will share with me after you die."

"*Words can deceive. But eyes we should trust.*" Albrecht stands firm.

I crouch down as a group of Blades fights off the beasts, staying away from the spreading fire. A Legion hisses behind me. I lift my Steel and cut the air. Claire is suddenly beside me and does the same. Both weapons catch the beast, exploding it into red cinder.

"Sweet hit." She smiles at me for the first time. But I don't smile back.

I could have cut her. They might not have a fear of striking one another with their weapons, but I do. I'm the only one able to break the Current in the Paradise Steel. She has no idea what danger she was in.

I nod at her and back away, working hard to reach Maddox and stick to my plan. As I get closer to the Well, the frigid air turns warmer and tastes of nectar, feeding my determination. I race around the growing fire.

Even from this distance, it's not hard to see Sage's jagged grin as he circles Albrecht on the side of the hill. "It is quite charming how you trust in the words of your ancestor Cesare. A man who could not defend the gate, who so tragically trusted a Blight—the very thing you swore in your heart you would never do. Yet, look how much lower you have fallen."

Sage's words break her. No longer poised, she launches at the monster with unbridled fury.

This is my chance. I run blind through the smell of burnt sugar and charcoal. I'm listening to the sounds of war, hissing Legions, and whirling Steel. A fat raindrop splatters on my head. I dodge, duck, and make my way across the lawn, determined to find Maddox.

I leap over a fallen body. The stench of blood and burnt hair trails behind me. I'm trying not to cry when I plow right into him. My palms land hard on his chest as he takes me by the shoulders. His intense eyes are terrified and relieved all at once. His face is covered in soot, his blond hair muddy and tangled. "What are you doing here? Go."

"This is our chance to change things, Maddox." Raindrops tap my head, my face. My hands won't stop shaking. "We can't rely on Sage to strike the Wall, or even believe that we could deflect his power from a shield to do enough damage. But I can do it. If I strike the Inner Wall when Sage is close enough." I gesture with the Steel. He quickly takes me away from a swarm of Cormorants. "But you have to warn the Awakened," I say, catching my breath as I scan the sky for creatures. Another raindrop catches my eyelashes. Stings my eyes. "Spread the word of what I'm about to do. When someone sees me about to strike, tell them to shout the command word: rise. They'll know to lift their shields and stay safe from the blast."

"Cera, don't." Light from the raging fire flickers shadows across Maddox's face. "Leave before—"

A Legion whirls in our direction. Maddox whips me behind him and cuts the air, exploding the beast. The rain falls faster.

"I'm not leaving," I tell him as we stand back to back. "This is our one chance to change the world. Together."

Maddox spins me around, ready to protest, when a streak of red lightning and the stringent scent of sulfur heats the air. The bolt lands not far from where I was standing. Sage fired a blast at the admiral but missed. And that shot nearly disintegrated me.

But Albrecht is pushing Sage closer to the Inner Wall. No time like the present to execute the plan. I risk my heart and do the one thing I've never dared. I throw my arms around Maddox's neck and bring him close. I kiss him in the steady rain. A kiss so bold and deep my feet leave the ground. No visions flash between us, only the wrenching ache of goodbye.

Our kiss breaks as Maddox is yanked back. Gray drags him away through the wispy smoke as a Legion swoops down. But I don't move fast enough, and the beast slams into my chest.

The Steel flies from my hand. I sail through the air and land hard on my back. Rocks dig into my spine. The sky spins. Rain pelts my face. My whole body radiates with searing pain. I lie in the mud as the battle swirls around me. I taste blood and ash. Feel heat from the creeping fire. I need to move. Run. Find the Steel. But I can't. I can barely breathe.

Legions circle wildly overhead, shrieking with joy. Stupid beasts are calling me out. I push to my knees. Barely get to my feet. When I rise, Sage claps. Slow. Mocking. Terrifying.

"Well done, *ma belle*." Despite his beastly form, that longing ache rises again in response to my father's essence. "I knew you were here. For, '*I feel thy power / Within me clear*.'" I grit my teeth, hating how he claims Milton as his own. With him less than thirty feet away, it's easy to see how his charred skin shines *with a glossy scurf*, and slithers with the screams of souls trapped inside. Perhaps my father is one of them. My stomach roils. *Noxious vapors* flow from the black smoke surrounding him.

The ache in me snuffs out.

Through my ringing ears, I hear Albrecht command my termination. Sage shakes his horned head with dissatisfaction. He whips his tail, keeping Albrecht and her team away. "*Queen of this universe*," Sage says to me. His voice is too gentle with Milton's words. Too kind. Too clear in my head. "*Do not believe / Those rigid threats of death*."

He raises a hideous arm, commanding a wall of hissing Legions ten feet thick to surround Albrecht and her troupe, blocking any path to me. They're trapped on the north part of the field, caught in the swarm.

"*Ye shall not die.*" Sage descends the hill. Carefully. Slowly. "*How should ye?*"

My feet twitch, begging me to run and slam the Steel into the Inner Wall. But a Legion beats me to it. The beast sails past me, aiming for the spot between the trees. It disappears right as a bright light explodes from behind the screen. The projected image blips, then blinks back. But it was enough for Sage to notice. He contorts his giant head. His gruesome tongue licks the air. He's searching for a scent.

I drop to my knees, scouring the ground, looking for the Steel as rain bullets down. Threads of the honey-colored light pour out from the Well and flow through the grass to fuel the Awakened. But even with the soft glow, the smolder and the thick haze make seeing anything on the ground four feet beyond me impossible.

Sage has figured out what we've done with the projections in a matter of seconds. He hurls his red current to the ground again and again and again, shaking the earth, splitting the field wide open, taking down the reflective images, and cutting out the soundtrack disorienting the beasts, destroying any advantage we had in the fight.

The incessant thrumming turns quiet, but there's still a lingering hum in my head. Smoke dances in front of the warping Inner Wall, highlighting exactly where the Well hides. Whatever confidence the Awakened army had suddenly evaporates. I don't stop searching through the grass for the weapon. Searching for anything to stop Sage.

Anything but the words from my mouth.

At the thought, my body suddenly shakes, as that insatiable, greedy power churns, restlessly demanding release.

Legions shriek. Cormorants take to the sky, ready for final victory.

Sage is too strong. His army, never-ending.

It's clear that our plans to defeat him will be next to impossible to carry out.

36
BATTLES AND REALMS

Sage glides through as if immune to the war, floating over the smolder *of rigid spears . . . and shields.* Unstoppable. The glowing threads from the Current pulse through the field and up the sloping terrain like lines of a fallen constellation.

Thunder crashes across the sky. The steady rain battles the growing fires. All while Sage picks off anyone who dares attack him. He tosses his current at a girl with a flower headband, sending her limp body tumbling into the Inner Wall. A bright spark kicks back, disintegrating her on contact. But the blast wasn't even strong enough to damage a nearby Legion who scurries out of the way.

And here I stand, weaponless.

Useless.

Soaked by freezing rain.

"How many, *ma belle?*" Sage remains at the base of the hill, a good distance away from me and the Inner Wall. The small bird, Ayala, drifts from his shoulder, fluttering between raindrops and dodging the flames. "How many have to die before you join me?"

Sage casts his red current at Grumpy the Blade, who is fighting off a Legion with all his might, almost victorious, until his body is struck. Grumpy wails in agony. His Steel falls from his hand as he collapses. The Legion swoops down, engulfing him. The caramel stream of light once puddled beneath Grumpy's body is smothered by the Legion as it greedily drinks the Current.

I feel sick. An uncontrollable tremble rises in me, spreading through every nerve. Every fiber. Every sinew of my being.

I will not let Sage win.

Ever.

Lighting flashes. The rain falls stronger, wrestling the flames.

"I didn't think you were such a monster, letting so many die." Shadows from the fire dance across Sage's gruesome face as he flicks his red current once again, picking off another Blade. But through the streaming rain, I can't tell who it is. "How much death and destruction will you allow before connecting the realms?"

Sage strikes again. This time it's Lance, as he and Maddox fend off Moloch. Lance crumples. I throw my hand over my mouth to stifle a cry as tears blur my eyes. I can't stand here and do nothing. But without a weapon, what can I do?

Lightning fractures the murky dark. Black fog seeps through the woods at the top of the hill. As soon as the rolling wave reaches the lawn, the Legions form. Ten times more than were at the gate.

Thunder breaks open the sky. Angry rain pelts my head and runs down my spine.

There's no way we will all survive. Albrecht and her team are swallowed, fighting off Legions. Who knows if they're even alive? Maddox is battling Moloch with the help of Gray and Devon, but now Belial and several other Cormorants join the fight. There's no way the remaining Awakened army can defeat this next wave of Legions.

And Sage knows it. He bows his head. *"Empress, the way is ready."*

My temples throb. I want to shout at Sage to stop quoting Milton. Stop reciting the archfiend's lines to a pre-fallen Eve, asking her to lead him to the forbidden tree. But for all I know, those words might be considered a dissenting command, giving Sage exactly what he wants.

What I need is a weapon. Something I can drive deep into his stony heart. I know it won't kill him. I know he'll eventually heal, but at least he'll feel the wrenching pain.

I run toward a group fighting uphill, trying to stand their ground against the swarming mass of Legions that descend. A Steel glistens in the dirt. My boots sink into the mud as I try to run and reach it. I'm less than five feet away when Sage strikes the weapon, blasting the Steel somewhere out of my sight.

I'm shouting through the rain, begging for someone to give me a weapon, but Sage commands Belial and a pack of stocky Cormorants to keep everyone at bay.

He wants me isolated.

Alone.

"My sweet, Lonicera," he says, as I stand near the base of the field. Biting rain drenches my clothes but doesn't snuff out the fires near me. "Let's not play games. This is what you want; this is everything you've ever wanted." Sage prowls near me. A few daring Blades attempt to reach us but Sage knocks them away with his ghastly tail. This close, and in the russet firelight, I notice for the first time his tail is covered with millions of eyes.

Sage whips his tail out of my sight. "Together, we can harness the power of the Empyrean Well, and there will be no more running or hiding. You will have a life without visions, a life worthy of love, where you can be beautiful and wanted. One simple act is all it takes and you shall resurrect as a queen. For you can change . . . everything."

A knife feels lodged in my throat. But I wish it were his throat so I could cut out the words he's stolen from Maddox. The words Maddox believes so much about me. About us. About changing the world, together.

"You will join me, will you not?" Sage narrows his sickly eyes.

"I'm sure you will. For I believe you will do anything for love."

How could Sage ever believe I would join him?

But then he does the one thing he knows will bring me to my knees. He raises one long finger. Red sparks lick the tips of his talons as he aims them at Maddox. Maddox, who is fighting Moloch in the rain—alone. A strong light billows around him. But with his back turned, he won't see the blast until it's too late. Gray and Devon are too busy battling their own monsters to intervene. Maddox will die.

Sage follows the path of my stare. "Say the word and the boy shall live."

Lightning forks the sky. Maddox hits the ground, rolling to avoid a cut from Moloch's talon. His blond hair turns muddy, the same way it appeared in my vision.

The acrid stench of sulfur burns my nose, tastes rancid in my mouth. I shout through the rain, sloshing in the mud, racing toward Maddox, searching for a clear path away from Sage. But the vile demon blocks me. I don't give up. I launch at him. Kicking. Punching. Fighting with my useless bare hands to get away. My desperate fight does nothing but exhaust me. And now I'm trapped in a ring of fire with Sage blocking my way out. His tail swishes as he looks at me with those flickering obsidian eyes and something that resembles pity. The rain slows its fight.

Hissing steam rises from the ground as he speaks. "All those acts of bravery weren't noble at all. They were simply a means to hide what you are. All this time you've been attempting to become something you were never created to be: a mere pawn for the Alliance's tyranny. Deep down you knew that no matter what you did, how good you were, how many lives you saved, they would never accept you. Never grant your heart's desire."

My blood turns to slow, creeping ice that the heat from the searing fire can't thaw.

Sage's fingers spark once more, itching to unleash on Maddox.

The same way my powers itch inside me, begging to command the beasts away. Or Sage himself to die in a thousand fires. Both sides of me are warring for control as I face the monster I know I can't destroy.

"One act will grant you everything you've ever wanted. One simple act will give you the power to save whomever you choose." Sage's voice softens with that gentle lilt he knows sounds like my father. I think of the photo of my dad, laughing. Those eyes that said he loved me. My knees weaken.

But the venom in Sage's words spirals in my soul. Bodies litter the ground. Not many are left standing. It will only be a matter of time before Sage has destroyed each and every one and siphoned their knowledge, giving him even more power. If I have the ability to stop all this destruction, stop the killings, stop this endless bloodshed, what would I be if I didn't?

The gold in Sage's eyes warms with a hypnotic glow. He sends a quiet blast striking a wounded girl nearby whose shaky fingers are prying open a vial of healing serum. She collapses into the mud before the glass touches her lips. *Reach, then, and freely taste . . . / Taste this and be henceforth among the gods / Thyself a goddess, not to earth confined.*

Taste? *Taste.* The word echoes, a cobra's hiss in my dizzy head. *Consume . . .* Consume what? The serum? No. Taste something forbidden, the same way as Eve.

Sage's voice is steeped with a promise. "Join me, Lonicera, and you will grant them life."

The greedy power inside me leaps at Sage's request, straining to break free.

The rain continues but struggles to snuff out the fires. Shields and swords of the fallen glisten in the hazy stench of battle. Without a weapon, there is nothing I can do to save the Awakened except give Sage what he wants. Belial circles above me, swooping in to attack anyone who tries to reach me. But when I hear Maddox cry out in pain, my heart nearly bursts. The temptation is too great. And Sage knows it.

I want to save lives. It's all I've wanted. I walked into the fight believing, *"at this last sight, assured that man shall live."* But here I stand, no different than the last Destroyer Blight. Sage has cornered me. And no one will survive unless I agree. If joining the realms is what it takes, then what other choice do I have?

The words to give Sage what he wants wrestle on my tongue. Heart and mind collide as heat from the flames grows hotter. Closer. Urging me to choose.

Choose. The word echoes inside me. Pop believed every choice would reveal who I am. Create what I'll become.

"Hey, Blighty!" A shout cuts through the battle, sounding too much like Cole. "Don't give up!" It *is* Cole. He should have been long gone. Why didn't the idiot head back to reconcile with his family and do the one thing he's wanted? Why is he here, in the haze of war, tucked under the barren branches of a willow tree?

Through the rising smoke his Steel glistens in one hand. He clutches something small in the other.

It's a tiny white bird.

No. A Cormorant.

Ayala.

37

DYING

"**S**age will negotiate." Cole swiftly sidesteps an oncoming Legion through the branches of the willow tree. "He won't let his beloved die. Will you, Sage?" Brawling flames give enough light for everyone to see Cole point the shimmering Steel at the tiny beast, taunting Sage.

Sage takes the bait. He releases a thunderous growl and slings red lightning at Cole. But Cole is nimble and avoids the hit, ducking behind the trunk. I want Cole to leave and let the tiny beast go, but then I look around.

Suddenly I understand.

The Cormorants are held captive in midair. Their wings flap in unison, but they don't dare move as they watch Cole deftly outstep each strike Sage sends his way. Even the Legions have slowed their pursuit.

Cole has given the Awakened army an advantage by creating the ultimate distraction.

"Give her to me!" Sage pitches another bolt, but he's careful not to strike the Inner Wall. Cole quickly dances around the tree trunk. Sage floats closer to Cole. Closer to the Well. Not only has Cole given me a chance to escape, but it's clear he's maneuvering hard to get Sage to strike the Inner Wall and create a splintering blast. So I won't have to.

Lighting breaks through the clouds as another storm approaches. Maddox is lying on the field, alive but wounded. A Cormorant the size of a mountain lion hovers over him with a talon inches from his chest. Although he's cut and bleeding, Maddox shanks the Steel deep into the floating creature's heart with incredible strength. The monster shrieks. Before it crashes down, Maddox shoves it aside, and then leaps to his feet, taking out another Cormorant that has trapped Devon nearby. Others soon follow Maddox's lead and take up the fight.

But it's Cole that has me worried. He navigates every strike of Sage's current with perfect ease, dodging, ducking, and daring, as each blast scars the earth. But how long can he keep this up before . . .

No, Cole will *not* die.

Thunder rattles my core. I race through large drops of freezing rain toward the base of the hill not far from the Well where several bodies lie. I need a weapon to join the fight. The burning air tastes acrid. I swallow back the vomit wanting to make its way up.

A Legion whips in front of me, shrieking madly. Stringy saliva sticks to its mouth. It gurgles, hisses. The outline of a face emerges from inside the flaking gray skin of the beast. Nausea grips me. It's a face I know. A face with one kind eye. Mark. Any resemblance quickly vanishes, transforming back into the inhuman being as other creatures surround me, hemming me in.

I rush the throng of Legions, trying to break through their wall. The fabric sizzles on impact, making the Legions recoil. It's enough to give me a clear path out and see that Cole is now on the south side of the Well, moving Sage near the willow tree, drawing him away from me.

Sage's fury is growing. Each toss of his angry lightning is faster. Stronger. Brighter. I don't know how much longer Cole can keep this up while holding the tiny creature in his hands.

"You will surely die!" Sage throws a bolt at Cole with such rage the willow tree catches fire.

Cole backs away from the shelter of the willow, closer to the marshy reeds that outline the Inner Wall. His head turns my direction and his movement stops. "Gray, don't!"

Don't? Don't what? I turn in time to catch something sailing through the dark, sparkling as it hurtles in my direction with raging speed.

It's a weapon. Paradise Steel.

By the time I register what's happening, it's too late. I'm hit with a deep punching wound between my ribs. Its force pushes me backward through the wintry air. I land hard on my back in the mud not far from the Inner Wall.

The sky opens, dumping sheets of freezing rain. The ground trembles as I lie there, stunned. While everyone was distracted, Gray accomplished the one thing he's wanted since I set foot in the Garden.

My chest aches. I'm afraid of what I'll see, but I lift my head anyway and squint through the stinging rain. But nothing is lodged in my chest. My shaking fingers touch the tender spot between my ribs, feeling for the incision.

There isn't one.

It takes half a second for it to click. Gray's toss was off. I was hit with the hilt by mistake. I push up on my elbows.

But Gray never misses.

As the battle rages, the scarring flames consume any sense of hope. Except that if the weapon wasn't impaled in my chest, it's somewhere nearby. I search blindly through the pouring rain, my fingers groping mud, carefully feeling my way for the Steel.

I find the sparking weapon near the Inner Wall. The vine-etched blade is a brassy metal. The handle ornate. Opal. It's Gray's Steel. The same weapon that cut me in the training room.

The same one Sage tried to destroy at the gate. The one Cole said would be strong enough to create the blast needed to destroy Sage.

The hilt burns with a fierce sting—ten times worse than any other Alliance weapon. I loosen my grip to lessen the pain and use the fabric from my sleeve as a buffer. I push to my feet as someone shouts my name. Through the sheets of rain, I see Gray. He's probably fuming that he missed and I'm not dead.

Except he's not. He nods with approval at the weapon in my hand and then runs off to help Maddox, who is still fighting for his life.

That can't be right. Gray sent the weapon on purpose? I teeter, stunned for a moment. Hope starts to rise in me again. Then I hear a cry that rips my heart open.

Sage's delighted laughter follows, slicing through the field, cutting deeper than a sword ever could.

The tiny white Cormorant, Ayala, takes flight.

No. Please no.

Through the shadows, *on a heap . . . overturned*, is Cole.

He is sprawled out, facedown. There is no sense of the Current flowing through the mud toward him. But it has to be there. It *has* to be.

I plunge through the drenching rain—over *armor strewn* throughout the field, dodging Awakened and Legions alike to reach his side.

"Cole." No response. "Cole!" No. I shake his listless body. "Cole, please. Get up!" There has to be a spark. Please, let there be at least an ember. I lift his heavy arm, searching the mud for anything that is not just darkness . . .

Lightning splits the sky above the barren tree. I fumble with the vial from his pocket. "You were supposed to leave. Go back to your family. Not come here." The shaky words swell inside my throat. I turn his head and pour the healing serum into his slightly open mouth. His eyes, once brilliant emeralds, stare dark and vacant somewhere beyond me. "Cole, no. Please. Please!"

Golden threads pulse from the Well in every direction, except near him. I toss the useless vial. I dig through the mud, desperate to catch a thread and force it back to Cole. "Come here!" I demand it. I'm hitting, digging, beating the earth with my fist as the cords slip around me, seeking new paths. "I said come back!"

My voice echoes through the field, but I'm left huddled next to Cole, surrounded by nothing but darkness. I scream into the pouring rain.

Legions flock, ready to siphon the wispy Current seeping from Cole's body. Fueled with nothing but rage, I attack them instead. Exploding embers ignite the air. Gray's Paradise Steel cuts with power beyond measure. One by one the beasts descend. The hilt sizzles my palm, but I don't care. I welcome the pain, letting Steel and Legion collide.

For Cole. I strike a monster.

For Pop. I kill another.

For Juniper. Another and another.

For Jess . . .

And every name of the dead. One after the other, I destroy the vile creatures with every ounce of strength I can muster. But with every one I take out, another takes its place. More Legions arrive—*lured / With scent of living carcasses.*

Footsteps splatter through the mud as someone runs in my direction, shouting something I can't hear over the screeching Legions.

It's Foster. With disheveled hair hanging in his soot-covered face, he joins me, and we fight the descending swarm of Legions clamoring for Cole's lifeless body. Foster attacks the Legions with thrusts and swipes as angry as my own. The vile beasts retreat, and I collapse next to Cole. Foster pulls me back.

"Be wary not to siphon any remaining power," he says to me, but his sorrowful expression lands on Cole.

I crawl back, sickened at the thought. I'd forgotten I could do such a thing.

More buzzing sounds approach. This time behind me. As I jump to my feet, I'm hit. I fall facedown into the mud, but keep hold of the knife. As Foster takes out the beast, I push up to my elbows.

Sage has backed away from the Inner Wall. He paces the base of the south hill, the entrance to the maze not far behind him. The battle rages, but at the moment, I don't have the strength to fight. Thankfully Albrecht and Silver Assassin make an attempt to attack Sage. But they're quickly knocked back by a hard swipe of his tail.

They're no match for his power.

No one is.

Sage glides my way *with horrid strides; hell trembled as he strode.* I stand. My hands shake. Do it. Take Gray's knife and lodge it deep into Sage's chest. Aim for *his* heart. I know that even though the weapon is made from the gate, it won't kill Sage the way Gray killed a Cormorant. I know Sage will eventually heal, but there is a possibility I can wound him enough to replace the ache in my soul with vengeful satisfaction.

Sage's army protects him from oncoming attacks as he approaches. *"Ye shall not die. How should ye? . . . / Look on me, / Me who have touched and tasted."*

Steam puffs from his flat nose. With each breath my loathing for him grows. The Steel vibrates in my hand. I force myself to face him, sulfur burning my lungs, overcoming the sweet nectar scent lingering under the oak tree.

The Inner Wall lies ten feet to my left. A magnetic force tugs the knife toward the Well. I hold it close to my side. But the tug is enough for me to realize that Sage is too far away. If I attack the Inner Wall, the strike won't do any good. I need to wait for the right moment.

With a jagged smile, Sage shifts his focus to the maze wall as his Legions descend, carrying something ghostlike through the pelting rain.

It's a slumped body in a white gown. The figure seems to float in the darkness. Not thirty feet away, the Legions hold the frail body between them. The tips of her bare toes scrape the mud. Her Current, fueled from the Well, is a burning ember about to die.

He found Mom.

"Grant me the power." All warmth is drained from Sage's voice, the *hiss returned with forked tongue.*

The knife burns my fist. I'm trembling. Sage will take everything from me until he gets what he wants.

Absolutely everything.

I ready myself to run and strike the Inner Wall as soon as Sage is close enough.

"Pathetic girl." He glances at the Wall as if he could read my thoughts. "Did you not hear what I said?" Sage's obsidian eyes turn hard. "*Ye shall not DIE!*" He lifts his hand. A raging red spark snaps through the air. No. No. No!

Mom collapses. Her tiny ember snuffs out.

A violent tremble rises inside me. The weapon shakes in my fist. Giddy Legions descend over her but Sage backs them away. He hovers at Mom's side and flicks his tongue. "This one, I've been waiting for."

My focus tunnels into one thing and one thing only: the monster.

I splash through the mud with a guttural cry. As Sage turns to fully face me, I leap into the air and shove the blade deep into his chest, stopping only when I get to bone.

Sage roars. I grip the hilt as my whole arm slides into his flesh, a stinging gelatin. Sage shoves my face and shoulder with such force, I fly backward through the sooty air, clinging to the Steel with a death grip. My arm is covered up to my shoulder with black blood—*beastial slime*—that burns with the venom of a million hornet stings.

Sage teeters back. Before Legions can descend, I throw myself over Mom's body, covering her from the Legions and from Sage. Warmth seeps out of her. Her caramel threads are evaporating. Lavender taints the air.

"Greedily she engorged without restraint." Sage's voice smiles, even as he writhes in pain.

I scoot back and spit at the ground, nauseated. *That's* what Sage wants me to do. Taste. First he offered the girl with the flower headband and now my mother's power. He wants me to join him in doing the unconscionable and siphon the Current.

I can't.

I won't.

Sage's beastly face contorts. "Very well, then." He lumbers over to my mother as black smoke engulfs his calves and feet. The wound on his chest bubbles and oozes but obviously has no deeper effect on him.

I stand in the darkness of his shadow, nothing but a puddle for him to trample on. All while Sage's army attacks anyone who tries to venture near. And he won't move close enough to the Well for me to strike.

I can't let the monster take the last of her. But I don't know how to stop him.

Sage carelessly plucks Gladys's hairpin from Mom's hair. When the metal sparks between his fingers, he tosses it into nearby flames. "Since you not only denied my generosity, but then inflicted me with this ghastly wound, I promise you no one shall survive this battle. Not a single one." He leans in to absorb the last bit of my mother's power. To take her thoughts, her memories, dreams—all that she is. But he will *not* have her.

"Sage!" I rise.

He stops, almost amused, as if he knows he's pulled the right trigger.

And he has.

My blood throbs in my veins. The Steel burns my palm. I force myself calm as a faint scent of the sweet nectar pushes its way through the ash, bringing clarity.

The vision showed that I would bridge the realms. Sage has seen that vision and knows what I will do. But he doesn't know that the three visions, when placed together, tell a bigger story.

The bridge *must* form, so it can break. Only then can it turn into the ladder, where something new will rise.

Sage waits for my answer, his charred mouth upturned in a grotesque smile. The Awakened, weary in the fight, can't hold much longer. If joining the realms can give them direct access to the Well and strengthen them the way Foster said, and this mainline power is the only chance they have to live, then I need to trust the path.

I have to make the terrifying choice.

I'll bridge the realms, but I'll never side with Sage.

I'm drenched by unrelenting rain. A honey-colored thread flows through the ground, pulsing beneath me for the first time.

I rise with Guardian strength and envision every creature on the battlefield. Then I speak the words that I know will change everything. "Destroy Sage."

The creatures hold still for a moment. Then, as if a rushing wind, they explode in a frenzy, attacking the vile monster as he fends off his own creatures, leaving my mother's body alone. The tiny wisps of her Current dissipate into the ground, vanishing forever.

I sink to my knees and gingerly take her hand. All warmth is gone. So is her lavender scent. I collapse beside her, my voice a whisper through the pouring rain. "I'm so sorry. I did the only thing I knew how. Mama, I love you . . ."

Lightning flashes through the charcoal sky as the world moves in slow motion. Sage is swarmed with his beasts as they push him to the base of the hill, but he is regaining control.

Thunder cracks as the scarring flames are doused by blinding sheets of rain. The weary Awakened army staggers through the valley. Some stunned, others wearing horrified expressions.

Stormy heat rises from my toes, runs through my veins, courses under my skin as *I feel new strength within me rise.* Powers collide, shadow and light, as both halves of me awake. I activated my dissenting inheritance by commanding the beasts. I made a Guardian choice to protect, knowing the cost, and did the very thing I feared—what everyone feared.

I believe with all my heart this is what the visions showed. This is the path I was supposed to take. But what happens now?

38

ONE REALM

Sage lifts his hands to the night sky and wields Milton like a wand as he approaches the Well.

"*Awake / My fairest, my espoused, my latest found . . . / My ever-new delight, / Awake; the morning shines and the fresh field / Calls us.*"

Fitting that he'd use Adam's line to Eve after her disturbing nightmare. Except this time, he's not talking to me.

On cue, the once-protective Inner Wall crumbles like wilting fabric. Any plans of splintering Sage evaporate into a silky puddle. The marshy reeds suddenly dissolve into plumes of silver smoke. Through the haze, something glistens. An image looms behind the dancing fog the same way as in my visions.

Thick liquid bubbles up from the dirt, rolling out from under the silver mist, filling the space between the two trees with molten glass—*Underneath a bright sea flowed / Of jasper or of liquid pearl.*

Milton's description is close. It's not a sea but a small lake. A pond. And the water isn't pearl, it's painted like a reflection of a breathtaking sunset, the sky upside down—*The portal shone, inimitable on earth / By model or by shading pencil drawn.*

Yes, capturing the full image of the portal would seem impossible.

In that moment, a clean silver light shines like a sunrise waking over a mountainside. The fog dissipates. And there, a defenseless shrub shyly glistens over a placid lake for all to see, the light casting on wondrous faces.

Sage brightens—*of that stupendous bridge his joy increased. / Long admiring he stood.* Admiring with prowling eyes and devouring the sight of an unruly shrub with a curved trunk.

The tiny sapling is plain and ordinary—except the leaves are liquid silver, and the tendrils pulse as if it had a heartbeat. The vines curl with the same pattern etched on the Paradise Steel. The vein-like roots dip in the water, stretching underneath the liquid sky.

This weak shrub, the same one from my vision, with its gangly vines and silver leaves, is what protects the Well?

Sage smiles with gnarled teeth as the tiny alabaster beast flits to his shoulder. "Now, Ayala, there is but *one realm, one continent / Of easy thoroughfare.*"

I'd like to slash Milton's words off his tongue, but instead I look around the battlefield that is smothered with the *stench and smoke* of war. The Awakened army is gazing at the glowing shrub, weapons hanging at their sides, battle halted as bright light illuminates the valley.

Steady rain is smothering most of the flames in the charred field. Silver Assassin staggers near the maze entrance. Not far from him, Tanji wipes her mouth with the back of her hand, stabbing one more Legion for good measure. Claire is slumped to her knees.

Further behind me, Gray is down, wounded, struggling to stand with a small knife in his fist. His Steel suddenly feels heavy in my hand. Across the lake, I can see Maddox under the barren branches of the willow tree. My heart leaps. He's alive, facing the glowing sight. Devon, battered and bruised, comes to help him rise, but Maddox musters the strength to stand on his own.

For the moment, the battle has ceased. No one dares move, not even the creatures, as everyone watches, waiting. Wondering what's next.

The shrub rustles as if blown by a spring breeze, but the freezing air is completely still. The silver leaves cluster together, forming a mosaic of mirrored pieces. Suddenly, the clean light brightens ten times its strength. The rivers of golden Current spilling from the Well gush faster, stronger. Each strand is fueled with mainline power, brighter than before, lighting the field in the waking hues of sunrise.

The surge feeds the Awakened army with new life almost immediately. Strength renews as they notice the light streaking through the grass and around their feet for the first time. Some begin to pull the injured to safety as others collect weapons and shields.

But Sage ignores their rush of power, fixated on only one thing: the glowing shrub. He moves closer to the Well with *belched fire and rolling smoke*. A crooked smile is plastered on his beastly face. I push to my feet as he reaches down and picks up a cord of the honey-colored light, twisting threads between three talons.

He brings the cord to his nose and inhales deep. "Lonicera." I shudder at the way he ingests my name. His voice is no longer tinged with a French accent, like my father's, but raspy like a tongue scarred by lava. "Lured to your own scent?" Sage turns to me, dangling the cord between his gnarled fingers, his skin slithering and hissing with smoke. "No matter where you hid, this scent is how I found you."

The scent from the arbor is mine?

My quickened breath streams into the frosty air. My head spins as the reality of what I've done sinks in. Red sparks hiss from Sage's fingers. *With delight he snuffed the smell / Of mortal change on earth.*

Sage pricks the honey-colored thread with a small flick of his red current, injecting it like a needle to a vein. *"In the day / Ye eat thereof your eyes . . . / Shall perfectly be then / Opened and cleared, and ye shall be as gods."*

A smug, satisfied look spreads across his gruesome face as the red current alters the stream of light from a soft glow to venom green, then slick black. The strand, once glowing bright, turns to adders slithering through the grass, seeking the heels of the Awakened.

The poisoned thread travels to the girl with the pretzel braid. As the venom reaches her feet, she drops her shield and collapses with a blood-piercing cry. The girl flails in agony. Legions swirl overhead. Crackling thunder drowns out their screeches. And my scream.

I slosh through the glassy water, leaping over silver vines and roots, trying to reach her, but her body has already turned to wispy black mist. Legions descend on me, knocking me away from Sage, who is beside her. I duck, roll, and cut the freezing air with Gray's Steel to get away.

Sage inhales the girl's Current and puffs out his chest. Two vellum wings expand from his hunched back. I'm sickened. My frozen fingers clutch the Steel tighter. The more power Sage consumes, the stronger he'll grow.

What have I done?

Sage releases the obsidian cord. As soon as it falls to the ground, the caramel light returns, searching for a new path in the grass. His greedy eyes zero in on the tiny shrub—*hope elevates, and joy / Brightens his crest.* The black misty cloud under his feet swells as he floats above the water, circling the glowing tree, assessing his prey.

The *fiery surge* of battle resumes. From the hill, Albrecht raises her sword with a battle cry. The Awakened do too. With powerful strength fed by the Well, they attack Sage—*the field pavilioned with his guardians bright,* rushing him all at once.

But Cormorants knock the Awakened army off their feet, clearing a twenty-foot perimeter around the glimmering pond. Sage has unobstructed access to the tree.

The growing smell of sulfur and ash swirls around me. I'm swallowed in the fight of oncoming Legions and pushed away from the Well. Gray's Steel is powerful, but not enough to overtake the two. Then three. And four Legions that surround me. I'm hit, slammed into the mud.

Red sparks fall with the rain as the Legions explode. "This isn't over," Devon's voice says.

Foster is helping me to my feet. He looks into my eyes. "The answer will become clear."

It's not clear yet. But somehow, seeing them rally around me after what I've just done renews my confidence.

I join them in the battle against Sage. But as soon as I reach the lake, something sideswipes me—Sage's tail, a Cormorant, or a Legion, who knows. Whatever it is, it knocks me into the air and sends me sailing toward the shrub. The Steel pulls from my hand as if magnetized by the tree.

I hold it tight as I splash into the lake. The knife sparks with explosive white light as I accidentally clip two drumstick-sized branches from the vine. The blast temporarily blinds me. The Steel burns my palms something fierce. I can't hold the sizzling weapon any longer. It plops into the painted water. No. No. No. I search for it wildly.

Through the scraggly vines, I see Sage stagger—*his head / Crested aloft and carbuncle his eyes.* His focus is on one thing.

"Happy realms of light / Clothed with transcendent brightness." His delighted laughter echoes as he dips his hands into the tepid water. His charred skin glows with soft golden liquid.

I'm plunging my hands beneath the surface, diving under, feeling blindly through the gentle water, searching for the Steel.

I come up for air and blink in disbelief. The weapon is floating strangely, not far from me.

I pluck the resisting weapon out of the water as the battle sounds increase. Albrecht is trying to reach Sage. Tanji is rushing through the smoke with a searing war cry. Maddox battles Belial while Kellan fights Legions. But it's no use. Sage is unharmed, hovering over the captured tree.

The monster lets out an agonizing cry as he slides his sizzling hands over the trunk of the silver tree, turning the bark a deep, endless black. The caramel water surrounding the charcoal trunk slowly transforms from warm honey to the venom green, into a *bituminous lake*, then obsidian black, darker than Sage's eyes.

The Awakened army manages to reach him. Albrecht launches at Sage, attacking him from behind, gashing his wing. He roars, blasting his red current reactively into the hazy sky.

I scramble back, finding solid ground before the infected stream reaches my skin because Sage's touch clearly *perverts best things / To worst abuse or to their meanest use.* Instead of bright, hopeful light flowing from the Well, haunting darkness seeps through the Garden, chasing down the creamy threads. The air is filled with a sickening stench of rotting death that will soon snuff out the sweet fragrance of the arbor forever.

I did everything I thought the visions showed. I know I did.

Yet now the world burns.

Sage has won.

39

A SPARK LIGHTS

I kneel under the oak tree, drenched and muddy. My hands are raw from holding Gray's Steel. My body aches. Cuts, bruises, and burns hide under my battered outfit.

Legions and Cormorants celebrate in swarming circles through the rain. Muffled thunder rumbles as the Awakened army staggers through the smoldering field. Small fires and what remains of the dim strands of the Current provide the only light in the swallowing darkness. Agonizing cries fill the valley as the venom reaches another victim. And then another. All while Sage hovers over the lake as if it's his throne. Untouchable.

But I know this fight isn't over, even though everything around looks as if it were.

Sage will not win.

I was *assured that man shall live.*

Sage can celebrate and believe he's won—for now. Because I know the bridge *had* to form so it could break and create a new path. *New hope to spring / Out of despair.* A despair painted on everyone's faces.

Then the bridge will break and a fierce blast will explode with white sparks where *the world shall burn and from her ashes spring / New Heaven and earth.*

Despite everything, I'm positive the vision is showing that a new Empyrean Well will rise and dwell in a separate realm once again. And the blinding light is the answer.

As Gray's knife hums in my palm, a thought hums in my mind. Gray's Steel. It's part of the gate. When I accidentally clipped the tree, white sparks burst forth, like the Circuit Wall. His weapon did nothing to destroy Sage because it was never meant to wound him directly.

It was meant to protect the Awakened. To do the very thing the Alliance feared.

Destroy the Well.

Something only I can do.

I don't know what will happen to everyone's power when it happens, but I *know* this is what the vision showed. And right now, we've got nothing left to lose. As I find the energy to stand, Pop's words float back with an affirming melody. No, it's a drumming fight song.

Casting off what winter hides
New life on the other side
From the ashes
Spring will rise

It's time for spring to rise. Even though the pitch-black Garden is steeped in winter, a blast from the Well will bring back what Sage's defiling power hides. But if the explosion will be as strong as it seemed in my vision, anyone unprotected by a shield will die. I might save the Empyrean Well from Sage's control, but anyone left fighting will be destroyed in the process. Including Maddox—if his Current hasn't already been consumed.

I look at the lake's edge. The Alliance symbol is fading. I don't have much time.

Bloodcurdling cries come faster now. I wince, feeling the agonizing wails in every part of my being. With every death, Sage grows stronger. Bigger.

Forget finding Maddox. I have to strike now. I have to trust that what I'll do will save the remaining Awakened around the world, because it's only a matter of time before Sage's power infects them all.

As I step into the oil-slick lake, Sage throws his red current two feet in front of me. I stand frozen. He doesn't need me alive any longer. I've given him what he wants. I slip Gray's knife out of his sight. The hilt throbs, tugging toward the tree.

"I promised no one shall live." Sage glides around the tiny tree to face me. "But since you granted me my heart's desire . . ." He nods at the tiny white Cormorant perched on a branch of the black shrub, *the middle tree.* The remaining Cormorants, including Moloch, swirl through the rain as if performing a ceremonial dance. One by one, they swoop down, diving into the obsidian waters. "Side with me, and I will spare your life and grant you all that you desire."

The Steel pulls harder. The cries of dying Awakened burrow into my core. But the answer is an easy one.

"Never." Not Ever.

"Very well." Sage sends his red current somewhere beyond the willow tree, lighting up the night. In the flash, I see Maddox. Alive. My heart nearly bursts. He's on the ground, ragged and weary, holding a shield as he stabs a Legion. Without warning, Sage flings the scarlet bolt from his fingers directly at Maddox the same way he did with my mother.

I scream, plowing through the water, straining to intercept the hit. I shout a command for Moloch to push Maddox back, for any beast to intervene, for someone—anyone—to save him. But nothing can hear me over Sage's roaring laughter.

I'm too far away. The red current cracks through the air, hitting the darkness where Maddox lies. Then somehow, the stream refracts into the night sky. Moloch screeches and tries to dodge the ray. She's not fast enough. Her tail disintegrates on impact. The rest of her spirals from the sky and smashes to the ground, exploding in *livid flames* not twenty feet from me—exactly how Martin painted it.

I hit the ground and cover my head with my hands. Maddox might have redirected the hit, but he may not be alive.

I push off of the soggy ground. Half of Moloch burns like a bonfire—an *inextinguishable fire*—heating the air. The remaining Cormorants scatter with fear. Sage calls them back. Maddox lies on the ground. His shield is busted from where it caught Sage's current. He's alive, but his light grows dimmer. And not more than thirty feet away, Sage's venom is hunting him down, devouring the faint thread leading right to him.

Maddox lifts his head. Despite the distance, our eyes lock. I raise Gray's knife in my hand and then look directly at the scraggly black shrub that once shared my scent. Please know what I'm about to do, Maddox. Protect the others and call out the code word: rise.

He nods with resigned sorrow and mouths something: "I trust you."

I slosh through the water and wade to my knees. Sage has his back to me, consoling Ayala, resuming whatever twisted ceremony the beasts are performing to restore her.

The blackened water stings my legs, but I continue on. I listen to the sounds around me, the way Cole taught me, hiding in the pouring rain. Sage doesn't hear me coming, and he's close enough to get the full measure of the blast.

Cutting the vines won't cause enough of a spark. I'll need to stab it the way Cole showed me. I crouch, dipping my whole body in the water. The pain is more excruciating, but I move closer. I'm less than five feet away. I need to get close enough so I can shank the knife deep into the bark, cutting through the outer layer, and strike deep, where hopefully the silver tree still lives.

Then I hear Devon cry out in agony. The venom must have

reached him. Forget stealth. I lunge for the shrub, but my splashes are way too loud. Sage turns and somehow his tail manages to find me before my hand can make solid contact with the bark. A spark kicks off the Steel. I've only clipped the tip of a charred vine. The obsidian stick falls into the water, revealing a tiny silver core.

Sage's tail wraps around my chest, dunking and then holding me under the water. My arms are bound to my side, and I'm so far below the surface, I'm surrounded by stinging darkness. But deeper down, there is light. He hasn't destroyed the Well completely. The silver vines look as if they're deeply rooted into the portal.

I'm desperate to breathe. My remaining breath claws inside my lungs. My hand burns with fierce fire from the weapon. But no matter what, I can't let go of Gray's Steel. Suddenly Sage releases me. I rise to the surface, gasping in the freezing air. My eyes widen as he topples back.

Albrecht has attacked him from behind, slashing his wing. Tanji and Kellan join the fight. But I can tell their threads are weakening as darkness overtakes the light. Sage spins around, sending a blast at Albrecht, which she barely avoids.

The acrid smell of burning hair swirls around Sage as his wing regenerates. His charred, flaky skin fills with a million tiny yellow eyes. Martin didn't even come close to capturing this beast on the canvas.

Despite the horror in front of me, I move to the thickest part of the trunk. Through the fire, I see Maddox. His eyes find mine. The venom has reached him. He's wincing, bearing the pain. I hope he'll make it—I pray he will. But I'll never see his face again. There's no shield to protect me from the blast.

This is it.

I raise the knife.

Maddox shouts the battle cry. His voice carries through the field. At once, silver shields twinkle across the meadow and up the hill as if the starry sky had descended to earth.

With Guardian power beyond my own, I grip the Steel. My palm sears as I thrust the knife deep into the black bark.

The ground trembles—*earth felt the wound*—shaking with a violent force.

Sage bellows with a deafening roar as terror flashes across his million yellow eyes. I collapse, submerging under the water.

Everything explodes with a clear blinding light.

Then total darkness.

40

AFTER THE STORM

I lie on soft sheets smelling of clean linen. A plush blanket strokes my cheek. Something thick binds my eyes, holding them closed. My arms feel weighted, heavy. But I reach up. My fingers touch rough bandages. Not only on my eyes, but around my head. And my hands. I peel my cracked lips apart, tasting blood. I try to ask, "Where am I?" but no sound escapes.

"She's awake."

I can't make out the voice over a constant ringing in my ears, although I'm sure it's Harper. Her rose scent hovers near me. "Drink," she says. A straw cuts my bottom lip, but I manage to suck in a sip. The cool water soothes my dry throat.

I remember a bright light . . . Sage . . . and . . . "Maddox?" His name comes out a hoarse whisper.

Warm hands that smell of baked bread tug at the bandage on my eyes. Lina. She's alive. Harper's alive . . .

"*Puedes ver?*" Lina asks me. My sticky eyes burn. Are they open? All I see is a purplish red.

A door opens. Someone enters the room, but they stay near the door. "Maddox?" I clutch the sheet.

"Cera." Harper's soft hand takes hold of mine. "You've been out for days. Calm down. You need more time to heal."

Why won't she answer me about Maddox? I squeeze her hand because I lack the strength to argue. Then a concerned voice says, "Sedate her once more." It's Foster. No sooner does the door close than a needle pricks my arm.

Three times they sedate me. Each time Lina asks if I can see. Each time I ask for Maddox. I wake up for the fourth time in who knows how many days. I have no idea where I am. Somewhere at the Estate, possibly. Not a hospital. The constant humming in my ears is quieter now, but I startle at the sound of wings. Not Cormorants but birds singing a soft melody. I smell flowers from a garden but not the scent from the arbor.

They don't tell me about Maddox. They don't tell me anything.

My heart rips with endless grief every moment I'm awake. Mom. Cole. I don't know how many were lost. Or who survived. I lie still, pretending to sleep, hoping to overhear any bits of conversation that might soothe the wrenching ache consuming me. Lina and Harper move through the room in silence. It must be a small room, because they don't move very far.

"*Otra vez*." Lina might be talking to Harper, but then her fingers touch the bandages on my face. Cold air brushes across my eyes. "*Abre*."

"Open your eyes," Harper says.

Aren't they open? They must be because the light is way too bright. A migraine splits my skull. I wince, squeezing my eyes shut, but that doesn't do anything to dim the blinding light. It's as if I've stared at the sun and burned the image inside my eyes. My already aching heart shatters a little more.

"*Bien?*"

Good? I think I'm blind—how on earth can that be good?

My head throbs as Lina helps me sit up. A glass vial touches my bottom lip. I smell Harper's sweet healing serum. It burns going down my throat. I want to ask about Maddox, but I'm afraid they'll knock me out again. So instead I ask, "Where am I?" hoping this is a less volatile question.

There's silence for a moment. I'm surprised when Foster answers. "We are on the east edge of the Garden."

Harper takes my hand. "It's the only part of the Estate that wasn't destroyed."

"But what happened? Did Sage . . ." I stop. Deep down, I don't know if my heart can bear the truth.

"Your actions caused an explosion, splintering Sage in the blast," Foster says. "We believe he was fragmented to the point of not being a threat for a very long time."

But one day, in who knows how many hundreds of years, he will come back. "And the Well?"

"We are not entirely certain."

"Everything is quiet," Harper says. "We think all the Legions and Cormorants are gone for now." Her voice drops. "But the Garden was ruined."

"The incident was perceived by the remainder of the world as an earthquake. Seven-point magnitude," Foster adds.

A knot strangles my throat as vivid memories come crashing back. "Cole . . ."

The room turns silent.

"He was an extraordinary young man." Foster's voice is somber.

"Cole was brave. No one could have pulled off what he did," Harper says, sounding as if she's consoling Foster more than me.

"I demanded more of him than necessary. But it was simply because he displayed all the markings of becoming an exceptional leader. I regret never telling him so." The lieutenant's slow footsteps walk away, and then he closes the door.

Harper squeezes my hand. "Devon said we lost a lot of Awakened."

Devon is alive. I exhale slightly. "What about . . . Maddox?"

"He's with Council."

"He's alive?" My heart nearly explodes. I wrap my bandaged fist around the soft blanket, wanting to rip it back and charge out to find him.

"Yes." A grave seriousness taints Harper's tone. "But before you get any ideas, with the exception of Foster checking in every now and then, Council isn't letting anyone but Lina and I near you."

"Why?"

She guides my shoulders to the wooden headboard, settling me back down. "They're still deciding what to do with you."

Council takes days to deliberate. I'm given freedom to walk around part of the Garden, but only because I'm blind and need a full-time escort, which usually ends up being Harper.

Every day she walks me to the field where bodies that weren't burned by the blast are buried. Mom doesn't have a grave, but someone has placed a plaque in her honor, along with the other fallen. Harper tells me a memorial was placed for Pop in the family plot. But that part of the Garden is off-limits for me.

I memorize the path as she hooks her arm through mine and leads me down a pebbled road, its rocks crunching under my feet. As we walk over a field of soft grass, I follow the growing scent of flowers to the evergreen tree where Cole's body lies. Every day the Awakened bring more tokens to his memorial. If only they knew how much Cole hated flowers. I wrap my arms around my middle with a bittersweet smile, and fight the tears stinging my eyes. The ground is cold as I kneel. I dig my hand in my pocket. Earlier, I asked Harper to find me a certain chess piece. I rub the smooth marble between my fingers, feeling the grooves. "You were never an expendable pawn," I whisper and then kiss the white knight. My fingers outline the smooth plaque, and I trace the etching of his name. "Hendrick Colton Tripton III."

I lie on the ground as my fingers rest on his nameplate. I think about what I could have done differently to save him. He was more heroic than anyone knew. His family would have been proud. The lieutenant had him recorded as a level one Blade, the highest rank for an Alliance member.

The ringing in my ears has lessened but not gone away. I can see light and dark, a few flashes of light every now and then, but nothing else. As the days go by, hope seems hard to find.

Lina keeps putting drops in my eyes that are supposed to help, but they only make my eyes feel on fire. After I recover enough for a full cleanup, it's a huge ordeal. Harper cuts off most of my hair because it's singed and tangled. I don't even want to know what I look like now. And sleep is difficult. Every time I lie down, all I can hear are the bloody cries as my mind replays images of Sage and the explosion.

I think it's been a week since the Well was destroyed. I've yet to see or hear from Maddox. The longer the days, the more I wonder if I'll ever get to speak to him again. According to Council, there's no need for him to see me. He was my interceptor, and I haven't had any visions since the battle. With Sage no longer a threat, my visions are probably gone. The irony. Ridding myself of visions was the one thing I wanted from the start, but I had no idea what it would cost.

And the Empyrean Well—I can only hope it isn't destroyed for good. It's a wonder Council hasn't killed me.

After a short walk through the Garden on the seventh day, Harper guides me back to the cabin. I've come to know the feel of the doorframe. There's a slight notch in the wood by the handle. Today, I don't feel like being here. Today the ache of losing my mom, losing Cole—the weight of it all feels too raw. And as soon as I step back into the room, I know Harper and Lina will be all over me, checking my eyes, asking if I can see.

This day is warmer than the others. The trees rustle with a gentle melody.

"I need to be alone," I tell Harper.

She hesitates. "I'm not supposed to leave you by yourself."

"Then can you sit me somewhere without letting me know you're around?" I know that sounds bad, but she seems to understand what I mean.

We go back down the pebbled path, but this time she leads me toward a different part of the field and sets me under a tree. My fingers press against the knotted trunk guiding me as I sit. Her quiet footsteps walk away.

I tilt my head back to stare at the sky. A sky I can't see. Only shades of dark and light and a few flashes of that creamy swirl. I imagine the blue sky playing hide-and-seek with me through thick pine-scented leaves.

Now that the bandages are gone, I run my hands through the soft grass. The coolness seeps into my empty palm where rough scars from holding Gray's Steel burned my skin.

Where is the Current now? I believed spring could rise, but the Well and the protective Walls are gone, and winter is starting to take over.

I sit still, playing scenarios over and over in my mind, but I try not to think about where I'll go without family. Without money. Or sight.

I lean my head against the bark and look up. "I hate this blindness, Milton." Not that he hears me anymore. In fact, any connection to him seems erased.

Someone walks through the grass. I can't smell Harper's rose scent yet, but she's probably still a good distance away. I look in her direction. "I need at least five more minutes." She doesn't respond but continues to come closer, then sits next to me. I bite back frustration. "I said I need to be alone."

A light breeze twirls around me, and I smell rain. When he places a warm hand over mine, I know it's him.

Maddox.

I sit up. My fingers feel their way over his T-shirt, collarbone, and along his neck and up to his face. I run my hands through his hair. It's shorter on the sides and combed back.

"Cera," he says, as my trembling fingers brush over his lips. My search pauses, but then I trail two fingers down his scar along his jaw—then across a new one, a smaller one on his chin.

"You're alive."

"And so are you." His breath brushes my cheek.

I trace the outline of his soft lips with my finger. He draws me close, his lips suddenly pressing to mine. Warmth soothes every aching part of me.

He rests his forehead against mine and holds me like he'll never let go. "They wouldn't let me see you. I tried. Harper snuck me in a few times, but you were out cold."

"They wouldn't tell me anything. I was terrified that . . ." I don't know why, but suddenly the need to justify myself is strong. "I did the only thing I knew to do, Maddox. I couldn't let Sage win. Everything seemed to keep changing. Gray threw me his knife. If it weren't for him . . ." I search for the right words. "I think all he ever wanted was to protect you." I run my hands along his chin, finding a rough scab. Tears sting as they well up, but I try not to cry. I want so much to see his face—his eyes.

"He came to see you once when he didn't think you'd pull through."

For a moment, I swear I can see two blurry cerulean spots until I blink away the burning tears. "He's alive?"

"And not happy with the changes Council is making."

Through the shadow, a golden flash flickers. I close my eyes. The flash is gone. When I open them again, the creamy light returns. My heart races. "Did you set your weapon down?" Another flash. This time in the grass. "Bright streaks keep appearing. I don't know if it's my sight or they're from something else."

"Those are probably streaks of the Current."

"What?" I press my hand into his chest to steady myself, feeling the muscles I know well, except this time I also feel a thick bandage.

"When you struck the tree, you didn't destroy the Well, you ushered a transfer," he says almost reverently.

Under my fingertips, his heart races as fast as my own. I know what he's saying is good news for the Alliance but not for me. I'm still a Blight—the enemy. I wish I could see those stormy eyes looking at me, and then I'd know how to read him. I can feel him staring at me, probably at my freakish eyes. Harper said the side effect of whatever drops Lina uses causes the iris to lose color, making them look like glass. But she's hopeful I'll see again. Someday.

"What?" I pull away at his silence. "I can't see. I can't read what you're thinking."

"Global Council asked me to help find the new location of the Wells." His voice is soft, as if saying words he knows might wound.

I run my scarred palm over a rough tree root. It takes a split second before his last word hits me. "Wells? As in more than one?"

Maddox's words now tumble out. "There's been a crazy amount of creative activity in different parts of the world since our battle. It's hard to tell for sure, but based on the three lanterns from your visions, Foster believes the Well didn't transfer into one location, but split into several. Possibly three portals. He thinks your visions showed how the Well was guiding you to attack it, so it could reform.

The power isn't concentrated in one area anymore but spread around the world."

I take in the news. "Overtaking three portals isn't as easy as one," I say slowly. "And it will take Sage centuries to reform, if not longer." Hope rises in me. "After everything was over, I expected the Garden to change back to spring. No wonder it didn't. Because the portal and protective Wall transferred somewhere else."

Maddox's denim jacket rubs against the tree bark as he shifts. "Council is training teams to find and protect the portals. They probably won't be discovered for a long time, but they asked me to join." He can't hide the excitement in his voice. "I'm now the youngest level one in active duty."

Somehow his words are a knife wound to the chest. He's chosen the Alliance. This is probably his way of saying goodbye, but that doesn't mean it doesn't sting.

He takes my hand, his fingers rubbing the scars. "I told them no."

"You're joking, right?" I laugh as an unwanted tear runs down my cheek.

He cups my face in his warm hands. His thumb wipes away the tear. "I'd rather find newly Awakened and use both art *and* training to strengthen our Bents. I want what we've learned to be passed down to others so they'll be ready when Sage returns." He is quiet for a moment. "I want to build a new Hesperian. With you."

"But I'm a Blight. There's no way—" His bold kiss dissolves my doubt, shooting like a livewire through my blood.

He pulls back, leaving me breathless. "We've changed things." His confidence grows stronger as he wraps both arms around me. "Sage isn't a threat now. Laws are changing. Gray's not thrilled with the thought of you being a part of us. He still can't trust the idea, so he's going his own way with his Steel.

He'll probably join the admiral and search for the Wells." Nestled against him, I rise and fall with his breath. "Stay with me. Together we can find others like you."

He brushes back my hair, tucking something near my ear to hold the strands in place. I feel a smooth metal prong. It warms my fingers, humming under my touch as I trace the small outline of the arbor flower. Gladys's hairpin. He found it, again.

"Okay, time's up." Harper's voice floats down from somewhere in front of us. But I only see two tree-like shadows.

"Miss Bossy Pants is back." I manage a smile. "And who else?" I catch a whiff of an earthy undertone complimenting her rose scent.

Devon laughs. "How you holding up?"

"Convince her to join us." Maddox rests his chin on top of my head. His arms stay locked around me. "She won't listen to me."

"She's a handful, that's why." Harper laughs, her voice light.

"Don't worry, Gladys will convince her," Devon says. "Now let's head out."

Maddox takes my hand, helping me to my feet. His lips brush against the curve of my ear as he whispers, *"The world was all before them, where to choose / Their place of rest, and providence their guide."*

That waking flutter returns. "You memorized Milton?"

"Maybe we could make it a song." His voice smiles. The sun warms my skin as he weaves a hand in mine. The gentle hum I thought was a ringing in my ears, wakens into a pulsing melody as he says, *"They hand in hand, with wandering steps and slow, / Through Eden . . ."*

"Took their solitary way." I finish.

"Only we're not alone," Maddox says as we make our way through the grass. "Devon and Harper are in front of us, walking across this mossy green field. Harper's arm is hooked through his. Her head on his shoulder."

I can picture it. Maddox doesn't have to tell me her hips sway as she walks. And Devon is probably walking with his head high, leading the way.

"Tree branches wave as you walk by. They're climbing over one another, reaching out, begging for one touch as yellow leaves toss their petals like confetti in your path." Maddox is clearly exaggerating, but sounds as if he's enjoying painting the scene in my mind. "The Awakened army line the road, bowing as you walk by. They're smiling. Even Tanji."

Now he's gone too far. I swing a playful fist into his ribs. "You're such a liar."

When we hit the graveled path, I shuffle because sometimes I can trip over the dips in the uneven trail. Maddox slides his arm around my waist, supporting me as a soft wind blows against my back.

Then distinct scents swirl along the trail leading back to the cabin. A growing presence fills the road. Was Maddox really serious? I try to sense the surroundings as we walk.

Their faces flash in my mind as I pass: The potter's clay strengthened by fire is Claire. Then it's Kellan's enduring leather with a dash of cologne. Amide is a spiced ginger with a gracious smile. And starched linen warmed by the sun—Foster.

Other fragrant scents collide in the crisp air, but I can't yet connect those to faces I know.

One hopeful scent stands out over the rest. Cutting through the light breeze, Maddox walks beside me with his arm around my waist. And I smell rain—after the storm.

"In ten, twenty, a hundred, or even more years from now, when you see the world in a way no one else can—when you think you're misunderstood and alone. Know that you're not. Consider it a sign. A clear indication that a new battle is brewing and you've been called to protect and fight. Don't let fear blind you to inaction. Trust that everything will come together. You've been Awakened. Take heart and know there are others like you waiting to be found."

— Cera Marlowe

ACKNOWLEDGMENTS

This story was born from a struggle of my heart, and it was a struggle to wrangle the words onto the page every step of the way. But I know that the story wouldn't have come to life without the continued love, support, and encouragement of so many people who believe in the power of storytelling.

So I give the biggest thank you possible to those who carried me along during this journey. First, to Steve Laube for seeing the potential and trusting the vision of this book from just the synopsis. To Lisa Laube, I'm forever grateful for your love of the story, taking time to talk through elements, and working your editing brilliance to tighten the manuscript, turning it into so much more than I could have imagined. A huge thank you to Trissina Kear and Jordan Smith and the Enclave Publishing team for the continued support and encouragement. To Kirk DouPonce for amazing and breathtaking cover design. To Lindsay A. Franklin for laboring over the manuscript and wielding your meticulous copyediting magic, as well as encouraging me along the way. I'm so thankful God has allowed me to be part of this family and given me a story to tell.

To Donna K. Wallace whose mentoring, guidance, and encouragement was the brightest hope when I didn't think I could take another step, prodding me to dig deeper and blessing me with the notion of a Ghost Army (thanks, Cierra!). To Jamie Downer for first-run editing, being a sounding board at the very start, and helping me claw my way out of a tangled mythology. To Susan Brower for plowing through the initial draft and urging me to finish the story. Carla Hoch for incredible guidance on the fight scenes and training sequences. To Judy McCarver for the French translations. To Wes for the motorcycle ride and answering my bazillion bike questions. To Jeremy for the battle strategy discussions. To my amazing beta readers: Sara Swinford, Elizabeth Gammill, and Isabelle Kenneke who helped make the story what it is.

And to Professor Angelica Duran for graciously reviewing an early draft in rough form and nudging me for deeper clarity, and for the unending support and belief in the story.

Of course I would not have made it across the line without the love and support of my Art House Dallas family and Fort Worth Writers Group. A huge thank you to fellow authors, Sarah Kay Ndjerareou and Krissi Dallas for being the best cheering section anyone could ever have, encouraging, checking in on me, and dousing me with prayers while I was swimming in chaos.

To Mary David, for the morning walks and hot meals so I could reach my deadlines. To Erin Turek for those long car rides, discussing the mythology and properties of the "gate," adventure trips, and enduring all my emotional ups and downs. And to Travis Turek for all the support and Sunday night gatherings. To Mary Gammill for talking me off several ledges and a few cliffs. To Annemieke for sharing too much coffee, and never letting me get out of hand.

To my children, Addison, Leyton, Siena, and Ethan for answering my bizarre questions, tolerating my daydreams, and packing patience during my deadlines. To my sisters: Juliana, Diana (your support has been beyond what I could dream), Claudia, and Camila for the kindness and understanding when I couldn't return phone calls and faded off the planet.

And a huge thank you to my readers whose comments and joy of the story make it take flight. Thank you for taking the time to read and share the story. Your support and kind notes drove me to make this half of the story the best I possibly could.

To Professor John Rumrich for sparking my love for Milton, encouraging me to continue the journey, and opening doors I never thought possible.

As always, to the love of my life, John, for the unending support while allowing me to spread my wings and dream.

ABOUT THE AUTHOR

Sandra Fernandez Rhoads is the author of *Mortal Sight*. She is a Cuban-Colombian living in Dallas, Texas with her husband and four children. She has a deep love for the artist community, and is an active part of Art House Dallas and the Fort Worth Writers Group. She holds an M.A. in English with a focus on John Milton and has an insatiable love for coffee, laughter, and adventure. And dinosaurs.

www.SandraRhoads.com
Instagram: @sfrhoads.author
Twitter: @sfrhoadsauthor
Facebook: Sandra Fernandez Rhoads - Author

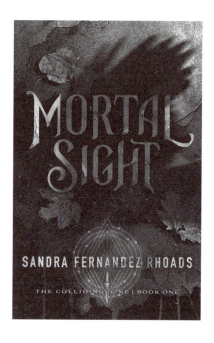 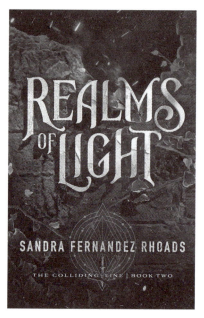